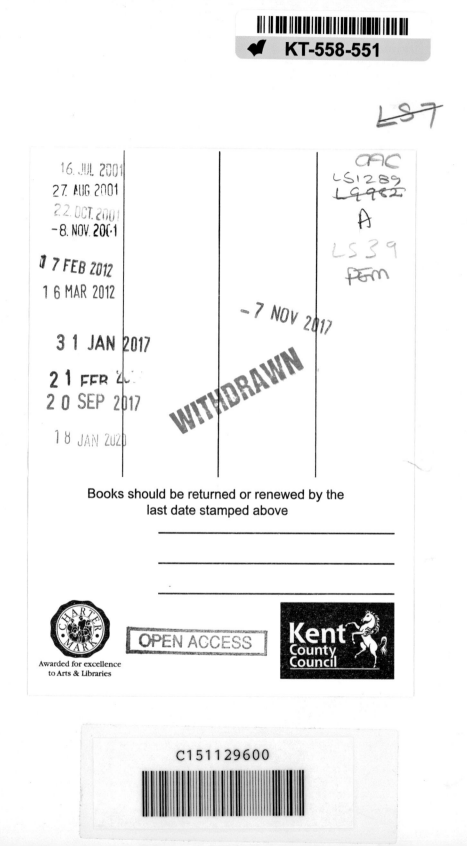

COBBLESTONE HEROES

When Susan, Jimmy and Billy Bairstow are found alive in the rubble of their home, they are nicknamed 'the miracle children'. But they don't feel lucky – they've lost their parents and Aunt Dorothy is a poor substitute for mam and dad. She cannot cope with all three children and Billy is sent to an orphanage. When she tells them that Billy has died, Jimmy and Susan decide to run away. They meet Freddie, and Susan feels the first stirrings of love, but Freddie is off to war and Susan realises that any home is better than none. She and Jimmy must return to their aunt's house…

COBBLESTONE HEROES

by

Ken McCoy

Magna Large Print Books
Long Preston, North Yorkshire,
BD23 4ND, England.

British Library Cataloguing in Publication Data.

McCoy, Ken
    Cobblestone heroes.

    A catalogue record of this book is
    available from the British Library

    ISBN   0-7505-1629-1

First published in Great Britain by Judy Piatkus (Publishers) Ltd.,
1999

Cover illustration © Gwyneth Jones by arrangement with
Artist Partners & Piatkus

The moral right of the author has been asserted

Published in Large Print 2001 by arrangement with
Piatkus Books Ltd.

Magna Large Print is an imprint of Library Magna Books Ltd.

Printed and bound in Great Britain by
T.J. (International) Ltd., Cornwall, PL28 8RW

To my father and mother, Wilf and Olive.

To Judith Murdoch.
For pointing me in the right direction.

Chapter One

Lily Bairstow sat on the top step crooning softly to baby William. On the step below sat eight-year-old Jimmy, the birthday boy. He was trying to read the *Beano* by the light of a flickering candle, laughing at the antics of the Bash Street Kids. Lily had left the cellar door slightly open to take the benefit of the heat coming from the fire smouldering wastefully in the recently black-leaded kitchen range. She jumped as a glowing ember spat out, its progress onto the hearth rug denied by the wire fireguard, one of the items on her check list. Doors unlocked (for quick getaway), lights out, fireguard up, wireless on (for any news), bottles of water for the kids. Baby William wouldn't need anything extra than her own built-in supplies. At strategic points down the cellar steps odd bits of candles were placed, all held in position by their own wax, and Lily prayed that the light wouldn't be seen through the broken coal grate. She couldn't afford another ten shilling blackout fine.

'Mam, will yer tell our Jimmy ter stop kicking me!' complained Susan, sitting one step further down, unhappy that her two-and-a-half-year seniority wasn't reflected in her position on the cellar steps. Jimmy had always been Mam's favourite, just because it was his birthday and he'd been poorly, it wasn't fair. She jabbed an elbow into her younger brother's thigh producing a loud howl of anguish totally disproportionate to the mild pain it caused.

'Ow! Mam, our Susan's just hit me. Will yer tell her ter stop!'

Lily shifted her position in an effort to free the limb required to exact her retribution, but her flailing arm was easily avoided by the much experienced Jimmy.

'I'll give yer both a good hiding if yer don't behave. Get down them steps into bed.'

'Aw, Mam!' moaned Susan. 'Do we have ter sleep on that mattress? It's all prickly!'

'Can't we stay here and listen to t'bombs?' asked Jimmy. 'I've never heard no bombs.'

'There won't be any bombs, it'll be a false alarm like it always is,' snapped his mother. 'Now, do as yer told and get into that damn bed!'

The word 'damn' was enough to spur the two children into action. It could well precede violent action from their mam if they didn't do as they were told. They both climbed reluctantly onto the horsehair mattress on the bottom bunk and pulled a heavy overcoat over the top of them. Everyone knew that the Luftwaffe never bombed Leeds, it was known as the Holy City – just out of range. It took them all their time to get to Sheffield. Still, there was no harm in taking precautions.

A man's first duty was to protect his family so the ceiling joists above them had been propped and reinforced by their joiner dad before he'd been mobilised to go and fight Hitler. Although up to now Adolf had little to fear from Fred

8

Bairstow, who was still at Becketts Park Barracks about three miles away doing his square bashing.

It was January 1941 and up to then Fred had been held back doing reserve work. Joiners who could put right bomb damage were far more in demand than soldiers. A couple of weeks before he got his call up papers he'd gone back to his digs in bomb-blasted Sheffield, only to find they weren't there any more, thanks to a German incendiary. A month before that he'd been working on a bomb-damaged warehouse in Hull, only to arrive one morning to find all his good work laid to waste by the Luftwaffe.

So displeased was he with his working conditions that he'd caught a train back from Sheffield to Leeds and told his employers where they could stick their job. Ignoring their threats to report him to the authorities, he took a job with another firm working on an underground ordnance factory near Wetherby. Shortly afterwards he was called up. Fred reassured his worried wife that at least being in the army was a damn sight safer than being a wartime joiner.

Contrary to army regulations, Fred had spent many unauthorised nights back in his wife's bed at number six Gorston Mount. A secreted bicycle had transported him there and back and he was in line for breaking the barracks' record for the number of times a new recruit had been put on report during basic training. Fred Bairstow thought the threats of dire punishment from his sergeant well worth it; after all, what were they going to do, give him the sack? The two bunk-beds were homemade but serviceable if you only wanted to lie on them for a couple of hours. According to Fred's brother, Tommy, any longer and you'd be picking horsehairs out of your arse for a week.

This was the sixth time in a fortnight that the air raid warning siren had sent them scuttling into the cellar and they'd yet to hear a single enemy plane.

'The minute you hear that siren,' Fred had instructed, 'you get yourselves straight down them cellar steps and you don't move till you hear the All Clear, understand?'

They'd all nodded obediently and saluted. Fred had grinned and saluted back saying, 'At ease men.' Then he picked them up one by one and gave them all a smacking kiss. Susan and Jimmy pretended to hide their faces in embarrassment when it came to Mam's turn.

'I bet we never rotten well get bombed,' grumbled Jimmy, yanking the overcoat away from his sister, provoking another complaint to Lily.

'Mam, will yer tell our Jimmy ter stop pulling t'overcoat off me.'

'I'll tell yer dad what you've been up ter when he gets home this weekend!' snapped Lily.

A hollow threat if ever there was one. Fred Bairstow was the only father in the street who didn't smack his kids. Not that Lily would have minded if he did. A bit of back-up from her husband wouldn't have gone amiss. Jimmy had been a worry, a bout of rheumatic fever had left him with a weak heart. It had been touch and go for a while but it hadn't affected his spirit. His pals at St Joseph's Roman Catholic Primary called him Sparky which pretty much described him. Susan watched over him like a mother hen. When it was thought he might not make it, she prayed continuously to the blue and white statue of the Virgin Mary in Mam and Dad's bedroom. She knew it was her who had brought him back from the dead like Lazarus and not the doctors, upon whom her mam and dad had heaped lavish, but misplaced thanks. She mustn't tell anyone though, or she wouldn't get her reward in heaven.

Lily was getting really fed up with these air raid warnings. She'd planned on going to the pictures that night with her sister-in-law, Dorothy, whose husband Tommy was Fred's older brother. Tommy could be called up himself before much longer. Dorothy was all the better for knowing. No children as yet, her and Tommy never said why – maybe they liked the good life too much to be saddled with kids. Or maybe there was another reason. If there was, they'd never opened up about it.

Hilda Braddock, from number thirteen, was coming with them. Her daughter Glenys, the one with the bad leg from polio, said she'd babysit for a couple of sweet coupons. They were going to the Bughutch, or the Western Cinema, to give its rightful but less apt name, to see Errol Flynn in *The Sea Hawk*. It would have been Lily's first night out in weeks. She craned her head round the door to look at the clock on the mantelpiece. It said ten-past-eight which meant it was ten-to. The Bairstow family clock was always twenty

11

minutes fast for some obscure reason. Susan and Jimmy had found it a bit confusing when they were learning to tell the time. Ten-to-eight, the second house was due to start in ten minutes. If the All Clear went any time during the next half hour they'd still make it, the manager, Lame Larry Gutteridge, wouldn't lose a house for the sake of a half an hour, there was a permanent notice on the cinema door to that effect. She might still get to see Errol Flynn.

'Can't we have a blanket, Mam?' pleaded Susan. 'This coat won't cover both of us.'

Lily was still sitting on the top step with William, vainly trying to catch a bit of warmth from the back room fire.

'Am I to get no peace from you two?' she grumbled. 'What do you want me ter do? Go upstairs and get some blankets off my bed? Is that what yer want?'

Susan and Jimmy grinned smugly at each other from behind adjacent lapels. They knew their mam was going to do just that. No way would she let her kids ever be cold in bed.

'Look after William – and don't have him crying or I'll give you two summat ter cry about as well.'

Two faces nodded obediently as Lily placed baby William gently between them. Jimmy's ears pricked up.

'Did yer hear that?'

'Did I hear what?' asked an impatient Lily.

'I thought I heard a plane.'

The three of them listened intently, but silence reigned.

'It means yer going daft when yer hearing things, doesn't it, Ma?' gloated Susan.

'Just try and behave for two minutes,' sighed their mother, 'I'll fetch a couple of blankets.'

Oberleutnant Kurt Weidling nudged his Dornier 17 through the night sky. The eastern coast of England was on his left. The Luftwaffe were really stretching it to the limits sending him this far north. Three of them had set off, but the other two had taken hits from a lone Hurricane, itself limping back across the channel with smoke trailing from its engine. The British pilot must have had a bad day to have taken on the three of them. The lunatic had hurled his damaged aircraft straight at them from underneath, taking them completely by surprise. Weidling had caught a glimpse of a wild-eyed, blood-streaked young face as the Hurricane roared up from below, cannons blazing as he blasted the complete tailplane away from Kesselring's Dornier. Weidling's nose gunner had returned the compliment and both the Dornier and the Hurricane ended up in the sea. Three parachutes opened from the German aircraft but none from the Hurricane. The third Dornier had taken a raking hit all along the underside and radioed to Weidling that it was turning back.

'The fool Englishman should have ignored us and gone straight home,' Weidling grumbled to his navigator. 'Such waste, no one will thank him for such foolhardy behaviour.'

He swung left well before they reached the batteries guarding the Port of Hull and headed for his target. The grim January night sky gave away no clues to their whereabouts. He knew that finding the Royal Ordnance factory to the north of Leeds would be well nigh impossible and they'd have insufficient fuel to come round again. Still, his was not to reason why. Drop the bombs somewhere in the vicinity and head for home, that's what Kurt planned to do. He wasn't one for heroics like the British Hurricane pilot. His wife and daughter back in Magdeburg wouldn't thank him for coming home a dead hero.

The clouds were now down to five hundred feet and as it made little sense to fly below them with all the danger that entailed, Weidling took his aircraft up to fifteen thousand feet where the view was much more pleasant. Let the navigator do the hard work, he thought, I'll just fly the plane and look at the stars. No point making this war any more unpleasant than it already is. Such philosophy preserved many a life on both sides during the war.

'We're over Leeds now, sir,' reported his navigator eventually.

'Tell me when we're precisely over the Royal Ordnance factory,' ordered Kurt, lighting up a cigarette and smiling to himself, knowing the impossibility of such an order. Leutnant Hans Eberbach, the new navigator, was a keen but nervous young man. He wouldn't know what to do if he couldn't locate their target precisely, which of course he wouldn't be able to. Most navigators would hazard a guess, the bomb aimer would thankfully release his load and the captain would turn for home, mission accomplished. If they were to drop the bombs ten kilometres off target why not let Eberbach take the blame?

'We are all ready when you are, Hans, and we don't have the fuel for a second try,' said Weidling. Eberbach was sweating, this was his first bombing mission. According to his calculations they could be right over the target, more or less.

'Now!' he blurted.

'Now? Are you sure?'

'No! Wait!'

But the bombs had gone.

Fred's chickens had come home to roost. His comeuppance had arrived in the shape of a sergeant-major who told Fred he must be joking if he thought he was going home on leave that weekend after all his bleedin' antics.

'The army needs you 'ere, son. We 'ave a pile of coal what needs whitewashing and as yer in the buildin' trade, you're the only man for the job.'

The escape bicycle beckoned. This was his last chance of freedom and conjugal bliss before his posting. It was a chance well worth taking and Fred took it. His indoctrination into army life was very much incomplete. Free thinkers like Fred were much in abundance in the British Army in those days, a quality sadly overlooked by those in authority.

It was little more than a fifteen minute ride home if he got some speed up. He was scarcely two minutes into his journey when the sirens went.

'Good,' he thought to himself. 'That'll clear the streets if nothing else.'

The blackout was particularly effective that night. The clouds were heavy and low. A recent purge, resulting in many ill-afforded fines, had had the desired effect and scarcely a chink of light emerged into the grimy black night, from any of the buildings he cycled past. A pair of dim, shuttered headlamps meandered noisily towards him, missing him by inches. The car driver happily oblivious to almost depriving His Majesty of one of his finest fighting men. Fred stopped and took his beret off. He'd asked for a six-and-seven eighths and they'd given him a seven-and-a-half saying he'd probably grow into it. Still, it kept his ears warm. But tonight he wanted to look dashing for Lily. He jammed it into his epaulette and took out a packet of Senior Service.

'Put that light out!'

The harsh order came from the other side of the street. Fred peered into the blackness and just made out a helmeted figure, standing on the opposite pavement. Probably an A.R.P. warden. He blew out the match.

'It's a Swan Vestas, not a bloody searchlight,' he called out cheerfully.

'They got binoculars up there, they can probably see your fag.'

Fred pedalled off before he was ordered to douse his cigarette. He was standing on the pedals for the short, final push up Paradine Hill when he thought he heard a drone. Then again it could have been his bike. Fred knew that the

Germans wouldn't choose a night like tonight to start bombing Leeds.

Turning into Back Gorton Mount, he swung off the bike and allowed the front wheel to bump open the gate of number six. He knew the latch was broken, he'd broken it himself by doing just this, time and time again, much to Lily's annoyance. He could hear the droning quite clearly now. It wasn't an aircraft noise he recognised, but that didn't mean much to Fred. To him they pretty much all sounded alike. A distant ack-ack gun fired off a few lively rounds, which made him wonder. The back door into the scullery wasn't locked. Fred opened it quietly, planning to surprise his family who would be in the cellar as per instructions or he would want to know why.

He caught a glimpse of Lily's back as she turned out of the back room to go up the stairs. Fred grinned to himself and tiptoed up behind her. He stood in the bedroom doorway watching her admire her self in the bedroom mirror, then she picked up their wedding photo from the dressing table and kissed it before placing it carefully back down, saluting and saying, 'At ease, soldier.' Fred undid his belt, dropped his trousers and saluted.

Lily had only been gone a few seconds when Jimmy heard the sound again. It was very faint, the plane must have been very high.

'Listen!' he said excitedly to Susan.

'It's not very loud.'

'It's high up that's why.'

17

'I bet it's not even German.'

Lily swung open the wardrobe door and looked at herself in the long mirror. She'd put on a few pounds since she'd married Fred twelve years ago but she didn't look bad for thirty-two. Eileen Garside was supposed to be coming round tomorrow night to give her a home perm. Lily wanted to look good for Fred. He'd be home at the weekend on proper official leave before he got his posting. Knowing the army, it'd be somewhere like Aldershot and she wouldn't see him till the war was over and at this rate that could be a couple of years. Catterick would be good. She might still see him at weekends if he got sent to Catterick. There was a photo of them both on the dressing table. A proper studio photo done at Hilton Studios for their tenth wedding anniversary. Tommy had paid the seven-and-six it had cost as his anniversary present to them. Jammed into the frame of the mirror was a photo of Fred and Tommy, with their arms around her and Dorothy. She remembered the first time the four of them had been out together to the pictures – well, there were six of them actually because Fred and Tommy had each brought a ferret along to liven up what promised to be a boring film. It livened up all alright – the four of them got thrown out. Still, it hadn't put Dorothy off Tommy, for all her snooty ways.

Fred smiled up at her from their studio photograph, causing her to pick him up and kiss him. Placing the photo carefully down she saluted smartly and said, 'At ease, soldier.'

'Yes, ma'am,' said Fred.

Lily swung round in shock, which turned to immediate delight at the sight of her grinning husband, standing to attention in the doorway in his ill-fitting khaki uniform, trousers round his ankles and saluting smartly, with his oversize beret pulled down over his ears. He'd decided against the 'dashing' look.

'Private 564896 Bairstow F. reporting for duty, ma'am!'

The first stick of bombs landed in the middle of Paradine Hill. The noise was deafening. Lily was blasted right across the bedroom into Fred. The windows came shattering in, cutting her on the cheek. She looked up into her husband's shocked face.

'What are you doing here?' was all she could think to say.

Fred was about to explain when a bomb dropped in the back yard, reducing numbers four, six and eight Gorton Mount, to a pile of rubble.

The first explosion had terrified the children who screamed and clung to each other. The second explosion numbed them into unconsciousness. They were the only survivors.

Thanks to Fred's reinforced cellar ceiling.

Chapter Two

For some inexplicable reason, kids' games were always seasonal. The conker season was the obvious one. This ran from September, pretty much up until Christmas. Cigarette cards followed in the New Year, whip and top and hopscotch at Easter, then throughout spring and summer, skipping for the girls and marbles, or taws, for the boys. Football, cricket and rounders were all played in the back streets, their traditional seasons strictly adhered to. The first newly chalked wicket never appearing on any self-respecting wall until after Easter.

One of the great ignominies of youth was in the selection of teams. A circle would form and two natural captains would automatically emerge from the ranks and make a selection, each taking turn in choosing players of reducing talent from the dwindling circle. The final ones to be chosen would be embarrassingly aware of their lowly status within the team.

Jimmy was always picked last. No one had more enthusiasm or courage than him, but no one had less skill either. His rheumatic fever had left him with a dodgy heart, as he called it, not wishing to be thought in any way an invalid. Jimmy's greatest attribute was that he was a 'good laugh'.

It was late summer, 1944. Three and a half

years since his mam and dad had been killed. They'd been famous for a while. The *Yorkshire Post* called them the 'Miracle Children'. Found alive after being buried for twelve hours. Fred and Lily had been found in the next street, still clinging to each other, Fred's trousers missing. Such was the black humour in those days that the word was that Fred and Lily had died 'on the job', and what a way to go!

It took three-and-a-half years and Leon Murgatroyd before this rumour reached Jimmy's ears. The wicket had been chalked on the wall which turned Broughton Terrace into a cul-de-sac, which was altogether too posh a word for the street where Jimmy and Susan now lived, with Auntie Dorothy and Uncle Tommy. It was just a couple of streets up Paradine Hill from the waste ground on which once stood their old house. The ten-feet-high wall separated the street from the local destructor, where rubbish was taken to be incinerated. The street's inhabitants took a certain pride in the fact that their destructor chimney was the highest in Leeds. There was something homely about the permanent mild pungency that descended on Broughton Terrace from its towering, smoke belching neighbour, but the residents scarcely noticed. It was a small price to pay for living in such well appointed dwellings.

Twenty terraced houses defiantly faced each other, ten either side, or backed on to each other in this case, as the cricket match was taking place in the back street. Each house had a back yard into which extended a single-storey lean-to,

21

containing a scullery and an outside lavatory. The steps to the scullery would be regularly scoured with a donkey stone and inside would be a deep rectangular Belfast sink, a twin gas ring and a cast iron bath which would be covered up by a well-scrubbed pine board when not in use. This obviated the need for the tin bath, which people in inferior dwellings often hung on their outside walls. The ownership of a personal, practically en-suite outside lavatory set the tenants of Broughton Terrace a cut above such as them up the road in Walton Street, who had neither back yard nor personal lavvie. Just a shared convenience to which some had to walk half the length of the street, which was a bit awkward at two o'clock of a winter's morning, hence the proliferation in such areas of the much maligned po.

The streets were paved with cobbles and many a Yorkshire batsman had learned his craft in these streets, having to pick out, at the last split second, the curious deflections the ball would take when pitched on to them.

Leon Murgatroyd hadn't been invited to play cricket that day. Murgy, as he was unaffectionately known, was never invited to play or do anything, and with good reason. He just turned up and decided he was going to bat. He'd been clean bowled several times and refused to budge from the crease. Protests fell on deaf ears. Murgy was a bully.

It was Jimmy's turn to display his unique bowling action. His arm completing three revolutions before releasing the balding tennis ball, which invariably set off more vertical than horizontal.

Fortunately he lacked the strength to send it any distance and the batsman frequently did more running before hitting the ball than after.

Murgy ran a few paces to where the ball was completing its descent before giving it an unnecessary swipe into Old Mrs McGinty's yard at number sixteen, thus ending the match, unless another ball could be found. Such was the terror in which Mrs McGinty, of the foul tongue and glass eye, was held.

'Get it, Bairstow!' demanded Murgy.

'Why me?' protested Jimmy. 'It were you what knocked it in there!'

'That's only 'cos you're rubbish at bowling. What's up, scared?' The last word was delivered with a sneer that got Jimmy's back up.

'Why don't *you* get it?' challenged Jimmy. 'You're scared as well.'

Murgy took exception to this.

'Who yer callin' scared, yer bloody cripple?'

'You, yer yitney!' proclaimed Jimmy, stoutly.

Murgy took an angry step towards Jimmy. He wasn't too sure about him. Jimmy was small but volatile and Murgy, like all bullies, didn't want to risk hitting someone who might hit back. He chose another strategy.

'At least me mam and dad didn't die shaggin' each other. At least my dad weren't a deserter like your dad.'

The other children went quiet. Susan was sitting on a nearby wall. Her sex didn't preclude her from playing, only the fact that she didn't much like cricket. If she had she would no doubt have been one of the captains. Susan excelled at all sports, much to Jimmy's annoyance. She slid down from the wall and walked over to stand beside Jimmy. Her question delivered with a quiet anger.

'What was that yer said, Murgy?'

'You heard. Yer dad were a deserter, everybody round here knows it. He deserted to come 'ome and shag yer mam.'

'My dad were never a deserter,' said Susan.

'Any road, your dad's in jail.'

'He's not, he's a prisoner of war is me dad.'

'He's a prisoner alright, he's in Armley jail. He's a thief is your dad.'

Some of the spectators sniggered. This angered Murgy, who was fifteen and the only kid there in long trousers. He was a year older than Susan and a good deal bigger. She was no match for him, or so he thought. He spat at her petulantly, and was much taken aback when she flew at him with a ferocity that initially counterbalanced their difference in size. The shame of being beaten by a mere girl forced Murgy to stand his ground, but not before he'd taken a couple of hefty blows to the nose causing it to bleed profusely. He made a grab at Susan, forcing her into a head-lock. The blood from his nose dripping liberally onto her fair hair.

'How about me an' you 'aving a shag?' he grinned up at the spectators, hoping for their approval. One or two grinned back uncertainly, but most felt uncomfortable at the course things were taking. Susan was choking from a combination of fury and the tight grip Murgy had on her.

Jimmy didn't say anything. He picked up the

discarded bat and swung it with a strength born of rage at Murgy's sneering face. The onlookers winced at the sound of the bat breaking Murgy's nose and teeth. He let go of Susan, a grunting sound coming from his mouth. He was just spitting out a tooth when Jimmy gave him another whack for good measure, this time across the side of his head, knocking Murgy to the ground.

The spectators moved slowly forward to view the damage as Jimmy and Susan moved cautiously back from the circle. Little Jackie Crombie knelt down and made a cursory diagnosis of the fallen combatant.

'He's dead,' he pronounced. 'Dead as a nit!'

'Dead?' The word went from mouth to mouth round the circle, finally passed on to Jimmy and Susan.

'He's dead!'

'Hey! That's murder, isn't it?'

'Jimmy Bairstow's murdered Murgy!' Murdered Murgy, a satisfying phrase that tripped nicely off the tongue. Someone tried another variation with unseemly relish.

'Murgy's been murdered!'

Jimmy and Susan backed away from the crowd in horror, before turning and running home as fast as they could. Once inside Susan locked the door and they sat side by side on the settee, faces white, eyes streaming tears.

'Do you think I'll get hung?' sobbed Jimmy.

'I don't know.'

Auntie Dorothy was out at the shops. After their parents were killed she'd reluctantly agreed to take in the three children. Then Uncle Tommy got called up and not long after that William was sent away to a home. They weren't sure why, something to do with it being the best place for him under the circumstances. 'It'll be like a holiday for him,' Auntie Dorothy had said at the time. Jimmy and Susan were a bit put out at first that William should go on holiday and not them, then when he didn't come back they began to miss him. They'd been to visit him a couple of times and it didn't seem much like a holiday place to them. William always cried and asked to come home which upset the two of them, especially Susan. It was because he got so upset that the visits stopped, according to Auntie Dorothy. It didn't stop Jimmy and Susan nagging her though. Every day they asked when he'd be coming home. Auntie Dorothy always got annoyed – but it never stopped them asking. Then came that awful day last July when Auntie Dorothy broke the news that William had died. She'd been shouting at them as she'd been doing a lot since Uncle Tommy went to war and she came right out with it.

'William's dead!' she'd screamed at them. Then she'd added, 'There, are you satisfied now?' as if it was their fault he'd died.

It took them a while to get over his death. What they couldn't understand was why they hadn't gone to his funeral.

Tommy was brilliant, the next best thing to their own dad, but Auntie Dorothy was a poor substitute for their mam and not just because of William either.

Susan made up her mind.

'We'll have ter run away,' she decided. 'Somewhere where they'll never find us.'

Jimmy nodded glumly. Running away was better than being hung.

'We'll take the rent money and leave Auntie Dorothy an I.O.U. Then it's not stealing.'

Jimmy nodded again. He didn't want theft to be added to his crime sheet.

'When we find somewhere we like,' went on Susan, 'we'll write and let her know we're okay.'

Behind the clock was a ten shilling note and some change which Susan exchanged for a neatly written I.O.U. and a note thanking Auntie Dorothy for looking after them and sorry for the times we were naughty but now they were leaving and please give our fondest love to Uncle Tommy when he comes home from the war.

They left by the front door, which was the one least used. It was early afternoon and the sun warmed their frightened faces as they made their furtive way from shop doorway to shop doorway, finally boarding a tram to town with a last backward look to check they weren't being followed.

Jimmy and Susan stood on the concourse of Leeds Central Station looking blankly up at the destination boards. It was crowded. Mainly with servicemen coming home on, or going back from leave. The expression on their faces told which was which. There were tearful farewells and happy hellos, weepers and greeters. Everywhere there was a great bustling clamour. Talking, laughing, shouting, crying – and a muffled voice over the loudspeaker telling them that the train now standing on platform six was for Scarborough, calling at York, Malton and Seamer. No one took any notice of the two desperate fugitives. Susan bought a couple of penny platform tickets from a machine.

'Where we goin'?' asked Jimmy.

'I don't know, I haven't decided yet. We'll have a look at the trains first.'

Hand in nervous hand they walked past a huge, intimidating locomotive. Steam hissing from somewhere behind its mountainous oily wheels. The equally oily driver leaned out and winked down at them, then pulled a lever that released a deafening blast of steam making them both jump and run out of range. They found themselves on platform six where a guard was walking the length of the train slamming doors shut and urging dawdling passengers to get on board.

'Off on yer holidays?' A grizzled old porter stood behind them, with a case in each hand and benevolent smile on his face.

'Yes, we're just, er – we're waiting for me mam, she went for a...' Susan couldn't think of what her mam might have gone for.

'She's gone for a pee,' chipped in Jimmy.

'Well, she'll have to be quick, it's off in a minute.'

'Oh, there she is,' lied Susan, looking back up the platform over the porter's shoulder. Then, as he turned round to follow her gaze, she exclaimed quickly, 'Oh, 'eck! She's got on up there, she must think we're already on.'

'Right then, quick as you can, jump on here and walk back up the train to meet her.' The

28

porter put down his cases, opened a door and helped the two of them on, waving goodbye through the window as the train moved off.

'Where we goin'?' enquired Jimmy.

'I think we're off on our holidays,' said Susan.

The train clattered happily through the sunny East Yorkshire countryside. Two young excited faces pressed against the window. Susan, her imagination running riot, pointing out the various points of interest like the seasoned traveller she wasn't.

Jimmy soon grew bored with his sister's travelogue and concentrated his attention on a faded photograph of the Yorkshire Coast above the seats opposite. Then he grew bored with that and decided to try and open a window.

The carriage window was held in position by a stout leather strap which could be loosened to let the window down. Jimmy attempted this and jumped back as the strap flew violently out of his hand, causing the window to drop with a bang. The only other occupant of the carriage, a young man in ill-fitting khaki, sat opposite, amused by his travelling companions. He took a bar of Cadbury's chocolate from his pocket and, without looking up, knew only too well that there were two pairs of eyes watching him unwrap it. He broke off a couple of pieces and offered one each to the children.

'No, thank you very much,' declined a cautious Susan, but she was too late. Jimmy was already wolfing his piece down with great relish. Susan jabbed him with her elbow.

'Greedy glutton!'

'Go on,' urged the young soldier, still holding a piece out to her. 'I've got plenty more.'

'Thank you very much,' said Susan, kicking her brother into remembering his manners.

'Yes, thank you very much,' said Jimmy, through a mouthful of chocolate.

'My name's Freddie,' said the man. 'I'm in the army.'

'I'm Susan and this is our Jimmy. I'm fourteen and he's eleven.'

'Eleven-an'-three-quarters,' corrected Jimmy.

'Pleased to meet you, Susan and Jimmy, are you on your own?'

The children lapsed into a suspicious silence. Maybe he was a secret policeman in disguise. Susan looked at Freddie's tanned, open face and decided he could be trusted. Freddie broke the silence.

'I'm going to Scarborough. I'm doing a signalling course. Do you know what that is?'

'No,' said Susan after some thought.

'I don't neither,' added Jimmy.

'I'm learning Morse Code and Semaphore.'

'Oh, right,' said Susan.

'Our dad was in the army,' said Jimmy. 'He were called Fred as well, but he's dead now.'

'We're running away,' confided Susan. 'Can't tell you why.'

'Won't your mother be worried?'

'We haven't got a mother,' explained Susan simply. 'Our mam and dad were killed by a German bomb. Nearly got us too, we were in the cellar.'

'We're The Miracle Children,' boasted Jimmy. 'I bet you've heard of us.'

'You're right, I have,' lied Freddie. 'But I'd like to hear the story from you.'

Susan told the story, with Jimmy butting in now and then to fill in any missing details. Neither mentioned the part where their mam went upstairs because *they'd* asked for extra blankets. They hadn't discussed it even with each other. The guilt was fading now.

But it would always be there.

She told how they'd gone to live with Uncle Tommy and Auntie Dorothy, but Uncle Tommy had been called up and Auntie Dorothy didn't like them very much – and she'd put their William in a home and he'd died.

The latter part of this information took Freddie aback but he thought it kinder not to ask them too much about it.

'So that's why you ran away, because you didn't get on with your Auntie Dorothy.' The soldier spoke a lot posher than their dad.

'Yes,' said Susan.

'No,' said Jimmy, simultaneously.

Freddie looked at them both and smiled, then his eyes grew distant.

'I ran away when I was your age,' he said. 'I was away for nearly a week. Thought I could live off the countryside, but I ran away in March and nothing had started growing so I practically starved.'

'How did you get back home?' asked a curious Susan.

'Walked into a police station, easy as that.

That's all you have to do if you want to go home. You might even get taken home in a police car.'

'I bet you had a mam and dad.' Susan was growing to like Freddie.

'Yes I have.'

'Are they posh like you?' asked Jimmy.

'Oh, much posher than me.'

'Blimey!' breathed Jimmy. 'I bet you can't understand nowt they say.'

Freddie laughed. 'They didn't understand anything I said, or anything I wanted to do. They wanted me to be an officer, at least my father did, but I don't like being in the army so why make a career out of something you don't like?'

Susan nodded her agreement to this philosophy. 'I want to be a comptometer operator,' she said sagely. She wasn't entirely certain what a comptometer did, but it was a word she'd recently learnt to get her tongue round and it sounded very grand.

'Really!' said Freddie, obviously impressed.

The train was pulling into Malton Station and an echoing loudspeaker was announcing that the train would be there for fifteen minutes if anyone wanted to get off for any reason. Freddie stretched and rose from his seat. 'Fancy a cuppa?' he asked.

Susan was still cautious. 'Do you promise not to give us away?'

'Promise.'

Susan sat in the sunshine on a weather-beaten wooden bench seat at the end of the platform. Her eyes watching Freddie as he and Jimmy went off to the station café for refreshments. She was only fourteen years old but Freddie was causing a strange, but not unpleasant fluttering in her stomach. The bench was beside the station garden. A mass of roses and fuchsias, the scent of which mingled with the smoke and steam coming from the train. Most of the passengers had alighted and were walking up and down the short concrete platform to enjoy the fresh air, to explore the limited amenities or simply to 'stretch their legs'.

When they came back, Freddie was laughing at something Jimmy had said.

'Hey! Susan!' shouted Jimmy. 'What did Hitler say when he fell through the bed?'

Dismayed, Susan looked round at the other disembarked passengers, who all seemed curious to know what Hitler had said. Knowing Jimmy it would be lavatorial and she didn't want Freddie to think she laughed at such things. She wanted him to think of her as sophisticated future comptometer operator.

'Poland at last!' yelled Jimmy loud enough for everyone to hear. 'Get it? Poland – po – under t'bed.'

One or two of the other passengers smiled, more at Jimmy's enthusiasm than his wit. Susan cringed as she accepted a mug of tea from Freddie.

'Excuse my brother,' she gave Freddie her most dazzling smile. 'He can be vulgar at times.'

'Oh, I don't know,' grinned Freddie. 'He's been making me laugh. He's a bit of a card is your brother.'

Susan blushed and went quiet, she didn't know how to deal with such situations. She'd never been in love before. Freddie took his tea across to a wooden fence and leaned over it, staring into the distance.

'I used to spend my summers not far from here. Mum and Dad had a country cottage...' He pointed above the adjacent houses towards a distant hill. 'Just beyond that hill. I used to walk it from this station for school hols. Takes about an hour, lovely walk. It must be, I don't know, three years since I last went there. Wonder what it's like?'

'Why don't we go and have a look?' asked Jimmy, simply.

'Because I'm due at the Grand Hotel in Scarborough at eight o'clock in the morning – and the army get very cross when you're late.'

'I know, they used ter get cross with me dad,' agreed Jimmy. 'He used to sneak out of the barracks and ride home on his bike to see us.'

'I think I'd have got on well with your dad,' smiled Freddie. 'We might have had a lot in common.'

'Maybe there's another train,' suggested Susan. A country walk with the man of her dreams seemed like such a good idea to her.

'I'll go and ask,' said Jimmy impetuously and before Freddie could give him an argument he was gone. With an amused smile, the young soldier watched Jimmy run off, his short grey trousers flapping loosely around his skinny legs. Freddie turned his attention to Susan, not noticing the adoration in her eyes.

'There's more to it than you've told me, isn't there?'

'More to what?'

'More to your running away. It'd take more than any old Auntie Dorothy to scare you two.'

'I can't tell you.'

'Okay, but if you need any help you'd better be quick and ask.'

'We'll be alright, thank you.'

No way was she going to involve Freddie in a murder charge. What sort of impression would that give?

Jimmy came hurtling back, skidding to a halt at the last minute as he almost ran straight past them.

'There's one at seven-twenty-three in the morning. Gets into Scarborough at seven-forty-two – or was it fifty-two?'

Freddie smiled and shook his head. 'That gives me either eight or eighteen minutes to get from the station to the Grand Hotel, and that's if the train's on time, which it never is. It'd be irresponsible of me to leave it so late.'

The disappointment on the children's faces was too much for him. 'So?' he added. 'What are we waiting for?'

Freddie lifted them over the fence one by one before vaulting over himself. Susan could have done the same with ease, but she much preferred this way.

It was early evening now and the late summer was warming their backs as the three of them headed towards the cottage. Freddie led the way, kitbag over his shoulder, whistling 'Pack Up Your

Troubles In Your Old Kitbag And Smile, Smile, Smile.' Jimmy walked beside him singing lustily. Susan walked just a few steps behind, her eyes firmly fixed on the man of her dreams. He was tall, taller than their dad, maybe six feet, but a lot skinnier. His hair was thick and shiny black and needed a good comb. The thing she liked most about him was his smile. It was one of those smiles that lit up all his face and made you want to smile back. A smile like the sun coming out, that's what Mam would have said. She used to say that a lot about Dad when he was away. Maybe that's why she liked Freddie so much, he reminded her of Dad, only a bit younger. Susan couldn't remember a happier time, shame about the murder they had hanging over them. Still, you can't have everything.

This was an alien world to Jimmy and Susan. Fields and hedgerows and cows and sheep and barns and farms were all the stuff of books. The gritty West Riding of Yorkshire was their world, which, in its own way was as attractive a playground to kids as any old green field. But they couldn't help but marvel at the beauty all around them.

'Ugh!' groaned a disgusted Jimmy, as his foot squelched into a cow pat. Susan laughed as her brother scraped his shoe clean on the grass. Jimmy remembered a joke he'd heard at school, which until now had meant nothing to him.

'Hey, Freddie! Did yer hear about that feller what lost his flat cap in a cow field? He tried two dozen on before he found his own!' Jimmy howled with delight at the newly revealed significance of this latest addition to his repertoire. Freddie laughed, more at Jimmy than at the joke.

The path Freddie led them along took them temptingly close to an apple orchard. The heavily laden branches of one tree practically overhung the fence which ran crookedly beside the path. Freddie hoisted Jimmy up onto his shoulders.

'Right, Jimmy, lad, it's apples for tea.'

Jimmy was oddly reluctant.

'Don't tell me a tyke like you has never been apple scrumping.'

'No,' said Jimmy truthfully. There weren't many orchards in Leeds. Not that he was above the odd bit of larceny. Many an illicit apple had found its way into Jimmy's pocket from the display outside Mallinson's greengrocers as Jimmy passed by on his way to school.

'He's wanted by the coppers,' explained Susan, who understood her brother's reluctance to be a party to further crime.

Jimmy gave her a look of horror at betraying their secret. He tried to repair the damage by changing the subject. 'It's alright,' he said, 'I'll get some.'

He reached out and plucked a dozen or so of the choice russet fruit and dropped them down to Susan, who caught them expertly, the late evening sun glinting off her long blonde hair as she darted laughingly about, catching the falling fruit.

'Oy!' The angry voice came from the other side of the orchard.

'Now there's a voice I haven't heard for a long

time,' warned Freddie, with some urgency. 'Quick, kids, best be off!'

The three of them beat an urgent retreat up the path as the orchard's owner arrived at the scene of the crime hurling loud and obscene abuse at the fleeing miscreants.

'An' don't think I don't know who yer are, yer thievin' young bugger. I'll be telling yer dad when next I see him!'

The three of them ran pell mell up the path, the odd contraband apple falling from their pockets, until they came to a stile where they stopped to catch their breath. Freddie sat down on the wooden step and smiled a nostalgic smile. 'It's like I've never been away. He threatened to tell my father every time I nicked his apples.'

'And did he?' asked Susan.

'No, he was frightened to death of Dad. Dad was a magistrate and old Dan Braithwaite back there was the local poacher. Mind you, if old Dan had had the sense to tell Dad, I'd have been for it.' Freddie looked up at Jimmy, who had climbed onto the drystone wall above him. 'Right, young James. It's about time you spilled the beans. What's all this about the coppers after you.'

'Oh that, it weren't nowt.'

'Well, if it weren't nowt,' said Freddie, gently mimicking Jimmy's broad accent, 'you won't mind telling me.'

Jimmy looked at Susan for guidance. She just shrugged and bent down to pick a nearby buttercup. 'He did a murder!' she said suddenly.

Freddie did a double take of Susan's face to check for any signs of leg pulling. The look she returned was all too genuine, she wasn't kidding. He looked hard at Jimmy. These kids were serious.

'Murder? Who did you murder?'

Jimmy's face crumpled under even such sympathetic questioning. His sister answered for him.

'Leon Murgatroyd. He were beatin' me up and our Jimmy brayed him with a cricket bat.' She turned to her tearful brother. 'There's no need ter cry. Freddie won't tell nobody.' Then to Freddie, 'Will yer?'

'No,' said Freddie, standing up and placing a comforting hand on Jimmy's thin shoulder. 'No, of course not. It sounds to me that this Leon Murgatroyd got what he deserved.'

'Well, I don't suppose he deserved to die – actually,' admitted Susan.

'And who says he's dead?'

'Jackie Crombie, he had a right good look at Murgy and said he were dead alright.'

'Jackie Crombie, eh? I suppose you mean *Doctor* Jacky Crombie?'

Freddie inclined his head and gave Susan the same look that her dad used to give her when she'd said something daft. She began to see what Freddie was getting at.

'And how old is this – *Doctor* Crombie?'

'Eleven,' she answered, almost embarrassed.

'Well now, perhaps you're not quite the wicked desperadoes you think you are,' smiled Freddie. He stood up. 'Come on,' he ordered. 'Onwards and upwards. Tomorrow we'll pick up a paper from Malton Station and see if there's any news of murder most foul in Leeds. If not, you're in the clear.'

Most of this conversation went on above Jimmy's head. As he trudged along beside Susan he whispered, 'What's he on about?'

'He thinks Murgy might not be dead.'

Jimmy visibly brightened at this news and took a noisy run at a herd of cows, scattering them with his whoops, treading into another cow pat and hopping around in disgust. Jimmy would never be a country boy.

The cottage, when they arrived, was something of a disappointment to Jimmy, who expected a thatched roof at the very least. It was nice enough as cottages go, but the years of neglect had taken a savage toll. Set in a large, untended garden, it was built of weathered, pale red brick with a stone slate roof in need of urgent repair and tiny leaded windows, also in need of some repair. Part of the wooden guttering had broken away, taking with it a rusting downspout, which leaned away from the wall at an impossible angle. The paint-work was cracked and peeling and the stone window ledges spattered with bird droppings. A rustic bower was attached to the front of the house, around which grew a mass of roses, strangulated and untended for many years. There presumably, to provide a scented welcome to anyone wishing to enter the doorway beyond, but defeating this object with a thorny vengeance.

Freddie absent-mindedly fingered the cracked wooden sign on the gate which read 'Fiddler's Cottage' as he viewed his childhood holiday home with a measure of disappointment.

'Does it still belong to your dad?' enquired Susan.

Freddie nodded. 'For what it's worth. I thought someone was supposed to be looking after it. You should have seen it when I was a kid, it was beautiful.'

'I still think it's beautiful,' said Susan. 'It's sorta – natural. Miss Formby who takes us for nature study said Mother Nature was the best gardener – and she never had a lawn mower.'

Freddie smiled in surprise at the poetry in Susan's urban soul. 'Then this is Miss Formby's type of garden alright. Come on, let's see if we can get in. I don't fancy getting scratched to death on those rose thorns, so maybe we should try round the back. We used to keep a couple of spare keys in the shed … that's if the shed's still there.'

The shed was very much worse for wear, but it was still there, so were the keys. However, it seemed they were unnecessary, the back door was already open. The lock violently smashed.

'Hello,' muttered Freddie. 'I think we've had visitors.'

'We never lock our doors at home,' said Jimmy.

'We never had owt to nick,' said Susan as they walked tentatively into the dark interior.

A loud flutter of wings brought a yell of fright from the children as a couple of frightened starlings made their getaway. Another bird, not quite so lucky, lay dead in front of the fireplace.

'They come down the chimney and can't find their way out,' explained Freddie.

He opened a couple of sets of curtains to let in

some scattered light and the three of them surveyed the room. The sunlight illuminated the disturbed dust rising in clouds from everywhere they trod, and glinted off cobwebs galore. There was a three-piece suite in cracked brown leather. An oak dining table with four ill-matching chairs and a tiled fireplace that had burned logs in its heyday. A brass oil lamp stood on the table and another lay cracked and useless on the floor, the oil from it had long since soaked into the threadbare Axminster, leaving a large black stain. Other dark brownish stains spattered the carpet, some leading to a small hallway.

'What's through there?' asked Susan, pointing towards the hallway.

'Kitchen, and – my old bedroom,' said Freddie. He smiled to himself. 'I bet it's still in a tip.'

Jimmy was already through there. Freddie and Susan made to follow him, when he appeared at the hall doorway, breathing in small gasps, his face chalk-white.

Chapter Three

Kurt Weidling sat at the controls of his Dornier. He was alone. It was August 1944 and the war was going badly. Especially for Kurt. His wife and daughter had been killed during the fire bombing of Magdeburg some months ago. He hated his job, he hated the war, he hated the Führer and today he hated the SS, especially

Colonel Otto von Manstein, for whom he was impatiently waiting on the tarmac of this God-forsaken hole. It was a secret mission, he'd been told. This was the third 'secret mission' he'd flown for the Colonel in as many weeks. Little fat Otto was feathering his own nest and the only person taking the risk was Kurt. His lone aircraft stood on an airfield just outside Brussels. Deserted now in the face of the Allied advance. His destination, Berlin.

Von Manstein had already been on board to bark out his instructions. He would be back in about half an hour. 'Guard this with your life!' he'd ordered, passing Kurt a small leather case. Kurt placed it on the empty navigator's seat and waited for the SS officer to return with the men carrying the rest of the booty. Kurt had a good idea what he was carrying, but it wouldn't be prudent to ask von Manstein for precise details. Mainly paintings and *objets d'art*, looted from houses all across France and Belgium. He'd been placed at von Manstein's disposal by his own commanding officer, Colonel Fischer, who, to Kurt's mind, was obviously in league with the SS man.

Kurt looked at his watch, 10.15 p.m., von Manstein and his men should be back in ten minutes. How much longer must this stupid war go on? When could he go home? He gave a hollow laugh. Home, to what? The so-called Third Reich had taken too much away from him. His wife, his daughter, his house – and for what? Still Oberleutnant after four years of combat missions. His promotion held back because of his

43

general attitude. Mind anywhere but on the job etcetera. What did they expect? If they wanted him to take an interest in the war they shouldn't put idiots in charge of him. And now these idiots were losing a war which, at the beginning, was theirs for the taking.

He picked up the leather case and weighed it speculatively in his hand. What was in it? Money? – probably not. Documents? – maybe. It was fastened with two buckled straps. Von Manstein had said nothing about not looking inside, only to guard it with his life. The least he could do was to find out what was worth more than his life. He scanned the perimeter of the airfield with his field binoculars to confirm to himself that he wouldn't be disturbed, then undid the two buckles and opened the case.

Inside was a large, black velvet bag, tied with a silk cord. Kurt undid the cord and emptied the contents onto the navigator's seat beneath him. Even in the dim cabin light the jewels shone with a brilliance that took Kurt's breath away. There were all kinds of stones, mostly diamonds though. Necklaces, bracelets, rings, two tiaras and many loose stones, too many to count. He stared at them for a while, not daring to touch anything. In the distance he saw the glow of hooded headlights approaching. Sweeping up the jewels, he put them back in the bag and the bag in the case. He'd buckled it up when he noticed the three rings still lying there on the navigator's seat. The headlights had entered the airfield now. He put the three rings in his pocket, telling himself, 'He'll never notice three rings out of all that lot – but what if he does? That'll be the end of Kurt Weidling's Luftwaffe career – what am I talking about? That'll be the end of Kurt Weidling.' With surprising clarity of thought, he started up the engine and taxied to the end of the runway. He could see the lorry clearly now, heading across the grass towards him. Von Manstein would wonder what he was doing. Kurt smiled to himself as he imagined the panic on little fat Otto's face when eventually he realised what was happening. He took off the brakes and sent the pencil-slim bomber rolling down the runway. The lorry turned awkwardly and tried to follow him, but Kurt was airborne. He thought he heard shots from the ground but he was free and clear – and rich. A manic grin lit up his face. As far as Oberleutnant Kurt Weidling was concerned, the war had ended early.

He headed north towards England, a plan slowly formulating in his racing brain. There was enough fuel for a long one-way trip. He would follow the route he took that time they'd sent him to bomb Leeds. Over the North Sea, far enough away from land to avoid the low level coastal radar. He couldn't guarantee landing it though, he'd have to parachute. No, forget parachuting, the very thought of that sent a chill up his spine. He'd parachuted out of his previous Dornier and spent three hours swinging from a tree until a French farmer, at the point of Kurt's Luger, had climbed up and freed him. Still, it could have been worse, at least he'd made it out alive, which was more than could be said for young Eberbach, who'd just been promoted to Oberleutnant that week. A hundred and eighty miles he'd travelled, on one engine. The damn thing packed in just ten minutes from base. Eberbach was already dead. Feldwebel Blomberg, the gunner, had cradled his head in his lap all the way back, unable to stem the blow of blood sloshing all over the cabin floor. He'd coughed his last breath just as the second engine packed in, weird that. Eberbach would have been twenty-one the following day. What a stupid waste of life! What a stupid war!

Once Kurt cleared the Channel he felt reasonably safe. All the action was going on behind him now. He found a deep bank of cloud and flew into it, maintaining this strategy like a thief in the night, dodging from door to door, or in Kurt's case, cloud to cloud. Eventually, far below on his left he saw the Humber Estuary and altered his course to 280 degrees. The North Yorkshire moors.

On his map there looked to be many possibilities of landing sites, anything to avoid another night up a tree – or worse. His final plan was to ditch the plane, bury the jewels somewhere where he could find them later, then give himself up. The English were notoriously decent captors, so that part of it should be alright. All in all it was a good plan – not foolproof, but good enough for a spur of the moment effort. Then the starboard engine began to splutter.

Landing on rough moorland with one engine was suicidal even for a pilot of Kurt's ability; so his options had narrowed. Setting the controls at straight and level, Kurt pulled on a parachute and opened the door. He stood for a while looking out at the night sky, thinking about his beautiful wife and daughter, and how he wished they could be with him to share this new found wealth. Why did they have to die? What sort of animals could callously drop bombs on such innocent people?

The few seconds it took for the parachute to open seemed like an eternity. Kurt released his pent up breath and looked at the darkness of the ground below him. He could well have qualified as the most useless parachutists in the Luftwaffe. Kurt had no control whatsoever over where he landed, otherwise he wouldn't have chosen to land on Freddie's cottage. He hit the roof with some considerable force, breaking several slates and his left leg. In great pain, he managed to release his parachute, which was swept away on the stiff breeze. Then he slid backwards off the roof and head first down the side of the cottage, ripping his side open on a sharp metal spike protruding from the wall, which in normal times was there to tie an innocent washing line to.

Kurt hit the ground in grave distress. The wound in his side pumping out blood. If he could only get inside the cottage, perhaps the people who lived there might help. He'd fallen right beside the back door. Raising himself on his good knee he banged as loud as he could, but there was no reply. He tried to open the door, but it was locked.

Taking out his pistol, Kurt emptied the chamber into the lock. Not caring who heard. As it happened the only person who did hear was Mrs Braithwaite, who woke her husband up with harsh instructions for him to investigate. Dan, who hadn't heard the shots, assured her it must be a fellow poacher about his clandestine business and good luck to him. He dropped back off to sleep with a stream of vitriol from his ever loving wife ringing in his uncaring ears.

The door swung open under the onslaught and Kurt dragged himself inside. Perhaps if he could find a bed to lie on he would be alright. Don't die now, Kurt, not now you've come this far. He dragged himself into the hallway and spotted Freddie's bedroom and the welcoming bed. A grim smile flickered across his lips, he'd be alright now. A good long rest and I'll be good as new. If only my side didn't hurt so much. His eyes suddenly slammed open in horror. The case! He'd forgotten the case! You stupid bastard, Weidling! No wonder you never got promotion, they were right, you're an idiot. He cursed himself soundly until he realised the truth of the situation. Then he smiled to himself, 'What the hell! I'm dying anyway. Better to be with my beautiful wife and daughter than hang around in this ugly world.' With a monumental effort he reached into his pocket and took out the three rings and held them up, one by one in the moonlight, the pale diamond light reflecting on his face as he died.

Freddie looked down at Kurt and shuddered. Susan and Jimmy stood in the doorway behind him, not daring to come any closer.

'Looks as though he's been dead a week or two,' guessed Freddie. 'Phew! He doesn't smell too good, does he? Bled to death by the look of it. He's German – Luftwaffe officer, a Flying Officer, I think. What the hell's he doing in my cottage?' He took a step back. 'Better not touch him, don't want to be accused of anything.'

'We're going to have to tell someone, aren't we?' said Susan, who could see this spoiling their romantic evening.

'Tomorrow maybe, not tonight,' said Freddie. 'We're not on the phone here. Besides,' he nodded at Kurt, 'he's not going anywhere.'

'I'm not spending no night with no dead German,' protested Jimmy.

'You don't have to,' said Freddie. 'There should be a tent in the hall cupboard. You two can sleep in the garden.'

'What about you?' asked a disappointed Susan, too young for any carnal inclinations towards Freddie, just an innocent childhood crush.

'I'll sleep upstairs.'

Susan's fear of sleeping in the same house as a dead German easily outweighed her infatuation with Freddie, so she elected to join Jimmy in the tent.

The sun had gone down over the distant hill by the time they'd got the tent erected. Or to be more precise, by the time Freddie had got it erected. Stolen apples, biscuits and chocolate from Freddie's kitbag and water from the kitchen tap went some way to satisfying their hunger. The three of them sat in the overgrown, moonlit garden beneath a vastness of stars, brighter and more majestic than anything the kids had ever seen before in the sooty skies above Leeds. They

49

sat and talked for a while. Freddie told of his childhood in India and then in London. And how his ex-soldier father had moved them all to Yorkshire at the outbreak of the war. Apart from the cottage they had a large house in Harrogate where his father and mother lived. Freddie was twenty-one and after the war intended to study medicine, which his mother thought was a marvellous idea but his dad, Brigadier Harry Fforbes-Fiddler, wasn't too keen.

'Fiddler?' Susan and Jimmy howled with laughing. 'You're called Freddie Fiddler?'

'Alright, alright, have your fun, I've heard it all before,' said Freddie. 'I must say, there was a time when I would have preferred to have been christened George or Jack or anything but Frederick. But it was my mother's father's name – I don't think anyone stopped to think how funny it would sound with Fiddler stuck on the end. Oddly enough, I've grown to like it – it has a sort of ring to it, don't you think?'

'I think it's a lovely name,' lied Susan, after she'd calmed down.

'Freddie Fiddler, Freddie – Fiddler' repeated Jimmy, trying to work out what sort of a ring it had to it. Then his face creased with a laugh he tried hard to control, but failed miserably, setting his sister off.

Freddie shook his head and grinned ruefully. 'It's actually Fforbes-Fiddler, if you really want to rub it in, with Fforbes spelt with two Fs.'

'You mean like Freddie F-Forbes Fiddler?' said Susan.

'That's a lot of effing Fs,' chortled Jimmy.

50

'Too many for me,' agreed Freddie. 'No, I answer to plain old Freddie Fiddler. The old man doesn't like it, says I'm letting the side down, he's a terrible old snob, bit of a bully too if he can get away with it. Typical army type.'

Presently Jimmy fell asleep. Freddie picked him up, laid him on a groundsheet inside the tent and covered him with a blanket.

'Right then,' he said to Susan. 'Better get some kip ourselves, early start in the morning.'

Susan nodded, disappointed the night ever had to end, then lay down beside her sleeping brother, to plan her life with Freddie. There'd be just the two of them living in Fiddler's cottage. No dead Germans of course, or even lavatorial brothers. Just the two of them. Mr and Mrs Freddie Fiddler – it had a ring to it. It was around four in the morning when an owl hooted, waking Jimmy up with a start. He shook Susan awake.

'What was that?'

The owl obliged with another hoot.

'It's a flipping owl,' grumbled his sleepy sister. 'Have you woken me up just to listen to a rotten old owl?'

'How was I to know it was a flipping owl? I've never heard an owl before.'

'Well you have now, so go to sleep.'

Dorothy sat at the old upright piano in the back room. Not exactly an accomplished pianist, she played more for relaxation than for entertainment. It was Tommy's piano and Tommy could set the thing on fire with his vibrant ragtime

51

style. The occasional bum note was of little concern to Tommy who played with his soul rather than his fingers. She smiled at the thought of him as she tinkled out her own simplified version of 'Morning' from Grieg's *Peer Gynt*. On the top of the piano in front of her were two photographs of her and Tommy, taken on Blackpool front. Tommy had managed to get the Tower growing out of her 'Kiss Me Quick' hat, and he was standing outside Gypsy Rose Lee's fortune telling booth with a look of despair on his face and a water pistol to his head.

The clock on the mantelpiece made a half-hearted attempt at chiming midnight but gave up after four-and-a-half pathetic bongs. They'd been gone over ten hours now. A disappointed Jackie Crombie had been round with the news that Leon Murgatroyd wasn't dead after all, only concussed with a broken nose and broken teeth. Dorothy wasn't absolutely clear why they'd run away, it had never occurred to her that Jackie's fatal diagnosis of Murgy's condition might have had something to do with it. At first she'd been annoyed at them for stealing the rent money, but now the anger had subsided, maybe she didn't blame them for running away, they knew she'd be no comfort to them, no matter what the problem was. Too wrapped up in her own problems, that was her trouble.

Dorothy had reported their disappearance to the police, who only became interested when they found an assault had taken place. Their interest waning dramatically when they realised who the victim was.

'It'll take more than a cricket bat to knock some sense into young Murgatroyd's thick head,' commented a sergeant drily, when the details of the incident were revealed. 'Bring your lad in when they turn up, I'll put the frighteners on him.'

'*If* they turn up,' complained Dorothy, annoyed at their lack of enthusiasm.

'They'll turn up, they always do.'

'Always?' Dorothy fixed the sergeant with a stern glare. He coughed with discomfort and dropped his gaze from this beautiful but angry face.

'I'll, er, I'll put the word out for my men to be on the, er, the lookout.'

'Thank you, sergeant.' She swirled round and flounced out of Paradine Hill Police Station followed by many admiring glances and a few lascivious comments, most of which she'd heard before. She stormed back up Paradine Hill consumed with anger and then with guilt at her treatment of Jimmy and Susan – and especially William.

William had been nagging at Dorothy's conscience for some time now. When Fred and Lily had been killed, the three children had been automatically brought to Dorothy and Tommy's house. It wasn't the ideal situation but what option did they have? They'd had a good time, her and Tommy. Neither wanted to be saddled with kids straight away, plenty of time for that, then the war broke out so they decided to start a family as soon as hostilities ended, even if it took a couple of years.

Tommy had been called up not long after and the whole business was a shock to Dorothy's system. Bringing up two boisterous children and a baby was difficult enough when they were your own, but to have to bring up someone else's and without a husband to help was above and beyond the call of duty. Each day she grew worse. She could see it in her own face – she'd burst into tears for no reason. Having a baby in the house meant she couldn't even get a part-time job to pick up a bit of much needed money. That's why she decided to send William into care. It would be only for a while to see how it went. That's what she told herself. That's what she told Tommy in her letter explaining what she'd done. She told Jimmy and Susan that he'd gone on holiday for a while.

She coped after that. A part-time job in Bretheridges Jam Factory helped supplement the money Tommy sent home and things went a little better. It was heart-rending to see William's face every time they went to visit. Susan would tell him she'd be coming to get him soon. So she'd stopped going. She convinced herself it was better all round not to keep upsetting the lad. Besides, her nerves were getting worse even with just the two of them to look after. The constant nagging by the children about when their baby brother would be coming home was driving her mad. Then Tommy went off to France and the uncertainty of everything got too much for her. Every day she heard of someone's husband or son or brother being killed or going missing. People she knew. The D-Day landings had taken a heavy toll, as had the fighting in the immediate aftermath. She hadn't heard from him for two months, not a letter, not even one of those cryptic crossed-out messages to tell her he was alive and well. The neighbours came round to tell her that no news was good news and still the children asked about William. Then Lord Haw Haw had announced over the wireless that the Polar Bear Regiment had been completely wiped out.

'Isn't Uncle Tommy a Polar Bear? asked Jimmy, as the evil propagandist delivered his crackling gloating message across the airwaves.

Mrs Crombie, who was listening with them, laughed. 'Ee, yer've not ter take no notice of owt he says, love. He's just saying it ter put the wind up yer. It's all lies.'

And it was lies, but no one knew for sure. Lord Haw Haw was cunning enough to sprinkle enough truth among his lies to sow seeds of worry amongst the listening population. They'd all been advised to switch off as soon as he broke into their programme. But many didn't.

As the ensuing days went by, Dorothy sank into a deep depression. Sitting at the window, watching and waiting for the postman to come with good news. News that didn't arrive – not in time anyway. And every day without fail, either Jimmy or Susan would ask about William. It was Susan who asked that day. The postman had been with an official looking letter which Dorothy had feverishly ripped open. It was from the Children's Home. William had had measles but he was okay now and was looking forward to a visit.

Riddled with despair and guilt she let the letter drop to the floor, the heading on the letter plain to be seen. *'Oxford House Children's Home'* Susan turned her head around to read it.

'It's about William, isn't it?' she cried. 'Is he coming home, Auntie?' As Susan bent down to pick up the letter, something inside Dorothy cracked. Before her niece could pick it up she stamped her foot on it.

'Leave it!' she commanded.

Susan jumped back. Startled by the sharpness of her auntie's voice.

'What is it, Auntie?' Susan looked first at Dorothy, then at Jimmy, who'd just come into the room.

Dorothy was breathing heavily now. Unable to understand what was happening to her. She'd been convinced the letter would contain good news about Tommy.

Why she said what she did shocked her.

'He's dead!' she screamed. 'Your brother's dead! Are you satisfied now!' Then she picked up the letter and ran upstairs where she dissolved, sobbing on the bed.

Jimmy and Susan looked at each other. Unable to take in the gravity of what they'd just been told. Then they put their arms around each other as they'd done all those years ago when the bomb dropped on their house. It was all they could think of.

Dorothy lay on the bed all day, undisturbed by Jimmy and Susan, who were coping with the news in their own way.

They'll get over it, she thought. As soon as I hear Tommy's okay, I'll tell them the truth. Pretend there's been some terrible mix up at the children's home.

Thus justifying her actions she went about her daily business. They'd missed the funeral, she explained to them, because the stupid bureaucrats in charge of things had told her too late. When in doubt always blame the stupid bureaucrats, that's what they're there for.

Jimmy and Susan, especially Susan, had cried on and off for days and then, with the resilience of the young, had accepted their baby brother's death. Susan prayed every night for the repose of his soul as well as Mam and Dad's and knew that they'd be looking after him. Jimmy felt better when Susan explained this to him.

A week after Dorothy had delivered the fateful news, she heard from Tommy – he was okay. That's all the letter said, but it was enough for Dorothy.

But she never told the kids the truth. They'd never mentioned William from that day and she was amazed at the burden this lifted from her. When Tommy gets home, that's the time to tell them, she thought. I can cope till then.

Gently closing the piano lid, Dorothy kissed the photograph of her husband and sat in the comfy chair. She didn't want the kids to find her in bed when they came home.

Jimmy couldn't sleep. He lay there thinking about the dead German.

'Betcha daren't sneak in an' look at him,' he challenged.

'You what? Look at who?'

'The dead German.'

'Look at him yerself!'

'I've looked at him. It were me what found him!'

'Well, I've looked at him as well! And I'd like to go to sleep now.'

'You didn't look at him properly like I did. He looked a lot deader than Leon Murgatroyd.'

'That's 'cause Leon Murgatroyd wasn't dead. You didn't hit him hard enough.'

'I hit him as hard as I could – betcha daren't go right up to him an' touch him.'

Susan hated being outdared by Jimmy. The trouble was, for a skinny kid, he was so flipping fearless. She decided to call his bluff. 'I'll go if you will!'

'Right,' said Jimmy, who now wished he hadn't started this.

'Come on then,' challenged Susan, convinced he'd back down.

'Right, you come on then.' Jimmy stood up with a look of determination that told Susan she wasn't going to get out of this one.

The two of them trod carefully and fearfully across the kitchen. A loud snoring came from upstairs, which destroyed many of Susan's romantic illusions about Freddie. A three-quarter moon shone through the bedroom window, bathing the dead German in an eerie light they could have done without. The children froze in the doorway, Jimmy moved in first and stood beside the bed, staring down at Kurt's face, which was very much worse for wear.

'I've never seen a dead person before,' he whispered to Susan who had nervously joined him.

'No, nor me. He whiffs a bit, doesn't he?'

'Phew!' agreed Jimmy.

Susan's eyes fell on Kurt's left hand, something was gleaming beneath his fingers.

'He's got something in his hand!' she whispered, as though not wanting to wake him up.

'Get it then!' urged Jimmy.

'You get it.'

'Why should I? You're the oldest!'

She knew he'd say that. Gently lifting Kurt's lifeless hand, she made a quick grab for what was underneath then ran out of the bedroom with Jimmy close on her heels. Neither of them stopping until they'd dived into the tent.

Susan opened her hand to reveal three rings. One, a large diamond solitaire, the second, a diamond cluster set round a larger central stone, and the third, a slightly smaller stone set in a heavy gold band and giving off a brilliant pale blue iridescence in the moonlight.

'Bugger me!' breathed Jimmy, who normally never swore in front of his sister.

'It's jewels!' exclaimed Susan.

'We're rich,' said Jimmy.

'No, we're not, they're not ours,' argued Susan, to whom dishonesty was the most mortal of sins. There were other, more interesting sins she found out about later in life, most of which she

59

would commit with enthusiastic regularity.

'Well, they can't be the German's, he's dead,' countered Jimmy. 'Anyway, he's our enemy so we wouldn't have to give things back even if he wasn't dead – which he is.' He added the last bit to give conclusive weight to his argument. Jimmy had his own sense of logic which always seemed to work to his advantage.

'We'd better ask Freddie, he'll know,' said Susan.

This disappointed Jimmy, who had a deep suspicion of all adults, even Freddie. 'Oh, alright,' he conceded. 'Have we to go wake him now, then?'

'Might as well.'

Their fear of the dead German forgotten as they rushed upstairs to where Freddie lay snoring away, happily oblivious to the twist this night would make to all their lives.

Freddie, being a sound sleeper, took some waking up. His tiredness was soon forgotten at the sight of the three rings. 'They belong to the German,' said Susan simply.

'He's dead, so they can't belong to him,' pointed out Jimmy, who thought he'd settled this argument already.

Freddie shook his head. 'Blessed if I know what to think. They were in his hand, you say?'

The children nodded. Their eyes fixed on Freddie as they awaited his decision as to ownership.

'My guess,' he said, 'is that they didn't belong to him either. I reckon that if we look round in the morning we'll find evidence of a parachute or some plane wreckage or something.'

'You've got to be in Scarborough,' Susan reminded him.

'I think finding a dead German's quite a good excuse for being late, even for the army. Anyway, I'm not going till I find out a bit more about our dead benefactor.'

Jimmy didn't know what a benefactor was, but it sounded encouraging. He walked to the window and looked out at the brightening landscape outside.

'It's morning now,' he announced, 'and I'm hungry.' Jimmy always had his priorities in order.

'Pass me my kitbag and we'll finish off the last of my provisions,' said Freddie. 'Then we'll see what we can find.'

It took them until lunchtime to find the parachute, which had blown into a nearby copse. They returned to the cottage to discuss what to do next.

'I'm convinced the jewels are stolen,' said Freddie to his two young companions. 'The proper owners may well be dead and if not would be almost impossible to track down. We could hand them over to the authorities, that would be the right thing to do. We might even get a reward – the odds are we wouldn't get anything.'

'What do you think he was doing with them?' asked Susan.

'Who knows?' replied Freddie. 'I've got a feeling they're not his though.'

'They're not much use to him now,' observed Jimmy. 'How much do yer think they're worth?' He wasn't the least bit interested in where the jewels came from.

'Quite a lot,' said Freddie. 'This big solitaire must be worth a few hundred at least, that's if it's genuine.' He picked up the shimmering two-carat solitaire and scratched it across the window, leaving a deep groove. He then held it up to the light allowing the facets to reflect their brilliance into the children's eyes.

'It's a beauty, they can't make paste diamonds like this.'

'I think we should keep 'em,' decided Jimmy.

'It'd be nice if we could get away with it,' said Freddie, who seemed to be on Jimmy's side. 'No one would miss them, let's face it, no one knows about them, except us.'

'Let's take a vote on it,' suggested Jimmy, who wanted to act before Freddie changed his mind. 'Hands up who wants to keep 'em.'

His own hand went up as he said it, Freddie looked at Susan, then slowly put his own hand up.

'That's it!' laughed Jimmy, triumphantly. 'Two out of three.'

'No,' cautioned Freddie. 'It has to be unanimous.'

Jimmy wasn't sure what unanimous meant but it sounded bad and his face dropped. Freddie looked at Susan and said gently, 'All three of us have to agree or it won't work.'

Susan's conscience disappeared under the onslaught of the young soldier's dark brown eyes. She raised her hand in the air.

'Right, spuds up,' declared Jimmy.

Freddie, whose public school education had

sadly failed to teach him the time honoured way of deciding 'who goes first', looked bemused. Susan and Jimmy already held out their two clenched fists at the ready. Freddie did the same but didn't have a clue why. Jimmy took it upon himself to do the honours. He went round the small circle of fists, banging each one with his own right fist, one at a time.

'One potatie, two potatie, three potatie, four,' he sang, at a rate of one potatie per fist banged. 'Five potatie, six potatie, seven potatie, more.' The word 'more' came as he banged down on Susan's right fist. With a small scowl she tucked it away behind her, if it happened again she was out. The last one in got to choose first. Not surprisingly it was Jimmy, who had long since figured out how to work this method of dipping to his favour, no matter how many were in the circle. Unfortunately his 'spuds up' expertise wasn't matched by his knowledge of jewellery. He chose the diamond cluster. Susan, who was next, had already fallen in love with the blue stone, leaving the large solitaire to Freddie, who felt guilty at being left with what looked to be the pick of the crop so to speak.

'You do realise you've probably left me the best one,' he warned.

Jimmy held his ring up to the light. 'Rubbish!' he chortled. 'You can't fiddle us, Freddie Fiddler!' He and Susan laughed, but Freddie shook his head and slipped the ring into his pocket.

As the midday sun forced its way through the unwashed windows, the three of them sat round the kitchen table. Freddie examined their faces one by one, inducing in the children a feeling of mild apprehension.

'What's up?' queried Jimmy, nervously.

'What's up,' answered Freddie, 'is you two, that's what's up. Both sitting there, each with a valuable diamond ring in your pocket, but what do you think you're going to do with them?'

'Flog 'em,' answered Jimmy, surprised at such a question.

'And what would a scruffy little tyke like you be doing with a very expensive diamond ring?' asked Freddie.

Jimmy wasn't sure what Freddie was on about, but Susan understood. 'We can't sell them, can we?' she said.

'Not straight away you can't. You'll have to hide them somewhere safe until you're much older – and what's more important,' he reached across the table and held both their hands to emphasise his point, 'you must not tell anyone – and I mean no one. Not even Auntie Dorothy or Uncle Tommy.'

'Especially not Auntie Dorothy,' said Jimmy.

'No one!' said Freddie. There was an un-characteristic gravity in his voice which took the children by surprise. He made them both swear a solemn oath of secrecy.

'What's the most sacred thing you can swear by?'

'Our Lady of Lourdes,' said Susan.

'Me mam and dad,' said Jimmy.

'Okay. Do you swear by Our Lady of Lourdes and your mam and dad that you'll never breathe a word of this to anyone so help you God and strike you down dead if you do?'

'I do,' said Jimmy and Susan together, although they weren't happy with the bit about God striking them down dead.

'Right then,' said Freddie. 'What you must do is keep them safe until the war's finished, then we'll meet up again and I'll see what I can work out.'

'But what if – you know?' asked Jimmy, uncertainly.

'You mean what if I don't come back?' He held up a hand to stop Susan's admonition of her younger brother. 'No, it's a fair question, there's a chance I might not.'

He didn't notice the look of panic on Susan's face. She made up her mind there and then to pray for Freddie's safe return every spare minute she had – and nobody prayed better than she did. Her panic subsided at this reassuring idea. Freddie rubbed his unshaven chin, his brows creased in thought. He held Susan in his gaze, unconsciously melting her beneath his thoughtful brown eyes.

'It'd be up to you, Susan,' he decided. 'When you're a young lady, say eighteen or so, you should take them, one at a time, to two different jewellers. But you'll need to dress the part and talk the part, not to arouse suspicion. We're talking about quite a lot of money. Enough to give you both a nice start in life, and God knows, you deserve it. I'm sure the previous owners of the stuff wouldn't begrudge you that.'

'*Dress the part and talk the part,*' odd words, but

65

fortunately they stuck in Susan's mind.

The walk back to the station took much longer than the reverse journey the day before. Neither of the children wanted this magic time together to end. Not Jimmy, who still had a possible murder charge to face; and not Susan, because she was desperately in love with Freddie and just wanted this time to go on for ever.

Freddie solemnly shook hands with Jimmy and kissed Susan lightly on the forehead through the open train window.

'When do you think we'll see you again?' asked Susan, fighting to hold back the tears.

'I've got your address. As soon as the war's over, I'll come and see you.'

'Promise?'

'Promise,' smiled Freddie.

He stood and waved to them until their train was out of sight, before sitting disconsolately down on a platform seat to await his own train and whatever the army had to say about his absence.

Freddie notified the authorities about the dead German who was taken away and buried with whatever ceremony was due to an enemy soldier, which wasn't a lot. His aircraft had already been found, crashed on the Yorkshire moors, forty miles north of Freddie's cottage. A local search had been carried out for the crew and it was thought that at least three of them could still be at large.

But why did they leave behind a case containing a fortune in jewellery?

On their way from the tram stop to Auntie Dorothy's, they passed Bramham Street cemetery where their mam and dad lay buried beneath a single, economically lettered, granite slab. Climbing over the low wall to spare themselves the walk to the gate, they made their sacrilegious way across various overgrown graves to where Lily and Fred lay buried. They waited quite a while until an old lady, visiting her last two husbands, buried in nearby adjacent plots said her tearful goodbyes, seemingly favouring the earlier of the two. The children wondered what was wrong with the second incumbent, who, according to the inscription, had certainly stayed at his post a lot longer than his predecessor. But who knows about such things?

Between the two of them they managed to lift up the slab until it was standing on end, then, with Jimmy holding it balanced in position, Susan using a sharp stone, scraped out a shallow hole, just big enough to take the tiny potted meat jar they'd placed their diamond rings in. Then Jimmy let it go with a thud, prompting the two of them to apologise to their mam and dad for all this noise and inconvenience.

With their arms around each other they gritted their teeth and made their way to number thirteen Broughton Terrace and whatever retribution lay in store.

Dorothy woke up with a jolt in the chair in which she'd spent the last few hours trying to catch up on the previous sleepless night. The clock was attempting to strike 6 p.m. but stopped after four-and-a-half bongs, it always stopped after four-and-a-half bongs, even at an hour when four-and-a-half were more bongs than necessary.

Pushing herself up from the chair with the resigned effort of a woman twice her age, she turned wearily towards the scullery to put the kettle on. She was just lighting the larger of the two gas rings when something through the window caught her eye. Her heart gave a great surge of joy at the sight of two familiar blond heads loitering beyond the wall. Dorothy rushed to the door, yanked it open and dashed out into the back yard, her eyes streaming with tears of intense relief. Without a word of welcome or admonition she took the two dumbstruck children in her arms and hugged them. The three of them bursting into tears.

It was the first time anyone had hugged them like this since their mam and dad had died and they stayed there until Dorothy eventually stepped back, blinking away her tears. Jimmy looked up at her with a worried expression on his face.

'Auntie Dorothy – Leon Murgatroyd – he's not dead or owt is he?' he paused, terrified what the answer might be. Dorothy smiled and ruffled his hair.

'Dead?' she smiled, a glimmer of realisation setting in. 'I'm afraid not, he's alive and kicking, worse luck.' Then she forced her face into a stern expression and added. 'But what you did was wrong. He's got a broken nose and broken teeth. The worst part about it all, was the worry you've caused me.'

The children looked bemused.

'Running away,' explained Dorothy. 'Didn't you think I'd worry?'

The children shrugged, in truth they didn't. Dorothy's face softened. 'Maybe I'm being unfair, maybe you'd no reason to think I'd worry – but I did – and I'm sorry I wasn't there for you when you needed me.'

'We weren't running away from you, Auntie Dorothy,' said Susan. 'We thought Murgy was dead. Jimmy thought he'd murdered him.'

'Ah! So you were running from the hangman's noose,' laughed their auntie. 'By the way, young Jackie Crombie filled me in chapter and verse about why you gave Murgy a crack with the cricket bat.'

The children looked embarrassed at what Jackie might have said. He just didn't care didn't Jackie. Dorothy turned her back on them to hide the grin of approval on her face and walked into the scullery. Thugs like Leon Murgatroyd deserved a good crack with a cricket bat now and again, and if it was a Bairstow that did it, then all the better. Suddenly she turned round, the grin still intact.

'I don't suppose he'll be saying things like that about your mam and dad again in a hurry.'

Over Dorothy's shoulder the kettle was beginning to show signs of boiling. 'Right,' she said, 'I'll make us some tea while you tell me all about what you've been up to.'

Jimmy's appearance at the police station caused many a raised eyebrow. Leon Murgatroyd was known to the constabulary as a local tearaway who needed a good clip from a dad. But his dad being in jail, wasn't there to give him a good clip. The sight of the waif-like Jimmy owning up to being young Leon Murgatroyd's chastiser caused a certain amount of hilarity among the policemen and Jimmy got the promised ticking off from the sergeant who did well to keep his face straight. As a chastened Jimmy turned to go, the sergeant gave Dorothy what he hoped was a conspiratorial smile. She gave him a withering look that wiped it straight off his face.

'We're leaving now,' she said frostily, 'so do you think it's possible, sergeant, for your men to keep their crude remarks to themselves, at least until I'm out of earshot?'

As Jimmy galloped off in front of her up Paradine Hill, happy at no longer being a wanted criminal and eager to enjoy the freedom this entailed, Dorothy's thoughts inevitably drifted to her beloved Tommy. It was three months since she'd last seen him and she hadn't much of a clue where he was. Somewhere in France probably – avid reading of the papers kept her roughly informed. In her pocket she fingered a censored communication. She'd received from him just over a week ago. It used to be letters but now it was just a piece of printed paper with lines through all the bits of inappropriate information. At least he was still alive – or he had been two weeks ago when it had been sent. How would she cope if anything ever happened to him? She shuddered and dismissed the possibility from her mind – mustn't think like that. It was bad enough when Jimmy and Susan had gone missing. How odd she should take it as badly as that, she'd just spent twenty-four hours with what seemed like a lump of lead in her stomach. And how guilty she was beginning to feel about the rotten way she'd treated them, then she thought about William and the guilt got just too much. Dorothy stopped and looked in Freeman's window, forcing such thoughts out of her head. Replacing them with thoughts of her lovely Tommy. If only he could come home, all their problems would be solved in a flash. She scanned the array of freshly baked confectionery on display and allowing herself to be drawn inside by the only tempting aroma on Paradine Hill.

Chapter Four

Gunner Bairstow T. sat down on a twenty-five pound shell, resting in its wooden cradle and lit up a Capstan Full Strength, almost immediately coughing out a lungful of smoke. He'd only been smoking a week and he still hadn't quite got the hang of it. His Battery had just arrived, after an arduous overnight march, at the new gun position. It was mid-January 1945. He was cold, he was fed up and his feet were wet. He hadn't seen his wife for nine months, nor his nephew and niece – and he was still unhappy about what had happened to his youngest nephew, William. Sending him off to a home wasn't his idea of

71

looking after his dead brother's child.

Despite all his weeks of training and months of preparation for the big push across Europe, the most invaluable piece of advice had been given to him by his comrade-in-arms, Gunner Nobby Clarke. 'All yer need, Tommy me old son, is ter keep yer bowels open and yer socks dry – all the rest is bollocks.'

This turned out to be sound advice and dry socks had become almost an obsession with Tommy, who spent much of his spare time finding new ways of drying them. The other part of Nobby's advice was adequately taken care of by spasmodic German shells. He pulled a dry pair of socks on and revelled in the comfort as he slid his size-nine feet back into the size-ten boots.

After moving up to join their bit of Montgomery's 21st Army back in early November, this was the first progress they'd made, if you could call half a mile progress. Word had it that Monty and Eisenhower had been otherwise engaged further south in the Ardennes region of Belgium, where the Germans had broken through the Allied front, in what came to be known as the Battle of the Bulge. Now that that piece of nonsense had been taken care of, mainly by the American tank divisions, it was back to the business of winning the war.

They were in a muddy Dutch field just north of Nijmegen, facing General Gustav von Zangen's 15th Army spread out around Arnhem, just a few miles to the north across the Rhine. Back in September, the British First Airborne Division had been all but wiped out trying to take the bridges at Arnhem. Information such as this did little to fire Tommy with much enthusiasm for a prolonged military career.

His sensibilities had become somewhat brutalised over the last few weeks at the sudden loss of many new friends. So much so that he'd made up his mind not to become friendly with anyone else. Lance-Bombardier Nobby Clarke's annoyingly cheery Cockney manner made that difficult. He was also a difficult man to say 'no' to. As many French, Belgian and now Dutch girls found out to their cost. Tommy, as part of the war effort, had remained faithful to Dorothy. And it *had* been an effort.

'Gizza fag, Tommy.'

'No, smoke yer own fags,' said Tommy, determined not to give in this time.

'That's nice, innit? An' who taught you how ter smoke in the first place? If it weren't for me yer'd know nuffink about the pleasures of nicotine. That's bleedin' nice, that is. Yer do a mate a favour an'...'

Tommy threw Nobby a cigarette just to shut him up. 'That's yer last one, then it's your turn.'

'Say no more, Tommy me old son, you're a scholar an' a bleedin' gentleman,' grinned Nobby, leaning happily against a field gun and lighting up his cigarette.

To Nobby, O.P. meant 'other people's' – a brand of cigarette so much more satisfying than smoking your own. Whereas to Captain Hetherington, approaching them from the Command Post, it meant Observation Post, which is what he had in mind that morning for Tommy and Nobby.

He pointed at a shell-damaged farm building on top of a piece of higher ground a couple of hundred yards ahead. 'Run a wire up to the farm and set up an O.P. There's a German gun emplacement up ahead. We need to knock it out before we go any further.'

Tommy and Nobby saluted more smartly than was necessary. 'Yes, sir, very good, sir,' said Tommy.

The captain hesitated a second, alarmed at Tommy's uncharacteristic alacrity and wondered if he should emphasise the urgency of his request, but foolishly decided it wasn't necessary. He returned their salutes before hurrying back, ducking as a German shell whistled overhead. As soon as the officer was out of sight, the two men resumed their previous positions. Nobby took a deep, satisfying drag on his cigarette.

'Didn't say "when", did he?'

'He didn't, did he?' agreed Tommy. 'Mind you, I think he meant today.'

'In that case, we'd best give him the benefit of the bleedin' doubt,' said Nobby. 'Teach him a bleedin' lesson if we didn't though. Coming here with half an order, must think we're bleedin' mindreaders.'

Half an hour later, after leisurely finishing their cigarettes and a warming mug of hot tea, the two conscientious young soldiers made their way towards the farmhouse. Between them was a drum of telephone wire through which they'd stuck a brush handle for it to turn on, unravelling the wire as they went. At the tops of their voices they sang the latest rude version of Colonel Bogey.

'Hitler, has only got one ball.
Goering, has two but very small,
Himmler is very similar,
but poor old Goebbels has no balls at all...'

They both heard it coming, but thought it would travel over their heads like all the others had done. In any case there was no cover to run to, so they just kept on walking, unravelling and singing. The shell exploded about twenty yards away. Nobby was partially shielded by Tommy who took the full force of the blast which carried the two of them through the air, across a road and into the next field. Miraculously Nobby was still alive, seriously wounded but not expected to last long.

Bits of Tommy were spread far and wide, making him just another statistic – and Dorothy just another war widow.

Chapter Five

The children had had no contact from Freddie since he'd waved them off at Malton Station the previous year. The war in Europe had ended over a month ago. Susan had half-expected him to turn up at the street party held at V.E. day. After all, he had promised to come and see them as soon as the war was over.

Rarities such as real eggs had been produced,

and chopped up with tomatoes to make the most delicious sandwiches. Jelly shivered on the street's long trestle tables, the first time most children had seen it. Bananas and other exotic fruit were still many years away from a regular spot on the greengrocer's shelves, but Jackie Crombie's grandad, who had something to do with the army stores in Catterick, managed to smuggle a huge box of such fruit and other delicacies through to the street, where they were shared out with a generosity of spirit peculiar to that happy time.

Mrs Bateson got drunk on apple cider and tried it on with Reg Byrne who'd avoided the armed services due to his feet. Mrs Byrne, who'd spent the war defending her stay-at-home husband from the caustic comments of service wives, took exception to this and threw a well-aimed custard tart at Mrs Bateson, who retaliated with a bowl of trifle which splattered Mrs Crombie's new cardigan. This was the start of the great food fight of Broughton Terrace, talked about for many years with little need for exaggeration. As the happy combatants retired to their kitchen sinks to clean up, Susan stood at the end of the street, looking in vain up and down Paradine Hill and wondering if she'd ever see Freddie again.

Dorothy, who hadn't even begun to get over Tommy, had given the festivities a miss. She'd walked up quietly behind her niece and placed a friendly arm around her shoulder. It didn't take a genius to work out Susan's problem. Dorothy had been in love herself at fifteen. An unrequited bout of passion with David Ableson, a handsome young Jewish tailor who made all her father's suits.

'If it's any consolation I don't think he was killed,' she murmured the words gently, so as not to startle her niece.

Susan turned and attempted a smile.

'They were all listed in the *Yorkshire Post,* Freddie wasn't among them,' continued Dorothy. She'd never met Freddie but she'd heard so much about him from both Jimmy and Susan. The way Susan talked about him spoke volumes and she knew no unwanted advice from her would be heeded.

'He said he'd come as soon as the war's over,' said Susan, trying to keep her emotions in check.

'Most men won't be home for months yet, some of them maybe not until next year.'

This thought didn't seem to have occurred to Susan who perked up visibly and gave her aunt a hug. Dorothy wanted to tell her that Freddie had probably forgotten all about her, that he was much too old for her; but these thoughts she wisely kept to herself. She remembered her own reaction when she'd been given the same advice.

It was now late June with no word from Freddie. Why hadn't he been in touch? Was he okay? Susan was beginning to fear the worst, then she saw his picture in the *Yorkshire Evening Post.* 'War hero's son comes home,' it said. She viewed the photograph with mixed emotions. Initial shock at seeing the love of her life in such a state, then relief at knowing at least he was still alive, then annoyance that the paper had neglected to mention that Freddie must be a hero. It was him that was swathed in bandages, not his dad. Brigadier Harry F-Forbes-Fiddler M.C. J.P. who was beaming into the camera as he wheeled his heavily bandaged son out of an ambulance, into the house. She devoured the tiny article, memorising every precious word. He'd been blown up by a grenade in Belgium, that's where Uncle Tommy had been killed. Doctors had given up all hope at first but he'd made a miraculous recovery and was now well enough to convalesce at home.

She showed Dorothy the article and her aunt decided on the only possible course of action.

'You must go and see him, both you and Jimmy. He'd like that.'

Dorothy wasn't entirely sure why she'd suggested it. Perhaps she thought that Susan might see Freddie in a new, less glamorous light – or perhaps Freddie might put Susan straight about the impossibility of any romance. Susan certainly thought it was a great idea – and so did Jimmy, who'd never been to Harrogate.

A quick scrutiny of the telephone book in Paradine Hill post office turned up Freddie's address and the following Saturday they arrived at Freddie's gate with a bar of Cadbury's Fruit and Nut for Freddie, and an air of youthful exuberance, although youth was not a word one would readily associate with such a place. It was a large, old, grey-stone house in a long street of similar large, old, grey-stone houses. There were old grey trees neatly lining the street planted in neatly tended verges. No children played in the street, or in the gardens for that matter. This was a most unusual state of affairs for a Saturday morning. They'd left Broughton Terrace a couple of hours earlier, amid the clamour of a fiercely contested rounders match, several noisy games of taws, and a bitter argument between young Mrs Harrison at number seven and big Mrs Veitch at number eight, about hanging out washing on a Saturday morning. Apparently Mrs Veitch was defending the rights of her children to play in the street on a Saturday, unhindered by washing lines. The children themselves didn't actually mind. It was quite good fun playing rounders in and out of Mrs Harrison's interesting underwear.

Jimmy looked around disapprovingly at his surroundings as they walked up the driveway of Freddie's house. 'There's more life in Murgy's vest,' he muttered.

They walked past a gleaming black Wolseley and a statue of a naked nymph which took Jimmy's admiring eye. Susan grabbed her loitering brother by his arm and dragged him away. She gave the door a confident knock. It was opened by Freddie's father, the Brigadier.

'Yes?' he demanded, as if one word was all that the situation merited.

'We've come to see Freddie,' smiled Susan. 'He knows us, see, and we've come to, er, to see him.' Her confidence faltered under the Brigadier's exasperated glare.

'Go away,' was all he said, and shut the door.

The children stood there, gobsmacked at such rudeness. They'd expect it from old Mrs McGinty at number sixteen, but she had an excuse, she wasn't all there. She used to sit on the outside lav with the door wide open and an umbrella up. But rudeness such as this was well beyond their scope of understanding.

'You rude man!' Susan addressed her angry remark to the door.

'What shall we do now?' asked Jimmy, as they walked back down the garden path.

'Well, we've come all this way to see him so I think we should!' said a determined Susan. 'We'll wait till old Bulldog Features goes out, then sneak round the back.'

'What if he doesn't go out?'

'Everybody goes out some time on a Saturday morning,' scoffed his sister, amazed at her brother's dimness.

Half an hour later, they were sitting on a low wall at the end of the street, wondering whether to break into the bar of chocolate, when the Wolseley came purring past them, with the Brigadier at the wheel.

'See, I told you he'd go out,' said Susan, getting up and walking off down the street, causing Jimmy to run to catch her up.

'What's the plan?' he asked excitedly. 'Shall we break in?'

'Don't be silly. First we'll go round the back and look through the windows – and see what we can see.'

This seemed an incomplete sort of plan to Jimmy, but he decided not to argue and followed his determined sister around the back of the house. A large window had been left open to allow in the gentle breeze, sighing through the poplar trees bordering the neat lawn. The children walked stealthily towards it, Susan in the lead. Cautiously she looked through the window, then turned round excitedly to her brother.

'It's him!' she exclaimed. 'It's Freddie, he's in here!'

She stood on her tiptoes and leaned in at the window. Freddie was lying in a bed just inside the room, his eyes closed, an open book lying on his chest beneath his sleeping fingers, its pages rippling over in the breeze.

'Freddie!' whispered Susan, as loudly as she dared.

Freddie's eyes flickered open and looked around the room's interior.

'We're here! Over here, in the window!'

With a painful effort, Freddie turned his head in her direction, his eyes opening in surprise at the sight of two excited children grinning at him through the window.

'Hiya, Freddie,' yelled Jimmy, then clasped his hand to his mouth as his sister shushed him.

'Hello, Freddie,' smiled Susan, as demurely as she knew how. 'Remember us?'

Freddie stared at them, his mouth opened – then closed, as if he'd changed his mind about saying anything.

'He doesn't remember anything!'

The voice came from behind them. The children cringed, not daring to turn round. But there was no menace in this voice, it was a woman's voice. Susan risked a look round, her brother slowly following suit. On the path stood a nice-looking, middle-aged lady, with greying hair and a vaguely amused smile playing on her lips.

'I suppose you're the children my husband was so rude to earlier?'

'Yes,' admitted Susan. 'Er no, well he wasn't really ru...'

'Yes he was,' insisted the lady. 'I scolded him for it afterwards.' She laughed gently to herself. 'He's gone off to his golf club in a bit of a huff, I'm afraid. Probably ruin his game and he'll blame me for it when he gets home. Still, I can handle him. His bark's a lot worse than his bite – and he's very protective of Freddie. He threatened one newspaper reporter with his shotgun, so you two got off rather lightly. Anyway, I think we'd better introduce ourselves, I'm Mrs Fiddler.' She spoke with the controlled confidence found only in ladies of quality and elderly Roman Catholic nuns.

'Not Mrs *Fforbes*-Fiddler, like your husband?' inquired a curious Susan.

'No, that's *his* name. I used to be called Fforbes, but when we were married, Harry decided to hyphenate us. Better for his army image and all that. I don't think he was ever happy with plain old Harry Fiddler. But I can't be doing with all that.'

'Too many effing Fs,' grinned Jimmy, as if he'd just thought of it.

'Precisely,' laughed Mrs Fiddler.

'I'm Susan, and this is my brother Jimmy,' said Susan quickly, wishing her brother didn't have to make a joke out of everything.

'Pleased to meet you Susan and Jimmy,' smiled

82

Mrs Fiddler. 'Look, come inside, where you can talk to your friend properly. I must say, I'm rather curious to learn how you know him so well.'

She led them through the back door, into a cool, spacious kitchen, fitted with gadgets completely foreign to the children. Gas cooker, fridge, electric kettle, washing machine, automatic mangle and two sinks and a picture of the King and Queen on the wall.

Pausing at the kitchen door while the two of them looked round, she smiled to herself, wondering what Harry would say if he knew she'd invited two tykes, obviously from what he would call the 'lower orders', into their house.

'Through here,' she directed, pointing towards what Harry called the 'drawing room' and she and Freddie rebelliously called the 'parlour'.

She herself had apparently married above her station, if Harry's parents were to be believed. Daughter of a village butcher, she'd been serving behind the bar in the Bell and Monkey when young Harry had fallen hopelessly in love with her, and she, surprisingly, with him.

Freddie was leaning up on one elbow, awaiting the arrival of his unexpected visitors. To Susan, his welcoming smile was just as warm and heart-melting as ever, but it was accompanied by a slight questioning of his eyebrows.

'Hello, Freddie,' she smiled, totally confident he would remember her – and how foolish poor Mrs Fiddler would feel when he did.

Freddie stared at them for what seemed an age then he gave an apologetic smile and said, 'I'm sorry, I know I should recognise you but I'm afraid I don't.'

'Perhaps if you reminded Freddie of where you know him from, it might jog his memory,' prompted his mother.

'Oh, right,' said Susan, and between them they launched into a breathless story about them running away because Jimmy thought he'd killed Leon Murgatroyd, but he hadn't actually, and the train journey and Dan Braithwaite's apples and the cottage and the dead German. Complete with interruptions and constant reminders from whoever wasn't telling the story at the time. But neither mentioned the rings, not while Mrs Fiddler was there. The oath Freddie had made them swear that day was the most sacred thing either of them had ever done.

They finished the story simultaneously and stood with bated breath for Freddie to smile and say how could he forget such a day. But he didn't.

'Oh, I wish I could remember a day like that,' he said, shaking his head sadly. 'How many marvellous memories such as that must I have locked up in here,' he tapped the side of his head, then lay back resignedly on the pillows. His eyes closed and he fell into a sudden sleep.

'He's on quite strong medication,' explained Freddie's mother, 'You mustn't think him rude.'

The visit was over. Mrs Fiddler walked quietly out of the room, Jimmy followed, but Susan hung back, gazing sadly down on Freddie's sleeping face.

'Freddie Fiddler,' she whispered. 'Maybe you don't remember me, and maybe you'll never love me, and maybe you think fifteen's too young for a person to say they're in love with someone. I happen to know that's what most grown-ups like to think. But if I'm not in love with you, then I don't want to be in love with anyone else, thank you very much, because this is bad enough for me – and if I'm not making sense it's your fault for confusing me.'

She moved her head away as a tear dropped on to his cheek. 'My mam and dad left me, and I loved them. Then Uncle Tommy and our William – and I loved them. And now you. And I love you, Freddie Fiddler, and I don't care if I am only fifteen.'

Susan picked up a corner of his bedsheet and wiped away her tears, then she backed away and took several deep breaths before turning to leave the room.

Chapter Six

Dorothy looked in the mirror and wondered how she could still be pretty after what had happened in the past months. Perhaps she wasn't pretty any more, perhaps it was wishful thinking. Her hand still shook as she put her lipstick on. Many's the time she'd gone out without make-up rather than go round looking like Coco the Clown. Not this morning though. This was the start of a new week. A new job. A new life. At least that was what she kept trying to tell herself. It was five months and thirteen days since she'd received the impersonal buff letter saying her Tommy was 'Missing in Action'.

To all intents and purposes he was still missing, insofar as he'd never been found, not much of him anyway, but the army had sufficient sensitivity not to mention that. He'd since graduated to 'Killed in Action' and Dorothy was now a proud war widow, complete with derisory widow's pension. A man from the War Ministry came and said he'd been killed in Holland and gave her some combat medals. He'd simply been in the wrong place at the wrong time, said the man. Dorothy had tearfully pointed out that being in Holland in 1945 was the wrong place at the wrong time and the man from the War Ministry chose not to tell her that he'd spent 1945 behind a desk in Huddersfield. He muttered a few words of embarrassed sympathy before leaving her to her grief and riding away on his motorbike, enshrouded in non-combatant's guilt.

In the aftermath of the war, four million service personnel descended on a Civvy Street that wasn't quite ready for them. Servicemen, who'd been looking forward to the day for years, arrived home only to be met by strangers. The young wives they'd left behind had become hard and old and independent, many having spent years on a factory floor. The men came home in their demob suits to children who didn't know them from Adam and resented this stranger who ousted them from their mother's bed.

Bright young men who'd gone off to war had returned damaged. Physically or mentally or both. For every happy rehabilitation there was an equally sad one. In many ways the post-war years were as difficult as the ones that had gone on before. Ex-Servicemen who were all treated like heroes during the conflict had now become something of an embarrassment.

Vera Bateson from number twelve had been notified that her husband Len had been posted 'Missing Presumed Killed'. Her grief was cushioned due to her not having seen him for over a year, so she took in a lodger who was employed in a reserved occupation at the same Royal Ordnance Factory that Weidling had failed to bomb, dropping his bombs instead on Fred and Lily Bairstow. At the end of the war Len Bateson turned up in a Polish P.O.W. camp.

Driven by that same love for Vera that had kept him going during his long hard time of internment, he walked halfway across Europe into France. Eventually returning to Broughton Terrace in something less than triumph, only to find his beloved Vera in bed with the lodger.

The charge against him was attempted murder, but the judge let Len go free, having much sympathy for him and little for the lodger. Stories like this abounded after the war.

This morning Dorothy was due to start a full-time job in the Thrift Stores on Connington Road. Not much of a job, but she'd promised Tommy she'd do everything in her power to make sure the kids got a proper schooling. When she made the promise she didn't know what she was letting herself in for. She did now though. Susan needed to stay on that extra year to take her School Certificate if she was to get a decent job. Dorothy could really do with the money Susan could bring in. But she had promised Tommy. Just the thought of him brought the inevitable tears to her eyes. The day she married him had been the happiest and proudest day of her life. The fact that her own family had boycotted the wedding cast a cloud over the proceedings, but marrying Tommy Bairstow made up for all that.

The Bairstow brothers, Fred and Tommy, had been legends down at the Hippodrome Ballroom. Where there was a Bairstow brother there was fun to be had. No one could dance the Jitterbug like them, or the Waltz, the Foxtrot, the Quickstep, the Palais Glide and so on and so on. Tommy was the singer. He'd be invited up on to the bandstand and the audience would shout out their requests. And Tommy could sing alright – he had a voice like an angel – only he never took himself seriously and neither did Fred. Fred would get up and stand beside his brother, doing his hilarious comic dance, pulling faces, anything to make the audience laugh – and every time Tommy turned round, Fred would be standing there innocent as you like and the audience would howl with laughter. They'd talked about going on the clubs as a double act after the war – after they'd done their bit for king and country. Ironically, the one thing you never saw a Bairstow brother do was fight. Not that they were cowards, it's just that they could talk their way into a fight and joke their way out with a practised ease. The Bairstows were not fighting men. Pity no one told the army that. The Bairstows never raised a fist in anger to anyone. They raised many a laugh though. Dorothy smiled through her tears at the memory. Now they were both gone – Lily as well. She'd always got on well with Lily, although they were different types. Lily had been quite a bubbly girl until the arrival of three kids, which had quietened her down a lot. Quieten anybody down, having three kids. It had only taken two of them to quieten Dorothy down. Oh dear, there was that guilt again.

Dorothy had been a little more sophisticated. She came from a wealthy family in Alwoodley which was a damn sight posher than Paradine Hill. But she wouldn't take their charity if they came to her on bended knee. Which they hadn't. Her life had been already mapped out for her by her builder father, Sidney Allerdyce, chairman and managing director of Allerdyce Builders Ltd. Even to the extent of finding a suitable husband in the form of Eric Westerbrook, the doctor son of an ear, nose and throat surgeon at Leeds Infirmary. Sid Allerdyce had dragged himself up from being a bricklayer to chairman of his own house building company and he insisted on his children turning their backs on the class of person he'd worked so hard to leave behind. He'd married the daughter of a wealthy publican, a boringly beautiful woman. Dull as she was she could surely have done better than Sid, who was no great catch in the beauty or personality stakes; but each seemed to know where they stood in the relationship. She was an unaffectionate woman, who looked on with a cold dispassion whenever her husband disciplined their daughter with regular heavy beatings.

The Allerdyce family had reckoned without the irresistible charms of Tommy Bairstow who swept their sophisticated daughter off her feet, with his outrageous sense of fun and not inconsiderable good looks. To look at they made a fine-looking couple. Dorothy was a real beauty. Well-educated, well-spoken and with a deep-rooted hatred of her brutish father.

A heavy knock on the front door made her jump. She looked at her watch, 7.45. Oh God! Who on earth could it be at this time on a morning? Front door as well, so it could be official.

Her heart quickened anxiously as she looked through the back window and saw her father, standing with his back to the door, surveying his lowly surroundings with obvious contempt. An expensive-looking, black Homburg was jammed unceremoniously down over his workman's head, his hair closely cropped right back to the folds of his thick, crimson neck. A shiny blue suit stretched across his fat back, pulling at his armpits and sitting uncomfortably on a body designed for overalls.

Pulling a small table away from behind the rarely used door, Dorothy took a deep, controlling breath and opened it. Her father turned round, his hand going to his hat by way of greeting, then changing its mind and returning to his side. Dorothy looked at the father she hadn't seen for years and opened with a line she'd rehearsed in her head for most of that time.

'By heck, Dad! Look at you – just goes to show, you can't buy class, can you?'

He gave a frown which meant he didn't understand what she was talking about, then beckoned to the Rover parked behind him. The only car in the street. His voice was harsh and uncompromising.

'Right, girl, yer've stuck it out long enough. I reckon yer've had yer come uppance and yer've paid yer dues. Get yer stuff together, yer comin' home with me.'

'Just like that, eh?'

'They'll be nowt said about this bloody mess yer got yerself into, but I reckon yer've only got God to thank for getting you out of it so smartly.'

'So that's what God's been up to is it? Getting me out of it. I was wondering where he was when I needed him.' She felt a surge of anger rising within her that she knew she'd have to control if she wanted to say all she had to say.

'Eric Westerbrook never got married, you know,' said her father, his unpleasant piggy eyes boring into his daughter. 'He never got over it when you wed that brainless pillock Bairstow. Got what were coming to him, if you ask me. Anyway, if yer play yer cards right yer could get back in with young Westerbrook.'

It was all Dorothy could do to stop herself from lashing out at her father, but that would spoil the moment.

'And what about Jimmy and Susan?' she said icily. 'Do you think *Young Westerbrook* will want a ready-made family?'

'Who's Jimmy and Susan? Look stop pissing

91

me about, I'm due on site in half an hour, I haven't got time for all this bloody chit-chat.'

'You know very well who Jimmy and Susan are – or at least you should. They're part of my family now.'

Sid scowled. It wasn't going as well as he thought. He figured she'd be overjoyed to be welcomed back after what she'd been through.

'Fred's brats,' he acknowledged grudgingly.

'My niece and nephew,' she corrected. 'Your great-niece and nephew,' she added, to rub salt in the wound.

'Hey! They're nowt ter do with me,' protested Sid, angrily. 'They're not even flesh and blood. No, he can't be expected to tek in anybody's brats. They'll have ter go into a home. That's what homes are there for. He'll want to father his own will Westerbrook's lad. Proper breeding, that's what counts.'

'*Westerbrook's Lad?* Breeding? You make him sound like a race horse. Mind you he's got the face for it and it'll take more than a couple of generations to breed an arsehole like you out,' retorted Dorothy scornfully, but still holding her anger in check. 'Anyway Jimmy and Susan already have a home. A better home than I ever had. They're decent kids – and that's a word you never learned from your posh pals.'

Her father's mounting fury had him struggling for words with which to retaliate, so Dorothy, being on a roll, jumped back in first.

'Tell me, Dad, do these posh pals of yours still laugh at you behind your back? Have you worked out why you're not a member of that precious golf club yet? Do you still use your fork like a shovel? Do you still fart like Flamborough foghorn? Are you still the big, loud-mouthed shithouse you always were?'

Dorothy had imagined this confrontation many times, so much so that she was surprisingly well rehearsed in what she had to say to him. There were many more insults in her repertoire but her father had heard enough. He exploded and took a violent step forward, his arm drawing back. Dorothy was ready, she slammed the door on him and had the bolt in place just before his heavy fist battered into it with frustrated rage. He pushed open the letterbox, through which he spat his parting message to his only daughter.

'You ungrateful little whoring bitch. Don't come grovelling ter my door from whatever gutter yer find yerself in. And remember this – if it's the last thing I do I'll make you regret them words! I'll say no more to yer!'

He turned to face the inevitable onlookers who'd all chosen that very moment to come casually out of a front door they hadn't used for months.

'She's no daughter of mine any more!' he roared, spraying spit all over his shiny black car. 'Do yer hear me? I don't know why I bloody bothered!'

Susan and Jimmy joined their auntie at the window to see what all the commotion was about. Dorothy looked down at them and smiled.

'That's your Great Uncle Sid. Wave bye-bye to Uncle Sid, children.'

Jimmy and Susan happily obliged as an enraged

93

Sid screeched over the cobbles and out of Broughton Terrace for the first and last time: and for the first time since Tommy had died Dorothy felt good about herself.

'Thanks for that, Dad,' she said to herself, loud enough for Jimmy and Susan to hear. They of course, though she was going potty.

Dorothy returned to the mirror to finish her lipstick. Her hands were steady now. She smiled back at Susan's reflection as she watched her aunt's technique with lipstick and powder.

'You want to try this, don't you? I know the feeling. I couldn't wait when I was your age. Maybe tonight when I get home from work.'

Susan blushed a little then said, 'I'd like that, thanks, Auntie Dorothy – and thanks for, you know...'

'What?' Dorothy ran her bottom lip over her top lip to smooth out her handiwork.

'You know, for letting me stop on at school to take my School Certificate.' Susan was referring to a recent visit from her form teacher at St Winifred's College where Susan was a scholarship pupil.

'Susan's one of our brightest girls,' Miss Briers had said. 'I know things must be difficult for you but that extra year would make all the difference in the world to Susan's career.'

Dorothy pulled a mock stern face at her niece's reflection. 'Just you make sure it's worthwhile.'

'I will.'

'Auntie Dorothy,' chirped Jimmy.

'Yes, Jimmy?'

'It's alright if you want me to leave when I'm fifteen, I won't mind, honest.'

Dorothy laughed. 'I'll bear it in mind. Oh, by the way you didn't tell me much about your visit to Freddie the other day. How is he?'

'He's a lot better,' said Susan, who didn't really want to talk about him. To her the visit had been something of a disappointment. 'But he can't remember anything,' she added.

'He didn't know who we were,' added Jimmy.

'Good Lord! He must have it bad if he doesn't remember you two, still at least he's alive, that's the main thing.'

'It is, isn't it?' agreed Susan optimistically.

Dorothy's relationship with the children had improved dramatically since Tommy had died. They'd been a tower of strength – and Jimmy was showing signs of becoming every bit as entertaining as his dad and uncle. This was where she belonged. Her father's false world was a million miles from where she wanted to be. She returned her gaze to the mirror to check on the finished product and gave herself a nod of approval. Thirty-three years old now and yes, she was definitely still a good-looking woman. A shadow passed through her thoughts and brought an unconscious frown to her brow as it had done increasingly over the past few weeks.

How on earth could she have told them their brother was dead? And when was she going to tell the children the truth? Not today that's for sure. The shock of Tommy's death had pushed it to the back of her mind, but gradually, as she came round to accepting life without her lovely

Tommy, the spectre of William began to emerge. She couldn't put it off much longer. Maybe next week. One step at a time, that's what they said, wasn't it?

Chapter Seven

Dorothy picked up the packet of butter she'd left behind the counter and dropped it casually into her overall pocket. The past four months had been hard, but she was managing, just. She'd settled into a routine. The wage she earned from the Thrift Stores wasn't a fortune, but together with her widow's pension they just scraped by. Not much left for luxuries, such as clothes. Susan needed a new blazer desperately, and both the kids' shoes needed cobbling. Larry Gill, next door but one would do that if she got him the leather. He fancied her did Larry. Better not let Mrs Gill find out or there'd be no more free cobbling from Larry. She smiled to herself at what sounded like a crude innuendo. If there was ever to be anything like that again in her life, it wouldn't be with the likes of Larry Gill. She wouldn't mind it with somebody though. It had been a long time now since her last night with Tommy. She'd had another letter from Oxford House Children's Home in Cleckheaton informing her that William was now formally in the care of the Local Authority and would shortly be transferred to somewhere more suitable, but they didn't say where. This should have set warning bells ringing but Dorothy kept telling herself that she still hadn't come to terms with losing Tommy and she owed it to herself to give herself time. Deep down of course, she knew this was just an excuse. There just didn't seem to be any way to tell them without making her seem like the Wicked Witch of the West. Perhaps she was living in hope of providence turning up an opportunity. Whatever happened, she was determined to tell them before Christmas and bring their brother home.

Harry Evans would never notice the butter. Besides what was he going to do, sack her? Well, hardly. He couldn't run the shop without her, anyway he was only the manager, it wasn't as if she was stealing from him. Not that that would worry her, the miserable old sod. Never a good word to say for anybody, never a word of praise for her and she knew she was good, all the customers told her. A lot better than Ethel, thick as two short planks was Ethel. He'd be retiring in a couple of years and they'd need someone to take his place. She quite fancied that, manageress. Nice title, more money. In the meantime she just had to supplement her wages as best she could. Wages! Slave labour more like. Two and a penny an hour less stoppages. She hadn't been so much as to the pictures in a year. No, the odd packet of butter here, the odd loaf there, and why not? She was entitled to it.

'I'm just nipping out for my dinner, Harry,' she called out to her boss who was in the storeroom round the back. 'So can you come through and serve? Ethel's late back – as usual.'

'Gimme a minute,' came the muffled reply.

Presently Harry came through, red faced from heaving boxes of sugar around. 'Before yer go,' he panted. 'There's just something I need to check.'

Dorothy looked at her watch, twelve-thirty-five. 'Hurry up, I'm five minutes into my dinner half hour.'

Harry was a small man, in his late fifties. He looked like a grocer, grocery had been his life; apart from four years in France in the Great War, where he'd been one of the very few who managed to stay clear of the fighting. The store had been his life. He'd once owned it but had sold out to the Thrift Stores Group and had regretted it ever since. Constantly looking over his shoulder, as he fully expected a younger man to push him into forced retirement, after which his life would have no meaning.

He gave Dorothy a funny look and without saying anything delved into her overall pocket and brought out the butter. 'What's this?' he demanded.

Dorothy tried to dismiss it. 'Oh heck! I stuck it there when I was tidying the shelves this morning. I must have forgotten it.'

'Like you forgot that loaf you took yesterday – and that bag of sugar on Monday.'

'Look, Harry, you'd better let me explain…'

Harry shook his head, 'It's been going on too long. I reckon you've been at it for weeks. It was Ethel who first saw you taking stuff.'

'Ethel? Good God, Harry – she's worse than me! If you suspected, why didn't you say something. At least it would have stopped me doing it.'

'Why did you do it?'

'For God's sake, that's a stupid question to ask a widow trying to bring up two children.'

Harry went to the till, took out three pound notes and some loose change. He grimly handed the money to Dorothy. 'I'm being more than fair to you. I could dock your wages to make up for what you've taken or I could report you to the police. But I'm not doing that, I'm paying you up to tonight.'

Dorothy looked disbelievingly at the money in her hand, then back up at Harry. 'So this is it then? I'm fired?'

Harry nodded and handed her the packet of butter. 'Here, you might as well have it.'

Dorothy took it dumbly. As she went out of the door she turned and said, 'You didn't answer my question. Why didn't you give me some sort of warning? That would have stopped me. You know I was good, you'll have a job getting anyone as good as me.'

'I don't want anyone as good as you. They were going to retire me early and give you my job. They'll have to keep me on now.'

'You're a bastard, you know that, don't you, Harry?'

Harry shrugged. 'But I'm a bastard who's still got a job.'

Raymond Donoghue came into Susan's life on the top deck of the number forty-two bus on her way back from school. It was October 1945 and she'd just started in the fifth form at St

Winifred's. Her school blazer was a source of amusement to a group of girls returning from the afternoon shift at Penny Hill Dyeworks, whose circumstances, by virtue of them being in work, weren't quite as straitened as Susan's. She still wore the blazer she'd been bought second-hand for the start of the fourth year. The cuffs had been turned down to the limit, as had the hem. But Susan was a tall girl and the sleeves ended a good three inches from her wrist. Her boisterous existence had occasioned many a not-so-invisible mend by Auntie Dorothy, whose skills as a seamstress were less than legendary.

'Thought she were the Queen of the bleedin' May when she passed her scholarship. Look at her now. Hey, Bairstow! Where'd yer get yer blazer? Off a bleedin' rag an' bone man?'

Susan's tormentor was Greta Birchall, who'd been in the same class as Susan at St Joseph's Junior School. Named after Greta Garbo and there the resemblance ended, for good looks could not be numbered amongst Greta's limited attributes. She had an older brother called Rudolph, who was no Valentino either. Only four girls out of a class of forty-six had managed a place at St Winifred's and Greta, being in what was euphemistically called the 'Transition Group' had not been one of them, she wouldn't have been one of them had forty-five managed places. Susan ignored them and gazed out of the window at the passing street below. A smoking paper boy stood beside a *Yorkshire Evening News* placard saying: SMOKING THOUGHT TO CAUSE CANCER. On the next corner a

Yorkshire Evening Post paper boy sold his papers beside the rival headline HERTFORDSHIRE TRAIN CRASH – MANY DEAD. Their bus driver hooted impatiently as he veered out to pass a slow-moving, pony-drawn Rington's Tea van, the pony evacuated its bowel in what appeared to be retaliation, causing all the kids on the lower deck to howl with amusement, as kids do at such things. A copper coin hit Susan on the forehead and it began to bleed slightly.

'Here y'are – "penny for the guy",' cackled one of the other girls, eager to crack the best joke at Susan's expense.

Individually, Susan was more than a match for any of them and as courage was never something she was lacking, she foolishly spun round and grabbed Greta Birchall by the lapel of her blouse, dragging her up from her seat.

'You're a big brave girl, Birchall, when you've got your pals with you. How about just me and you?'

Greta's sneer turned to shock at the ease with which Susan dragged her out of her seat. Then she glanced over Susan's shoulder and sniggered. An arm came around Susan's neck and dragged her down the aisle of the bus onto the long back seat, where Greta and her three friends laid into her. Susan fought back like a tigress but was held down by sheer weight of numbers as Greta stood over her, gloating.

'Right, Miss Snotty Nose Susan Bairstow, let's see how stuck up you are without any clothes on.'

Pulling Susan's shoes off, she threw them out of the bus window. She then dragged her blazer off, stuck her finger in a recent small tear and then, to a chorus of laughter from her friends, ripped it right across the back before throwing that out as well. As she made a grab for her skirt, Susan kicked out violently with a shoeless foot and caught Greta in the throat, sending her choking to her knees. The other three girls, seeing the acute distress their crony was in, momentarily let Susan go; long enough for her to push her way past them and vault over the rail on to the stairs. Almost immediately she heard a scuffle behind her.

'She's getting away, get her!'

'Leave her alone, she's had enough.'

'What's it ter do with you? Mind yer own bleeding business and get outa the way!'

Susan looked round at Raymond Donoghue who'd positioned himself stubbornly between the three remaining tormentors and Susan. He was a tall, broad lad who had little difficulty halting their progress. The girls were screaming atrocious obscenities over his shoulder, causing the conductor to tell them to watch their language or get off the bus. Violence, it seemed was okay but bad language was not.

'Sorry I didn't step in earlier,' apologised Raymond, as they stepped off the bus together. 'But with it being lasses – you know – it were a bit awkward. Here, I got your satchel for you, you left it on the seat when you...'

'When I made an idiot of myself and grabbed Birchall. Thanks anyway.' She took the satchel gratefully, it was real leather, she wouldn't want to lose that. A jubilant Uncle Tommy had bought her it when she passed her scholarship exam.

'A brainy Bairstow!' he'd laughed. 'That's a new one!' She'd turned up for school that first day wearing a brand new uniform, proud as a peacock. Greta Birchall had been right, she had been the Queen of the May back then. And now?

They were retracing the bus route in an effort to retrieve Susan's coat and shoes, their pace quickening as it dawned on Susan that someone might take a fancy to them. Even a torn school blazer would be of value to someone in those days.

Raymond picked up the blazer from a puddle in the gutter. Susan thanked him then looked at the badge on Raymond's dark blue blazer.

'My brother's at St Tommy's, he's in the second form.'

Raymond nodded. He knew he couldn't be expected to know a second former. 'I'm in the fifth,' he said. 'Same as you, I imagine.'

Susan nodded. 'That's right, I'm at St Winnie's. Not that you could tell, looking at this blazer.'

'I hope your mam's good at mending,' he said awkwardly.

'I haven't got a mam. It's my Auntie Dorothy. She'll not be so pleased when she sees this. She's only just finished mending it.'

'There's one of your shoes,' called out Raymond as he ran into the road and picked up a scuffed black shoe with a hole about to appear in the sole.

'Thanks,' replied Susan. 'The other one's over here.'

With her shoes back on, the pair of them

turned and headed for home once again.

Raymond introduced himself. 'I'm Ray – and I reckon I know your name, Snotty Nose Susan Bairstow, isn't it?'

'Just Susan, thanks very much. By the way, I do know who you are, your sister was in the year above me at St Winifred's. I've seen you with her. She was supposed to be clever, why didn't she stay on to do her A levels?'

Her new friend kicked a tin can noisily along the footpath and replied. 'Same reason as I reckon you won't be doing yours – we're a bit skint. Me dad says there's no point doing you're A levels unless you're going on to university and we can't afford to send her there.'

This was the first time Susan realised the limitations that lack of finance could place on her future and the idea of retrieving the jewels crossed her mind, as it had several times recently. She held up her blazer and groaned.

'I think it's beyond all hope – what do you think?'

'I think you're right,' agreed Ray stopping at the corner of Crawley Grove. 'I live up here.' He pointed up the street, similar to Susan's festooned with washing lines under which three small boys kicked a tennis ball around.

'Oh, right,' Susan felt oddly disappointed that he had to leave her. 'See you, bye!'

Ray walked up the street a few steps then hesitated. 'Hang on!' he shouted. Susan stopped and turned to him. 'Our Eileen's got an old blazer. Shall I ask me mam if yer can borrow it till yer get yours mended?'

Susan shrugged, 'Yes, if you like. It's alright if she doesn't want to though.' She followed Ray to a small terrace house and waited at the door as he went inside and shouted up the stairs.

'Mam, do you know where our Eileen's old blazer is?'

'Under t'stairs, what do you want it for?'

Susan took a step back as she realised the voice was coming from above her. Mrs Donoghue was sitting on the bedroom window sill, with her feet inside and her well upholstered bottom protruding above the street as she busily cleaned the windowpane. She looked down at Susan and gave a toothless smile. Ray stepped out and looked up at his mother.

'Can Susan borrow our Eileen's blazer? Some lasses on t'bus tore hers.'

'Hang on, I'll come down.'

Mrs Donoghue disappeared inside and clattered noisily down the uncarpeted stairs. She appeared at the door, teeth back in and wiping soapsuds onto her pinny.

'Hello, love, I'm Raymond's mam. Now then what's all this about your blazer.'

Susan handed over her blazer for Mrs Donoghue to examine. She shook her head. 'I think it's beyond mending, love.' She looked closely at Susan. 'Aren't you Lily Bairstow's girl?'

Susan nodded, 'Yes, she was killed in the war. Me dad as well.'

'Yes, I know all about that, love. I remember that night myself. By heck! It were a beggar of a night were that. Sounds to me like your troubles are still not over.'

Susan nodded her rueful agreement. Mrs Donoghue smiled at her. 'I remember your dad. Went out with him once. Mind you, so did most of the lasses round here. By heck! He were a beggar were yer dad – and that brother of his, Tommy – they made some sparks fly when they got together them two.'

'My Uncle Tommy got killed as well.'

'I know, love, I heard about that as well.' She shook her head sadly, then smiled at some fond memory she'd no intention of revealing to the children.

'Tell yer what, come inside and I'll get our Eileen's blazer for yer. She's no use for it and it's only gathering dust. You might as well have it.'

Susan knew only too well what a sacrifice this was. Although the blazer was old, she could easily have got seven and six for it by selling it at the school. Second-hand blazers were at a premium.

'Thanks, Mrs Donoghue, I'll tell my Auntie Dorothy to give you something for it.'

'You'll tell her no such thing. I'm giving it to you, so let that be an end to it.'

Susan tried on the blazer, which was much nearer her size and a vast improvement on the one Greta had ripped. Mrs Donoghue cocked her head to one side in appreciation. 'Very nice, mind you, I reckon you'll end up with the sort of figure that'll look good in owt. By the way, yer can tell them lasses on that bus if they rip that one they've me to answer to.'

Auntie Dorothy seemed pre-occupied as Susan told the story of the girls on the bus and the

106

ripped blazer and how Mrs Donoghue had given her their Eileen's blazer which was a good fit and didn't have a single mend in it.

'I'm sorry, Susan, what were you saying? It's just that I've got a lot on my mind at the moment, what with one thing and another.' Dorothy was sitting on the settee, staring blankly at the *Yorkshire Evening Post*, miles away.

Susan chose not to repeat the story but went up to her bedroom to give her new blazer a good brush. She'd moved up into the attic when it was decided that a young lady should sleep in a separate room from her curious younger brother. As she passed Jimmy's room he poked his head round the door.

'She's been crying,' he said simply.

'Why?'

'No idea – she were crying when I came in from school. She didn't see me at first then she tried to let on she had summat in her eye.'

'I wonder if I should go see what's up?' asked Susan.

'I think it's private.'

Susan nodded her agreement to this assessment and sat down on the bottom attic step. She didn't want Auntie Dorothy to be upset. She'd grown to like her quite a lot and she certainly did her best for her and Jimmy. Maybe it was time to get the rings. Every time she thought along these lines she remembered the oath they'd sworn and shuddered at the very thought of breaking such a sacred vow. No way could she sell the rings without the help of an adult, besides, hers was to be her engagement ring. Jimmy, on the other hand, would have no such compunction and had tried to persuade her on numerous occasions to 'dig 'em up and flog 'em.'

Jimmy was in the second year at St Thomas's College, having amazed everybody, not least himself, by winning a scholarship place there, in the face of fierce competition.

'Shouldn't she still be at work?' Susan said suddenly.

'No idea,' answered Jimmy, sitting down on the step beside the sister he hated and loved with equal passion. 'Is that a new blazer?'

'Nearly. Raymond Donoghue's mam gave it to me. It's alright, isn't it?'

'Raymond Donoghue? Who's he then? Is he yer new boyfriend, then?'

'Don't be so soft,' protested Susan, rather too loudly. There was only one man in her life. Unfortunately he couldn't remember who she was. She carried a mental picture of Freddie, lying in bed, with one of her tears on his cheek.

'I think she's crying again,' said Jimmy. 'Listen!... Told yer. She's crying again.'

Dorothy felt Susan's arm around her shoulder and straightened up as her niece sat beside her on the settee.

'Is it something very bad, Auntie Dorothy?'

'Oh, no. It's just me being silly.'

'Is it Uncle Tommy?'

Dorothy nodded. It wasn't such a lie. Tommy was always in her thoughts, maybe not at the forefront at the moment. But he was in there somewhere.

'I still cry about Mam and Dad,' said Susan comfortingly. 'So does Jimmy. Not so much as we did though. I try and remember what she looked like. She was very pretty, wasn't she?'

'She was beautiful was your mam.'

'My dad was funny, wasn't he?'

'They both were, him and your Uncle Tommy.' She smiled to herself at some distant memory. 'Did your mam ever tell you about the time they took a couple of ferrets into the pictures? I still laugh about that, even today.'

Jimmy, who'd been listening from the stairs, came across and sat on the floor in front of them. An expectant grin on his face at the prospect of another story about his dad and Uncle Tommy. Dorothy smiled down at him and continued:

'Your mam was just married to your dad at the time and I'd gone along to make up a foursome.' She looked at Susan and winked. 'Actually, you came with us. Just a big bump in your mam's tummy, but she carried you with some pride, I can tell you.'

Susan smiled back, she'd already worked out the date of her conception and figured she must have gone to Mam and Dad's wedding as well.

'God knows where they got the ferrets from,' continued Dorothy. 'They must have had them hidden in their jackets when we met them outside the pictures. We'd gone to see Al Jolson in *The Jazz Singer.*'

'Seen it,' interrupted Jimmy. 'Made in nineteen-twenty-seven starring Al Jolson and Mary McAvoy, first ever talking picture.'

'I wish you'd stop talking,' scolded Susan,

109

before her brother launched himself into his version of 'Mammy'. Jimmy was an avid Al Jolson fan.

'It was on at the Crescent Picture Palace as it was then, on Atherton Street,' went on Dorothy.

'They call it "The Vogue" now,' interrupted Jimmy once again. Susan gave him a dig this time.

'Anyway,' said Dorothy, patiently. 'It was first house on a Saturday night and the place was absolutely packed. I knew they were up to something by the way they were wriggling about in their seats. Then all of a sudden these two big furry animals appeared. I've never seen a ferret before, nor since come to think of it – and I don't think too many people at the Crescent knew what they were either. They let them go under the seats and I tell you what, they were fast. One minute there was a commotion in the back stalls and two seconds later there were screams coming from the front stalls, then the side, then back to the middle – honestly, you've never known such pandemonium. Your dad and Uncle Tommy thought it was hilarious – so did your mother, I thought she was going to have you there and then!'

'What about you, Auntie, did you think it was funny?' laughed Susan.

'Well, I did and I didn't. You have to remember, this was my first date with your Uncle Tommy. What would you think if your boyfriend did a thing like that on your first date?'

This point of view had the children laughing even louder. 'What happened then?' asked Jimmy.

'I'll tell you what flipping well happened then,' went on Dorothy. 'The house lights went up and the manager came round. Some of the younger lads were rushing round trying to catch these ferrets, a woman in front of us was having hysterics, Al Jolson was singing, "Toot Toot Tootsie Goodbye" and some people had just had enough and were asking for their money back from this poor manager. Then as soon as he clapped eyes on your dad and Uncle Tommy he went absolutely potty. He knew it had to be them. They were so well-known for playing daft pranks like that. Anyway, we were kicked out, all four of us – banned from ever going back there as well. As far as I know I still am banned. Funny sort of first date when you come to think of it.'

Jimmy and Susan rocked with laughter at their auntie's story.

'Hey! Our Susan must be banned as well then,' deduced Jimmy. 'She were with yer!'

Even Dorothy laughed at this, her problems momentarily lifted.

'Everybody says they were funny,' said Susan proudly. 'I was talking to Mrs Donoghue today and she said that.' Susan paused then added, 'She said she used to go out with my dad.'

'There's lots of girls can say that, they could say the same about your Uncle Tommy as well.'

'But he picked me mam, didn't he?' Jimmy chipped in, 'And Uncle Tommy picked you – so you two must have been the best then.'

Dorothy smiled and ruffled Jimmy's hair. The Bairstow charm was safely in the hands of the next generation.

111

Chapter Eight

Dorothy sat down in the chair opposite Frank Sackfield the builder. She'd heard that Molly Butterworth, who'd been doing Frank's books was due to pack it in owing to a bout of pregnancy and Dorothy was hoping to step in before the job was advertised.

'I worked for Sid Allerdyce for five years as book-keeper cum secretary,' she chose not to mention that Sid was her father, as she feared it might not help. Sid was not a popular man. 'I know pretty much all there is to know about the business.'

Frank sat back in his chair and gave Dorothy an appreciative smile. She was a vast improvement on Molly Butterworth, in looks anyway – and if she'd held down a job with Sid Allerdyce she'd need to be a good worker. He'd asked her one or two questions but he knew more about setting on bricklayers than employing secretarial staff.

'I really need the job, Mr Sackfield,' she decided to pull out all the stops now. 'My husband was killed during the war and I'm bringing up his dead brother's children.'

'Your husband? Bairstow? Not Tommy Bairstow? Tommy and Fred Bairstow!'

'You knew him then?' It was probably a silly question, everyone in a mile radius of Paradine Hill had heard of Tommy and Fred Bairstow.

Frank chuckled to himself as everyone did when Tommy and Fred's names came into the conversation. 'Look, Mrs Bairstow,' he said. 'Right now there isn't a job. Work's a bit thin on the ground and to be honest with you, Molly getting pregnant's a blessing in disguise – but,' he added, seeing Dorothy's face drop, 'in the new year, things might be different. If there's a job going you'll get first refusal, before I even advertise.'

They stood up together and she took his proffered hand, 'Thanks, Mr Sackfield,' she said. 'I'd appreciate that.'

He watched her leave and knew there and then he was going to employ her before much longer – whether he needed to or not.

The first indication of a downturn in the Bairstow family fortunes was the non-appearance of pocket money. It was over a week since Dorothy had been sacked and all she'd managed to find herself was a cleaning job, two hours a day, three days a week and she didn't know if she could stick that. On her second day she'd heard the woman she worked for refer to her as a servant, which took Dorothy aback. She seriously toyed with the idea of telling Mrs High and Mighty Oldfield where she could stick her mop, and which end to put in first, in fact she might just stick it there for her. Dorothy did not have the mentality of a domestic.

Mrs Veitch opened the scullery door to Jimmy's businesslike knock. 'Have yer any empty jam jars

113

ter take back, Mrs Veitch?' he asked politely.

'Mebbe one. I'll have a look.' She reappeared with an empty jar of Bretheridges Strawberry Preserve. 'You'll need to wash it out a bit before you take it back, you know.'

'I know, thanks, Mrs Veitch.'

Susan was working the other side of the street, which was a bit demeaning for a fifteen-year-old young lady, but if she wanted to see the Saturday matinée that afternoon, then needs must when the devil drives, as Auntie Dorothy had said earlier. In truth she was probably growing too old for the Saturday matinée, but she just wanted to see if Flash Gordon managed to escape from the Emperor Ming. She had a bit of a crush on Buster Crabbe. Nothing like her love for Freddie, of course.

Between them they collected just eight jam jars, which, at a penny each, would realise just eightpence. Fourpence short of their target. It cost sixpence each to get into the Bughutch. Normally they'd be given ninepence each every Saturday morning. Threepence for two ounces of sweets from Mrs Barrett's corner sweet shop and a tanner into the pictures. But not today.

'Sorry, kids,' Auntie Dorothy said sadly. 'I just can't manage it today. Maybe next week, eh?'

Susan and Jimmy accepted the situation with equanimity. They weren't the first kids in their street to go without pocket money. And there were other ways of doing things. Jam jars, for instance. There were strict territorial rules about the collecting of jam jars. Stick to your own street, pretty much outlined it in a nutshell. So, eightpence it was then, fourpence each, better than nothing.

Off they went to Bretheridges Jam Factory with eight glistening jam jars clinking away in a shopping basket. As they approached the front entrance, they passed the gate to the factory yard. A high iron gate with vicious looking spikes on the top, interlinked with barbed wire and locked with a massive padlock; the type of padlock that said 'don't even think about it' to any would-be lock picker.

'Somebody's left the key in the lock,' observed Susan in passing. 'Anybody could walk in there.'

'Oh yeah! And who'd want ter nick a load of empty jam jars?' scoffed Jimmy.

They both stopped in their tracks. Just inside the gate were dozens of crates, all stacked with empty jam jars. The children retraced their steps, the yard was deserted. In the padlock were two keys, one in the lock and one dangling on a chrome ring. With Jimmy acting as lookout, Susan took the key from the lock and tried the other one. It fitted, they were identical.

Susan unlocked the gate as Jimmy went inside and filled up the shopping bag with jam jars. The whole operation took just a few seconds. He was out and whistling his nonchalant way down the street as Susan clicked the padlock back into place. Leaving one key in the lock and slipping the spare key into her pocket.

Jimmy heaved his bag of jam jars onto the scarred wooden counter, as he had many times before, to supplement his pocket money. Susan leaned forward and shouted into the office at the back where a jovial looking man in overalls and a surgical boot sat engrossed in the *Daily Mirror* crossword.

'We've brought some jam jars back, mister!'

'That's what I like ter see,' said the jovial man, folding his paper and clumping towards them. 'Properly washed jars. You should see the state o' some of 'em. I refuse ter take 'em. "Take the buggers back and give 'em a wash," that's what I tell 'em – one came in last week half full o' bloody fungus.' He leaned forward and added confidentially, 'Mind you, yer'd expect no better – they came in from Camp Road.'

Susan curled up her nose in disapproval at the state of Camp Road jam jars. Jimmy thought a joke might be appropriate.

'Me Uncle Tommy used ter be a window frame cleaner up Camp Road,' he said it with a dead-pan face which creased into an appreciative gin as the man laughed uproariously at this juvenile comedian.

'Right then,' he said at last. 'Twenty-two jars at a penny each – that's one and eightpence.'

'One and tenpence,' corrected Jimmy and Susan.

The man laughed. 'Just testing, there'll never be no fooling you two, will there? I can see I shall have to watch me step with you two. Right, one and tenpence it is then.' The man counted out the coins onto the counter under the close scrutiny of the youngsters, who knew not to trust jovial men with surgical boots.

'Thanks mister,' called out Jimmy over his shoulder. 'See you next week.'

As they walked out into the grimy street Susan said, 'He tried to diddle us, didn't he?'

'I know,' agreed Jimmy. 'Diddling a couple of hard working kids, disgusting that!' They both burst into gales of laughter as they ran to Mrs Barrett's sweetshop and thence to follow the fortunes of Flash Gordon, Hopalong Cassidy, and the Three Stooges.

Dorothy watched guiltily through the bedroom window at Jimmy knocking on Vera Bateson's door and willed her to give him an empty jar. When Mrs Bateson shook her head and closed the door on a disappointed Jimmy, she burst into absurd tears.

She was letting them down. No matter how hard she tried. That business at the Thrift Stores was typical of her. All she had to do was keep her nose clean and she'd have been made manager. If she had, Ethel Styren would have gone, that's for sure. She'd a good mind to write to the Thrift Stores Head Office and tell them it was a put up job just so Harry and Ethel could keep their jobs. It probably wouldn't do any good though. Her word against theirs. She'd have to lie through her teeth to get away with it and she was no good at lying. Honesty is the best policy, that's what they say. From now on she'd be honest Dorothy Bairstow – and she'd make damn sure the kids followed suit. The thought of having to clean for Mrs Oldfield again next week, and whatever other jobs she could pick up, depressed her even more. Jimmy and Susan came noisily into the house rattling jam jars.

117

Dorothy daren't go down because she knew she'd weaken and give them their pocket money out of the rent tin. Not that it'd make any difference. The fifteen shillings in the tin wouldn't make it till Thursday anyway. God knows what was going to happen if she didn't get some more money coming in.

When Jimmy and Susan came in late that afternoon they didn't tell Auntie Dorothy precisely how they'd made the money to go to the pictures. They knew she wouldn't approve. She'd already told them all about what happened at the Thrift Stores, including the little plan that Harry and Ethel had cooked up between them. In a way, confessing the truth to them did her no harm at all, as the kids embellished the story very much in her favour and spread it all around the neighbourhood, prompting many sympathisers to boycott the Thrift Stores in favour of the newly opened Co-op.

'You managed it then,' she smiled, giving them both an embarrassingly long hug.

'Yes, we er, we went to another street,' explained Susan.

'Oh dear, I thought that wasn't allowed. I hope you won't get into any trouble.'

'We won't, Auntie,' Jimmy assured her. 'What's for tea?'

'I thought we'd have beans and spam.'

Jimmy nearly said, *what again?* But was stopped by a glare from Susan. The menu was becoming very limited lately and consisted largely of potatoes done in a variety of ways. Bread, untoasted or toasted on a fork by the fire. Tinned soup, tinned beans, spam and the very occasional egg.

'It's daft, is this,' complained Jimmy, later that evening, as they sat on the attic steps. 'We'll have ter tell her about our diamond rings.'

'You know what she said about not being honest. It cost her her job at the Thrift. That's why we're in the state we're in. If we tell her about the rings she'll most probably tell us to hand them in.'

Jimmy nodded, she was right.

'Tell you what,' went on his sister. 'If things don't get better between now and Christmas I'll try and sell one myself.'

'You? You heard what Freddie said. They'll be suspicious if a scruffy kid goes into a shop with an expensive diamond ring and tries to flog it.'

'Maybe, maybe not,' smiled Susan mysteriously. She wasn't happy at selling her engagement ring – still, maybe it wouldn't be necessary, there were *two* rings after all.

The rent didn't get paid that Thursday. At the usual rent collecting time the lights were turned out and everyone sat in the dark, waiting for Mr Simpson's very individual knock, one loud, two soft, three loud. Jimmy and Susan saw the funny side of this and Dorothy was constantly shushing them lest they were heard. She held her hand across Jimmy's mouth when the knock came. When he got no response Mr Simpson knocked again in reverse order. Three loud, two soft, one loud. Dorothy kept her hand firmly in place until she heard Simpson's footsteps leave the back yard and the gate slam angrily behind him.

On being released Jimmy exploded into muffled hysterics setting his sister and auntie off as well. They left it another half an hour until the landlord had collected his other rents in the street, then switched the lights back on. Dorothy smiled at the two giggling youngsters – but she knew it couldn't go on.

Neville Simpson knew she was in. He could have called back later and doubtless found the lights on, but he had other plans for Dorothy Bairstow. Neville was due to get married next year and his bride-to-be, Maggie Newton, of the 'Newton's the Butcher' family, was determined to be a virgin on her wedding night. This was causing Neville no end of frustration and he needed a spot of occasional relief to see him safely through to his wedding day. Vera Bateson was currently performing this service for him, but she was looking a bit haggard nowadays and Neville had his eye on someone far more attractive. The following week he called early and gave a different knock. Dorothy's face when she opened the door told him all he wanted to know.

'Good evening, Mrs Bairstow, I seemed to have missed you last week, so that'll be two weeks...' He said all this without looking up, his face studying his rent account book. Dorothy stood there, not knowing what to say. Neville looked up and smiled innocently.

'Is there a problem, Mrs Bairstow?'

Dorothy looked nervously at him. He was an unhealthy-looking man with a pale complexion and bushy ginger hair, and a nose that had been broken and badly set. She often wondered why he'd never been called up. He was the right age, probably not much older than her. His dad owned the business, but old Mr Simpson, who was much more of a gentleman than his son, never came round any more.

'I er, I was wondering if I could give you double next week,' said Dorothy nervously.

'That'd be treble actually – forty-five shillings. Are you sure you'll be able to manage that next week?' He was still smiling, but his teeth were yellow and crooked and his breath wasn't exactly fragrant. 'Look, may I come in?' he asked. 'We might be able to sort this out another way.'

Dorothy stood back from the door to let him pass. He put his account book down on the table and turned to face her. She was even better looking close up, in a tired sort of way. A lot better looking than Maggie Newton; still, he wasn't marrying Maggie Newton for her looks. He glanced around.

'Are the children in?'

'No, they're out playing.'

'Good – look, I'll get straight to the point, Dorothy.' He hesitated, 'Can I call you Dorothy?'

She nodded, at a loss to know what was happening.

'The truth of the matter is,' he went on, 'that you can't pay the rent. Nor will you be able to in the near future – not until you get another job. Am I making sense so far?'

Dorothy shrugged her agreement, she hadn't a clue what he was on about.

'You're a fine-looking woman, Dorothy, and

121

many women in your position would take desperate steps in order to take care of their family.' Neville paused, needing to choose his words carefully. 'Some women would even sink to going on the streets.' He held up his hand as he saw Dorothy was about to intervene. 'Now – I wouldn't dream of suggesting that you'd sink so low – but if someone came along with, say, a private arrangement. Once a week say, in lieu of rent – something like that. How would you feel about it?'

His face was flushed with an almost orgasmic excitement at having made such a proposition. Dorothy was flushed with anger.

'You dirty-minded bastard! You want me to have it off with you to pay the rent? I'd beg on the bloody streets first. Get out of this bloody house, you filthy pervert! Good God! If your father knew what you were up to he'd have a heart attack!' She picked up his account book and threw it at him.

Neville backed out of the house, aghast at her reaction. As he went out of the door he turned and shouted nastily, 'Forty-five shillings next week, or notice to quit!'

Kicking the door shut behind him, she continued to vent her anger and despair on it until a crack appeared in the bottom panel. Then she sat down at the kitchen table and dissolved into floods of tears.

Dorothy had deliberately removed all her make-up and tied back the shining auburn hair which usually cascaded down over her slim shoulders.

She'd taken Mrs Crombie up on a long-standing invitation to have Jimmy and Susan round for tea. So Dorothy was alone when the knock came on the door the following Thursday. Neville stood there, uncertain of his reception. Dorothy said nothing.

'Well?' he asked. 'Have you got it?'

She shook her head.

He took a piece of paper from his pocket and handed it to her. 'Notice to quit,' he said without emotion. 'You've got a week.'

Dorothy took a deep breath. 'You'd better come in,' she said dully.

A half-smile of elation crossed his face. Things seemed to be going his way. Without saying another word to him, she led the way to the stairs, pausing to make sure he was following her. He needed no further hints. Hers was the front bedroom. The one she'd shared with Tommy, whose photograph was turned face down on the dressing table. The curtains were already drawn, to prevent neighbours putting two and two together. She didn't turn the light on for the same reason, but it was early evening and the thin curtains let in sufficient light for them to see by. There were no bedclothes on the bed, just two large bath towels covering the mattress. Dorothy had thought of nothing else all week. Trying to come up with an alternative. But there was no alternative. If she lost the house the kids would be taken into care and she'd end up in lodgings.

Neville sat on the only chair in the room and stared at her, making her feel uncomfortable.

'What would you like me to do?' she asked

uncertainly, trying to detach herself from the reality of the situation.

'Well, I, er – I'd like you to get undressed, please,' he replied hoarsely. Not quite believing she would actually do as he requested.

She kicked off her shoes then turned her back to him and slipped out of her blouse and skirt before sitting on the bed to unhook the stockings from her suspender belt. He made no move to start undressing himself, his breathing was quite audible now, tiny beads of sweat appearing on his forehead. Dorothy looked at him.

'What about you?' she asked. 'Are you just going to sit there?'

'Oh! R-right, y-yes,' he stammered. 'I er, I thought I'd let you go first.'

Having no make-up and severely tied back hair did little to hide the beauty underneath it all that had once turned Tommy Bairstow's head. Her figure was slightly fuller now, but still elegantly proportioned, statuesque even. Neville took a grimy handkerchief from his pocket and wiped his brow as Dorothy took a deep breath and stood up to finish what she had started. She turned her back to him once again.

'No, no,' he demanded. A desperate urgency creeping into his voice. 'Turn to face me. I want to see...'

She steeled herself and turned as he instructed, wishing for the first time in her life that she had an ugly body. Dorothy desperately wanted Simpson to be disappointed in what he saw. But she knew he wouldn't be. Reaching behind her back she nervously fumbled her brassière fastener, unhooking it at last. Then fixing her gaze at a point over his head, she very slowly, and with a tantalising reluctance, dropped her brassière, until her breasts were exposed to his lecherous gaze. She stood there for what seemed an age, trying to summon up the courage to take off her panties and knowing this awful man was drinking in every inch of her. Hooking her thumbs into the waistband, she inched them down with painful slowness, dreading the point at which she finally revealed herself to him. She lowered her gaze onto his sweating face as she finally let them drop to the floor. His eyes were transfixed between her legs as though he'd never seen a naked woman before.

And he'd certainly never seen one this beautiful.

Dorothy stood there facing him for a moment, hands on hips, almost defiantly, then lay down on one side of the bed and stared blankly up at the ceiling.

She heard him stand up, fumbling with his buttons. His breathing becoming increasingly heavy now. Dorothy expected him to get on the other side of the bed and was mildly surprised to see him standing over her. His naked body was unusually pale and without the vaguest hint of muscular definition. His was the body of a man who'd never done a hard day's work in his life. She turned her head away from the stink of his perspiration as he placed a damp hand on her breast, causing her to cringe with revulsion. His other hand went on to her stomach, then moved slowly down between her thighs. She instinctively brought her legs together and trapped his hand there, preventing any movement. Then she looked up into the sweating face of this foulest of men.

'Mr Simpson,' she asked quietly, but with barely concealed disgust. Deliberately using his surname to maintain some sort of incongruous formality. 'After, after this, I won't owe you anything – will I?'

He nodded vigorously. 'Oh no!' he gasped. 'Nothing at all – we're definitely quits after this.'

She relaxed her grip and prepared herself for the worst, closing her eyes and trying to imagine what the kids would be having for tea at Mrs Crombie's. He climbed onto the bed and knelt between her legs, forcing her thighs apart with his knees until she was concealing nothing from him. Suddenly he let out a loud moan and she felt a warm spattering on her breasts and stomach. She opened her eyes and saw that Neville was finished – no longer a threat to her.

He looked embarrassed, he even apologised. 'Sorry about that, I'll, er – well, yer know.' He got off the bed and turned his bony backside to her. Picking up his underpants and hopping comically on one leg as he tried to get them on. Dorothy took the towel from the other side of the bed and quickly wiped him off her, then covered herself up until Neville was dressed. He left her there, saying something about same time next week but Dorothy didn't hear him, she was already crying quietly. Consumed with self-loathing. She couldn't do it again.

But she knew she must.

As soon as she heard the door close behind him she hurried downstairs, still naked, and slammed on the bolt, cursing loudly at this disgusting man she was locking out. She yanked off the wooden board covering the bath and threw it tearfully on the scullery floor; then turned on the taps and sat weeping in the bath as it filled up around her.

She was still there an hour later when Jimmy and Susan banged on the door asking to come in.

Chapter Nine

The jam jar scam was paying dividends for Jimmy and Susan, who'd taken another two dozen back the following Saturday and once again the jovial jam jar man had complimented them on their spotless product. He held one up to the light.

'Just look at that! Hardly need put 'em through our washers, keep 'em coming, I wish we had more kids like you.'

Jimmy and Susan took this compliment with a modesty and good grace that further impressed the man. Sunday morning was the best time to acquire the jars. The factory closed on a Sunday and an early morning expedition before ten o'clock mass was all too easy. Susan had already mentioned stealing jam jars in confession, but Father O'Flaherty had dismissed it as a third-rate venial sin, worthy of only two Hail Marys.

Perhaps if she'd filled him in with details of the whole scam, her penance might have been more severe. She made up her mind to make her next confession to Father Proctor, no point boring Father O'Flaherty with the same old sin every time. She hadn't mentioned the ring yet, as she hadn't actually stolen it.

If Dorothy was pleased at them providing their own pocket money, she didn't seem to show it. Since losing her job at the Thrift Stores, she'd become more and more withdrawn. Snapping at them like she used to in the early days. Even raising her hand to Jimmy on one occasion, before withdrawing it and running out of the room and up the stairs. They'd been for tea at Jackie and Maureen Crombie's and had had to wait outside for ten minutes while she got out of the bath. Jimmy hadn't grumbled much, not enough to merit her nearly hitting him. They didn't need to listen at the bottom of the stairs to know she was crying. They looked at each other and shrugged helplessly.

'Wish we had a grandma and grandad like Jackie Crombie,' said Jimmy wistfully. 'I bet it's great having a grandma and grandad.'

'We might have for all we know,' said Susan. 'Dad's mam and dad are both dead, but me mam never knew who her mam and dad were. They might be still alive for all we know.'

'I hope they are. Did me mam ever tell you what happened?'

'Just that she were put in a home when she was a baby.'

'That's rotten that is,' muttered Jimmy. 'They

can't be very nice people then – to do that, can they?'

'Maybe, maybe not. We don't know what the circumstances were. That's what me mam said.'

'Oh, yeah, that's right, we don't, do we?' accepted Jimmy, who knew what Mam said was always right.

'Do you know what we ought to do to cheer Auntie Dorothy up?' decided Susan, before going on to answer her own question. 'Pay next week's rent, that'd cheer her up no end.'

'That's fifteen bob! Where we goin' ter get fifteen bob from?'

'Where'd you think?' grinned his sister.

'We can't take fifteen bob's worth of jam jars back – that's,' he began a mental calculation that Susan beat him to by a split second.

'A hundred and eighty,' she said triumphantly. 'If we really fill up our shopping bag, we can probably get thirty in – that's er,' she stopped to think for another couple of seconds, 'six trips. Easy.'

'They're bound ter get suspicious if we take all them back at once.'

Susan considered this then said brightly, 'Ah! – but we don't take 'em back at once do we? What we do, next Sunday we get a hundred and eighty jam jars, we'll take a shopping bag each and make three trips. Then we'll hide them in the cellar like we have been doing and take them back next week, one bag each a night. First you go, then I go. We've only got to do it for three nights and we've got our fifteen bob.'

So the plot was hatched there and then. The

129

fact that a variety of different personnel manned the empties counter during the week helped allay any suspicion and by Wednesday evening they had a bagful of change adding up to the magic figure of fifteen bob shillings. Mrs Crombie changed it into a ten shilling note and two half crowns, so the presentation could be made properly.

Dorothy came in from doing for Mrs Oldfield the following afternoon and sank gratefully into a chair. It was Thursday and Simpson would be round again. She intended telling him it was the wrong time of the month and could he come back next week. No man ever argued with that. Jimmy and Susan were already home, having both made a special effort to get back quickly. A steaming cup of tea appeared and their auntie accepted it suspiciously.

'Come on,' she demanded, 'what have you been up to?'

'Nowt,' protested an affronted Jimmy. 'We haven't been up ter nowt, have we, Susan?'

'We have actually,' admitted his sister.

'I thought so, come on, what is it?'

'Well,' said Susan, smirking at her grinning brother. 'You know we've been collecting jam jars?'

Dorothy's eyes narrowed. 'Yeess, I know you've been collecting jam jars – what's the problem?'

Jimmy couldn't contain himself any longer, 'We've got yer rent money!' he blurted, much to Susan's annoyance; he was always doing this.

'What?' exclaimed Dorothy.

'We've got this week's rent money,' repeated

Susan, handing her auntie the fifteen shillings. Dorothy looked down at the money in shocked surprise.

'But how? How did you? Good grief!' She sank her head between her hands and stayed like that for a long time.

'Are you alright, Auntie?' asked a concerned Jimmy, who swore he would never understand grown-ups.

Dorothy nodded from where she was, not wanting the children to see her tears. They approached her from either side and, very tentatively, each put an arm around her shoulder.

'I'm sorry,' she sobbed. 'Don't think I'm not grateful. You must have gone to an enormous amount of trouble to do this for me. It's just that – well, I don't seem to be able to do much for you.'

'You look after us,' argued Susan kindly.

'After a fashion I do,' she lifted her head and wiped away her tears on her sleeve. 'I sometimes think you deserve a lot better than me.'

'Would yer like us to go out an' play?' asked Jimmy, who was not without tact at times like this.

Dorothy nodded. A knock came at the door and she looked up with a worried start. Susan ran to answer it, as though she knew who it would be. Ray stood there awkwardly, it was the first time he'd called on Susan. It was actually the first time he'd called on any girl.

'Oh hiya, Ray,' she greeted. 'Auntie, I'm going out with Ray, I'll be back about si...' She grimaced at Ray as her aunt interrupted her.

'Bring him in then, let's have a look at him.'

An embarrassed Ray entered the kitchen and presented himself for inspection. He was tall and pleasant-looking with dark, tousled hair and the beginnings of acne. Dorothy nodded her approval.

'If only I was a couple of years younger,' she smiled. Then to Susan. 'Back about six then, have a nice time and…' Susan looked back at her auntie who looked on the verge of tears again. 'Thanks.'

Jimmy followed his sister out, leaving Dorothy to her confused thoughts. She looked at the clock, ten to five. He'd be here in twenty minutes. At least she wouldn't have to go through *that* again. Just pay him the rent and use the time of the month excuse next week and maybe even the week after. And then? Well, half an hour's unpleasantness for forty-five shillings. It seemed daft *not* to do it when she put it like that to herself. But it wasn't as easy as that, and she knew it.

He was late. It was nearly half-past. She wouldn't have been able to accommodate him anyway, with the kids coming in for their tea in half an hour. The knock came. Same stupid knock. She opened the door and he stood there grinning and holding out a pathetic bunch of chrysanthemums.

'Here,' he said. 'Gotcha some flow … errs.'

'Oh, God,' she thought. 'The pig's drunk, just what I need.' She stood back to let him through and took the rent money out of her pocket.

'I've got the rent,' she said. He looked down at

132

the money, stupidly.

'What? W-hat yer talking about? I haven't come for the rent.' He made to grab her but she took a quick backward step, positioning a dining chair between her and him.

'I don't want to do it, just take the rent and go, please.'

He didn't seem to hear her. 'I've had a little drink,' he explained, 'to make me last longer. Don't want a repeat of last week, do we?' He sniggered to himself as he took off his coat and threw it on the settee.

Dorothy thrust the money at him angrily. 'There won't be a repeat of last week because I'm not doing it,' she shouted. 'Just take your bloody rent and go!'

Her anger had a sobering effect on him. Realisation sinking in. 'Wotcha talkin' about, yer stupid cow? Course we're doin' it again. That's what we agreed last week. Anyway I didn't get me money's worth last week. Shot me load before I got it in.' He grabbed hold of the chair Dorothy was using for protection and snatched it away from her, flinging it across the room, his drink-sodden eyes fixed excitedly on hers, advancing on her until she was backed up against the wall. She tried to push him away but he grabbed at her blouse, tearing it open, then pulled viciously at her brassière, exposing one of her breasts, his fingernails leaving livid scratches. Dorothy was frightened.

'Come here, yer whore!' snarled Neville. 'I want me money's worth. Three pounds you owe and I want it out of your body, here and now!'

'But – but how can I owe three pounds after last week? You said we were quits, you got what you wanted. Please leave me alone,' begged Dorothy, crying now.

'Quits, my arse!' he roared. 'I want me three quid or I want you!'

The door opened and Susan stood there horrified at the sight of her Auntie Dorothy, blouse ripped open, being attacked by the landlord. Neville turned and leered at her. He released his grip on Dorothy and advanced on Susan.

'Your auntie doesn't want to play today – but why should I settle for mutton when there's a nice bit of lamb on offer?'

He made a drunken grab for Susan, who was taken completely by surprise and failed to get out of the way in time. She fell to the floor, taking Neville with her. He laughed at their predicament, belched loudly and tried to force himself on the terrified girl, kneeling over her as he attempted to unbuckle his belt. Dorothy felt a crimson rage envelop her. She picked up the piano stool and smashed him across the back with it, weeping with fear and fury. He half stood up and turned, as if to see who was hitting him. The pure hatred on Dorothy's face provoking fear on his. He staggered to his feet, backed out of the door and ran into the street, chased by an hysterical Dorothy, desperately trying to land just one telling blow with the stool.

'You filthy perverted bastard, I'll kill you for that,' she screamed.

Constable Greenough couldn't have chosen a

more opportune moment to be passing the end of the street. Or *in*opportune, depending upon your point of view. The sudden violent screaming giving him quite a start. He looked down the street and saw a terrified man emerge from a back yard, closely followed by a screaming woman. He couldn't believe what he was seeing. It was Tommy's widow, Dorothy Bairstow, unless he was very much mistaken. Alan Greenough had been a good friend of Fred and Tommy and he always thought Dorothy was a sophisticated sort of woman. A bit too classy for Tommy in a way. But she looked far from classy now, her blouse ripped open, and even from this distance he could see her naked breasts.

'I'll kill you, I'll kill you!' she was screaming.

The terrified man stumbled, his arm coming up a fraction too late to ward off the stool, arching vengefully down onto his head and smashing into it with a sickening thud. P.C. Greenough winced. The man collapsed, blood pouring from a gash in his skull. Dorothy dropped the stool from her trembling hands, mortified at what she had done. Susan came running out and flung her arms around her auntie as they both looked down, horror-stricken at the lifeless-looking form of Neville Simpson.

Chapter Ten

Jimmy was just rounding the corner into the street when he was almost knocked down by Jackie Crombie, desperate to herald the news of Simpson's demise to the neighbourhood.

'Yer auntie's just murdered Simmo,' he gasped happily. 'She brayed him with a stool – yer should've seen it. She didn't half fetch him a bleedin' clout! There's blood all over t'street!'

Jackie had no time to elaborate further, he dashed down Paradine Hill, pausing here and there to breathlessly deliver his increasingly gory news. A crowd had gathered by the time the ambulance came. P.C. Greenough was bending over the still figure of Neville Simpson and a second constable was standing by a pale and dazed looking Dorothy, with a firm grip on her arm. Susan stood nearby, crying and being comforted by Mrs Veitch. No one could make any sense out of what had happened.

Jimmy watched horrified as his Auntie Dorothy was led away and taken the short distance to Paradine Hill Police Station, watched by many a curious eye, and with wild speculation hurrying from mouth to mouth. The ambulance came and went, with lights flashing and bell ringing, followed by Jackie Crombie, a dozen other whooping children and two barking dogs. Simpson was still alive but he didn't look too good and in the opinion of most onlookers in the know, 'It's only a question of time.' Constable Greenough took Susan back into the house to take a statement and Jimmy followed them in. The policeman looked up at the shocked boy standing quietly in the doorway.

'Do you think you could make us all a cup of tea, son?' he asked kindly.

Jimmy nodded. Things couldn't be too bad if the police could still think about mundane things like tea. He busied himself in the scullery, listening carefully to what his sister had to say.

It was hard to make her out through the sobs. But what he did hear made him angry beyond his years. Susan and P.C. Greenough sat opposite each other at the table, the policeman licking a thumb to open a stubborn page of his notebook. 'What exactly did you see when you came in?' he asked gently.

'He was shouting and swearing and pulling at Auntie Dorothy's clothes – and Auntie Dorothy was crying, and I think he was drunk, and then–' Susan stopped to regain her composure.

'Take your time, Susan, there's no rush. I just want to get it all down while it's still fresh in your memory.'

The policeman turned to Jimmy who was pouring out the cups of tea, unsure why his hand was shaking so much.

'Thanks Jimmy,' he said, taking two cups and giving one to Susan. 'Right, love, in your own time, what happened after that?'

Susan took a deep breath and continued. 'He came after me! He knocked me down. I was

137

struggling, I couldn't move and he was laughing at me and...' She paused and looked across at Jimmy, wishing he wasn't listening to this. 'And he was trying to get his trousers off – and Auntie Dorothy hit him with a stool and he got up and ran out and...' Susan's words flooded out in a tearful torrent, halted only by the sound of Jimmy dropping his cup in anger, causing the other two to turn round. Susan was the person closest to him in the whole world although he would be loath to admit it.

'Auntie Dorothy did right,' he blurted. 'I hope the bloody bastard's dead!'

He ran past them and sat on the stairs to plan his vengeance on Simpson, who he hoped would survive in order to suffer whatever Jimmy had in store for him.

There was a knock on the back door and he heard P.C. Greenough talking to a man called Sackfield. He was asking after Auntie Dorothy and would she pop in to see him as soon as she'd got the time.

'Do you mind if I ask what it's about?' asked the constable.

'Er – yes. I came to offer her a job – if she's still interested.'

As he left he was passed in the yard by Mrs Veitch who was promising to keep an eye on the children until Dorothy came home from the police station.

'It might not be tonight,' warned the constable.

'That's alright, we'll manage,' Mrs Veitch assured him.

P.C. Greenough went off with a feeling of dread

inside him. He'd have to tell the story as he saw it, and what he saw was Simpson running away from Dorothy and her attacking him. He firmly believed Susan's side of the story, but facts were facts, and it was Simpson who was lying in hospital not Dorothy.

Dorothy didn't hear the cell door slam shut behind her. She didn't hear the custody sergeant ask her name and address. The accompanying constable had to help out on that one.

The mattress on the cell bed was hard but it suited her just fine. She didn't want to be comfortable. Her mind was swimming with a mixture of different awful images. Of *him* watching her get undressed, of *him* kneeling over her naked body. Then kneeling over Susan, then lying in the street with blood gushing from his head. But what she'd done hadn't purged her hatred of him. She needed to know he was dead. Or was it herself she hated for taking this loathsome creature into her bed? The bed she'd shared with her lovely Tommy. She was little more than a common prostitute. She sobbed well into the night before falling into a disturbed sleep.

The cell door clanged open early the next morning and an unpleasant-looking police-woman came in. Or rather she wobbled in with the knock-kneed gait of the unathletic obese. An outsize woman with two chins, a wispy moustache and a cup of tea which she placed sloppily on the floor beside the bed. Any fleeing villain would have little difficulty escaping this officer's pursuit. Dorothy awoke suddenly, completely disorientated. Then she remembered where she was and why, and a cloud of despondency enveloped her. The policewoman, who had seen this happen before, found it oh so amusing.

'Forgot where you were, dear?' she smirked. 'Thought you were at home in your nice warm bed snuggled up to your husband?'

She turned to leave then had another thought. 'Oh, by the way. Simpson's still alive but not expected to live, so with a bit of luck we've got a murderess on our hands. Don't think we've ever had a murderess down at Paradine before.'

Dorothy hurled her tea at the grinning policewoman, the cup smashing on the cell door. 'Get out, you stupid bloody woman,' she screamed. 'Just get out!'

She wanted to think of something clever to say to wipe the silly smile off that woman's face. But she couldn't. The policewoman left, silly smile intact, locking the cell door on a tearful Dorothy. She opened the hatch in the cell door to fire in one final shot.

'By the way, if you're hoping to get bail this morning, keep hoping, but it won't do you any good. Magistrates never let mad women like you loose on the streets!'

'Why don't you get a shave, you fat freak!' was all Dorothy could manage in return. It had the desired effect, although Dorothy couldn't tell from where she was.

Mrs Veitch knocked on the door early. Jimmy and Susan were already up, debating whether or not to go to school.

'Best place for you,' insisted Mrs Veitch. 'Your auntie's up in court this morning, most likely she'll get bail. Probably be home by the time you get back.'

The children nodded at the logic of this. With a bit of luck the news wouldn't have reached school so at least they'd be out of the way of idle gossip.

They couldn't have been more wrong. St Winifred's was rife with rumour. The story of a rent man being beaten up by a mere woman went down well at a girls' school and by lunchtime Dorothy was being hailed as a heroine of the working classes, much the predominant class at St Winifred's.

Jimmy didn't fare quite so well. Scoggy Andrews and his pals from 2A had always looked down on the inferior beings from 2B, Jimmy included. The taunting began at morning break.

'Hey! Bairstow! Can yer get us tickets to yer auntie's hanging?'

Jimmy knew if he reacted he'd finish off second best. He walked away followed by the baying mob. Scoggy ran in front of him and pretended to have a noose around his neck, choking and lolling his tongue out. Jimmy wished he were bigger and stronger. Scoggy Andrews' nose was just waiting to be hit. If he could just get one clean blow in, then run, he might just get away with it. Running was something he was good at.

Then Scoggy overstepped the mark. 'Hey, Bairstow! When yer auntie kicks the bucket there'll be nobody left in your family. D'yer think

God's trying ter tell yer summat?'

Jimmy's fist exploded on the end of his tormentor's nose. Every ounce of strength in his puny body went into that one venomous blow and Jimmy was a lot stronger than he looked. Scoggy yelped in pain as blood poured from his nose and obscenities from his mouth. Jimmy was already much too far away to hear any of this but unfortunately for Scoggy, Father Leitrim on one of his playground profanity patrols, did.

Dragging the shocked Scoggy by the scruff of his neck, the hard-faced priest took him away for the appropriate punishment. Bad language at St Thomas's was the language of the devil and must be mercilessly beaten out of any boy using it. And Jimmy knew that for once, justice was being done.

But today, the fortunes of the Bairstow family were mixed.

An ashen-faced Dorothy ascended the steps leading to the dock of Court Number Three in Leeds Town Hall. She looked across the courtroom and recognised the sympathetic faces of Valerie Veitch and Mrs Crombie. She found herself racking her brains to remember Mrs Crombie's first name and her confused mind was still running through the alphabet when a clerk appeared with a Bible for her to swear on.

Alan Greenough was nowhere to be seen. He'd told her in the Black Maria on the way that he didn't think the police would be opposing bail. 'Most of the lads down at Paradine are on your side,' he'd assured her out of the side of his mouth lest the other travelling felons heard.

The charge was read out by a short, bilious-looking man in a black gown with a huge tear in it. The magistrate in the middle of the bench stared across at her as though she were some unpleasant kind of life form.

'Dorothy Anne Bairstow. You are charged with Attempted Murder, how do you plead?'

It sounded so much more than it was, she'd only clonked Simpson over the head with a stool. They made it sound as though she'd hacked him up with a machete.

'Not guilty, sir,' her voice was barely audible.

'Could you speak up, Mrs Bairstow?'

'Not guilty, sir,' she almost shouted this time.

'Mr Mitchell?' The magistrate in the centre looked over his glasses at the prosecuting solicitor. 'Do we have a case to answer?'

'Yes, sir, I wish to call P.C. Greenough to the stand.'

Alan Greenough walked briskly into the court, scarcely looking at Dorothy, and took the oath.

'Constable Greenough,' inquired Mitchell. 'Where were you at five-thirty on the evening of Thursday the fourteenth of November nineteen-forty-five?'

Alan Greenough took a notebook from the top pocket of his uniform. 'I was on foot patrol up Paradine Hill, sir.'

'Did you pass the end of Broughton Terrace?'

'Yes, sir.'

'And did you see anything unusual going on?'

'Yes, sir. I saw Dorothy,' he grimaced to himself at this unprofessional slip up, 'I mean Mrs

143

Bairstow – chasing a man out into the street.' He stopped and looked across at Dorothy, then lowered his eyes to his notebook.

'Carry on, Constable Greenough,' insisted Mitchell.

'She looked very distressed, her blouse was torn and her...' he gave a dry, embarrassed cough. 'And her breasts were exposed!'

'Was she carrying anything?'

'Yes, sir, she had a piano stool in her hands.'

'Piano stool! That would be quite a heavy stool, would it not?'

'I imagine so, sir.'

'Go on, what happened then?'

'The man tripped and fell to the ground.'

'This man – was he acting in any way aggressively towards Mrs Bairstow?'

'Er, well, no, sir.'

'Did he look frightened?'

'Yes, sir.'

'Tell me what happened then, Constable Greenough.'

'Well, sir, she raised the stool in the air and struck him with it.'

'How many times?'

'Oh, only the once, sir,' Alan assured him earnestly, this being the only thing he'd said which went in Dorothy's favour.

'Was it a violent blow?'

Alan took a deep breath before saying, 'Yes, sir, quite violent.'

'Enough to kill a man?'

'Depends, sir.'

Mitchell ignored Alan's fudging, sensing he was

144

on Dorothy's side. 'And was she shouting anything as she struck him?'

Alan's face dropped again. 'Yes, sir.' He looked across at Dorothy again and shrugged apologetically. 'She said she'd kill him!'

'Thank you, constable, that's all we need to know.' Mitchell sat down, well pleased with himself.

The magistrate looked down at Dorothy's solicitor. 'Do you have anything to ask this witness, Mr er…'

'Baldwin, sir. No, sir, I've nothing to ask the witness but I would like to explain to the court as to why my client acted in a manner totally out of character.'

'You may proceed, Mr Baldwin.'

'The reason my client's breasts were exposed was because the alleged victim had been attempting to rape not only her but also her niece who chanced to walk in on the incident.'

Mitchell sprang to his feet. 'It is the view of the prosecution that no rape was intended. The accused, having been caught in an act of promiscuity with my client by her niece, decided to recover her reputation by accusing him of rape.'

'And is this niece in court?'

'No, sir, she is not.'

'Pity.'

Dorothy had been adamant that Susan didn't become involved at this stage. She could say her piece when the matter came to trial.

The magistrates withdrew and reappeared ten minutes later to announce that the case was to be referred to the Assizes, to be heard in the new year at a date to be decided. This was of little concern to Dorothy who had a naïve faith in the British legal system and was convinced that when they heard her side of things she'd be found innocent.

Her solicitor stepped forward to apply for bail. He looked across at her and gave a reassuring smile that told her all was well, for the time being at least. The magistrate looked across at the prosecuting solicitor who was whispering to a uniformed police inspector who had just walked in the court.

'Is there a problem with bail, Mr Mitchell?' asked the magistrate.

'Yes, sir,' replied the prosecuting solicitor. 'We've just heard from the hospital that the victim has taken a turn for the worse and may not recover. The implication being that a more serious charge may be brought against Mrs Bairstow and in view of this we wish to oppose bail.'

'Do you really, Mr Mitchell?' mused the magistrate.

Dorothy's heart stopped. Surely there'd been some mistake. She looked pleadingly across at her solicitor who gave a helpless shrug. It was for the magistrates to decide, not him. He made one final plea.

'In view of the fact that it is my client who is the victim in all this, might I suggest that she is scarcely a danger to the public and hardly likely to run away from being tried for a crime she did not commit.'

The magistrate accepted his plea with a curt nod and leaned over in turn to his colleagues for their contribution. A series of nods followed as they coldly discussed Dorothy's immediate destiny. Her eyes were glued ferociously on them for any clues as to the outcome. Their eyes in turn looked studiously away from her as they came to their decision.

'In view of the potential seriousness of the crime, the court refuses bail. Take her away.'

The silence was replaced by a steady murmur as the court callously prepared itself for the next case.

Take her away. The finality of it staggered Dorothy. How could three ridiculous old duffers just have her *taken away*. Where to, for God's sake? It hadn't even been discussed. In desperation she ripped open her blouse and thrust her breasts towards the bench. The livid scratch marks that Simpson had left could be seen clearly across the court. The murmuring halted abruptly as every eye in the court was fixed on Dorothy's magnificent chest.

'Look at this!' she screamed defiantly. 'This isn't promiscuity, you idiots! This is rape!'

'You tell 'em, Dorothy love!' shouted Mrs Crombie.

'Nice tits, missis!' shouted a grinning, unkempt spectator from the back of the court, shortly before Alan Greenough led him unceremoniously out of the door.

The two policemen on either side of Dorothy stepped forward in unison and pinned her arms to her sides, spinning her round, and hurried her back down the steps to the cell that, only a few minutes ago, she'd thankfully vacated for what she thought was the last time.

Mrs Veitch and Mrs Crombie were still sitting at the back as the crowded court emptied. The clerk was reading out the next case. Drunk and disorderly. 'How do you plead?' – 'Guilty, yer Honour' – 'Fined five pounds and bound over to keep the peace.' It all seemed so insignificant compared to what had happened to their friend who didn't even belong amongst the riff-raff passing through this place. And what would happen to the children? No one had mentioned that. It was as if the court didn't know about them.

'Don't worry about the kids,' Mrs Crombie had yelled as they took her away. 'We'll keep an eye on 'em!'

Dorothy had looked across at her and seemed to nod her thanks before disappearing downwards.

'I should button your blouse up, Mrs Bairstow.'

The voice was Alan Greenough's who'd followed down to the cells. Still in a tearful daze, she took his advice.

'What are they going to do to me?' she said quietly, as she fumbled with the buttons. She sounded so helpless, like a small schoolgirl. 'What's happening to me?'

Alan Greenough turned sadly away. Nothing he could do or say would help. She was in for a hard time and how she survived it was up to her. Not for the first time in his life he was disillusioned with the justice system he had sworn to uphold.

There were six of them in the Black Maria bound for Ashinghurst Women's prison just outside Wakefield. Four convicted criminals and two prison officers, one male, one female. Dorothy was handcuffed to a brazen-looking young woman who spat on the floor as she entered the vehicle, narrowly missing the boots of another prisoner already seated.

'Watch it, yer slag,' snarled the seated prisoner. A mountainous woman with close cropped hair and startling white teeth which seemed at odds with the rest of her.

Dorothy's handcuffed companion grinned at the woman. 'As I live an' bleedin' breathe, it's Dildo Delma the Drighlington Dyke. Who'd nick yer new gnashers off, Delma? Trigger the fucking Wonder 'orse?'

Dorothy's short time in captivity was beginning to inure her to such language and she made a mental resolution not to allow these words to creep into her own vocabulary.

'That's enough of that, you two,' grunted one of the female warders. 'I'm not at me best today so we'll have a nice restful journey. I'm sure neither of you want to pick up a black mark before we get there.'

An innocent sounding threat, but enough to shut these two aggressive women up – for the time being at least. After a while, her handcuffed companion gave Dorothy a double take.

'First time?'

'Is it that obvious?'

149

'You could say that, darlin'. I'm Rita, Rita Doidge. Part-time prossie and failed fraudster.'

'Hello, Rita, I'm Dorothy Bairstow,' she returned politely, wondering if she should add her own criminal qualifications, but Attempted Murder had a certain incongruity to it when associated with her.

'I'll call you Dolly then.'

'Watcher in for, Dolly darlin'?' sneered Delma. 'Fartin' in church?' She laughed at her own joke and earned a second admonition from the warder.

'I hit a man over the head with a piano stool, he was trying to rape me and my niece. They think he might die.'

The last sentence earned Dorothy a certain kudos from two of her fellow prisoners.

'Serve the bastard right – I hope the bastard dies,' announced a small woman sitting at the other side of Rita. Her thin, tinny voice tailing off under the warder's glare.

'Don't talk so bloody stupid,' admonished Rita. 'If he dies, they could top our Dolly. An' we don't want our Dolly topped, do we, girls? – we've only just met her.'

Rita turned her attention to Delma. 'Did yer hear that, yer fat faggot? Did yer hear what our Dolly does ter them what tries it on with her? Better watch yer step with our Dolly, yer fat fu...'

'Quiet! roared the warder.

'Sorry, Miss,' apologised Rita, who didn't sound sorry at all.

Chapter Eleven

Jackie Crombie was waiting at the end of the street as Jimmy and Susan walked up Paradine Hill together. His skinny, short-trousered white legs shivered inside a pair of Wellingtons, recently handed down from sister Maureen. Having two children of different sexes made a difference to the economy of the Crombie household insofar as they were limited as to what could be handed down from sister to brother. Although they didn't always let this stand in their way, as Maureen's old knickers were currently doubling as Jackie's underpants, adding to Jackie's dread of ever getting knocked down by a car. His eyes constantly blinked from behind a pair of circular glasses, one of the lenses having been covered up with elastoplast in order to bully his other 'lazy' eye into doing a bit more work. Jackie's dad had cut his hair the night before and Jimmy was eternally thankful that Auntie Dorothy hadn't taken Mr Crombie up on his kind offer to cut Jimmy's hair for nowt.

'There's only a week between a good hair cut and a bad 'un,' were the words which rang in Jackie's ears every time his father sent him out to brave the world with mutilated locks. In Jackie's case a month was nearer the mark, by which time his dad was at it again.

Jackie's mother had told him to keep his big

151

mouth shut about their Auntie Dorothy, and just ask them to pop in and see her. But news such as this was just too much for Jackie to keep to himself.

'Hey! Yer auntie's bin sent ter prison!' he yelled, as though having an auntie sent to prison was something to be proud of.

'Jackie Crombie, if this is one of your stupid lies I'll…' Susan didn't finish her threat. She saw Mrs Crombie appear at her gate with an expression that told her Jackie was telling the truth for once. A beckoning arm ordered Jackie to come in.

'Jackie! What did I just tell you? Come in here, NOW!'

As her son ran past she gave him a well-timed clip behind his ear then looked up at Jimmy and Susan.

'You'd best come in.'

They followed her in to her house knowing full well what she had to tell them. Auntie Dorothy wasn't coming home.

'What's going to happen to us, Mrs Crombie?' asked Susan with an air of resigned practicality.

'I'm not going into one o' them homes,' announced Jimmy. Jackie agreed with him wholeheartedly.

'They lock yer up in cupboards and don't give yer nowt to eat for a week, just for giving 'em a bit of cheek,' declared this happy harbinger of doom and gloom.

His mother aimed another blow to his head, which he rode with practised ease.

'Next time!' she warned. 'And it's up ter bed, my lad, and no tea nor supper.'

Jackie sat back, not quite realising what he was doing wrong, but kept his mouth shut all the same. Mrs Crombie turned her attention back to Jimmy and Susan.

'Right, you can have a bit of tea with us tonight. Mrs Veitch is going to help out as well – and it's Saturday tomorrow, so we've all got the weekend to sort out what to do for the best.'

'Thanks Mrs Crombie,' said Susan.

'Yes, thanks, Mrs Crombie,' echoed Jimmy as he dashed out of the door with Jackie.

Mrs Crombie bustled about in the scullery as she shouted through to Susan. 'We'd have you to stay with us but it'd be a bit crowded.' She didn't see the look of relief on Susan's face. 'You see, you'd have to share with our Maureen but she's only got a single bed, same with our Jackie.'

'It's alright,' assured Susan. 'We'll not come to any harm in our house – and I am nearly sixteen.' She was hoping Mrs Crombie didn't know when her birthday was. 'You're old enough when you're sixteen, aren't you?'

She didn't explain what you were old enough for at sixteen, but Mrs Crombie nodded all the same. She glanced approvingly at the assured young lady sitting in her kitchen and fatuously hoped that her Maureen, a year Susan's junior, would turn out as well.

'Mrs Crombie,' said Susan quietly, 'you do know why Auntie Dorothy hit him, don't you?'

'I don't know the full story, love, but I could see from the state of your auntie what he'd been up to. He was drunk, wasn't he?'

'Yes ... he tried to attack me. That's what made

153

Auntie Dorothy so mad.'

Mrs Crombie put a comforting arm around Susan. 'I know, lass. He's tried it on with a few round here that's been behind with their rents. I'm naming no names, but there's them what's let him get away with it as well. Vera Bateson for one. If her Len ever found out, he'd have finished him for sure!'

'When it all comes out in court, do you think they'll let her come home?'

'Course they will,' consoled Mrs Crombie, who didn't believe it for a minute.

That evening Jimmy and Susan sat on the attic stairs. An overcoat around both their shoulders to ward out the biting November cold.

'You know what we've got to do, don't you?' said Susan. Jimmy nodded. 'Run away. Do you think Freddie will help?' Susan gave a faraway smile. The idea of Freddie helping appealed to her. A knight in shining armour would come in handy right now. But this was the real world. 'No, not run away,' she said. 'We've got to sell one of the rings to pay the rent. Whatever we do, we mustn't let ourselves be kicked out. There's got to be a house for Auntie Dorothy to come home to.'

'And for us to live in,' added Jimmy.

'That too. So we'll do it tomorrow.'

'Right ... g'night.'

'Where do you think you're going?'

'I'm off ter bed, where d'yer think I'm going?' asked a puzzled Jimmy.

'I think you're going to the cemetery with me. I

154

can't get the rings on my own! If we're going to sell the things tomorrow, we'll have to get them tonight. There'll be too many people about in the morning.'

'Blimey! Sounds a bit creepy!'

'Course if you're too scared!' Susan knew she'd got him there.

'I never said I was scared!'

'Right then, let's get our coats on.'

Dorothy sat on the bottom bunk and viewed her surroundings with horror. A decorator might have had the temerity to call the colour of the painted brick walls Eau de Nil, the residents called it puke green which was nearer the mark. It was littered with pencilled graffiti, an indication of the intellect of previous inmates who'd passed through. It ranged from the chillingly obscene to the pathetic cry for help, to the witty, and to the illiterate – mostly the latter. During the day the cell was illuminated by a high window, small enough to merit just a single bar down the middle. In the evenings they would be lit by a dismal forty-watt light bulb diffused behind a rectangle of reinforced glass and controlled by some outside hand that threw them into darkness at two-minutes-to-eight each night, provoking complaints that they'd been switched off early. Every second of light being precious. The cell measured perhaps ten feet by seven and was home to two people. The door, which was mercifully left open during waking hours, was painted dysentery brown, presumably to complement the walls. It was made of steel with a small sliding hatch controlled only from the outside. The floors were tiled and hosed down daily and woe betide any inmate who left anything not waterproof on the floor.

Dorothy's eyes were constantly drawn to the seatless w.c. in the corner. No amount of bleach would ever remove the ingrained stains that caused the water to look permanently discoloured. A lever on the wall controlled the desultory flush which would only rarely completely remove the waste. Two consecutive flushes took several minutes.

'Rule number one,' announced Rita from the bunk above. 'No crappin' in the lavvie. Save yer solids for the bog block during the day.'

Unknown to Dorothy, the warders had deliberately placed her with Rita simply because they didn't want another suicide on their hands. All remand prisoners were taken back to court once a week and it was embarrassing to have to explain to a magistrate that another of their charges had committed suicide. As they viewed Dorothy as one such potential embarrassment, they thought it a good idea to stick her with someone who'd keep her mind occupied. And there was no one better than Rita Doidge for that job.

Dorothy didn't answer. She didn't appreciate being lumbered with the loud-mouthed Rita. She eased herself onto the bunk and stared up at the bulge formed by her cellmate.

'There's worse places than this, yer know,' persisted the voice from above. 'Holloway – that's an arsehole of a place. Like a posh hotel this, compared to Holloway. Mind you, that's where you'll end up if yer get done fer murder.'

'They hang you for murder, you cretin!' snapped Dorothy.

Rita's head suddenly appeared, upside down. 'It's got to be pre-meditated for 'em to hang yer. Nobody pre-meditates a murder wiv a bleedin' pianna stool!'

Having delivered this piece of legal logic, Rita disappeared. This was of no comfort to Dorothy who at that moment didn't care whether they hung her or not. She just wanted to go home, away from this nightmare of stained toilets and strip searches and locked doors and fat dykes and loud-mouthed cellmates. Her determination to keep a stiff upper lip was finally deserting her. She felt the tears rising to the surface.

The hatch in the cell door slid noisily open and a face inspected the two occupants before slamming the hatch shut and moving on with a cheerful whistle. A simple act which infuriated Dorothy. She ran to the door and hammered on it.

'Stop whistling, you callous bastard,' she screamed hysterically.

The whistling stopped as the warder listened to what she was shouting. Returning to the hatch she looked back in, but this time couldn't see Dorothy who had slumped to the floor, blubbing like a baby.

'Everything alright in there?'

'Yes, Miss,' said Rita. 'First night nerves that's all.'

'Right, lights go out in five minutes.'

The hatch slammed shut again and the whistling recommenced. Dorothy had managed to get back to her bunk just as the lights went out. Just another inconvenience forced on her by this inhuman place. Try as she might she couldn't stop weeping.

'Christ Almighty, I hope I ain't been lumbered with a bloody screamer,' moaned Rita. 'Pull yerself tergevver, Dolly lass. It's bad enough bein' locked up wivout bein' locked up wiv a bloody screamer.'

It was two hours before the late winter dawn when Dorothy finally dropped off, eyes reddened with tears and her throat hoarse with sobbing. Her plight not helped by the contented snoring from the bunk above.

Chapter Twelve

'Bugger me! It's freezing.'

'Jimmy Bairstow, just watch your language,' snapped Susan. 'Just because there's no one looking after us doesn't mean to say you can start swearing.'

'It is cold though, isn't it?' shivered Jimmy.

'Yes – bloody cold!'

Jimmy opened his mouth to caution his sister, then saw the grin on her face. He returned the grin as he pulled his Uncle Tommy's flat cap right down over his ears, then turned up his collar against the biting wind as they headed down Paradine Hill towards Bramham Street Cemetery. A policeman, thankfully ending his lonely beat, glanced up the road at this huddled couple advancing on him. He might well have asked what a pair of youngsters was doing out and about at this late hour. An awkward question for which they didn't have a ready answer.

'Keep walking,' whispered Susan.

A wise strategy as it turned out, the policeman called out a cheery 'Goodnight' to them as he stamped his feet and disappeared into the warmth of the police station. They were both tall for their age and from a distance could well have been adults.

'He thought we were grown-ups,' chirped a delighted Jimmy.

'I hope the jeweller thinks the same tomorrow,' said Susan.

'Have you figured out how you're going ter get away with it?' asked Jimmy.

Susan smiled to herself. 'Just you wait till tomorrow, you'll see.'

Jimmy shrugged his shoulders in mild frustration. He hated mysteries, but he knew there was no point in trying to get anything more out of her. Best to pretend he wasn't bothered. At least it didn't give her the satisfaction of knowing how curious he was.

The cemetery gates were locked, which was a bit pointless, as the iron railings which had once enclosed it were long gone. Dismantled at the beginning of the war and sent away for re-cycling as tanks, bullets, ships and suchlike. The wall on which they had once stood was only three feet high and provided the cemetery's only protection. Any corpse wishing to escape would have no problem.

It was a clear night. The cold wind sending what clouds there were scudding across the wintry moon and casting eerie moving shadows over the graves. A brave, flickering gas lamp illuminated the grave of Sidney Tobin and his wife Florence April Rose, a fragrant name until you worked out her initials. Jimmy walked behind Susan and shuddered half with cold, half with apprehension.

'It's a bit spooky, isn't it?'

Susan nodded, she felt it as well. A yellow-eyed cat glared at them from an overhanging tree branch, hissing and leaping down as Jimmy lobbed a twig at it.

For the hundredth time they read their mam and dad's names etched into the moonlit grave-stone.

FREDERICK WILLIAM BAIRSTOW
1909-1941
AND HIS BELOVED WIFE LILIAN
1908-1941
GOD BLESS.

The children stood there reverently for awhile, hands clasped in silent prayer, before Susan spoke.

'I hope you don't mind, but we're going to have to disturb you again, aren't we, Jimmy?' She looked to her brother for support.

'We won't be a minute though,' said Jimmy.

They crossed themselves, perhaps hoping for

some sort of advance absolution, then dug their hands under the slab and heaved it upright. Susan held it in position as Jimmy retrieved the jar. Then with a final apology she let it go with a thump that cracked it right across the middle.

'Bugger me!' blasphemed Jimmy, then clasped his hand to his mouth at such sacrilege. Susan burst into tears and knelt beside the broken slab which had cracked right between their dad's name and their mam's name.

'Oh heck! I'm ever so sorry.'

'She is, she's ever so sorry,' confirmed Jimmy.

Susan glared at her brother. 'It wasn't entirely *my* fault, you know. You dropped it last time, I was only doing what you did.' She returned her attention to the grave.

'What we'll do,' she explained to her parents, 'is when we sell the rings, we'll get you a proper headstone, all nicely engraved and all that, with all our names on, including our William's – won't we, Jimmy?'

'Yeah, we will,' said Jimmy. 'And a big crucifix on top with angels and stuff...'

'Alright, alright,' interrupted Susan, who didn't want her brother making promises they couldn't keep. 'Anyway, Mam and Dad, we'll have to go because it's late. So, sorry again and see you later.'

The two of them walked contritely away from the grave, Susan a pace in front. After a while she stopped and held her hand up, silently signalling Jimmy to do the same. Ahead of them was a marble tombstone, watched over by a weeping angel who had much to weep about insofar as both her arms were missing. One amputation obviously had occurred quite recently, as the broken limb lay on the ground beside her. Below the angel were a pair of shadowy figures locked in a feverish embrace. Susan pulled Jimmy behind a tree from where they both had a concealed view of the proceedings.

'What's happening?' whispered Jimmy, who wasn't nearly as naïve as he pretended.

'I think they're, you know, having it off.'

'Having what off?' whispered Jimmy, enjoying this.

'They're having...' she hesitated, stuck for a genteel word.

'Having a shag?' suggested Jimmy, who didn't know any genteel words. 'I've never seen anyone having a shag before.'

Susan blushed in the moonlight at having to witness such things in the company of her younger brother. The woman was writhing about in a most unladylike manner and pulling the man's trousers down with unbecoming urgency; her own underwear was already around her ankles in preparation for the big moment. It became apparent that the man was having difficulties, due mainly to drink. Words of passion from the woman turned from words of encouragement, to words of exasperation and then to coarse criticism, which Susan and Jimmy couldn't quite understand.

'I've heard o' Brewer's Droop,' grumbled the woman, 'but this is ridiculous. Bloody hell! It's like trying to push a marshmallow into a money box.'

She giggled at her own coarse wit. Jimmy made a mental note to use it himself once he found out what it meant. The woman's cackling grew louder and coarser and her criticism of his manhood, harsher. The man lost his temper, drunkenly slurring his speech. The woman stepped back, still laughing at him. He just stood there swaying uncertainly. A ridiculous figure, trousers round his ankles, thin white legs shining in the moonlight, recklessly exposed to the bitter elements and cursing intemperately at this cackling woman who was now bent over, pulling her knickers up. Suddenly the man bent down as if to pull up his trousers. As he straightened up, he had the weeping angel's broken arm in his hand. Time and time again he brought it crashing down on the woman's head, weeping with anger and frustration and battering her at last into a bloody and deathly silence.

He stood over her for what seemed like an age. The angel's arm dropping from his nerveless fingers. Jimmy and Susan were frozen with shock, scarcely daring to breathe. A twig broke beneath Jimmy's foot causing the man to look up. They both dodged back behind the broad trunk of the tree. Surely he'd be able to hear their hearts pounding with terror. The man started weeping and moaning to himself.

'What have I done? What have I done? Oh, my God, I didn't mean ter kill yer. Yer shouldn't have laughed at me, yer silly bitch. Oh, may God for- give me.'

He was still pulling up his trousers and moaning to himself when he ran past them, stumbling through the darkness, tripping up and crying with pain as he fell on something hard, then picking himself up and hurrying on. They waited until he was long gone, then set off running in the opposite direction. Not stopping to look at the woman he'd just battered to death. They didn't stop or speak to each other until they were back in the house and breathlessly huddled together in Jimmy's bedroom.

Susan was finding it very hard to take in. First Auntie Dorothy hitting Mr Simpson and then this, and both to do with the same thing – sex. She secretly renewed her vow of celibacy, until such time as her marriage to Freddie was consummated.

'Jimmy,' she said eventually. 'Did you recognise that man's voice?'

Jimmy thought for a moment. 'It sounded like Mr Bateson.'

'That's what I thought.'

There a long silence, broken by Jimmy.

'We ought ter tell the police.'

'I know,' agreed Susan reluctantly. 'But if we do, they'll ask us what we were doing in the cemetery at that time of night. We'll get put in a home for sure.'

'We'll most likely get put into a home, any road. Most likely an orphanage or summat,' grumbled Jimmy.

'Not if I can help it!' declared Susan with some determination. 'Tell you what, let's ring them up – *anonymously.*'

Jimmy very much liked the sound of this.

St Stephen's clock was just striking midnight as

they ventured out once again to the telephone box on Glossop Street. The one on Paradine Hill being too close to the Police Station.

Susan nervously dialled 999.

'Emergency, which service please?'

'There's been a murder in Bramham Cemetery,' she announced, with surprising calmness, holding a handkerchief over the receiver to disguise her voice. A ruse she'd seen so many times on the pictures.

'That'll be the police, I'm putting you through now.'

But Susan had already put the phone down. It was enough. As they turned into the top of Paradine Hill they saw policemen dashing out of the Police Station at the bottom, heading with some urgency towards the cemetery.

'Blast,' cursed Susan, as they got back in the house.

'What's up?'

'I forgot to tell the police it was Mr Bateson that did it.'

'Mebbe it wasn't him. Mebbe it was just somebody what sounded like him.'

'Maybe,' acknowledged Susan. But she wasn't convinced.

Jimmy woke to a loud hammering on the back door. He cautiously peeped through the bedroom curtains and looked down into the back yard at Jackie Crombie, jumping up and down in excitement and looking up at Jimmy's window.

'There's been a murder!' shouted Jackie. 'Come on or we'll miss it!'

Jimmy couldn't work out what there was to miss, but he dressed hurriedly and shouted up to the attic to Susan who was already moving around.

'Jackie's at the door, he knows about the murder.'

'I know, I heard him.' Susan appeared at the top of the stairs already fully dressed. 'Pretend we don't know anything,' she said with a note of caution. 'I don't think we can afford to get involved in this.'

'Okay,' agreed Jimmy, with a certain reluctance. He would have loved to have gloated over Jackie Crombie just once, but he knew she was talking sense. He opened the door, and Jackie burst in like a tornado.

'This woman's been murdered in t'cemetery. I think she were a prossie. She had her throat cut from here to here!' He dramatically demonstrated the length of the cut with a sweeping finger. 'Oh! Me mam said I've to ask yer if yer want any breakfast at our house, but yer won't, will yer? 'Cos yer'll miss it if yer do!'

'We'd love some breakfast,' said Susan, stepping into the back room. 'Wouldn't we, Jimmy?'

Jackie's face dropped as Jimmy nodded. Then he turned and shot out of the house as fast as he'd come in.

There was not much to see when Jimmy and Susan walked tentatively past the cemetery an hour or so later. In the distance, at the scene of the murder, they could just make out uniformed figures moving around. At the gate an irritated-looking policeman was fending off Jackie's persistent questions.

'Look! Clear off, you flaming nuisance, before I tan yer little arse for yer!'

Jackie looked away hurt but his face brightened when he saw his friends.

'We're not allowed in,' he explained. 'I told him I only wanted to visit me dear old mother's grave.' He turned his back to the policeman and gave them a huge conspiratorial wink.

Susan was mildly shocked at such tempting of providence, but Jimmy couldn't help but admire such an enterprising lie.

'If he carries on telling stories like that, his mam'll be coming to visit *his* grave,' grumbled the policeman.

'I think he knows who you are,' said Jimmy.

'Just take him away,' beseeched the policeman, 'before we have a double murder on our hands!'

The three of them trudged back up Paradine Hill, leaving a relieved constable guarding the gate.

'Are you off to t'Bughutch this afternoon?' inquired Jackie. 'There's Hopalong Cassidy on.'

'No, we, er...' started Jimmy.

'We've got something else to do,' cut in Susan.

'Yer mean yer've got no money,' commiserated Jackie genuinely. 'Me mam said you wouldn't have no money. She says yer'll most likely get kicked out of yer house. Specially with yer auntie braying Simmo like that.' He stopped and kicked a stone across the road. 'I wish I had an auntie like that,' he added admiringly.

This stark assessment of the situation, albeit from Jackie Crombie, gave Susan an added determination to go through with the selling of the ring that day. Leaving Jimmy and Jackie at the end of the street, she returned to the house, making Jimmy promise faithfully to meet her back there in an hour.

Rita swung down from her bunk as the wake-up buzzer sounded. There was no slopping out in this wing of the prison, thank God. She looked down at Dorothy.

'Just wait till yer doin' proper time, madam. Yer'll know what it's all about then.'

Hard as she'd become over this past couple of years, she still felt a pang of sympathy for Dorothy, but dismissed it from her mind as a weakness she couldn't afford in this place. It was Rita's third stay courtesy of His Majesty, and prison held few fears for her. A warder appeared at the door and looked down at her sleeping cell-mate.

'Leave her,' she decided. 'She was still blubbering at two o'clock this morning. Been at it all night by all accounts. She'll not mind missing breakfast.'

'You're all heart, Miss Netherton,' said Rita, who'd met this warder before.

'It's her first day. We'll not make such a fuss of her again.'

'I'll tell her what you said, she'll really appreciate it.'

'You do that.'

Dorothy woke to the clamour of the wing. It took her a few seconds to come round. The little sleep she'd had in the last two nights wasn't nearly enough. Rita walked in with a tin mug full

168

of lukewarm tea which she handed to Dorothy.

'You looked so peaceful lying there that me an' Miss Netherton decided ter let yer have a lie in.'

'Who's Miss Netherton?' asked Dorothy dully, taking the tea without a word of thanks.

'She's our hostess. Caters to our every whim does Miss Netherton. I thought we'd have a game of tennis before elevenses, would you like to make up a foursome? I know a delightful couple on the bottom landing.'

'Piss off!'

'Aha! You've been swotting up on prison lingo, good for you,' exclaimed Rita cheerfully.

As both she and Rita were remand prisoners they weren't required to do any work. Unfortunately the same applied to Delma Albright who appeared at their cell door accompanied by a marginally smaller woman who, as it turned out, had similar sexual proclivities to Delma. She leered at Dorothy.

'I'll have you fer Christmas, Dolly darlin' – that's a promise.'

Dorothy felt a shiver of revulsion as she looked up at the fat slavering face ogling at her. She opened her mouth to speak but the words wouldn't come. Rita spoke on her behalf.

'She'd like yer to bugger off, yer big ugly mess, but she's too polite ter say it, aren't yer, Dolly?'

Delma took a menacing step towards Rita but stopped in her tracks when Miss Netherton appeared behind her.

'Back in your own cell, Albright,' commanded the stern-faced warder, 'NOW!'

Delma was the only who didn't jump at the last

shouted word. She merely turned and gave the warder a smile that displayed every one of her stolen teeth.

'Just bein' friendly, Miss. There's no law against bein' friendly.'

'There is if you try and get too friendly.'

'No such thing as too friendly where I come from.'

The warder regarded Delma coolly. 'You're confined to your cell for twenty-four hours, Albright.' She looked at her watch, 'Starting in thirty seconds. If you're not back by then it's forty-eight hours and so on until I'm spared your obnoxious company altogether!'

Delma opened and shut her mouth, then spun round and hurried back to her cell with the warder close on her heels.

'I don't wish to appear naïve but what did she mean when she said, *I'll have you for Christmas?*' asked Dorothy, still trembling.

'Not quite sure, Dolly love, but she's a mean bastard is Delma. Best keep out of her road.'

'I mean, how can one woman have another? I mean, it's not as if they've got anything to – you know – stick in you or anything. She can't do anything to me – can she?' Dorothy was rambling, seeking some sort of reassurance from Rita.

'Look, Dolly love, Delma's a bleedin' headcase. The way she upsets the screws she'll spend most of her time banged up. The rest of the time, just don't go near her.'

When Jimmy returned at the appointed time, there was a young woman in the front room,

170

standing with her back to him. When she turned round, he gasped in amazement.

'Flippin' heck, our Susan! What have yer done to yerself?'

She was wearing Auntie Dorothy's best frock, suspiciously full at the bustline, a pair of high heels, nylon stockings, and long black gloves, all from the best end of Auntie's sparse wardrobe. Her long blonde hair was topped with a neat little pill box hat and around her neck was a delicate gold necklace, a birthday present from Uncle Tommy to Auntie Dorothy. She'd copied her auntie's stylish make-up right down to the slash of crimson lipstick showing off her dazzling white teeth. Jimmy was more than impressed.

'Yer look brilliant, our lass.' This was probably the first compliment he'd ever paid his sister.

'Thanks,' she said graciously, adopting the aloof air she hoped would see her through the job in hand. Her auntie had been an unwitting tutor. Dorothy's pseudo-middle-class upbringing had imprinted a certain style upon her that life in Broughton Terrace hadn't quite rubbed out. Susan had watched with occasional admiration, the way she dressed, the way she spoke and the assured way she dealt with people. There were exceptions to this of course, or she wouldn't be locked up in Ashinghurst Prison, but in general there was a lot to be admired about Auntie Dorothy.

Jimmy pointed curiously to the new, curvacious bustline. 'That's not all you, is it?'

Susan grinned and reached inside. She pulled out two pairs of knickers, one from each side,

171

leaving the bustline empty and sagging.

'I needed a bit of padding,' she admitted rue-fully.

Jimmy laughed out loud. 'Blimey,' he chortled. 'They were barrage balloons!'

'Do you think they're too much?' she asked worriedly, turning to the mirror to look at herself after she completed the re-padding.

Jimmy cast a critical eye over her. 'No,' he said reassuringly. 'They're not as big as Jane Russell's.'

Susan picked up her auntie's best dark blue coat and slipped it on, then looked loftily down at her brother.

'Come along, young man,' she said elegantly. 'You and I have business to attend to.'

There were three jewellers on Briggate. The smallest, but most exclusive and respectable being Blackstone's (of London and Leeds).

Leaving Jimmy looking through the window, Susan swept through the door as she imagined Auntie Dorothy would, and with her heart in her mouth, walked up to the oldest of the three assistants, a middle-aged man with odd strands of hair carefully arranged across his marble-white bald head. His eyes lit up at the sight of this beautiful, elegant young lady.

Susan stood there, soulfully. She'd rehearsed this moment time and time again. Freddie's words still fresh in her mind. 'Dress the part and talk the part.' How much more confident she'd have felt with Freddie beside her.

'Can I help you, madam?' asked the man, expansively. Displaying an array of dazzling white tombstone teeth that looked to have been made for a mouth much bigger than his.

'I, I don't know,' replied Susan, hesitantly. 'I have a ring I wish to sell ... I don't know whether I've come to the right place.'

'You most certainly have, madam. Providing the ring is of a certain, shall we say, quality.'

Susan took the ring out of her auntie's purse and placed it lovingly on the glass counter. The man screwed a glass into his eye and picked it up. His examination took longer than he expected. He put it back on the counter and looked at Susan with added respect.

'My word, a blue diamond,' he said. 'I don't think I'm personally qualified to assess its value. However, our managing director, Mr Blackstone, who is an expert in such things, is in this morning so if you'd allow me to take it to him?'

'I'd rather it didn't go out of my sight,' said Susan, not quite knowing why. 'I mean no offence, but I am aware of its value.'

'Quite,' said the man, somewhat unctuously. 'Perhaps if madam would like to follow me?'

He led her down a flight of stairs to a dingy basement, completely at odds with the elegant shop they'd just left. On either side were two long benches littered with parts of watches and clocks and various items of jewellery. An old man sat on a stool at the far end, hunched over an expensive-looking antique clock, whistling to himself as he worked. He had a skeletal face, a shock of the purest white hair and a magnifying glass screwed into his eye as though it belonged there. He was the oldest-looking man she'd ever seen.

'This is Mr Blackstone,' said the assistant awkwardly. 'Our, er, our managing director.' The old man removed the glass from a luminescent blue eye and held out a long bony hand.

'Delighted to meet you Miss er...?'

'Bairstow, Susan Bairstow,' said Susan, lightly holding the ends of his fingers, perhaps afraid she might snap something off.

'Delighted to meet you, Miss Bairstow. I must say you're the most decorative thing we've had down here in a long time.'

Susan smiled at the old man's charm.

'And how can I help?' he asked.

The assistant handed him the ring. 'Miss Bairstow has brought this ring in to sell and I explained that you'd be better qualified than me to assess its value.'

Mr Blackstone re-positioned his eye glass and held the ring in the light of a bright lamp. He whistled once again, this time tunelessly, more an expression of admiration. He looked up at Susan, his eyes twinkling.

'Would I be right in thinking that this is an engagement ring?'

Susan summoned up the tear which gave the old man his answer.

'He must have loved you very much.'

'He was killed in the war. He was a pilot.'

Up to now she hadn't told a lie. It helped her act along, but she was prepared for anything.

There was genuine sympathy on the old man's face. 'My grandson died too,' he said. 'It's hard to bear.'

Susan nodded. She knew as much as anyone about family grief.

'And now you wish to sell the ring?' Was he admonishing her? She looked at him searchingly.

'I need to get on with my life,' she said firmly. 'And I need the money.' Her heart was pounding all the time, but the two men interpreted her nervousness as sorrow at what she was having to do.

'Of course, please don't think I'm criticising. It's just that we both know what you have here. It's a very old, very rare jewel. I've never seen a blue diamond of such quality.'

'I am aware of its value.'

'I'm sure you are,' smiled Mr Blackstone. 'But we can't give you its full retail value. We're in business to make money ourselves.'

'I'm aware of that too – and I'm also aware that there are other jewellers in this town to whom I can take it.' It could have been Auntie Dorothy talking. Susan was beginning to enjoy herself.

The old man picked up the ring once again. 'Would you mind if I removed the stone?' he asked.

'Please do.' She'd no idea why he needed to do this.

He deftly removed the diamond and placed it on a small pair of scales.

'Point eight of a carat,' he announced. 'But as we both know the real value is in its colour and quality. Were it an ordinary diamond I'd value it at maybe a hundred. But if we were to sell this ring we'd be asking, oh – a thousand pounds for it.'

Susan suppressed a gasp. She was hoping for fifty quid at the most.

'But of course I can't offer you that,' he looked at her and rubbed his chin speculatively. 'Seven hundred,' he said suddenly.

'I was hoping for a little more than that,' responded Susan, mainly to disguise her elation at such an offer. 'Would you go up to eight hundred?'

'Seven-fifty.'

Susan smiled and shook his hand. 'I would like it in cash please.'

'What else?' said Mr Blackstone, who'd really taken to this young lady and he wished he was sixty years younger. 'However, we'll have to send out to the bank for such a sum. Perhaps you'll have a cup of tea or coffee whilst you wait?'

'Coffee would be lovely, thank you,' said Susan, who thought a young lady of her standing wouldn't be caught dead drinking anything as common as tea.

Susan was in something of a daze as she walked out of the shop, nervously clutching the seven-hundred-and-fifty five-pound notes in her auntie's deep coat pocket. Jimmy was waiting outside expectantly.

'Did yer sell it?'

'Yes, I sold it.'

'Great. Did yer get enough ter pay the rent for a bit?'

Susan looked around at the bustling street to check that no one was paying any attention to this odd pair. An unmanned tram was waiting beside the underground toilet in the middle of the road, the exit of which was the focus of all the passenger's eyes, some of whom cheered sarcastically when the unconcerned driver emerged, looking at his pocket watch as if to say it was just about time he was setting off.

'Just put your hand in my pocket,' she said surreptitiously. 'Don't take anything out, I don't want everybody knowing.' Jimmy did as she asked.

'Blimey!' he exclaimed. 'Are these all pound notes?'

'No, they're all fivers. I got seven-hundred-and-fifty quid!'

'SEVEN HUNDRED AND FIF...!'

'Quiet!' Susan scolded. 'We don't want everybody knowing I'm walking round with a fortune in my pocket.'

'We're rich, aren't we?'

'I think so, and we've still got your ring to sell.'

They walked along in excited silence towards the tram stop. Then Jimmy said.

'Does this mean we can stop nicking jam jars?'

Susan pondered the question for awhile. 'Why should we? It was good fun nicking jam jars. Tell you what thought, I've got no change for the tram and I daren't give him a fiver. Let's go get you a new blazer, you scruffy little arab.'

'Well, it's one way of getting change,' grinned a happy Jimmy.

Susan considered buying a new blazer for herself, but decided that such ostentation would draw unwanted attention and settled for new shoes and a new school shirt each. They arrived home as they'd left, through the rarely used front door. It was Saturday afternoon and the streets were empty apart from Mrs Harrison scouring her front step, obviously expecting company. Everyone who was anyone would be safely ensconced in the Bughutch, cheering on Hopalong Cassidy.

They sat in the front room and opened a celebratory bottle of dandelion and burdock. Inside them that distinct glow of confidence which comes from knowing you're the richest people on the street.

Delma's friend appeared at Dorothy's cell door after first ensuring she was alone. Rita was down below playing table tennis, a game she'd grown quite expert at during her time in prison.

'Message from Delma,' she sneered, approaching Dorothy with beads of sweat glistening on her smirking face.

Dorothy backed away until the woman had her cornered. She made a grab for her and Dorothy froze with fear, just like she had when Simpson had attacked her less than forty-eight hours ago.

'Please leave me alone,' she pleaded fearfully.

'Them weren't my instructions. Delma wants to know what yer taste like!'

She felt the woman's tongue licking the side of her face, then her slobbering lips pressing hard against hers.

'Very nice, darling' – but Delma wants ter know what yer feel like as well!'

She forced her hands up Dorothy's skirt and inside her pants causing her to weep with fear and disgust as the woman ran her lips and tongue all over Dorothy's tearful face. Instinctively she pulled her head away from her vile attacker, then with all her strength she smashed her forehead into the woman's face, again and again until she felt the hands drop away from her and saw the woman staggering backwards with blood pouring from her nose and yelping with pain. Dorothy couldn't speak, her heart was thumping, her breath was coming in short bursts. Rita rushed in, alerted by another inmate, and stepped to one side in amazement as the fat woman staggered out, weeping in pain with blood all down the front of her shirt. A crowd had gathered at the door.

'Bloody hell, Dolly,' gasped Rita. 'Yer don't like people messin' wiv yer, do yer?'

Seeing the distress Dorothy was in, Rita turned and shielded her from the women at the door.

'Show's over, folks. Lesson number one – don't mess around wiv my mate Dolly, she gets ever so bleedin' cross if yer do.'

Rita sat for a long time with her arm around Dorothy, not speaking, just waiting for the sobbing to subside. Eventually Dorothy braced herself and sat up straight, then turned to Rita.

'I don't know, Rita,' she sighed.' Sex isn't what it used to be.'

Rita began to laugh and banged her new friend on the back. 'Good girl, Dolly, you'll survive this shithole yet!'

Chapter Thirteen

Almost a week had gone by and no one had been to take them away. No one at their respective schools had asked any questions. Everyone, it seemed, thought that someone else must be looking after their welfare. The police had Dorothy listed as having no children and up to now, Dorothy had made them no wiser. As far as she was concerned, the longer the children could be kept out of the clutches of authority the better. She'd already consigned one child to a home, she couldn't be a willing party to sending the other two.

Inevitable though it might be.

Susan, with the great optimism of youth, wrote regular letters to Freddie, keeping him informed of events, so that when his memory returned he'd be fully up to date. There was no doubt in her mind that Freddie's memory loss was anything more than a temporary state of affairs.

Mrs Crombie had made it her business to check on the welfare of Neville Simpson who had regained consciousness and would make a full recovery. 'So, at least they won't be hanging your auntie,' she said comfortingly.

An official knock at the door startled Jimmy and Susan, who looked at each other with some concern. Susan looked through the window into the yard where two large men stood beside a stern-faced woman. It was raining heavily, bouncing noisily off the dustbin and causing obvious discomfort to the visitors. Jimmy and Susan went to the door together, standing side by side to face the intruders.

The two large men wore matching black overcoats, trilby hats and gloves, dwarfing the woman standing between them, who wore a belted raincoat and a strange brown hat. Her nose was long and narrow and her little mean eyes very close together, topped by just the one long, bushy, caterpillar eyebrow. The rain had collected in the brims of all three hats and was overflowing steadily.

'Good evening,' said the woman, patronisingly, 'and you are?'

'Never mind who we are, who are you?' retorted Susan. Her experience at the jewellers had given her a depth of self-confidence she didn't know she had. That and the money hidden away upstairs. The woman made to come in out of the rain but Susan barred her way.

'May we come in?' asked the woman sharply.

'No,' said Susan with matching sharpness.

'Oh, my name is Miss Newton. I'm here to represent Mr Neville Simpson, who as you probably know is in hospital,' snapped the woman, unhappy at being kept out in the rain by this cocky schoolgirl.

Susan looked at the two men. 'And who are these gentlemen?'

Miss Newton was clearly annoyed. 'These are court bailiffs, here to enforce a notice to quit given to Mrs Bairstow a week ago for non-

181

payment of rent.'

'My auntie Dorothy tried to pay the rent last week, but she was put off a bit when Mr Simpson tried to rape her.' Susan held the woman in a cold gaze and continued, 'Then he tried to rape me so Auntie Dorothy hit him with a stool.'

Miss Newton was flustered at Susan's icy calmness and Susan knew it. Jimmy was highly impressed with his sister. The rainwater gutter above Miss Newton was blocked and over-flowing, causing the uncomfortable trio to take evasive action every time a gust of wind blew the dripping water towards them.

'Don't talk ridiculous, child. Mr Simpson's not only a respectable businessman but he's also my fiancé. He and your aunt had an argument about rent which got totally out of control.'

'I was there, Miss Newton. You weren't,' said Susan. 'Besides, why should my aunt need to argue about rent? She has lots of money.'

'Now *that* I find very hard to believe, you and I know that aunt was flat broke,' snapped Miss Newton, regaining some of her composure then losing it as a sudden squall left the three of them soaked. Jimmy stepped out of sight so they wouldn't see him laughing.

'Really?' countered Susan. 'She was so flat broke she left us well provided for until she sorts out this nonsense with our rapist landlord. Just how much was she supposed to owe?'

Miss Newton shook the water from her hat and squinted through the rain at the two bailiffs. One of them shrugged and said, 'By law you must give the debtor an opportunity to pay.'

Taking a book out of her raincoat pocket, Miss Newton examined a set of figures with a sigh of exasperation as the rain immediately obliterated the ink.

'Three pounds fifteen shillings, including this week's rent,' she smiled damply, 'payable *now!*'

'And if we pay this money, do you promise these men won't try to rape me, like your nice fiancé tried to do last week?' asked Susan sweetly.

The two bailiffs shuffled uncomfortably. They didn't like being in this situation one bit. It certainly wasn't what they'd been told to expect. Susan took a five-pound note from her pocket and handed it to one of the men.

'Here, take for next week as well. I believe it comes to four pounds ten shillings.'

Miss Newton was completely taken aback by this unexpected turn of events. She snatched the money from the bailiff and fumbled in her bag for the ten shillings change.

'Keep the change, dear,' gloated Susan, loftily. 'Buy yourself a decent hat.'

Susan allowed the bailiffs inside to make out a receipt. As they left they politely tipped their hats to her; and Susan detected a smile of admiration on the face of at least one of them as they escorted the damp and defeated Miss Newton away.

For the first time in his life Jimmy gave his sister a kiss. Not much of a kiss, but coming from him it meant a lot.

'Susan Bairstow, you were bloody brilliant!'

'Jimmy Bairstow, watch your language. I was though, wasn't I?'

'Did you see her face when you told her to buy a decent hat?'

'Did you see her face when I said her fiancé was a rapist?'

'What about when they all got soaked?'

The two of them were still laughing when Mrs Crombie knocked and dashed in out of the rain.

'Are you two okay?' She looked puzzled. 'I know a bailiff when I see one. Who were that woman?'

'That was Simmo's lady friend,' explained Jimmy. 'Our Susan put her straight on a few things, didn't you, Susan?'

'I just told her the truth that's all,' said Susan. 'She's entitled to know the truth about the man she's marrying, isn't she, Mrs Crombie?'

'So, they didn't kick you out then? What about the rent?' asked Mrs Crombie.

'We paid it.' Susan gave her a challenging look that told her not to question how.

'Oh, I see,' said Mrs Crombie, who didn't see at all.

Chapter Fourteen

A flurry of snow sent most of the inmates scurrying back inside, but Dorothy merely turned up the collar of her coat and wrapped it around her neck. This daily freedom was far too precious to lose because of a few harmless snowflakes. Rita was sitting beside her on the wooden seat behind the canteen block, donated, according to the carved inscription, by the Friends of Ashinghurst Prison 1936.

'Soft sods,' commented Rita, Dorothy nodded her agreement. Most of the inmates were nowhere near as hard as she'd imagined they'd be. Many were sad recidivists, locked up by frustrated judges who'd been left with no option. There were cheats, liars, thieves, habitual prostitutes, but very few violent criminals. Dorothy was very much on her own in that respect – she and Delma Albright.

Delma was psychopathic thug who should have been locked up somewhere a lot more secure than Ashinghurst. Accused of beating up a young prostitute who didn't want Delma as a client. Delma's fat friend was just an incompetent thief who looked upon Delma as some sort of soulmate. In truth they had much in common, unpleasant, revolting to behold, and not a bit jolly as most fat people are supposed to be. Delma glowered at the pair of them as she trudged past.

'Soon be Christmas, Dolly lass!' she sniggered, sending a shiver of revulsion through Dorothy.

It was two weeks before Christmas and Dorothy's fourth week inside. She'd viewed Simpson's recovery with mixed feelings. She would have felt no remorse at his death, although she was relieved to be spared the threat of the hangman's noose. The memories of his attack on her were still fresh in her mind, although confused somewhat by the subsequent attack by Delma's fat friend. The fact that she'd given as good as she got on both occasions somehow diluted the aftershock of the attacks. The damage she'd inflicted on Delma's friend kept away many an unwanted advance by sexually frustrated inmates who would otherwise have looked upon the demure Dorothy as an easy victim.

Delma Albright excepted.

Rita was in for theft and fraud. As a part-time prostitute she'd stolen a client's chequebook and written herself a cheque for fifty pounds. It had worked as well, but she didn't leave it there. With incredible stupidity, which she still couldn't believe herself, she walked back into the same branch a week later and tried to draw out another fifty. The client, who was married and prepared to accept his initial loss in order to keep his marriage intact, had stopped all the cheques, and the bank security man had stopped the empty-handed Rita on her way out.

'Rita – what made you become a prostitute?' Dorothy blurted out the question she'd been dying to ask Rita since they'd first met. 'Sorry,' she added immediately. 'Stupid question, tell me to mind my own business.'

Rita huddled herself up against the cold and brushed a few snowflakes out of her hair. It was a while before she decided to answer.

'Me old man left me,' she said. 'High an' bloody dry, went off ter war an' never came back.'

Dorothy nodded, ready to accept this as the full and final answer to what probably was an impertinent question.

'He ended up in Malaya,' Rita went on. 'Three bleedin' years I'd been on me own. We never had no kids, thank God. Do yer know, he never sent

186

me a soddin' penny. He used ter write ter me and tell me he were savin' it all up so we could buy an 'ouse of us own when he got back. The lyin' bastard!' She spat out the last remark malevolently.

'I wouldn't care, but I'd been faithful to him. I'd gone three bleedin' years without. Not that I couldn't have – there were plenty what fancied me.'

She brushed more snow from her hair, it was coming down harder now and Dorothy wondered at the wisdom of staying out in it. But Rita was oblivious to any discomfort and continued with her story.

'Anyway, just after V.E. day I got this letter saying he met this slant-eyed bint – only he didn't put it that way – an' he were setting up home with her an' he weren't comin' back. He sent me a five-pound note an' d'yer know what I did? I burnt the bastard. I could have done with it an' all.'

Rita went quiet then, it seemed to Dorothy that she was fighting back the tears so she put her arm round her.

'Did you love him?' she asked gently.

'Aye,' admitted Rita. 'I bleedin' well did!'

She laid her head on Dorothy's shoulder as the snow came down ever faster. Neither bothered to brush it away, it had a purity alien to the world in which they found themselves. Rita sat up after a while and continued.

'So that were it, really. I had no money – an' I'd been buying stuff on tally, thinking my Tony'd settle up when he got back. It were t' tally man what started me off. I let him shag me a few times an' finished up wi' a clean slate.' Dorothy felt herself shudder at this, and not because of the cold. 'Seemed easy,' continued Rita, 'he weren't a bad lookin' bloke neither. Anyway, word seemed ter get round and I were at it every week. Not anybody mind. I were a bit picky an' I worked from home.'

'There, but for the Grace of God go many of us,' remarked Dorothy with feeling.

Rita didn't understand what her friend was talking about, and went on. 'Got done a few times for keeping a brothel, couple o' stretches, four weeks and six weeks. This is different though, could get two years for this when they take me previous into account.' She stopped and looked round at Dorothy. 'Bet yer think I'm a bad bastard, don't yer?'

'I think your language leaves a lot to be desired but on the whole you're okay.'

'Language? Oh aye, that's prison for yer. If yer can't beat 'em join 'em. I'm not as bad when I'm on the outside.' She grinned at Dorothy who was sitting there like a snowman, then shook some of the snow off herself. 'We're a couple o' barmy buggers when yer come to think of it.'

Dorothy blew a snowflake off her nose and grinned back. 'This is the best time I've had since I came in here. I think we should stay here until they come and dig us out.'

There was another long period of snowy silence, broken by Rita. 'Yer'd never guess,' she challenged.

'Never guess what?'

'I'm in t' Sally Army!'

Dorothy turned to her snow-covered cellmate. 'You're right – I'd never have guessed.'

'They taught me to play t' cornet – I'm pretty good an' all. They know all about me, but they reckon I can be saved.'

'You mean you're in the band?'

'Yeah – we play every Sunday morning – one of 'em came ter see me last week. She told me there'd be a place waiting for me when I get out. She brought me cornet thinking I might want to keep it up while I'm inside.'

'I think you should,' encouraged Dorothy.

'What? Yer mean you wouldn't mind?'

'Why should I? Maybe you could teach me.'

Rita smiled, then said suddenly, 'I bet you've never done nowt really bad, have yer? I'm not talking about braying that pillock wiv a pianna stool, sounds ter me like he got what he deserved.'

Dorothy went quiet for a long time. A silence undisturbed by Rita, who sensed Dorothy had something to get off her mind. The snow fell gently and silently, the flakes had increased in size now and had completely covered the prison garden. A robin hopped around by the bins, burying its head in the snow and pulling out a crust of bread much too big for it to fly off with. Rita pursed her lips and attempted a bird whistle which only succeeded in scaring the bird onto the top of a hut from where it looked longingly down at the crust.

'I told my step-children their baby brother was dead!'

It sounded awful the way she said it, but she

wanted it to sound awful, so she left it at that until Rita made a comment.

'I didn't know you had any step-children,' was all Rita could offer by way of reply. She didn't feel qualified to condemn something she didn't understand.

'I've got two,' said Dorothy, 'Jimmy and Susan. I sent their brother to a home because I was too useless to look after him.'

Such self-flagellation was not uncommon inside jails and Rita just shrugged. 'I think yer a bleedin' saint takin' two of 'em on. Why did yer tell 'em he'd snuffed it?'

'They were forever nagging me to bring him home. I just cracked in the end.'

'What're they like – the two yer've got?' asked Rita, who figured this would have some bearing on the matter, especially if the two she'd got were a couple of toerags.

'They're great. I wouldn't want them any different – I love them!' Dorothy added the last bit in a tiny voice, spitting away a snowflake that had landed on her lower lip. 'I suppose I'd love William as well – if I had him.'

There was a long silence as Rita considered her advice. She hadn't been asked for advice but felt it incumbent upon her to at least make an effort.

'I reckon yer should tell 'em as soon as yer can. At least that bit'll be off yer mind. Tell 'em their kid's still alive – make up some excuse if yer want – but yer've got ter tell 'em.'

Dorothy could see the truth in this, she'd always known she'd have to tell them, but to-morrow always seemed to be the best time.

190

'I'll tell them when they come to visit me,' she determined. 'And when I get out of here, which I will, I won't rest until I've got him back.'

Officer Netherton watched them from the warmth of the canteen window and shook her head at the two animated snow-covered lumps sitting on the bench. From the window above, Delma Albright looked down on them with an ugly sneer on her face; she turned to her fat friend. 'You can have Randy Rita fer Christmas – I'm gonna give her stuck-up pal a Christmas she'll never bleedin' forget!'

Dorothy scarcely recognised the two young people, sitting apprehensively at the table, awaiting her arrival. Betty Crombie and Valerie Veitch had already been, and to be honest they'd been little comfort. But the sight of Jimmy and Susan, looking so well-dressed, lifted her spirits no end. She'd half-expected they'd be taken into care and was more than curious to know how they'd managed to avoid this. No doubt the neighbours had been rallying round, they did at times like this. Up to now she'd refused all visits from them, feeling they'd have enough to put up with without worrying about her. But now she had something to tell them.

They looked so out of place in this room. Two innocents sitting uncomfortably at a table surrounded by thieves, prostitutes, women of violence – *and these are just the visitors,* she joked to herself. It was this grim humour that had enabled her to survive this place.

'Hello, you two,' she smiled and held both their

hands. Of all the people in the world, these were the two she was closest to. 'I've been terribly worried about you. How have you been managing?' She scarcely dare ask them about the unpaid rent.

Susan gave her a comforting smile. The prison seemed to have robbed Auntie Dorothy of all her glow.

'Actually we're managing very well indeed, aren't we, Jimmy?'

'We're brilliant,' agreed Jimmy.

'You've not ter worry about us,' reassured Susan. 'We've got everything organised. We're paying the rent and we've got enough money to live on till you get out. We've bought some new clothes as well.'

Dorothy looked at them in amazement. 'I daren't ask,' she said.

'Best not,' grinned Susan. 'But we're not doing anything illegal.' They'd agreed not to mention anything about the money for the ring, as they didn't know how she'd react.

'Is it anything to do with milk bottles?' Dorothy knew it couldn't be, but it was all she could think of.

Jimmy and Susan laughed heartily at this and for the first time in weeks, Dorothy laughed as well. Jimmy looked around, surveying the roomful of chattering felons, then leaned over to his aunt. 'Are there any murderers in here?'

Dorothy laughed at his natural curiosity. 'I've no idea, Jimmy. Anyway, this is the Remand Wing. Everyone here is technically innocent, like me.'

'We're going ter get you off when you go ter court. Our Susan's got this plan,' confided her nephew.

'Oh, right,' whispered Dorothy. 'I hope it's a good one,' Dorothy was only half-humouring Jimmy as she wouldn't put anything past these two.

'It is a good one, isn't it, Susan?'

Susan nodded. 'We don't want to get your hopes up too high, Auntie, but I think it might work.'

Dorothy couldn't imagine what the plan was, any more than she could figure out where they were getting their money from. All she knew was there were two special young people waiting for her as and when she did get out. Or would they be? She held them both in her gaze, knowing she couldn't keep her dreadful secret from them any longer.

'Look, kids,' she said almost hoarsely. 'There's something I've got to tell you – and you may not like me after I've told you, and to be honest I wouldn't blame you.'

Jimmy and Susan sat there quietly, not knowing what to expect. Dorothy took several deep breaths.

'William's not dead!' she said in little more than a whisper, averting her gaze, not knowing how they'd react.

It took a while for what she'd said to sink in. Susan spoke first.

'But – of course he is! He died two years ago – didn't he?'

Dorothy shook her head, guiltily.

Jimmy's face broke into a slow smile. 'Yer mean our brother's still alive? Honest?'

'Honest.'

Jimmy and Susan looked at each other then back at Dorothy.

'When did you find out?' asked Susan.

Dorothy examined her hands nervously. 'I've always known,' she admitted.

Susan was incredulous. '*Always* known, how do you mean? always known, I don't understand. You told us he was dead! You must have lied to us, Auntie. Why did you do that?'

'Why *did* you do that?' echoed Jimmy, who was confused now, not knowing whether to be happy or sad.

Dorothy sank her head between her hands, as they'd seen her do so often. 'I don't know if I can explain,' she said, tearfully. 'Not in a way to make you understand. I'm not sure if I understand myself.'

'I think we'd like you to try,' demanded Susan, who, like Jimmy, was totally confused.

'I was ill,' said Dorothy. 'Sad, depressed – call it what you like. If I hadn't been so useless, William wouldn't have gone away in the first place. I couldn't even cope with you two, much less a baby. It was at *my* insistence that he was sent away.'

'Uncle Tommy told us it was for his own good,' said Susan. 'I never understood that.'

'Uncle Tommy told you that to cover for my uselessness. The whole business of the war and your Uncle Tommy having to go away – and I just couldn't handle bringing up someone else's baby.'

Susan nodded, trying her best to understand. Jimmy copied her. 'But why did you tell us he was dead?' she asked.

Dorothy took a deep breath and continued, avoiding their eyes now. 'You just kept going on about him. When's he coming home, Auntie? When can we go to see him? Where's he living? Will they be looking after him? Not a day went by without you asking endless questions about him. You were driving me mad – so I...' her voice tailed off.

'So you thought you'd put a stop to all this by telling us he was dead?' Susan's face was colouring up. 'That's it, isn't it?'

Dorothy didn't reply.

'Isn't it?' repeated Susan, shouting now. 'Where is he, Auntie Dorothy? Where's our baby brother?'

People at the other tables broke off their conversations and looked at Susan, who was standing up, shouting at her auntie. A prison officer looked hard at them, wondering whether to intervene. Jimmy was still sitting, but looking most uncomfortable. Tears steamed down Dorothy's face as she looked back at her angry niece.

'I don't know,' she sobbed. 'I'm sorry, Susan, but I honestly don't know where he is. Please don't be angry with me.' She stood to walk round the table towards Susan. The officer moved swiftly over to restrain her, but Susan had already taken a pace backwards.

'We cried for days after you told us. How could you do that to us?'

'I'm so sorry,' wept Dorothy. 'I thought it was

for the best. Tommy was in the army, I was just trying to cope as well as I could. I would have told you the truth when Tommy came home. We were going to get William back. I just – I just wanted you to stop going on about him.'

She struggled to free herself of the officer's grip, but Susan moved further away from her.

'Don't come anywhere near me,' she said tearfully, then turned and went, leaving Jimmy sitting there, not knowing what to do.

'You'd better go after her,' said Dorothy.

Jimmy shrugged and opened his mouth to apologise on Susan's behalf then thought better of it.

'See you,' he said simply, then left.

Dorothy sat on her bunk pretty much at the end of her tether. Another mess. She should be used to it by now. But beneath all the self pity she felt a morsel of relief that the kids were alright. The news she'd given them was good news after all. They'd got their brother back, or they would one day. It seemed they were alright financially, God knows how, but they were. The only thing they had to worry about was having an idiot for their closest living adult relative. In an odd sort of way she felt relieved. Ah well, it'd soon be Christmas.

She gave a smile of resignation, picked up Rita's cornet and gave a blast into her dozing cellmate's ear. 'Right,' she said, 'I'm ready for my trumpet lesson now.'

Susan didn't speak to Jimmy all the way to Leeds on the bus. She couldn't believe anyone could be so cruel as to tell someone that their brother was dead just to stop them nagging.

They were waiting for their tram to Paradine Hill when Jimmy broke the silence.

'We did nag her a lot,' he muttered.

'You what?' snapped Susan.

'I know she shouldn't have done what she did, but we did nag her a lot. 'Specially me – I went on a lot when you weren't there.'

'Doesn't excuse what she did.'

'No, I don't s'pose it does,' accepted Jimmy. 'Still, it's great that our William's alive.'

It was as though Susan had forgotten this aspect of things. 'We'll find out where he is,' she said determinedly. 'We'll get him a brilliant Christmas present.'

'Yeah we'll send him a cake with a file in it,' chortled Jimmy.

'We'll ring up that last place he was at,' decided Susan. 'That place in Cleckeaton, can you remember what they called it?'

'Oxford House.'

'Oxford House, that's it. We'll ring up Oxford House and try and track him down from there.'

Thus decided, the two of them climbed onto the tram and headed for home. One with more forgiveness in his heart than the other.

'Susan?'

'What?'

'Yer know that plan you were talking about.'

'What plan?'

'That plan you said might get Auntie Dorothy off.'

'What about it?'

'You never told me what it was.'

'I know.'

She was so infuriating at times. If he thought he could get away with it, Jimmy could have cheerfully thumped her. It was four days since they'd visited Auntie Dorothy, since when, Susan had scarcely spoken about her. They'd drawn a blank when they rang up Oxford House, apparently the person who dealt with such things wasn't there that week, so could they ring back next week. Jimmy poured more milk onto his cornflakes and turned over another page of his *Adventure*.

'Are you not going ter bother then?' he asked.

'Bother about what?' asked Susan, idly looking through Dorothy's ration book.

'You know what – your plan ter get Auntie Dorothy off.'

'I haven't made up my mind yet.'

'In a way she's locked up because of you. It was Simmo starting on you that made her go potty.'

Susan ignored this observation and stopped at the sweet coupon page.

'Have you been buying sweets without telling me?'

'Why?'

'There's some coupons missing, that's why.' She put the ration book in her school satchel. 'How can you afford extra sweets out of your pocket money?'

Jimmy grimaced. She was worse than Auntie Dorothy. 'There was threepence in the bottom of the rent tin,' he explained sheepishly.

'You're not supposed to do that,' insisted Susan. 'I thought I explained it to you. We mustn't let people suspect we've got a lot of money in the house.'

'It was only flipping threepence.'

'I don't care.'

Jimmy wasn't going to win this one so he returned to the previous discussion.

'Anyway, you're supposed to forgive people.'

'Go on then, I forgive you,' said Susan graciously.

'I'm not talking about me, I'm talking about me Auntie Dorothy.'

'Oh.' Susan was finding it hard to have any charitable thoughts about Auntie Dorothy. How can you forgive the unforgivable?

Jimmy decided to give it one last try before he went back to his comic.

'If Simmo had died me Auntie Dorothy might have been hung – and she was doing it to protect you.'

'I don't think she was thinking that far ahead at the time,' retorted Susan.

'I think you should write to her and forgive her, 'specially with it being Christmas. You should send her a Christmas card.'

'Look, we'd best be off,' she said, neatly changing the subject. 'No point being late on the last day of term.'

What Susan didn't know was that Jimmy had already sent their auntie a Christmas card from both of them. Dorothy cried tears of misplaced joy when she read it.

Chapter Fifteen

Neville Simpson came out of hospital a week before Christmas. The fifteen stitches holding his head wound together had been painfully removed. His fiancée, Maggie Newton, drove him home and was once again more withdrawn than usual, as she had been for the past couple of weeks. Neville scarcely noticed this. Maggie's moods were of little concern to him. The only thing of interest about Maggie was that she was her wealthy father's only daughter, otherwise Neville wouldn't have looked twice at her.

Maggie, for her part, knew her limitations. Cosmetically she was very much third division and although Neville was no Clark Gable, he was better looking than her. But Susan's version of events had been worrying her, and as much as she didn't want to believe it, she knew the girl could well have been telling the truth.

She stopped the car outside Neville's father's house and switched off the engine, just staring contemplatively through the windscreen, making no move to get out. Neville's mother came to the door of the ugly Victorian edifice, the ground floor of which was occupied by the three Simpsons. The other two floors being divided up into six flats, the occupants of two of these had come to their windows to watch Neville's homecoming, more out of curiosity than affection.

'What's up?' asked Neville. His head was still swathed in bandages, completely obscuring his carroty hair.

'She's going to say you tried to rape her, isn't she?' Maggie's eyes were still firmly fixed on the street in front of her.

Neville shifted uncomfortably in his seat. 'How the hell do I know what the mad cow's going ter say?' he argued irritably. 'Do you mind getting the door for me, please, or am I supposed ter try and manage meself?'

'What exactly happened, Neville?'

Neville was becoming agitated. That bloody policeman hadn't seemed too happy with his explanation, but he could have done without Maggie becoming suspicious as well. If that bitch Bairstow had jeopardised his marriage he'd make sure they threw the bloody key away.

'I've already told yer,' he complained. 'She couldn't pay the rent and when I threatened her with eviction, she went barmy. She picked up this stool and chased me out into the street!'

Maggie swung round in her seat and gave him a challenging glare. 'Couldn't pay the rent? How come she left the kids so well provided for, then? They came up with the rent without any trouble when you sent me round. Made me look a right idiot in from of the bailiffs.'

Neville began to lose his temper. How dare this ugly bitch question him? Didn't she know how much of a favour he was doing her in offering to marry her?

'How do I know?' he snarled. 'She certainly didn't have any money when I went round there

201

– besides, whatever I did ter her was in self-defence. There's a big difference between raping someone and just scratching their tits a bit.'

'You did what?'

Neville sat back, chastened by his own big mouth.

'Are you trying to say you scratched her tits in self-defence?'

'I didn't say that!'

'That's what it sounded like to me.'

A wave of revulsion grew inside her as she looked at him, seeing for the first time what a vile little man he was. 'You bastard! You did it, didn't you? You tried to rape her, and her niece.'

Neville's head was beginning to ache. 'No, no, it wasn't like that,' he protested. 'You've got it all wrong. Look, all this aggravation is giving me a headache.'

'Get out of the car, Neville!'

Neville looked at her and knew the engagement was off. He couldn't resist delivering a parting shot.

'It'll be a pleasure. I've been dreading waking up opposite your ugly mush, so I'll just have me ring back, please.' Maggie had already hurled it through the car door, which she pulled shut behind him, before driving off with a roar, leaving him scrabbling around looking for it, to the consternation of his mother and the amusement of two of his tenants.

Delma caught Dorothy's eye in the canteen during dinner and gave a slavering leer that almost made Dorothy throw up. Prising her enormous girth from her steel chair she waddled across to Dorothy's table.

'Make the most of your last week!' She spat out the words and sent a cold shiver of dread down Dorothy's spine.

'Take no notice,' advised Rita, without much conviction.

Delma waddled off, smirking. Her plan was foolproof. Doing it was all that mattered – she hadn't planned on getting away with it, just doing it. That's why it was so foolproof.

Needless to say, Jackie Crombie saw it first. He'd watched the man from the estate agents putting it up, bombarding him with a million questions until the man told him to piss off. He was waiting at the end of the street for them, jabbing an excited forefinger towards the sign fixed to the wall beside their front door:

FOR SALE
WITH VACANT POSSESSION
Simpson's Properties
Leeds 36428

'Yer house is up fer sale. This feller came round an' put this sign up. He told me ter piss off,' announced Jackie cheerfully. 'An this other feller's been looking for yer, so I told him you were at school and he said he'd come back in half an hour.'

Susan and Jimmy looked in consternation at each other. What was going on? They walked to the house in silence, punctuated only by persistent questioning by Jackie.

'Will yer get kicked out? Where you gonna live? Will yer have ter go in an 'ome?'

'Look, Jackie,' said an exasperated Susan. 'You know what that man asked you to do?'

Jackie nodded uncertainly.

'Well, why don't you do it!' she yelled.

Jackie shrugged and mooched away to see if his tea was ready.

Jimmy and Susan were just going in through the back door when they heard a knock at the front. Susan looked through the curtains, then back at Jimmy with a huge smile on her face.

'It's Freddie,' she said excitedly. 'He can walk!'

He stood there on the pavement, beaming up at them, supported by two walking sticks. His father's car parked behind him.

'Freddie!' breathed Susan. 'You're better!'

'Well, I wouldn't exactly say that,' grinned Freddie. 'But I reckon I can manage these two steps if you invite me in.'

Susan blushed. 'Oh, sorry, yes, come in.'

Freddie mounted the steps slowly and with much grunting, until he stood in their front room with a look of triumph on his face. Susan offered him an easy chair but he chose a dining chair instead.

'I need to plan ahead,' he explained. 'It'd take me ten minutes to get up out of that chair. Still, mustn't grumble. The old pins are coming along nicely.'

Jimmy and Susan hovered in front of him, forcing him to smile at their awkwardness.

'Right, kids,' he said. 'First of all, thanks for

your letters. Plenty of people wrote to me whilst I was laid up, but none of their letters matched yours for excitement.' He directed his comment at Susan, his smile was making her heart race. 'At first, I thought they were a product of an over active imagination,' he went on. 'Fortunately, the old brainbox has made a bit of a break through and I remember enough to believe every word you wrote ... I also remember something about the rings, but for the life of me I can't remember what I did with mine.'

'You can have a share of ours,' said Susan impetuously. An offer that Jimmy felt he should have been consulted about.

'No, no, no wouldn't dream of it,' laughed Freddie. 'But thanks for the offer anyway.' His face became serious. 'It occurs to me that you need all the help you can get.'

'It's occurred to me as well,' said Jimmy, forcing another smile out of Freddie. 'Simmo's put our house up for sale.'

Freddie nodded. 'Yes, I saw the man putting the sign up. By the way, who's the kid that never stops talking? I thought the sign man was going to throttle him.'

'That's Jackie Crombie,' said Jimmy. 'He's alright.'

'In small doses,' added Susan, sitting down beside Freddie at the table.

'Anyway, first things first,' continued Freddie. 'Regarding your recently resurrected brother. I rang Oxford House to see if I could begin to track him down.'

'So did we,' said Susan. 'They said the person

we needed was away this week.'

'Yes, that's what they told us,' said Freddie, 'at first. Then Dad took it upon himself to do a bit of red tape slashing. He rang the woman back and gave her an almighty ear bashing. Threatened her with God knows what, and demanded to speak to her superior.'

'Your dad did this for us?' queried Susan. 'I got the impression that he didn't approve of us.'

Freddie laughed at her bluntness. 'He read about you in the papers and seeing as you've got some connection with me, he decided to take up the cudgels on your behalf. And believe me, he's a mean man with a cudgel.'

Susan's eyes were glued to him as he went on with his story.

'Apparently he was moved to an orphanage in Huddersfield a few months ago. They couldn't tell me much over the phone, but reading between the lines it occurs to me that young William's having a hard time of it.'

'Hey! It'd be great if we could get him back for Christmas,' exclaimed Jimmy.

'It's not as simple as that,' cautioned Freddie. 'He'd need to have a stable home to come to. You'd have to wait at least until your aunt got out of – came home. Even then the authorities might question her suitability, if she wasn't completely acquitted.'

Susan nodded, still not taking her eyes off Freddie. 'It's important that Auntie Dorothy's found not guilty then?' she concluded.

'Very important,' said Freddie. 'But from what you tell me she *isn't* guilty.'

'Well, she did clobber him,' admitted Susan.

'I should think she *did*,' said Freddie. 'I'd have clobbered him myself under the circumstances.'

'Would you?' breathed Susan dreamily, just for a second picturing Freddie as her knight in shining armour springing bravely to her defence.

'Yes, I damn well would,' said Freddie, cutting through her thoughts, unaware of the effect he was having on her. 'By the way,' he asked, 'tell me it's none of my business if you like, but where are you keeping the money?'

'In the attic,' replied Susan.

Freddie shook his head. 'I was worried about that. It's time you opened a bank account.'

'I think I'll need your help for that,' smiled Susan. Freddie smiled back and saw, for the first time, a lovely young lady instead of the pretty tomboy he'd been so taken with, back at Fiddler's cottage. Susan lowered her eyes under his gaze and wished they were alone.

'Oh, before I forget,' remembered Freddie, 'You're both invited to Harrogate for Christmas lunch.'

The phone rang in Neville Simpson's office. He'd promoted himself into his father's chair when the old man had been taken ill. He picked it up and answered in his flat, West Riding vowels.

'Hello, Simpson's Properties – yes, that's correct. Three bedrooms including the attic. The price is four hundred and fifty for a quick sale.'

The caller was a solicitor, ringing on behalf of a client. 'My client is a businessman like yourself, Mr Simpson, and he's prepared to make a cash offer for a quick sale. But your price would have to be much lower.'

Neville's hatred of Dorothy Bairstow festered inside him like a cancer. She'd wrecked his intended marriage and robbed him of the woman of his dreams, the sole heiress to sixteen butcher's shops and a mansion in Pudsey. On taking over the reins of his father's business it had become obvious that Simpson Properties was practically insolvent. All the properties were mortgaged up to the hilt, many in a state of disrepair. Thousands of pounds' worth of rent arrears, incurred during the war, had been written off by his father as bad debts. In short, the business needed an injection of cash to keep it afloat, hence his engagement to the homely, but wealthy, Maggie Newton. Now that bitch Bairstow had ruined it. She needed teaching a lesson. He had no reason to sell her house, other than to cause problems for her and her brood; and if they insisted on paying the rent, then he'd sell the house from under them.

'Would your client continue to rent it out or would he want it with vacant possession?' asked Neville. The answer to this was of paramount importance to him.

'My client would require vacant possession on completion. Why, is this a problem?'

'No, no problem whatsoever,' oozed Simpson. 'The tenants will have moved out before you take possession.' Kicked out more like, with my own size tens, he sniggered to himself. 'I'm prepared to drop to four hundred for a quick completion.'

'My client won't go higher than three hundred and fifty.'

Three-fifty? Jesus Christ! He'd only put it in at four-fifty to get rid quick. His hatred of Dorothy got the better of him. 'Okay,' he conceded. 'I'm giving it away. Three-fifty it is then. Can I expect a signed contract tomorrow?'

'I'll have one sent round to your solicitor, subject to the usual searches of course.'

'Of course.'

Simpson gave details of his solicitor, then put the phone down and rubbed his hands gleefully. 'Got them, the bastards,' he said, to no one in particular.

It was the morning of Christmas Eve when he rang his solicitor for confirmation of exchange of contracts.

'That's correct, Mr Simpson, we exchanged about an hour ago. The purchaser had personal searches done to expedite matters. We've set the completion for the first of January, if that's alright by you. Give your tenants time to move into another of your properties, I expect.'

Neville put the phone down and reached for his coat. He looked in the mirror and fingered the livid scar on his head to remind him how much he hated that Bairstow bitch. A brown-toothed smirk flickered across his face.

'Here comes old Ebenezer bleedin' Scrooge,' he sniggered, then howled with laughter at his clever analogy.

Jimmy and Susan had bought each other modest Christmas presents in keeping with their frugal budget. Both presents were wrapped up and sitting on the kitchen table inviting guesses from their curious recipients.

'It's a book,' decided Susan, it had to be a book.

'Aw, no, did yer want a book? I was gonna buy you a book, but I didn't know you could read.'

Susan slapped his arm playfully. Another present sat on the dresser in the front room, cuff links for Freddie. William's train set and Auntie Dorothy's cardigan had already been posted, William's being the most expensive present of the four.

The knock was one they'd heard a hundred times before. Susan winked at Jimmy. 'It's him, I'll get it, you go upstairs.'

She opened the door and gave Simpson a smile he didn't expect. 'Hello, Mr Simpson, how nice to see you. Won't you come in?'

He stepped through the scullery into the back room and handed Susan a piece of paper. There was whisky on his breath.

'Whew! Your breath smells, Mr Simpson!' she gasped, taking a step back. Then looking at the paper she added, 'What's this?'

'Notice to quit,' he snapped. 'By law I don't have to give you notice as you're not the legal tenants. That would be your aunt, who's hardly likely to be a tenant of anyone other than His Majesty for some time to come.' He sniggered to himself at this. 'You have one week from today to remove yourselves and your belongings, such as they are.'

'But, but it's Christmas, Mr Simpson!'

'I know,' smirked Neville. 'Good, isn't it?'

'And, will you be wanting to rape me? Like last time?'

Neville didn't know what to make of this, although the prospect was quite exciting. Susan gave him a look of disappointment.

'No? That's a shame. Still, from what I hear you're all talk. All mouth and trousers, that's what I've heard.'

This touched a raw nerve with Neville. He reached out and grabbed her by her blouse.

'Listen, you little bitch!' he snarled. 'If your whore of an aunt hadn't hit me with that bloody stool I'd have given you a screwing you wouldn't have forgotten in a hurry. And I'd have done a lot more to your precious auntie than pull her tits out!' He released his grip and pushed her away contemptuously, then followed as she backed away. He was shouting now, out of control. 'I'd have screwed her arse off if you hadn't disturbed us! It's your fault she's in jail, another five minutes and I'd have finished the job and nobody would have been any wiser. She'd have kept her mouth shut or she'd have been out in the streets, and you lot with her!'

There was a hint of madness in his malevolent eyes. Every word was accompanied by a spray of spit, which Susan struggled to avoid. She backed away from him, her face ashen. She'd gone a little too far with her taunting.

'It's okay, Susan, we've heard enough,' said P.C. Greenough stepping out of the small hall-way at the bottom of the stairs. Behind him was Maggie Newton and Jimmy who hurled himself at Neville, kicking and gouging until Alan

211

Greenough pulled him off.

'Jimmy, Jimmy, calm down, it's over!' said the policeman pulling the boy off the cowering Neville. With a restraining hand on Jimmy, P.C. Greenough read a shocked Neville his rights.

'Neville Simpson, I'm arresting you for indecent assault. You do not have to say anything, but anything you do say may be taken down and used in evidence.'

Neville's mouth opened and shut like a goldfish. He flopped down on a chair, totally defeated. Alan Greenough yanked him roughly back to his feet. 'Come on, you,' he growled. 'We've a nice little room for you to spend Christmas in!'

Neville glared at Susan, his eyes full of wild hatred. Then he gave her a twisted sneer. 'It doesn't alter things for you, you smug little bitch. A week today and you're out on the streets. This house is sold!'

'I know,' gloated Susan. 'I'm the one who bought it!' She took the contract out of a drawer and waved it under his nose. 'And I'd like to thank you for selling it to me at a knock-down price. I was told I'd have to pay five hundred for it.'

Neville howled with frustrated rage and tried in vain to struggle free of the policeman's grip.

Jimmy, Susan and Maggie Newton listened as his hysterical screams disappeared down Paradine Hill.

'You're well rid of him, I suppose,' observed Susan.

'You suppose correctly,' agreed Maggie. 'I'll

speak against him in court and hopefully never have anything to do with him again.'

'Oh, and sorry about being rotten to you before, you know,' apologised Susan.

'Apology accepted. You did me a favour in the long run.'

'When do you suppose Auntie Dorothy will come home?' asked Jimmy.

'Well,' cautioned Maggie, 'I'm afraid with it being Christmas Even there's not much we can do to get her home for tomorrow. But I think with this new evidence she should be let out on bail until her trial comes up. That's if there is a trial now.'

'Thanks, Maggie,' said Jimmy.

'Anytime,' smiled Maggie. 'Oh, and by the way.' She pulled a hat out of her pocket that was equally as atrocious as the brown affair they'd first seen her in. 'I bought this with the ten bob you gave me.'

'It's lovely,' lied Susan.

'You should have given her more,' said Jimmy, through smiling teeth as they waved Maggie goodbye. They sat down at the table and grinned at one another.

'What do you think of my plan then?'

'Quite good,' conceded Jimmy grudgingly, who'd been scared stiff for his sister when Simpson had lost his rag with her.

Chapter Sixteen

Hark the Herald Angels sing!
Beecham's Pills are just the thing.
Move ye gently move ye mild,
Two for an adult one for a child.
Regular administration,
Just the thing for constipation...

Dorothy had never heard this version before that Christmas morning. She was, it seemed, the only person in the canteen who was singing the traditional words. Rita was playing her cornet, accompanied by a spoon-playing shop-lifter and a warder playing the mouth organ.

All in all it was a happy morning. Delma's threats had come to nothing, and there was to be turkey for Christmas dinner. A far better meal than most of them would have got on the outside. She saw Delma's fat friend approaching out of the corner of her eye and decided to ignore her. The fat friend had kept her distance from Dorothy since coming out of the hospital wing with a misshapen nose and a reputation as a loser.

'Netherton wants ter see yer in her office,' she grunted in passing. 'Says it's important.'

Dorothy watched her waddle away, wondering what on earth Netherton could possibly want her for on Christmas morning. Maybe she had some

214

good news – why not? It was about time she had some good news. With an optimism brought on by the spirit of Christmas, she climbed the iron stairs to Netherton's office. It was in the corner of the first floor landing where Dorothy and Rita lived. Little more than a converted cell, the main difference being that Netherton's door locked from the inside. The door was partially open when Dorothy arrived so she knocked and walked straight in. Netherton was lying on the floor, her eyes closed and a pool of blood around her head. Dorothy froze for a second, long enough for a truncheon to come flailing out from behind the door and smash across her right shin, breaking both tibia and fibula in one vicious blow. Her shriek of pain was drowned by Rita hitting the high notes and the canteen choir singing the last two scatalogical lines of the hymn,

How to art can man aspire?
When his arsehole's not on fire.

Dorothy went down as it poleaxed, the pain in her leg almost unbearable. She looked down and could see the smashed bones sticking out at a sickening angle. A large shadow fell over her and she knew without looking up who it was.

'Not so full o' yer bleedin' self now, are yer? Yer stuck up cow.'

Dorothy had never felt less full of herself than she did at that moment. The intense pain had vanished, replaced by intense terror. Miss Netherton was lying beside her, frighteningly still, her blood beginning to soak into Dorothy's blouse. Delma was standing astride her, like an obscene colossus. A gigantic mess of a woman, smiling contemptuously down on Dorothy with those gleaming horse teeth of hers. Swirling the black truncheon in her fat hand.

'Now then, where would yer like me ter stick this, Dolly darlin'?'

She lowered herself astride Dorothy. Heaving with one leg to push aside the body of the warder.

'I think we'll have rid of her. Don't want dead screws cramping our style, do we, Dolly darlin? No need ter say goodbye, yer'll soon be joinin' her!'

She heaved Netherton over her shoulder like a small child and walked out onto the landing, waving at the inmates gathered below, stunning them all into silence as they looked back at the horrific sight above them. With a great flashing equine grin, she raised the body above her head and with a shout of, 'Merry Christmas, girls!' hurled the mortal remains of Miss Netherton down on top of them, before calmly strolling back into the dead warder's office and turning the key in the lock.

Freddie's car arrived at eleven o'clock on Christmas morning. Jimmy and Susan were already waiting at the open door, both dressed in their school blazers and latest finery. Susan locked the door and walked casually down the steps, secretly annoyed at Jimmy, who was already on the front seat where she wanted to sit, chattering excitedly to Freddie. Although Susan would never admit it, this was the first time in her life she'd ever been in a car. Of course there was no need for Freddie to know that. She opened the back door and slid demurely onto the back seat as though it was an everyday occurrence.

'We've never been in a car before, have we, Susan?' chirped an excited Jimmy.

Not for the first time, Susan could have throttled him. '*You* might not have,' she argued.

'Oh yeah! And when have you been in a car before?' challenged Jimmy.

Freddie butted in to save Susan's obvious embarrassment. He looked in the mirror at Susan's blushing face.

'Yes, madam,' he said with mock servility, 'and where would madam wish to go this morning?'

Susan smiled back and quickly regained her composure. 'Take us to Harrogate, my good man,' she instructed, loftily. 'And don't spare the horses!'

'Very good, madam,' replied Freddie, touching a forelock.

The journey to Harrogate was an interesting one. The morning bright and frosty. For reasons best known to themselves, someone had chosen Christmas morning to transport a wagon load of cows from Harewood towards Harrogate. Behind the cattle truck was a bowler-hatted man hunched over the wheel of his Austin Seven and behind him drove Freddie and his Christmas guests. A young man in an open-topped M.G. drove up behind Freddie and hooted impatiently. Freddie politely cursed him, but in the spirit of the season, signalled him to pass and as he did so the Austin Seven took it upon himself to put his foot down and slowly overtake the cattle truck, pulling out in front of the M.G. who'd had ambitions to roar past all three of them.

The hooter started again, urging the Austin Seven to get a move on, because by now both cars were on the wrong side of the road. At this point, one of the cows decided to relieve itself, sending a steaming spray out between the slatted sides of the truck to disperse itself in the cold slipstream all over the M.G. driver. Freddie, spotting the M.G.'s predicament, drove up close behind him, trapping him in position, so that he might receive the full benefit of the cow's Christmas present. A classic manoeuvre which filled Jimmy with unbounded admiration for Freddie.

They were all agreed that this was possibly the funniest thing they'd ever seen in their lives and they were still laughing when they pulled up outside Freddie's house. Christmas was off to a good start.

'Welcome,' boomed the Brigadier, as they walked through the front door.

'Merry Christmas,' said Jimmy.

'Nice to see you again,' said Susan, who still hadn't forgotten his rudeness, but was prepared to forgive and forget in the spirit of Christmas. Freddie's father gave her a smile, half of admiration for a pretty girl, half of puzzlement, wondering where he'd seen her before.

Freddie led the way through to the 'parlour', pointing out various items of interest with his walking stick. 'That's my paternal grandfather,' he said, pointing to a painting of a rather stern military man, glowering down at them from the staircase wall. 'And that's my *maternal* grandfather,' he jabbed his stick at a faded sepia photograph of a young man in shirt sleeves and collarless shirt, leaning against a farm cart with a tankard in his hand. 'Guess whose side of the family I take after?' he grinned. 'Right, I'd like you to meet our Christmas dinner guests.'

The parlour was a large warm room with a fireplace as big as the Bairstows' scullery. Heavy gold satin curtains hung from ceiling to the thick, patterned carpet on which stood a variety of easy chairs, a settee as long as a small car and two low coffee tables covered with bowls of nuts, fruit and sweets. In the corner stood the biggest Christmas tree they'd ever seen. The fairy on top was just touching the ceiling some twelve feet above them and from the branches hung small parcels and lights and bright decorations.

A group of guests broke off their conversations and turned to greet the new arrivals with welcoming smiles. Jimmy and Susan tried to contain their embarrassment as Freddie introduced them as the 'Miracle Kids of Leeds and very good friends of mine.'

'I believe you've already met Mother.' Mary Fiddler smiled and gave them a warm handshake.

'And this is my Uncle Ben, Auntie Maude, my cousin Beatrice, my old schoolfriend Tricky Dicky Dodsworth and last but by no means least ... my lady friend, Elizabeth.'

Susan was still smiling hellos to her fellow

guests when she heard the last introduction. As soon as she looked down at the sophisticated beauty smiling back at her, Susan's young heart was pierced with a pain she'd never known before.

'Hello, Susan,' said Elizabeth, patting the seat at the side of her. 'Freddie's told me so much about you. You must sit next to me and tell me more. My life seems ever so dull compared with yours.'

'Everyone's life's dull compared to Susan's, with the possible exception of young Jimmy over there,' laughed Freddie.

Jimmy had been taken under the wing of Tricky Dicky Dodsworth, an unconventionally dressed young man, who was already laughing at Jimmy's story of the cow and the M.G., brilliantly told as usual, in his unselfconscious Leeds accent.

Susan was fighting back the tears whilst trying to be polite to Elizabeth, whom she found to be infuriatingly nice. Who had she been fooling? How on earth could a schoolgirl like her hope to win the heart of a wonderful man like Freddie?'

'I understand you're doing your School Certificate this year?' asked Elizabeth, deciding to keep the conversation on a light note and avoid some of the more controversial aspects of Susan's complicated life.

'Yes,' she answered politely.

'She'll walk it,' cut in Freddie. 'Bright girl, our Susan. Not like me, got through by the skin of my teeth.'

'Well, you're not an academic, darling,' smiled Elizabeth, taking his hand. 'But I suppose I'll just

220

have to love you as you are.'

'What you see is what you get, Lizzie my love,' laughed Freddie.

Lizzie? Oh God, he's got a pet name for her. Susan was having one of the worst times of her life. She smiled grimly throughout this badinage. Her end of the conversation was little more than monosyllabic, which Elizabeth took to be shyness in the face of a roomful of adults, and understandably so.

'Perhaps you'd like to chat to Beatrice?' suggested Elizabeth, patronisingly, Susan thought. 'She's more your age. You don't want to be sitting round talking to old fogeys like us.'

'Old fogey – you?' bellowed the Brigadier, listening in on their conversation. 'What does that make me then?'

'An ancient old fart!' called out his brother Ben from the other side of the room. The laughter this produced was too much for Susan to bear. She stood up and rushed out in floods of tears. A concerned Mary followed her as the rest of them fell into an embarrassed silence.

'You should watch your language in front of young gels,' admonished the Brigadier.

'Perhaps I should go and apologise,' said a chastened Ben. 'I didn't mean to offend.'

'I don't think it was you, Uncle Ben,' consoled Freddie. 'I think it may be more to do with her aunt having to spend Christmas in prison simply for trying to protect her from this rapist chap.'

'Quite,' agreed the Brigadier. 'Sensitive young soul like that, seeing us all enjoying ourselves, while her poor aunt's incarcerated. She's bound to feel guilty, stands to reason.'

'Annoying thing is,' said Freddie, 'that the man she clobbered was arrested yesterday for assaulting her, but with it being Christmas we can't get her out on bail.'

'Really?' growled the Brigadier. 'You don't think so, eh?'

'You're a magistrate, Harry me boy,' said Ben, relieved to be absolved of blame for Susan's tearful exit. 'Don't you have any influence in such things?'

'I'll make a phone call,' decided the Brigadier. 'See if I can stir things up a bit.'

As the Brigadier went from the room with Freddie, Jimmy gave a puzzled frown. He didn't know what was wrong with Susan, but he knew it was nothing to do with Auntie Dorothy. He shrugged his bafflement at the behaviour of women in general and resumed his conversation with his new-found friend, Tricky Dicky Dodsworth.

Mary Fiddler found Susan sitting in the kitchen, weeping quietly. She stood behind her and placed her hands on Susan's shaking shoulders.

'I suspect you and I have something in common,' said Mary gently. She took a handkerchief from her pocket and gave it to Susan.

'What's that?' asked Susan, wiping her eyes fiercely, as though annoyed at her silly weakness.

'Perhaps I should have said some*one* in common.'

'Oh dear,' sighed Susan, 'is it that obvious.'

'Only to me.' Mary sat on the chair beside

Susan. 'You see, I heard you talking to Freddie when you came last year – you know, when he fell asleep and you thought you were alone with him.'

Susan blushed. 'It's alright, Mrs Fiddler,' she said. 'I won't embarrass Freddie. I'm happy for him, honestly I am. Elizabeth seems very nice.'

'Yes, she does *seem* very nice, doesn't she?' agreed Freddie's mother. '–Still, you never know,' she added mysteriously.

Susan gave a rueful grin as she stood up and walked back to the dining room with Mary.

Dorothy opened her eyes then closed them quickly, as she couldn't believe what she'd seen the first time. She vaguely remembered Delma standing over her in Netherton's office, then seeing her heave the warder over her shoulder and carrying her to the landing rail. With her broken leg trailing behind her, Dorothy had pulled herself out of that room of horror, hard on Delma's unsuspecting heels. As Delma was shouting her Christmas greetings to the inmates below and tossing the dead warder down on them, Dorothy, with tears of pain and terror streaming down her face, was hauling herself into the cell next door, out of Delma's sight. She'd heard the shouts from below as Netherton's body went crashing down, then the slam and locking of the office door and then the rush of feet up the stairs.

Rita was in the lead. She'd seen Dorothy crawling out behind Delma and needed to get to her friend before Delma did.

A roar of rage came from behind the office

door. Delma burst back out into the throng of inmates and warders, lashing out at everyone with great ham-like fists. Dorothy kept well out of sight as the battle raged; she saw Delma stagger past the cell door with one warder clinging to her back with her arms around her neck and another retreating backwards, belabouring Delma with a truncheon as she went, causing her gleaming teeth to fall out and bounce by the side of the cowering Dorothy. As the turmoil progressed to the other end of the landing, Rita popped her head round the cell door.

'You're a right bleedin' bother-causer you are,' she grinned. At that point Dorothy passed out.

Dorothy opened her eyes again. Susan was standing there, so was Jimmy, and two older people she'd never seen before. The last time she'd seen Susan there'd been a look of hatred on the girl's face, and for good reason.

'Where am I?' she asked, inevitably. The anaesthetic still dulling her senses.

'Told yer she'd say that,' grinned Jimmy, who'd apparently won a bet.

'You're in the prison hospital, Auntie Dorothy,' said Susan. 'Lucky to be alive apparently – which is more than can be said for the other poor lady.'

'Oh dear,' sighed Dorothy with genuine sadness. She'd quite liked Miss Netherton.

'We're just happy that you're okay,' said Susan, with a gentleness that told Dorothy all she wanted to know. The hatred had gone. She smiled up at her concerned niece.

'Are we friends again?'

Susan squeezed her hand and nodded. 'Friends,' she said. 'Mind you, there was no need to go to these lengths.'

Dorothy held out her other hand to Jimmy. 'Merry Christmas, Jimmy,' she said. 'It is still Christmas, isn't it?'

'Yes, it's still Christmas, Auntie,' Jimmy assured her. 'About half-past-five. We had a great dinner at Freddie's, turkey and everything, and we got some presents off the tree – yer should have seen their tree, it was massi...'

'Jimmy!' Susan stopped him there. 'Auntie Dorothy doesn't want to know about Freddie's Christmas tree!'

'Not at all,' smiled Dorothy, trying to clear her mind. 'I expect it was a beautiful tree. As a matter of fact, we were supposed to have turkey, but I expect I've missed it now.' She looked up at Freddie. 'I reckon you must be the famous Freddie Fiddler they're always going on about?'

'Pleased to meet you, Mrs Bairstow,' greeted Freddie, shaking her hand lightly. 'I've heard a lot about you as well. Oh, this is my father.'

The Brigadier stepped forward and instead of shaking her hand, he gave her a smart salute. 'I gather you're a fighter, Mrs Bairstow. I salute that. Know a bit about you, like what I hear.' He stepped back, having said his piece.

A nurse bustled impatiently through and shooed them all away while she drew the curtains around Dorothy's bed. A few minutes later she opened the curtains and announced curtly to the waiting quartet, 'You can take her now,' then hurried away.

225

'What did she mean?' "take her now"?' asked Dorothy.

The four of them grinned. Freddie took it upon himself to explain. 'Your niece here very neatly trapped the wicked Mr Simpson into confessing to your assault. With a policeman and his own ex-fiancée as witnesses.'

'And me,' added Jimmy.

'Sorry, Jimmy, you as well,' laughed Freddie.

'Anyway,' continued Freddie, 'my redoubtable parent here,' he inclined his head in the Brigadier's direction, 'being a magistrate of some standing, has been bullying people all afternoon into letting you out on bail – including the Chief Constable of Leeds, halfway through his Christmas pudding.'

'So, what are you saying?' asked an incredulous Dorothy.

'We're saying you're free to go home,' explained Freddie. 'Or rather you would have been if you could walk. Anyway, we're free to take you to a civilian hospital.'

'You're going to St Jimmy's for a few days, then it's back home. You'll be well looked after,' assured Susan. 'You've spent long enough looking after us, it's the least we can do.'

'Do you know,' said Dorothy tearfully, grimacing with pain as the anaesthetic began to wear off, 'this is one of the best Christmases I've ever had.'

The four of them stared at her in disbelief. Dorothy saw the funny side of what she'd said and burst out laughing, prompting them to join in. As they were lifting her onto a stretcher she looked at Susan and asked, 'Is there anything else I don't know about?'

Susan shook her head, 'I can't think of anything, can you, Jimmy?'

'We bought the house,' said Jimmy.

'Oh, yes,' remembered Susan. 'We bought our house off Simmo. Cheap as well.'

Dorothy lay back in the stretcher. She'd no right to believe such nonsense. But somehow she knew it would be true.

Chapter Seventeen

It was late February and Dorothy was faffing about, as she would call it, in the tiny scullery. There was no room for her wheelchair so she'd propped herself on a crutch, as she attempted, with her one good leg, to cook the children a hot meal for when they got in from school. The snow was quite heavy now and she knew they'd be glad of something warm inside them.

She was still trying to come to terms with their new-found wealth. Just as well really, because with her being out of work, things would have been desperate, despite the Brigadier's assurance that he'd do everything in his power to ensure that proper compensation would be awarded to make up for her recent troubles. She smiled to herself as she chopped the potatoes that Susan had peeled the night before. What a good man to have on your side.

The balance of Susan's money had been placed in what Susan insisted being called a 'family account'. To be administered by her and Dorothy. Dorothy had sold Jimmy's diamond ring to Blackstone's for two hundred and fifty pounds and the money placed into a separate account in his name, that he couldn't touch without Dorothy's signature.

Frank Sackfield had been round to congratulate her on her release and to tell her there was a job waiting for her as soon as she felt ready to start.

Freddie and the Brigadier had been round just once since she came out of hospital and stayed just long enough for it to become perfectly clear to Dorothy that Susan was besotted by Freddie.

'I know it's hard,' she explained to her tearful niece, who'd broken down under the gentlest of questioning by her aunt, 'but it's something you're going to have to accept.'

'Would you have accepted it?' challenged Susan, 'if Uncle Tommy had been going out with another girl when you met him?'

'No,' she admitted, 'probably not!' There was no *probably* about it, she'd fallen for Tommy the first time he'd winked at her from the bandstand of the Hippodrome.

'So, what do you think I should do?' agonised Susan.

'I honestly don't know what you can do, love. He's in Harrogate, you're in Leeds. He's a twenty-two-year-old, practically engaged man, you're a fifteen-year-old schoolgirl.'

'Sixteen soon!'

'If you call July soon,' said her aunt. 'But if you really want my advice you'll try and forget him. From a romantic point of view anyway. You're much better off with someone your own age. It's much safer in many respects.'

'Never,' declared Susan.

'Now why am I not surprised?' sighed Dorothy.

William was apparently in a children's home in Huddersfield. Dorothy, Susan, Jimmy, Freddie and the Brigadier had had a long discussion as to what to do about him and concluded that nothing could or should be done until Dorothy was completely in the clear. When they made their move to bring him back they wanted no unforeseen obstacles to add to young William's trauma. The prosecution had applied for a *sine die* adjournment pending the outcome of the case against Simpson.

'What does that mean?' she'd asked Alan Greenough, who came round to give her the news.

'In a nutshell, it means we have to nail him before you can apply for the charges against you to be dropped.'

'And how long's this likely to take?' she asked, mindful of not being able to get William back while the charge was still hanging over her.

'Could be a few months – even then we can't be certain of a prosecution. He's claiming you willingly had sex with him the week before,' explained Alan, 'and that he didn't try to rape you, it was just a lovers' tiff that got out of hand!'

'He's lying,' she retorted angrily. Despite there

229

being a vague element of truth in Simpson's claim, no way was Dorothy about to admit to it.

'I know that and you know that, but if it gets to court, there'll be a lot of unpleasant things said about you that might well reach the papers.'

'I suppose you're right,' she admitted. 'You're trying to tell me something, aren't you?' She could see by his fidgety manner that there was something on his mind.

He nodded. 'It's just a suggestion, but if you drop the charges against him, I understand he'll do the same for you.'

'My word, that's good of him!'

'And it'll leave the way clear for you to get William back.'

This of course was the clincher.

'Where do I sign?' asked Dorothy.

Alan Greenough smiled. 'He didn't exactly get away with it though, did he, Mrs Bairstow?'

Dorothy laughed and looked round at the house her niece had almost conned Simpson out of.

'You don't know the half of it, constable,' she laughed.

With the charges against her withdrawn, they planned to make their move to get William the next week. Jimmy burst in first. He sniffed appreciatively. 'Ooh, that smells great, Auntie. What're we having?'

'Sausage and mash, with bread and butter pudding to follow. Where's Susan?'

'Talking to her boyfriend. Just passed 'em on me way back.'

'Boyfriend? Who?' Dorothy asked suspiciously. Susan was turning into an exceptionally pretty young lady and she'd need to vet all prospective suitors. She didn't want her niece latching on to just anyone on the rebound from Freddie.

'Ray Donoghue.'

'Raymond? Ah yes, I quite like Raymond.' Dorothy was relieved that Susan had found an alternative to Freddie – a one-sided love affair if ever there was one.

'He's great at fighting,' enthused Jimmy. 'School boxing champion. Yer should've seen that fight he had with Boothie. I thought they were goin' ter kill each other. Boothie's in t' sixth form, two years older than Ray – but Ray knocked hell out of him.' Jimmy winced as the unintentioned expletive slipped out, but Dorothy didn't seem to notice.

'You shouldn't make heroes out of people, just because they fight,' she admonished. 'Look what happened to me?'

Jimmy failed to understand this. 'What do you think would have happened if you hadn't hit Simmo, Auntie?' he reasoned, innocently.

Dorothy narrowed her eyes. Trapped by his thirteen-year-old logic. 'What I meant to say was, you mustn't fight without good reason – and I had good reason, I doubt if Raymond had.'

Jimmy disagreed but let it go.

Susan held her breath as Ray walked up to the pay box. 'Two back stalls, please,' he asked commandingly.

The woman looked up momentarily, but long

enough for Susan to wonder if they'd get in. They were at the Dominion Cinema to see Lana Turner and John Garfield in *The Postman Always Rings Twice*. It was an 'A' certificate and Susan was still well short of her sixteenth birthday, but eager to see what was described on the posters as M.G.M.'s 'raciest film ever'. Ray was just sixteen and therefore technically old enough to take Susan in as an accompanying adult. Providing they believed he was sixteen.

'Two and six, please,' sniffed the uninterested woman, sending a couple of tickets shooting out of the machine.

A gum-chewing usherette led them down the aisle, pointing out odd vacant seats in the otherwise-full auditorium.

'Haven't you got two together?' asked a disappointed Ray.

'Can't see none, love.'

There was a shout from the back row, followed by a violent slap, as a woman stood up and pushed her way out past a dozen sets of reluctant knees, closely followed by a protesting gentleman friend, much to the amusement of the audience.

'Seems you're in luck,' grinned the usherette, pointing her torch at two recently vacated seats in the middle of the back row.

Ray and Susan settled down in the cramped and creaking seats to watch the Pathe News and learn that Al Capone had died and Crown Prince Gustaf of Sweden had been killed in a plane crash. Above them, the projector beam flickered down towards the screen, illuminating the constant clouds of cigarette smoke billowing through it, not to mention the occasional tab end, flicked by some playful youth in the hope that it might drop down someone's neck.

As the main feature came up, Ray slid a tentative arm around Susan. Maybe it wasn't as pleasant as she imagined Freddie's arm would be, but it was pleasant all the same. He gradually drew her to him until her head was resting on his shoulder. Perhaps she was better off with someone her own age. Ray was nice and uncomplicated. If she *had* to have a boyfriend, it might as well be him. He wasn't interested in the film, she knew that. Ray had other things on his mind. She knew that as well. What she didn't know were her own thoughts on the matter. She looked up at him and caught his attention. He nervously leaned across and gave her a tentative peck on the lips, before drawing away to test her reaction. Ray was as new to this as she was, but he wasn't going to tell her that.

'Is that it then?' she whispered. 'Is that all I'm going to get?' She was amazed at her own promiscuity, kissing a boy in the back row of the pictures. She'd heard about girls like that but she didn't realise how much fun it was.

They were still kissing when the national anthem came on at the end, urging them, reluctantly, to stand to patriotic attention.

As they moved to leave, a man on the row in front leaned over to them and commented drily, 'Good picture that. You want to come back tomorrow night and watch it!'

Susan and Ray grinned at his sarcasm as they walked out into the icy street, past a queue of people gradually moving forward to catch the second showing.

'Rubbish that, what do you think, Susan?' said Ray, loud enough for all the shuffling cinema-goers to hear.

'Worst picture I've seen for ages,' replied Susan, convincingly.

They trudged away, giggling to themselves, leaving in their wake a queue of people wondering at the wisdom of their choice of film that evening.

'What shall we do now? It's only ten-past-eight,' asked Susan.

'We could get some fish and chips and take them back to our house,' he suggested hopefully.

'You sure know how to spoil a lady,' laughed Susan, who was happier than she'd been for a long time.

'Well, me mam and dad have gone to the Empire with our Eileen. They won't be back till late. We'll have the house to ourselves.'

'Oh.'

Susan found the unspoken implications of such privacy quite exciting. She'd enjoyed their flirtation on the back row and she rather fancied continuing it. The fact that it might lead to something else gave the whole affair an added frisson.

They ate their fish and chips in front of the roaring front room fire. Ray had thrown some more coal on to the smouldering embers that had greeted them; it had been damped down by Ray's father, pending their return from a rare visit to the Empire Variety Theatre.

'We've got some dandelion and burdock, if

you'd like some,' offered Ray.

'Yes, please.'

Ray poured the red-brown liquid half way up a pint pot stamped, 'Melbourne Breweries' then poured himself some into a glass emblazoned, 'John Smith's Magnet Ales.'

'Me dad collects them,' he explained cheerfully. 'Brings one home every Saturday night – sort of a hobby.'

They finished their fish and chips and lay back on the settee, arms around one other. Comfortable in each other's company. Ray leaned over and kissed her. This time more passionately than in the pictures. Susan wasn't sure of this, she gently pushed him away.

'Phew! I couldn't breathe,' she said, by way of excuse.

'Sorry,' Ray blushed.

She'd never seen him blush before and felt slightly guilty. 'It's not your fault,' she consoled. 'Come here.'

She pulled him towards her and kissed him with the same passion as he'd been kissing her.

'You're a good kisser, Ray Donaghue,' she announced, breaking away for a moment. 'I bet you've kissed lots of girls.'

There was something in her voice that told him to answer carefully. If he told the truth, that she was his first girlfriend, it might jeopardise his prospects. Girls liked men with experience. But then again, if he lied, she might finish up asking all sorts of awkward questions. Ray was useless at lying.

He settled for, 'I realise now that I've never

actually kissed any girl before.' The accent on the word 'any', designed to make Susan feel special. It appeared to work.

'I'll believe you, thousands wouldn't,' she pulled him back towards her, satisfied now that she was his first girlfriend.

They kissed with renewed vigour, Ray's rising passion getting the better of him as he pressed his hand against her breast, giving it a gentle squeeze.

She jerked away, whether with guilt or shock, she didn't know. Instinctively, she grabbed her half drunk glass of dandelion and burdock and threw it at him. Liberally dousing him and causing him to spring to his feet in acute embarrassment.

'Sorry, Susan, I didn't mean to, er – I just got carried away.' Ray cut a pathetic figure. His best shirt dripping wet, his face crimson, not knowing what to say or do.

Once again Susan felt guilty. She stood up and held him. 'No, it's me who should be sorry. You were only doing what it's natural for a boy to want to do.'

Raymond nodded his agreement through his discomfort, completely baffled by Susan's rapidly changing emotions. 'I think I'd better take me shirt off though,' he said. 'Blimey! you don't do things by halves, do you?'

He removed his shirt and placed it on the fireguard to dry.

'I'll wash it for you if you like,' offered Susan.

'No, it's okay. Me mam'll wash it in the morning.'

Raymond lay down on the floor in front of the fire and studied this complex girl smiling down at him. His pale-skinned body much better muscled than most sixteen-year-olds, mainly due to his love of sport. She knelt beside him and kissed him lightly on the lips, then said,

'I'm not ready for – you know what. It's nothing to do with you.'

'That's okay,' he accepted. 'I'm a bit scared myself. Certainly of going, well, all the way and all that.'

'All the way and all what?' she teased, gently running her fingers across the hard muscles of his stomach.

Ray closed his eyes to enjoy the tenderness of the moment as her fingers wandered over his body. His relaxed concave stomach leaving a small space between the waistband of his trousers, into which she allowed her hand to teasingly venture before withdrawing it, then gently caressing his stomach and his chest and his neck and his face. Unconsciously aroused by her little game, she allowed her hand to venture downwards time and time again, each time a little further. Ray was becoming quite disturbed and could feel himself rising up to meet her. He opened his eyes, but she wasn't looking at him, her eyes were fascinated by the daring of her own hand, her face was flushed with an excitement matched by his own.

Reaching under her dress, he placed a hand on the inside of her thigh. It felt glossy and warm and she froze momentarily, as though making a momentous but reluctant decision.

'Don't you dare, Raymond Donoghue!' she said eventually.

Ray retrieved his hand, wondering whether to protest about the unfairness of it all, but decided against it. Their eyes met and Susan held him defiantly in her gaze as she ran her hand downwards once again, this time just touching him. Both hearts were thumping now as she stroked his stomach. Then, with a tantalising slowness, she allowed her fingers to move downwards once again, reaching down to hold him. There was a smooth, velvety feel to him that surprised and pleased her and she held him and caressed him with an exquisite gentleness he would probably never know again.

With her free hand, she undid his trousers, partly to release his erection and partly out of curiosity – she exposed him just as he exploded in a great moan of ecstasy, leaving her aroused and frustrated and knowing there was nothing left for her.

Susan hurried home that night engulfed in remorse and self-recrimination at her weakness. What must Raymond think of her? What would Freddie think if he knew? What if she'd gone all the way and lost her virginity? What would Freddie have thought of her then? She could still picture Raymond as she'd left him. Still lying there, eyes closed, a half smile on his face. His erection slowly subsiding in the light of the flickering fire.

Fancy a good Catholic girl like her being seduced by the sins of the flesh. And why did the memory still excite her? Did she really want to repeat it? Perhaps next time go a little further. Confession and absolution was the only answer. But who would she confess to? Certainly not Father O'Flaherty nor Father Proctor. They both knew here too well. They even called her Susan in the confessional where she was supposed to be anonymous. No, it had to be Father Helliwell in the school chapel, where confessions were heard every Friday. She rarely went there and anyway she could always disguise her voice a little. Her identity would remain secret.

'Good film?' asked Dorothy, looking up from a book as Susan came in and flopped down in a chair.

'Yes, thank you.'

'Where'd you go afterwards? Anywhere nice?' Dorothy wasn't trying to pry, but she was new at this parent business and felt she should keep herself informed of the whereabouts of her two charges.

Susan felt like telling Dorothy to mind her own business. Despite having told her aunt that she was forgiven for the William episode, she would probably hold it against her until the day they got their brother back, at least. However, she chose to be polite.

'Went back to Ray's house.'

'That's nice, meet his mam and dad, did you?'

She caught Susan blushing and instantly knew what she'd been up to. Smiling, she held Susan's hand. 'I was your age once, you know. They weren't in, were they?'

Susan said nothing. Dorothy knew she'd need to pick her words carefully – if she was to say anything at all.

'Look, Susan,' she said. 'I'm not a Catholic as you know, and I know it's difficult for a pretty young girl like you to, er – to resist her natural biological urges, if you get my meaning.' She was blushing now and Susan was squeezing her hand.

'It's alright, Auntie. It's not quite what you think – we didn't go all the way. In fact, we didn't even go half way.'

'Oh good, I, er – I was hoping you hadn't. Apart from anything else, you're under age.'

'It's just that…' started Susan.

'Just that what, love?'

'I'm going to have to go to confession.'

'Ah!' said Dorothy, wondering where the half way point was.

'I thought I'd go to the school chapel, Father Helliwell doesn't know me as well as the priests at church.'

'Sounds like a great plan to me. I know that's what I'd do – if I were a Catholic. You could disguise your voice as well, you're good at voices.'

'Hmm! Do you think God might object to that?'

'I think He'd regard it as a definite plus – making good use of your God-given talents and all that.'

'I'll do my Irish.'

'Oh, yes – that's your best one. Let me know how you go on, won't you?'

Susan laughed, 'I most certainly will not!'

Dorothy shrugged, disappointed. Susan stood

240

up to go upstairs to bed. She turned back to her auntie.

'Auntie Dorothy,' she said.

'What, love?'

'Thanks.'

Dorothy went back to her book, happy at having been able to offer such useful parental advice.

'Bless me, Father, for oi have sinned. It is two weeks since me last confession Father...'

Susan had chosen to adopt the lilting County Mayo brogue of Sister Claire. Mimicry being a talent of Susan's. Especially her impersonation of the pretty young nun who taught geography and history to 5A.

'Father, oi've committed a sin of der flesh wid a young man!'

She heard the old priest catch his breath. 'Go on, my child,' he said quietly.

'Oi touched a part of his body dat's forbidden, causing him to,' she paused, wondering if she should use the word in such a holy place, '... to ejaculate, Father!'

She cringed half expecting a bolt of lightning to come crashing down on her.

'Is that all, my child?' asked the priest gently, as though trying to coax more out of her.

She felt like saying, 'Isn't that enough?' – it was certainly her most productive confession to date.

'Yes, Father,' she replied truthfully, her accent still in place.

'Nothing else?'

'No, Father.'

There was a long silence before the priest said, 'For your penance I want you to say a Rosary each day for seven days. Now make a good Act of Contrition!'

Seven Rosaries! This was tantamount to capital punishment in confessional terms. Even Mary McAllister had never been given seven Rosaries and she'd definitely been 'all the way' with Kevin Murray from St Thomas's. Susan finished her Act of Contrition and stood up to leave.

'Thank you, Father Helliwell,' she said politely.

'Goodbye, Sister Claire,' sighed the shocked priest.

Chapter Eighteen

Dorothy read the letter twice. Assuming she'd misunderstood it the first time. But there was no mistake.

...We are obliged to inform you that William Bairstow has been successfully placed for adoption. It is the express wish of his adoptive parents that their identity is not to be revealed and we are bound by their wishes in this respect...

She handed the letter to Susan who read it with increasing concern.

'They can't do this, can they, Auntie?' she gasped.

'I don't think so – but it appears they have.' She buried her head in her hands. The letter was from the Fairbank Home in Huddersfield, the last address they had for William. She'd written to formally request that William be returned to them immediately.

'I'll go and talk to them,' decided Dorothy.

'And how the devil are you going to get there?' snapped Susan resentfully. 'Hop there on one damn leg?'

'If I have to,' replied Dorothy softly. 'One way or another, William's coming back to live with us. It's just a question of time.'

Susan took some time to regain her composure, but she didn't apologise to her auntie for snapping at her. She read the letter again.

'I'll ring Freddie,' she said. 'His dad'll know what to do.'

'And I'll ring a solicitor, we need to find out what's going on as soon as possible – then I'll go talk to them, on one leg if need be!'

Her last remark was lost on Susan, who was already on her way out, leaving Dorothy hopping around frustratedly. 'I think the first thing we need in this house is a bloody telephone,' she cursed to herself as she finally got her coat on and hobbled off on her crutches to the phone box on Paradine Hill.

She was due to start her new job with Frank Sackfield in a few days. He'd been round and congratulated her on her release and told her the job was still on offer. 'It was pretty common knowledge you'd been badly done by. I knew if I hung fire for a while, the barmy buggers'd see sense. Didn't reckon on you coming home with a broken leg though!'

243

'I don't need a leg to do your book-keeping,' said Dorothy. 'The worst part is limping to work.'

Frank had offered to give her a lift until her leg was fully mended.

'You'll do no such thing, Mr Sackfield,' argued Dorothy. 'You've been good enough to give me a job. I'll do the rest – you'll not be disappointed in me.'

Susan was just emerging from the phone box as Dorothy arrived.

'The Brigadier asked why it had been so long since anybody had been to see our William,' she said, with uncharacteristic coldness. 'I didn't know what to say – I could hardly tell him we'd been told he was dead.'

Susan's words cut into Dorothy like a knife.

'I thought you'd told Freddie the truth,' she sighed.

'I did, but he didn't tell the Brigadier.'

'I'll tell him then. He needs to know the full story – the most important thing is to get William back. What he thinks of me is unimportant. I'll ring the solicitor first.'

She rang Mr Baldwin, the solicitor who'd represented her in court. Not that she'd been particularly impressed by him – just that he was the only lawyer she'd ever had anything to do with.

'Mr Baldwin,' she asked, after telling him the details over the phone. 'All I want to know is – can they do this?'

'I honestly don't know, Mrs Bairstow. You'd better come in and see me, oh, and while you're in here, there's the question of suing for compensation and injury for your stay in prison.'

'I'm not worried about that.'

'It's me that's worried, Mrs Bairstow – you'll need some money to pay me.'

'Oh!'

'Friday morning at ten okay?'

'That'll be fine, thank you.'

'I've been on to Fairbank Home,' began Victor Baldwin, 'and they seem to think everything's above board. They don't think they've done anything wrong.'

'But surely I should have been told.'

'It seems you weren't his legal guardian.'

'I'm his aunt, for God's sake.'

'Not a blood relative, and apparently...' he hesitated, trying to put this next bit as delicately as possible, 'no one went to visit him for a period of two years!'

Dorothy felt an intense dejection. Susan, sitting beside her, didn't trust herself to say anything.

'Look – it's maybe not as hopeless as it seems,' he added. 'Family matters are quite delicate things, and the feelings of William and his brother and sister may have to be taken into account. Also it could well be that the people who adopted him may want to give him up when they find out the true circumstances. I understand he's a bit of a handful.'

'How long's it all going to take?' asked Susan.

'If we have to go to court it could be months – but,' added Baldwin, trying somehow to soften the blow, 'it may well be that we can deal with this outside court. The only thing I ask of you is, please – no matter how frustrated you feel – don't interfere. This is a very delicate matter. I'll keep you informed.'

'Every step of the way,' insisted Dorothy.

'Every step of the way,' agreed Baldwin.

Chapter Nineteen

This was the first time in the two weeks since she'd started working for Frank Sackfield that Dorothy had attempted the journey to work without crutches and she wasn't finding it easy. The journey had been somehow easier using crutches but now she walked with a stick, cursing regularly to herself, a legacy of her time in prison, eyes glued to the pavement in dread of slipping on some unseen crack in the pavement. She cursed her own stupidity at attempting to walk to work with a broken leg – and she cursed Victor Baldwin.

Baldwin's idea of keeping her informed 'every step of the way' had amounted to just the one letter she'd received that morning saying he'd now applied for a court hearing date and that there was no point him approaching the Fairbank Home as the matter was now *sub-judice*, whatever that meant.

To cap it all, this was the morning her dear old dad chose to stop and have a chat with her. It was almost as if he'd been waiting for her. She was just rounding the corner from the bottom of

Paradine Hill on to Eccleston Road when his car swished to a halt beside her. She glanced to her left before carrying on. She'd planned on resting on the seat beside the tram stop but gave up that idea as it would mean talking to her father.

'Bugger off!' she snapped brusquely.

'Oh, I'm buggering off alright,' he sneered. 'I just hope you remember that promise I made a couple o' years back.'

Dorothy remembered Sid's threat only too well, but she wasn't about to give him that satisfaction. She jabbed the end of her walking stick viciously towards his open window, making him jerk his head away. His face turned ugly momentarily until he realised this was the reaction she wanted. The sneer returned.

'Oh, and give my regards to Frank – tell him it's nothing personal, not between me and him anyway.'

He drove off, still sniggering to himself leaving Dorothy wondering what the hell he was up to.

Frank Sackfield walked into the office later that Monday morning, slamming the door behind him with a bad-tempered bang. A frown creased his usually cheerful face. He was a joiner by trade, although since returning to his business after being invalided out of the army with various 'hard to get at' bits of shrapnel still embedded in his body, he'd decided against going back on the tools and left the hard graft to fitter men than himself.

Dorothy was there to greet him, pouring boiling water into a chipped teapot. They shared the inner office which was mostly occupied by a huge desk with a chair at either side. On Frank's side was a telephone, four large pebbles weighting down a site plan, various scale rules, several cigarette packets, a pub ash tray, three cluttered wire trays, labelled, IN, OUT and SHAKE IT ALL ABOUT and a battered tin mug. Dorothy's side was well ordered; invoices ready to write up, a couple of ledgers, an antique Remington typewriter, a jam jar full of pencils, a bottle of Stephen's ink and a fountain pen.

'Problem, Frank?' asked Dorothy, who'd been working there long enough to spot a change in her boss's mood.

'You might say that,' replied Frank. 'You know that site on Moorcroft Road in Harrogate?'

Dorothy nodded. He was talking about a building site he'd just bought for a quality twenty-two house development. His most ambitious project to date.

'Well, someone's just bought the big field at the back and there seems to be a big problem with my drainage rights. If I can't drain through that field, I'm what's known in the trade as well and truly knackered!'

There was a fifteen-acre building plot at the back of Frank's site on which he had a verbal agreement with the owner to buy in small lots once he'd finished building on the first sight.

'I thought you were buying that site, Frank?' asked Dorothy.

'Apparently not,' said Frank despairingly. 'Money talks in this business. Sid Allerdyce came right out of the blue and bought the whole lot.

Doesn't make sense. He builds bread and butter houses, always has. This is choice land, he must have laid out a fortune for it. It'll take him three or four years to sell a site that size in this day and age. That's a hell of a lot of money to have standing around doing nothing. Unless he knows something that I don't!'

Dorothy's heart sank. So that was it! The lengths her father would go to just to get back at her. There must be more to this than pure revenge, there'd be something in it for Sid, that's for sure.

'Look, Frank,' she said. 'You know I said I'd had experience in the trade when you interviewed me?'

Frank nodded, 'You did – and you obviously weren't waffling. You know more than most of my men.'

'I learned all I know from my father – Sid Allerdyce.'

'What? You're Sid Allerdyce's daughter? That's good, isn't it? Why didn't you mention it before? Come to think of it, why are you working for me and not for him?'

Dorothy looked at Frank, waiting for him to answer his own question. 'Oh no! You don't get on with him, do you?' he moaned.

'That's putting it mildly, I'm afraid,' replied Dorothy. 'My father is an ignorant, arrogant pig of a man!'

'And those are just his good points,' grumbled Frank. 'So, there's no truth in this business of blood being thicker than water then?'

'None at all.'

'And we can't expect any favours from him on your account?'

'Quite the opposite, I'm afraid.'

'What? Surely you don't think he's doing this to have a go at you?'

Dorothy eyed Frank sadly. He was a nice-looking man, tall and strong with powerful arms developed by years of hammering and sawing. A thick head of hair going grey now, above a good-humoured, weathered face. His marriage, like so many others, had been a casualty of war. Elaine, his ever-loving wife, had ended up loving a visiting Yank and now lived in Ohio with Frank's beloved son and her new husband.

'I don't think, I know, Frank,' Dorothy said apologetically. 'It seems I'm a liability to you – if you want me to, I'll leave.'

'I think it might be too late now. Sid's got the smell of a quick profit and I don't think you leaving's gonna make much difference now.'

'Sorry, Fra...'

Frank waved her apology away. 'Not your fault, shame though – I was beginning to look upon you as one of my biggest assets. Strikes me you can run the company as well as I can.'

'Well, maybe from a business point of view,' she agreed. 'You do tend to be a bit, well, slap-dash – but I know damn all about the practical side.'

'That's why we'd make such a great team. I'm useless at business, always have been. All I can do is build good houses.'

'What happens if my father refuses you drainage rights?'

'Apart from me going bankrupt, you mean?'

'That bad?'

'Bad enough,' said Frank miserably. 'It turns a twenty-two house development into a site for four pairs of semis, mind you everyone would have a back garden as big as a football pitch. Might just make enough to pay the bank back for the land. Assuming they give me building finance – which they won't.'

'So you'd have to sell it as a site for eight houses?'

'Correct,' said Frank. 'That's the new valuation the bank's going to put on it as soon as they find out what's happening.'

'And that's the price my father will get it for when the bank puts it up for sale,' concluded Dorothy. 'Doesn't make it such a bad deal for him then, does it? Seems to me there's method in his madness.'

She walked over to a wall on which was pinned a location plan of the site. 'Which is my father's field on this plan?'

Frank picked up a red pencil and outlined an area behind his site. 'All this lot,' he said dejectedly. 'Right up to Finnestone Lane.'

'And that's his access, is it?' Finnestone Lane?'

'At the moment. He might well choose to use Moorcroft Road if he buys my site.'

Dorothy sat down, chewing the end of a pencil and staring back at the plan. Something wasn't right here. A germ of an idea was beginning to form in her sharp brain.

'What are you thinking?' asked her boss. 'There's something going on inside that brain of yours.'

Dorothy scratched her head with the point of the pencil. 'Has my father actually bought the land?'

'Bought and paid for, in full as far as I know,' replied Frank.

'No, he'd never do that if he could avoid it,' mused Dorothy, chewing the end of the pencil off, picking it daintily out of her mouth and dropping it in the ashtray. 'He could have offered the owner a similar deal to you, only on better terms. He's taking a gamble, is good old Sidney. He's like that. Something to show off about in front of his business pals.'

The telephone rang and Dorothy picked it up, still staring at the plan.

'Good morning, Sackfield Builders. I'll see if he's in, who shall I say is speaking? One moment, Mr Pomeroy.'

She covered up the earpiece with one hand, 'It's a Mr Pomeroy? Needs to speak to your urgently!'

'Bloody hell! How's he found out this quickly?'

'Not your bank manager?'

Frank nodded grimly and took the receiver from Dorothy. 'Hello, George, how are you? Good, the Moorcroft Road site? Yes, I'm expecting planning permission any day now. Pardon? You've heard what? No, there's probably some mistake. Tell you what, I'll check into it and ring you back as soon as I know anything – yes – tomorrow at the latest, bye, Mr Pomeroy.'

Frank sank back into his chair, pale with worry. 'He's found out. I didn't know myself till an hour ago. Who the hell's told him?'

Dorothy eyed him sadly. 'Do you really need to ask, Frank?'

She started on the end of another pencil. Sid was playing tricks. He was out to destroy Frank just because she worked for him, *and* make some money into the bargain. She knew it was a gamble her father was taking, and where there was a gamble there was a catch – and she'd a good idea what it was. She picked up the phone and dialled Freddie's number in Harrogate.

Dorothy looked around the table at her surrogate family. Susan's attitude to her over this past month had been lukewarm at best. Jimmy was the same old Jimmy, often bridging the rift between her and Susan and oblivious, it seemed, to any bad atmosphere in the house.

'Saw your dad today,' mentioned Jimmy in passing, as he excused himself from the table.

'My dad?' queried Dorothy, her dessert spoon hovering an inch from her open mouth, dripping custard onto the tablecloth. 'How do you know my dad?'

'From the time you asked him if he still farted like Flamborough foghorn,' grinned Jimmy.

'Would that be the time she asked him if he was still a big loud-mouthed toilet?' inquired Susan of her brother.

'Do you know, Susan, I do believe it was, only she didn't say toilet, she said sh–!'

'I know what I said!' interrupted Dorothy quickly. 'I just didn't realise you were listening.'

'The whole street was listening, Auntie Dorothy,' said Susan, getting up to leave the table. 'You certainly seem to have a way with your relatives!'

'If you knew him you'd realise why I...!' Dorothy started to explain, but Susan was gone. Dorothy looked at Jimmy, 'He's not a nice man,' she said.

'I know, Auntie Dorothy, so does our Susan. She's just bein' awkward.'

Dorothy nodded, maybe Susan had good reason to be awkward. 'Anyway,' she said, 'where did you see my father?'

'This morning on the way to school,' said Jimmy. 'He was just coming out of that bank on Priest Lane. He's put a lot of weight on.'

'You what? The Northern Bank? I wonder what he was doing in there, he's always banked at the Yorkshire Penny.'

Dorothy got up from her desk when she heard Frank arrive the following morning. She was standing at the outer door of his wooden office cum store room as he climbed out of his van.

'Are you in the mood for a gamble, Frank?' she called out to him.

'I'm actually in the mood for slitting my throat,' he called back, as he walked across the yard. 'What sort of a gamble?'

'One of the kids saw my father coming out of your bank yesterday morning.'

'That figures,' said Frank, following her back into the office. 'Pomeroy had to get the information from someone involved in the deal. It'd suit your dad to blow the whistle on me. Hurry things along a bit.' He sat down and lit up a cigarette, then remembered his manners and offered Dorothy one.

'That's what I thought,' agreed Dorothy, declining his offer with a wave of her hand. 'Then I thought, "Why didn't my father just ring Pomeroy up with the information? Why bother to go in and see him?" My father hates bank managers, he'd never go near one if he could help it. That was his accountant's job. My father's only ever happy when he's up to his knees in mud.'

'What're you getting at?' asked a mystified Frank, flicking through the morning post and putting it all down in disgust when he saw no cheques were there.

'I think Pomeroy and my father are cooking something up between them,' said Dorothy.

'Could be. Your dad's account's a pretty good one to have. I've known managers bend the rules to secure smaller accounts than that.'

'How much do you owe the bank?' asked Dorothy.

'Not a fortune, about a thousand, but if they call it in I'm out of business – and that'll cost me a lot more than a thousand quid.' He looked curiously at Dorothy, 'Anyway, what's this gamble you want me to take?'

Dorothy took a cigarette from Frank's packet, lit it up and blew a contemplative cloud of smoke over the top of her boss's head.

'Ring Pomeroy back and tell him you've found a way around the problem. If he asks how, just blind him with science – but make it sound convincing! Then when my father makes you an offer for your land, call his bluff, kick him out on his ear! Don't let him think you're in the least bit worried.'

Frank looked at her and nodded slowly. She had a quick, devious mind, much quicker than his. She was able to view the situation more dispassionately, see aspects that were clouded to his blinkered vision. All Frank could think about now was avoiding going broke, a damage limitation exercise. Sid Allerdyce knew Frank well and was relying on him reacting in a certain way; anything else and Sid would be worried. But Dorothy knew her father well and planned on playing him at his own game, albeit with Frank's money.

Frank was in the yard when Sid arrived later that morning. Sid arrogantly walked uninvited into the office and sat himself down in Frank's chair. A half smoked cigar protruding from his rubbery mouth dropped ash onto his suit. Frank let him there for ten minutes before he came in.

'Thought I'd try it out for size, Frank,' smirked Sid, jabbing his cigar out in Frank's ash tray among Frank's Senior Service stubs.

'You'll need a much bigger chair for your fat arse, Sid. Is there something you want, I'm a bit busy at the moment?' Frank retaliated with an air of impatience, elbowing Sid to one side as he took something he didn't need out of a drawer.

'I won't beat about the bush,' said Sid. 'That's not my style.'

'No, the only thing you beat are small children!' cut in Dorothy hotly, sitting down opposite her father.

'Not often enough by the look of things,' sniggered Sid. He returned his attention to

Frank, pushing back his chair to allow himself room to put his feet on the desk. 'Your bank's about to foreclose on your overdraft, Frank lad. They've found you've included in your list of assets a piece of land that's only worth a quarter of what they thought it was worth, you naughty lad!'

Frank returned Sid's belligerent gaze with a mildly bored expression, which had the desired effect of unsettling Sid, who continued. 'When they do, and your creditors find out, they'll all be down on you like a ton of bricks. Ever been bankrupt, Frank? Unpleasant experience so they tell me.'

The telephone rang, Dorothy picked it up and pressed a button to transfer it to the outer office. 'It's for me, Frank,' she explained, 'I'll take it through there.'

'I don't know,' sneered Sid. 'Allowing your staff to take private phone calls. No wonder your business is in the shit. Tell you what I'll do. I'll give you a grand for your bit of land. Pay off your overdraft, what do you say?'

'I paid three times that much for it!' snapped Frank, dropping his guard for a second. 'Anyway, how do you know how much my overdraft is, unless you're in league with Pomeroy?'

Sid held out his arms, and shrugged his shoulders, 'If you think I'm doing something illegal Frank, sue me, phone the police. I'm a businessman, just looking for the best deal.'

Frank knew he had him there. He was doing nothing illegal. Just unethical. A word alien to most businessmen. Sid took out his chequebook.

'Look, Frank lad, as an act of good faith I'll write you a cheque out now, just sign this contract to transfer the land to me and your bank's off your back just like that.'

He took a contract from his inside pocket and laid it on the desk in front of Frank, who made no move to pick it up. Sid looked up at him patronisingly. 'It's either this or let the bank foreclose. They'll have to sell to me. No one else is likely to show an interest and you'll finish up with, what? Nothing, after all the vultures have picked at what's left!'

Frank stared at the soles of Sid's shoes. Left to his own devices, this is when he would have capitulated. Accepted that he'd been done over by a craftier businessman. He then looked round at Dorothy as she spoke on the telephone in the outer office, she turned and winked at him and he felt a surge of relief that she was on his side.

'I see, and just how long have you been planning this, you fat-arsed bastard?' said Frank sarcastically, picking up the contract and tearing it down the middle. 'Get out before I kick you out! I'd sooner give the land away than sell it to you.'

'The bank won't let you do that, Frank,' retorted Sid, unsettled that Frank hadn't backed down as he expected. This wasn't the Frank he knew. 'The Northern's got first charge on it. Pomeroy won't be too pleased when I tell him you've turned down my offer!'

He stamped out of the office past Dorothy, who was just saying, 'Thanks, Freddie,' before putting the phone down. 'Bye, Sidney!' she called after

Sid, who hated being called Sidney. Frank joined her at the door as Sid roared off in a cloud of dust.

'He offered me a grand for the land,' he said grimly. 'Trouble is, that's all it's worth without drainage rights onto his land.'

'Maybe not,' said Dorothy cheerfully, walking back inside. 'I've got some interesting news. That was a friend of mine on the phone. His father's one of the Harrogate Planning Committee – and no way will my father be allowed access on to Finnestone Lane. It's apparently much too narrow to take all the additional traffic. The only viable access is through your site.'

'Do you think Allerdyce knows this?'

'Oh yes, I'm absolutely sure he does,' said Dorothy, 'He'll have known before he applied – you see that's his big gamble. He needs both your bank and you to think he can get access to his site from Finnestone Lane, even though he knows he can't.'

'Christ! It's a hell of a gamble he's taking! So why don't we just tell the bank all this?'

'Because we're not supposed to know. It'll be at least a month before his application's officially rejected, during which time he'll have got your bank to force you out – and he'll be able to pick up your land for next to nothing!'

'The crafty old bugger,' There was a hint of admiration in Frank's voice.

Dorothy shrugged, not sharing Frank's grudging admiration of her father. 'That's how he's always done business. He won't see it as much of a gamble though, not with your bank manager in

259

his pocket.' She eyed Frank seriously. 'You'll have to act quickly to stop the bank foreclosing. He'll sit on Pomeroy until he's got his hands on your land. Without your bit, his land isn't worth that!' She snapped her fingers.

Frank was shuffling through a sheaf of papers he'd just taken out of a drawer. He picked out one and studied it carefully.

'Seven days' notice,' he said dejectedly. 'They can give me seven day's notice then foreclose.'

'I think your call to the bank probably bought you a bit more time,' reasoned Dorothy. 'Pomeroy's not going to be too sure of anything now. He won't do anything until my father jumps on him and convinces him you're bluffing. I reckon we could have as much as a couple of weeks to raise the thousand pounds.'

The phone rang again. It was a man wanting his roof repairing, she handed it to Frank. 'In the meantime,' she smiled, 'we carry on as normal.'

Dorothy eyed her family as they finished their meal, wondering whether she was about to be fair to them.

'My boss is in trouble,' she announced. 'He needs money to stop my father taking over his business.'

'Your dad would kick you out if that happened, wouldn't he?' said Susan.

'Yes, he would. But that's not what I'm concerned about. If Mr Sackfield could find a thousand pounds now, it would be worth a lot more in a few months' time.'

Jimmy was about to leave the table; this conversation was of little interest to him, but Dorothy stopped him. 'Stay here, Jimmy, this concerns you as well.'

'I've been thinking about us giving him the thousand pounds, in exchange for a share in his business.'

'We haven't got a thousand pounds,' said Susan sharply.

'*I* certainly haven't,' agreed Dorothy. 'But you two have. We'd have to take a mortgage out on the house, and give Frank the money from your two accounts.'

'How's this going to help us get William back?' asked Susan illogically.

'This has got nothing to do with William, as well you know,' sighed Dorothy impatiently. She'd made a vow never to lose her temper with Susan, no matter how much she goaded her about William. Deep down she knew she deserved all she got. 'We're doing all we can to get William back. The solicitor's waiting for a court hearing date. I'm as frustrated as you are, believe me.'

'Then why bother with Frank Sackfield?' retorted Susan. 'Haven't we got enough to think about? And why risk our money on someone we hardly know?'

'If I thought it was a risk I wouldn't let you do it,' persisted Dorothy. 'Anyway, I'm not going to argue with you, it's your money and I've no right to ask.'

An embarrassed silence followed before Jimmy piped up, 'You can have my money, Auntie Dorothy.'

'Thanks, Jimmy, that's kind of you, but I'm afraid it's not enough. Let's just forget I ever mentioned it.'

Susan was shifting uncomfortably in her chair. All this talk of finance was way above her head. Freddie had organised the buying of the house for her and she knew she needed to be guided by Dorothy on many matters before she felt confident to face the world on her own. She knew she was being unreasonable, petulant even, but the anger she felt against her aunt for placing her baby brother in this awful position wouldn't go away.

Dorothy stood up to leave for work, taking her coat from the hook on the back of the scullery door and waving goodbye with her stick she went out of the door.

'I think you're rotten,' said Jimmy.

'I don't care what you think,' Susan answered sullenly. 'She shouldn't have done what she did!'

'She'd no need to look after us neither,' argued Jimmy. 'She could have sent me an' you to an 'ome.'

'Wish she had – at least we'd all have been together!'

'And she'd no need ter belt Simpson wiv a stool neither,' persisted Jimmy. 'She might have got hung fer that – and she only did it fer you. I think yer rotten!'

'Ohhh – go tell her we'll do it then!' snapped his sister. 'I'm getting ready for school.'

Jimmy didn't hear the last bit, he was already out of the door in pursuit of his aunt whom he seemed to understand better than most.

Frank was already there when Dorothy arrived, looking more relaxed than he'd been for a couple of days.

'I've found a commerical bank who'll lend me six hundred against the land,' he said. 'That leaves just four hundred to find.'

'Frank!' said Dorothy, trying to contain her exasperation. 'Under the circumstances, you need to own the land outright. You're just robbing Peter to pay Paul. We're heading for a stand-off with my father. We can't afford to have other interested parties.'

'Oh,' said Frank, gloomily. Dejected that his scheme was so easily shot down.

'Don't worry,' smiled Dorothy. 'I think I can raise the money. However, there is a catch.'

'There's always a catch,' moaned Frank, 'go on, what is it?'

'I want to buy into your company, or at least my family does. I'm offering you a thousand pounds for a fifty-per-cent share in Frank Sackfield Builders.'

'Fifty-per-cent? Blimey! You don't do things by halves do you?'

'Well, yes actually,' she laughed.

'Oh, right,' said Frank, realising what he'd said. 'You know there's a bit of your dad in you, don't you?'

'Don't start insulting me, Frank, or I'll withdraw my offer,' she said sharply. She didn't like being compared to her father, even jokingly.

'If you'd offered me twice that last week I'd have kicked you out on your ear,' grumbled

Frank. He held out his hand, 'Forty-nine-per-cent and it's a deal. The extra one-per-cent means a lot to me.'

'It's a deal,' said Dorothy, taking his hand.

Frank looked at her as he shook her hand warmly and knew he was going to like being her partner.

As Dorothy forecast, the nervous Mr Pomeroy procrastinated almost a week before he put Frank on seven days' notice to clear his overdraft, giving Dorothy just enough time to raise a quick mortgage through the commercial bank Frank was going to use. On the seventh day they were sitting in the office as her father's car pulled into the yard.

Allerdyce, Pomeroy and a third man entered together. Sid was making no attempt to conceal his glee at what was about to happen. Pomeroy was long and thin with a cheap pin-stripe suit and the constipated expression of a man with something nasty under his nose. He pompously placed a piece of paper on the table.

'Mr Sackfield, this is a possession order for the land at Moorcroft Road, Harrogate. It comes into force at close of business tonight. I thought I'd present you with the opportunity to clear your debts now by selling on to Mr Allerdyce, thus avoiding bank and solicitor's charges, which can be quite prohibitive. I've brought my assistant, Mr Ellis, along to witness the signatures.'

'Could you all wait in the outer office, please, we're on our tea break,' said Frank impatiently.

'But...' protested Pomeroy.

'Out!' roared Frank.

Dorothy stood and ushered the three of them into the outer office, where they waited, not knowing what was happening. The outer office, as it was called, contained a kitchen table, a telephone, a sink, a worktop and gas ring, on which was balanced a battered kettle. The only place to sit was on a pile of cement bags, left there for reasons best known to the yard man.

'Sorry about that,' apologised Dorothy with studied insincerity, 'but this is not a good time for Mr Sackfield,' she said.

'No, quite,' said Mr Pomeroy.

'Bloody awful time, I hope,' growled Sid.

'It's his haemorrhoids, you see,' she explained. 'He's a martyr to his haemorrhoids. Oh, by the way, while you're here. I wonder if you could put this cheque in his account? Save my legs and all that.'

She casually handed Mr Ellis a banker's draft for a thousand pounds.

'And if you'd like to sign this receipt, just to say it's safely in your hands. We wouldn't want anything to happen to it, would we?'

Pomeroy went pale. Sid's mouth opened and shut with shock. Ellis, who had nothing to do with the subterfuge, happily signed the receipt, leaving Sid pacing up and down, clenching and unclenching his fists. Frank appeared at the door.

'Our solicitor will be in touch, Mr Pomeroy, instructing your bank to release us from the charge. Will there be anything else?' he asked innocently.

'Yes, there damn well is something else!' roared

265

Sid. 'I need that bloody land and by hell I'm going to have it!'

'Tell me, Sidney dear,' sneered Dorothy. 'Did you plan all this just to have a go at me? Shame you had to drag Mr Pomeroy into it – you've probably cost him his job now.'

Pomeroy was now in a state of shock, with Mr Ellis looking accusingly at him. Sid was storming up and down kicking at anything in his way and shouting obscenities at Frank's yard man, who was quietly brewing himself a pot of tea in the corner.

Dorothy continued to bait her father. 'We all know you won't get permission to access your site on to Finnestone Lane! That application of yours is a cheap sham to fool the banks. Your only access is through Frank's site!'

She then turned to Pomeroy, whose jaw had fallen open with horror, at this piece of information. 'Surely not even you were fooled by that transparent little ruse, were you, Mr Pomeroy?' Dorothy put her hand to her mouth, as though shocked, 'Oh, dear!' she went on. 'I do believe you were!'

Pomeroy flopped down on the pile of cement bags.

'I wouldn't sit there, Mr Pomeroy,' warned Dorothy, 'that's how you get piles. You see, Mr Pomeroy, my dear daddy was banking on you kicking Frank off his land so he could buy it for next to nothing. What the silly man forgot to tell you, was that without Frank's land, his own land's worth, to use banking terminology, practically sod all! Will you still be wanting to take his account, Mr Pomeroy? I'm sure the Yorkshire Penny Bank will be only too delighted to hand it over!'

Frank was silently hoping that Dorothy would shut up at this point as Sid seemed to be taking things quite badly. Foolishly, however, she just couldn't resist one final taunt. Confronting her father, whose face was contorted with rage, she announced smugly:

'By the way, Daddy dear, as Frank's a member of that golf club that keeps turning you down he'll be able to tell all your friends there what a big brainless shit you really are!'

This proved too much for Sid. He punched Dorothy full in the mouth, then flung himself at Frank, who fell backwards into his office, punching wildly in self defence. Sid had gone berserk. With a strength born of madness, he had Frank on the floor with his hands around his throat, squeezing tighter and tighter until Frank's arms stopped flailing about.

A full milk bottle smashed over Sid's head causing him to release his grip and soaking his now unconscious body with Co-op Dairies sterilised milk. Mr Ellis, a youngish, broad-shouldered man, threw the broken bottle to one side, then heaved Frank over on to his stomach, frantically trying to pump air back into the builder's choking lungs.

Dorothy was just coming round, her face a mass of blood, when Frank coughed back to life. She staggered to the phone and dialled 999 asking for police and ambulance. The sight of her father lying unconscious and Mr Ellis tending to

Frank, gave Dorothy a fair idea of what had happened.

'Thanks, Mr, er…?'

'Ellis, Peter Ellis, I'm afraid I had to hit your father with a bottle, to stop him choking Mr Sackfield – I was sort of trained to do this in the army.'

'What? Hit the Germans over the head with milk bottles?'

'Well, we were taught to improvise,' he explained.

'I'm sure the bank will be very grateful to both you and the army, Mr Ellis. I know Frank will be.'

Frank sat up and squinted at Dorothy through an eye that hadn't quite closed yet. 'He's a bad loser your dad, isn't he?' he croaked. 'Mind you, Dorothy, you did go on a bit!'

Dorothy was nodding painfully as the police and ambulance arrived. Mr Ellis advised the police to take away both Sid and Mr Pomeroy, as he suspected possible bank fraud. He then climbed into the ambulance taking Dorothy and Frank to hospital.

'You're probably wondering why I came along,' he ventured.

'There was no need for it,' assured Dorothy. 'You did enough for us back there.'

'I'm looking upon this as a damage limitation exercise,' he said. 'Under the circumstances I'm sure the Northern Bank will wish to review your account favourably and seek to help you in any way they can.'

'Providing we keep our mouths shut about your

Mr Pomeroy?' grumbled Frank cynically.

'Well, I doubt if he'll be with us much longer, but yes, we would appreciate a certain amount of discretion,' admitted Mr Ellis.

Frank was about to tell him where the bank could stick their discretion, when Dorothy placed a gentle hand across his mouth.

'We'd like you to arrange us a meeting with Mr Pomeroy's replacement as soon as possible,' she said sweetly, but looking daggers at Frank. 'Wouldn't we, Mr Sackfield?'

Frank nodded, knowing his fifty-one-per-cent was never going to be enough to out-vote Dorothy.

Peter Ellis looked up and smiled at the group of people who'd just come into his office.

'Ah! So it's you, is it?' grinned Frank. 'They said there was a new manager. I suppose congratulations are in order.'

'Thank you,' smiled Peter. 'Oh, and thanks for pushing my promotion along. Anyway, how are you all?'

'Couldn't be better,' announced Dorothy. She was still walking with a stick and a large plaster covered her nose which, although swollen to twice it's normal size, was unbelievably not broken.

'Speak for yourself!' complained Frank who had two black eyes, bandages on his head and around his throat and a bandage around his wrist, which he'd sprained with the one good punch he'd managed to land on Sid.

'And how's Mr Pomeroy?' inquired Frank.

269

'Unemployed,' answered Peter with a satisfied grin.

'Right,' said Frank. 'I thought I'd bring my new business partners along to see you, with it being their half term holidays.'

He introduced Jimmy and Susan. Peter Ellis solemnly shook hands with them.

'Delighted to see Sackfield Builders pursuing a youth policy,' he approved.

'They own forty-nine-per-cent, which Dorothy administers on their behalf.'

'I think you've made a wise move, Frank,' said Peter. 'Your business expertise was always a worry to us. We only backed you because you're such a damn good builder.'

Dorothy sat down on one of the two chairs facing Peter. 'I'm glad you see it like that, because we need your help to squeeze my father off his land. Legally this time.'

Peter nodded, serious now. 'Depends on your proposal, what have you got in mind?'

'My father paid fifteen thousand pounds for his land. How much of that do you think his bank put up?'

'Off the record, we know they put up five and your father the other ten.'

'Knowing my father, that'll have stretched him to his limit and if his bank find out they've lent money on a piece of land that's worthless without Frank's bit they'll grab at any opportunity to get out, wouldn't you say?'

'With both hands,' confirmed Peter.

'In that case we'd like to make him an offer of five thousand, through his bank of course – but we'd need you to put up the lot.'

'You realise we never lend a hundred-per-cent on anything,' replied Peter.

'You'd be lending just a third of the land's value, of course you can lend us it,' countered Dorothy firmly.

Peter held her in his gaze. Underneath that plaster was a shrewd and beautiful woman. 'Okay, I think the bank could live with that,' he conceded. Then, 'You're a ruthless business woman, Mrs Bairstow.'

'Only where my father's concerned.'

'And how would you suggest we appraise his bank of their perilous situation?' he asked.

'I believe you people call it the "old boy network",' suggested Dorothy. 'As soon as you've "appraised" them, we'll make our offer. I imagine they'll be quite relieved.'

Peter smiled admiringly. 'Is there anything you haven't thought of?'

'I don't think so.'

'So, you're planning on screwing your own father out of ten thousand pounds, that's my salary for twenty years. It could well ruin him. Don't you feel a twinge of guilt?'

'I feel my nose,' she replied, 'and I remember who caused it.'

'You can see where she gets it from,' said Frank.

'I've told you not to compare me to him,' snapped Dorothy.

'Leave it with me,' said Peter. 'If you can force your father to sell for five thousand, we'll put the money up. On one condition.'

'What's that?' asked Dorothy.

'That you sell the land immediately, to give yourself some proper working capital. You don't have the resources to develop a site that size. I want you to sell off to one of the big boys and buy something smaller.'

'You've been reading my mind,' laughed Dorothy. She turned and gave Frank a smug 'I told you so' look.

'We've been arguing about that all the way here,' grumbled Frank.

'Not any more you're not,' announced Peter. 'You've lost, and somehow, I don't think it's going to be the first time!'

'Does this mean we're rich, Auntie Dorothy?' asked Jimmy.

'No, it means for the time being we're skint, but at least we've got good prospects,' answered their auntie.

Good prospects mean very little to boys, whatever their age, and Jimmy decided against asking Mr Ellis if he should open an account for their thriving jam jar business.

Chapter Twenty

Dorothy jumped when the telephone rang for the first time. It had been installed over two weeks ago and this was their first incoming call. Altogether it had been used no more than half a dozen times, including a frustrated screaming match with the Fairbank Children's Home in Huddersfield when Dorothy had got to the end of her tether one day. It was Susan who'd taken the phone from her and stiffly reminded her of Baldwin's strict instructions about not interfering. Although secretly she was pleased that her auntie was becoming so passionate about getting her brother back as there was no questioning her auntie's tenacity. Frank Sackfield had confided in Susan one day that her auntie was the most 'bloody-mind female' he'd ever come across and he wouldn't like to get on the wrong side of her.

'Leeds three-oh-three-two-eight,' Dorothy recited her phone number for the first time.

'Mrs Bairstow?' It was a woman's voice, a timid, frightened voice.

'Yes.'

There was a silence for a while which Dorothy broke. 'Hello,' she said. 'Dorothy Bairstow here, who's speaking please?'

'Is it you what's trying ter find William Bairstow?'

'Yes, it is – do you know something?' Dorothy felt her heart pounding.

'He's not been adopted if that's what they're tellin' yer. They sent him away. They weren't supposed ter do it so they marked him down as adopted.'

'Where did they send him? Hello?'

The phone went dead and Dorothy looked at it dumbly as she'd seen people do on the pictures. She sat down for a while to collect her thoughts. Susan, who'd half overheard the conversation,

273

came into the room.

'Was that about William?' she inquired hopefully. There'd been no mention of William on Dorothy's end of the conversation, but Susan had a fixation about her baby brother.

'It was a woman,' said her auntie. 'She said he wasn't adopted. She said he'd been sent away.' Dorothy was in a daze.

'Whereabouts? Did she say whereabouts?'

Dorothy repeated exactly what the woman had said, adding that she sounded frightened but genuine. Susan, for the first time in months, hugged her auntie. Jimmy walked in to find them both in tears, clinging on to one another.

'What's up?' he asked.

'We're going to get William back, that's what's up!' declared his auntie with tearful determination. 'I don't know how, but we're going to get him back!'

'Thanks for this, Frank,' said Dorothy as the car swung out of Broughton Terrace. Susan and Jimmy had wanted to come but there was too much uncertainty about what they were going to do and how long it was going to take, so the two children had already reluctantly left for school.

'We'll keep in touch,' she'd promised them, miming the making of a phone call.

She knew they'd be able to fend for themselves, even if she and Frank didn't get back that night. There was something about the mystery phone caller's voice that told her getting William back wasn't going to be easy.

Frank looked across at her and gave a big

274

friendly grin. 'I think we can afford a day off after the deal you've just done,' he said.

'I've got something else in mind for that money as and when it comes in, so don't start getting big ideas,' warned Dorothy, settling back in her seat and pulling a pack of Craven A from her pocket. She took out two and lit them both at once, handing one to Frank, as she'd seen Paul Henreid do for Bette Davis in *Now Voyager.*

Had it not been for the job in hand, the journey would have been a pleasant one. Frank was an affable companion, easy-going and humorous. It was hard to understand why a wife would ever want to leave such a man. Dorothy was secretly betting his ex-wife was already regretting it.

The cold spring sunshine brightened up the grey stone walls of Huddersfield. There was a grim solidity about the place that you couldn't get in the south. Perhaps in the soft south it wasn't needed. It was mid-morning and all the workers were already in their places. At their looms and lathes and tending their furnaces. The lucky ones had jobs that took them outdoors, where they could breathe the damp air gusting down from the bleak Pennines. Frank weaved his car through the narrow streets looking for a sign that would direct him towards Slaithwaite, which the natives had abbreviated to Slawit, just so that they could look pityingly on foreigners who pronounced it how it was spelt.

He was relieved to see the sign that saved him from stopping to ask. He'd lived in Yorkshire long enough to know they'd pretend not to know what he was talking about if he pronounced it wrong.

Yorkshire people can be like that.

The Fairbank Home was a mile outside Huddersfield. Quite a pleasant-looking place, very much at odds with its immediate derelict surroundings. Frank drove up to the entrance and parked in a spot reserved for the H. Parkinson, Chief Warden.

'Chief Warden,' read Frank out loud. 'That's a comforting title for homeless kids. I bet they feel right at home here.'

He and Dorothy knocked loudly on the door. There were no children about as it was a school day. The door was opened by an officious woman in a blue nurse's uniform.

She greeted them with a shocked 'Oh, dear, you've parked in the warden's spot. He won't like that.'

'Well, that's okay then,' breezed Frank cheerfully. 'I don't think I want him to like me!'

Dorothy wasn't sure if this was the right approach but had no option but to go along with it.

'Is the warden in?' she asked.

'No, but he'll be back shortly. I think you should move your car.'

'Oh, don't worry about that, there's a perfectly good spot right at the side of it,' Frank assured her. 'Where's his office?'

'Oh, dear. I suppose you'd better come in,' she said dismally. Turning and leading the way along a cream-coloured corridor and opening a door to a small office.

'This is Mr Parkinson's waiting room. I'll send him along as soon as he arrives.'

Frank and Dorothy sat down on the stiff, office-type chairs and surveyed their immediate surroundings. There was nothing homely about it. No pictures or flowers or evidence of the existence of children. More like a well-scrubbed office block. A vague smell of cooking pervaded the air.

'Not exactly "home from home", is it?' commented Frank.

Dorothy shook her head in agreement. She noticed the door to Mr Parkinson's inner office was slightly open.

'Keep an eye out, Frank,' she cautioned. 'I think I'll have a quick look in his desk before he comes.'

Frank grinned and needed no explanation. Nothing felt right about what had happened so far and he knew they'd have to fight like with like. He stood by the window and saw Parkinson's large black Humber arriving almost immediately.

'Get your skates on, Dorothy love, he's just parking up now! Florence Nightingale's dashed out to talk to him – he's on his way in!'

Dorothy was riffling through the desk drawers as neatly as she could. She tugged at a large drawer only to find it locked.

'Damn!' she cursed. 'I wouldn't mind a look in there.'

She pulled open the shallow central drawer, took out a small notebook and stuck it in her cardigan pocket just as two sets of hurried footsteps clattered along the corridor.

Parkinson entered the outer office to find Frank and Dorothy sitting expectantly in their

277

chairs. He was a tall man in late middle-age, who might have looked distinguished had his hair not been going bald in such a haphazard fashion. Neither Frank nor Dorothy stood up. Frank had already decided to adopt an unpleasant attitude from the start. He found it worked well when dealing with uncooperative workmen and he saw no reason to treat Parkinson differently.

The warden stood glaring down at them both; their attitude to his matron and the parking of their car did not endear them to him.

'Just who are you and what is your business?' he asked brusquely.

'This is Mrs Dorothy *Bairstow*,' announced Frank, emphasising her surname and searching Parkinson's face for any reaction. There was none from him but the matron gave an involuntary nervous glance in her boss's direction.

'I see you recognise the name, madam,' pressed Frank, 'as well you might. A small boy of that name appears to have gone missing from the face of the Earth and we're here to find out why.'

Dorothy was impressed with Frank up to now. Pity he didn't use the same forcefulness in his own business dealings.

'I'm William Bairstow's aunt,' she explained in as cold a voice as she could muster.

'Ah, the one who never came to visit him. Shame that – cried his eyes out every visiting day, didn't he, matron?' observed Parkinson scathingly.

Matron gave a disapproving nod. Parkinson's words were like a stab through the heart for Dorothy. Frank came straight back at him.

'For reasons I wouldn't expect you to understand, Mrs Bairstow was unable to contact her nephew. We expected you to do the job you were paid to do and look after the boy until such time as a home could be provided for him.'

'And that's precisely what we did,' retorted Parkinson, with a smugness that had Dorothy clenching her fists. 'A suitable home was found for the boy and, as I told Mrs Bairstow over the telephone, I believe the boy is very happy there.'

'Happy where?' demanded Dorothy angrily.

'I'm sorry, madam. I cannot disclose that information for reasons I gave you over the telephone.'

Frank, who hadn't introduced himself, stood up and confronted Parkinson with a steely-eyed glare that forced the warden to take a step back.

'In view of reliable information we've received, I've been engaged by Mrs Bairstow to follow a report that William Bairstow has not been adopted by anyone and was in fact transferred to another home! I'll be checking this story with absolute thoroughness and if it's true, criminal charges will follow – against both of you!'

He shouted the last three words in the matron's face, causing her to blanch and look up at her boss with a startled expression on her face.

'Would you kindly leave now,' demanded Parkinson. If Frank had got him worried he certainly wasn't showing it.

'With pleasure,' said Frank. 'But I doubt if this is the last you'll be hearing of us.'

As the two of them left the office, Dorothy stopped beside the matron. 'I don't know what you're up to,' she said, looking the woman squarely in the eye. 'But surely it can't be worth it!'

The frightened look in the matron's eyes told her all she wanted to know. Dorothy looked back at Parkinson and asked sharply, 'I wonder what she's so worried about?'

'Well? What do you think?' asked Dorothy as they sat in the parked car, planning their next move.

'They're lying through their teeth,' replied Frank.

Dorothy took the stolen notebook from her pocket and flicked through it.

'Hmmm, this could be handy. It's an address book.' She read a few pages. 'Doesn't say exactly who everybody is, but there's certainly a lot of them.'

'It's something, I suppose,' conceded Frank, who didn't fancy spending the next few days knocking on the doors of strangers. 'If only we could get a friendly name – we could maybe match it up with an address.'

'The name of the woman who rang me, you mean?'

'She'd do for starters,' he agreed, pressing the starter button and reversing out of the warden's parking spot.

As they stopped at the end of the short driveway, about to turn into the road. Dorothy saw a group of youngsters approaching. She looked at her watch. 'Dinnertime,' she said. 'I bet they're from the home, coming back from school for their lunch. I could smell something cooking back there, couldn't you?'

Winding the window down, she signalled the group to approach. Her smile was all that was needed – especially for the boys.

'Hiya, kids,' she greeted them cheerily. 'Are you all from the prison camp here?'

Her gamble paid off. All the children laughed, happy to hear an adult share their opinion of the place. They gathered round the car, perhaps wondering if any largesse might be coming their way. An icecream van pulled up at the opposite side of the road, the driver standing by the door and ringing a handbell to announce his arrival.

'Buy us an icecream missis!' demanded one short-trousered cheeky face, grinning through the window at Dorothy.

Dorothy laughed. 'Go on then, just for your cheek.'

Frank pulled the car into the road and stopped behind the icecream van. Dorothy got out and counted the heads.

'Six cornets? Right.'

'Seven, missis – Bernard Harrison's just comin'.'

'Seven then.'

'Can I have one, missis?' They were turning up in droves.

Frank joined her and went to the van window. 'Just keep on sending them till I say when,' he said to the icecream man.

The icecream man grinned back, happy to oblige. Dorothy leaned against the side of the van, licking the vanilla icecream from her cornet, surrounded by happy kids.

'Who's your favourite over there?' she asked casually.

The children jostled one another, eager to be the one to answer.

'Nobody, missis,' chirped the cheeky one who'd first demanded icecream. 'They're all arse'oles.'

'Mrs Atkin's not an arse'ole – she's alright is Mrs Atkins. She never hit yer or nowt,' argued a slightly older girl.

All the kids agreed that Mrs Atkins was the best of a bad bunch and definitely not an arse'ole. One young boy proudly displaying a livid bruise on his arm he'd received at the hands of one of the workers in the home. His display was greeted by a cry of derision from another youth.

'That's nowt that. I've got a better one than that!'

'Show us then,' challenged the first youth.

The second youth grinned and blushed slightly. 'Can't,' he admitted, 'it's on me arse!'

This revelation was greeted with howls of laughter. Then a teenage girl said something that had Frank and Dorothy looking at each other with excitement.

'She's not here no more isn't Mrs Atkins. She left t'other day. I reckon old Parky sacked her! She were alright were Mrs Atkins.'

'Oh dear,' commiserated Dorothy. 'I wonder if she's got another job – any idea where she's gone?'

'No idea. She didn't live in t' home. She lived in 'uddersfield somewhere.'

'Do you know if she was married or anything?' inquired Frank.

All the kids howled with laughter once again. 'Married? Mrs Atkins – blimey! Who'd marry her?'

Dorothy thought it time to ask the all important one. 'Did any of you know William Bairstow?'

They all shook their heads at first, then one shouted out. 'Hey! I bet she means Billy Bisto! His proper name were Bairstow – he told me once.'

'Oh aye missis. Yer mean t' Bisto Kid – he were a little bugger were Bisto!'

'Anybody know where he is now?'

'Don't know, missis. They never tell us where no one's going. He went a few weeks ago.'

'Do you think he might have been adopted by someone?'

'Nah – no one ever gets adopted from here. Not unless yer a right little kid. Sometimes right little kids get adopted.'

The answers came from different children all eager to supply information. But none with anything helpful – apart from the interesting news about Mrs Atkins.

Frank and Dorothy watched the noisy mob stream through the gates of Fairbank Home.

'Funny, isn't it,' mused Frank, 'how kids always manage to adjust to whatever's going on around them.'

Laurence Parkinson watched through the window as Frank drove out through the gate.

'Shit! They're talking to the kids now!' He spat the words out with a vehemence that made the matron cringe.

283

'It'll be that bloody Atkins woman – she'll have been blabbing. She was in the office when that Bairstow bitch rang up!' He spun round on the matron. 'It's your bloody stupid fault for sacking her! She's trying to get her revenge. What's her address? I'll go round to shut her up.'

'But, you told me to sack her, you said she was too namby-pamby with the children.'

'I expect you to use your initiative, woman, and not create problems for me!' rasped Parkinson. He stormed into his office and began searching through his drawers for his address book.

'Have you taken an address book from this bloody drawer, you stupid bloody woman?'

'I haven't been near your drawers, Laurence. If you want her address I've got it in my office – and I'll thank you not to talk to me like that!'

Even the matron, who was unfortunately besotted by her boss, had a limit to just how much she'd take from him and was rapidly approaching that limit. Parkinson glared at her. He'd taken advantage of her in every way, for the seven years he'd been warden. No way would he ever marry the ridiculous woman, despite their having been engaged for three of those years.

'You don't think one of them took it, do you?' he asked at last, having regained his composure.

'How would they know where to look? They were only in there two minutes before you arrived.'

Parkinson nodded. She was probably right – anyway he was always losing things. She stood tentatively behind him and placed a hand on his shoulder. 'It will be alright, Laurence, won't it?'

Parkinson placed a reassuring hand on hers. 'Of course it will, matron – don't be such a worrier.' But he didn't sound too sure of himself.

Matron thought it was about time her fiancé started calling her by her Christian name.

Dorothy looked up at the house and then down to the address book. 'This is it. Seventy-six, Glenstone Terrace. Hilda Atkins.'

It was a long, neat street of small stone terraced houses. A street with no money and a lot of working class pride. Two small boys, too young for school, were having a peeing contest up a lavatory wall, both attempting to reach a chalked record set by a previous contestant called Razza.

'Could you beat that, Frank?' asked Dorothy playfully as they stopped opposite the peeing boys.

'I'll have you know I was Mill Street Junior School record holder for two years running. Mind you, I'm lucky if I can manage a horizontal stream nowadays. The water pressure drops as you get older.'

'Frank Sackfield, you smutty old man!'

'You started it!'

Dorothy's amusement turned to tension as they approached the door. This could be the last step before they located William. But the house looked lifeless. Not just that no one was in, it looked as though no one lived there. It was hard to tell why. There were still curtains up at the windows and an empty milk bottle on the step which had been recently scoured – it just gave out the message that no one lives here any more.

'If yer lookin' for Hilda, she's done a moon-light!' The raucous information came from an upstairs window next door.

Frank and Dorothy stood back and peered up at the woman in the open window. Curlered hair and gigantic bosom. What Tommy would have called a Dead Heat in a Zeppelin Race.

'Do you know where she's gone?' shouted up Frank.

'Warra you? T' tally man or t' rent man?' she gave a loud toothless laugh. 'I shouldn't bother if I were thee, old lad. She hasn't a tanner ter scratch her arse wi hasn't Hilda! Buggered off last night – God knows where.'

'We're not after money,' called out Dorothy. 'Look, my name's Bairstow, Dorothy Bairstow from Leeds – she knows who I am and what I want. Tell her to give me a ring and I'll be able to help her out if she needs any money.'

'We all need brass, love. Yer can give some ter me – I'll give it to her when I see her.'

'So – you will be seeing her then?' persisted Dorothy hopefully.

The woman gave another toothless grin. 'Doubt it, love – I were just taking t' piss that's all.'

Without saying any more she slammed the window shut on Dorothy's hopes.

'Damn!' she said, with feeling. 'I could have sworn we were getting nearer.'

'Never mind,' consoled Frank. 'We've still got a book full of addresses to work on.'

Dorothy hopped over the low wall dividing the

miniscule gardens and knocked on the toothless woman's door. The woman opened the door with a slightly annoyed look on her face which disappeared when Dorothy handed her a pound note.

'Here,' she said, 'this is for your help so far. I'm searching for my nephew who lived at the children's home Hilda worked at. He's left there now and I'm fairly sure Hilda knows where he is. You get her to ring and tell me, and there's twenty-five quid each in it for you.'

The woman looked suspiciously at Dorothy, then at Frank, then at the car. It was the car and Dorothy's accent that convinced her that she could afford to back up her words with cash. She nodded. Twenty-five quid was a lot of money – a month's wages for her old man, when he was working.

'Twenty-five quid *each*,' she clarified.

'*Each*,' confirmed Dorothy.

'I'll keep me eye out,' she said at last.

'Thanks,' smiled Dorothy. 'It's in a good cause. Here's my telephone number.' She handed the woman a scrap of paper on which she'd already written her number, then turned and let herself out of the low wooden gate.

'If it's owt ter do wi that bloody kids' 'ome yer mebbe right,' called out the woman as Dorothy got in the car.

'Would it be rude to ask where the fifty quid's coming from?' inquired Frank.

'Company funds,' explained Dorothy. 'Call it an investment. I'll work better when William's back.'

'Oh, right – you don't mind me asking, do you?'
'Not at all.'

They spent the rest of the afternoon calling at the addresses in the book. With exception of a window cleaner who'd seen one of the boys being severely beaten, no one was able to enlighten them. Frank suspected that many of the people they were calling on would be reporting their visit back to Parkinson. This didn't bother him as anything that unnerved Parkinson was a good thing, but as dusk fell there seemed to be a growing futility about the whole exercise. On a hunch he headed back to Glenstone Terrace and knocked once again on the toothless woman's door.

By now she had her teeth in and her hair combed out, ready for her weekly visit to the West Huddersfield Working Men's Club.

Frank instinctively doffed his trilby hat, a gesture she appeared to appreciate.

'Sorry to trouble you again,' he said. 'But would you mind telling me if anyone else has been round looking for Hilda?'

Flashing him a mouthful of ill-fitting teeth she nodded her head. 'Aye, mister. Big long streak of a feller, came in a big black motor. Ignorant bugger if yer ask me – wouldn't believe me when I said I didn't know where she'd gone.'

Frank doffed his hat again. 'Thanks, missis,' he said, 'that's all I want to know.'

He was turning to go when the woman shouted after him. 'He wanted to know if a man and a woman had been asking after her.'

Frank stopped in his tracks. 'What did you tell him?'

She cackled, 'I told him ter piss off. I didn't like his bleedin' manner.'

'You did the right thing,' Frank assured her. 'I hope to see you again.'

'Hilda's definitely the one we're looking for,' he announced as he got back in the car. 'Parkinson's been round looking for her, but your busty friend told him to piss off.'

'I think that quid might well have been one of my better investments,' replied Dorothy. 'Let's hope we have to fork out the fifty before much longer.'

Chapter Twenty-One

It was over a week since their trip to Huddersfield and each time the phone rang at home Dorothy, Susan or Jimmy had it off the hook before it finished its first ring.

'I'll give it one more week,' promised Dorothy, after the latest false alarm turned out to be a wrong number. 'Then we'll get on to the police. I'd prefer not to because I think Parkinson's somehow prepared for it – but if it's all we can do, then,' she shrugged and looked at Susan's disappointed face. 'Look, Susan – William's alive and kicking and out there somewhere and if you don't think I can get him back then you don't know me very well!'

Oddly enough she had great faith in herself; sadly, Susan didn't share that faith.

'We've got company!'

Dorothy had heard the car pull angrily into the yard and knew before she looked through the window just who it belonged to, and she was just in the mood for him.

'Who?' asked Frank.

'It's Sidney, and he doesn't look best pleased with himself.'

'Can't understand why,' grinned Frank.

Sid came through the door like a petulant child. The telephone rang and Dorothy took the call with her back to her father.

'He's busy right now, can I take a message?' Dorothy said to the caller. She could feel her father quivering with emotion behind her as she wrote down the telephone message.

'Bastards!' he almost wept.

'Did someone come in?' asked Dorothy, putting down the telephone and looking at Frank, who wished she didn't get so much pleasure out of baiting her father.

Frank stopped writing and regarded Sid coolly. 'Don't you ever knock, Allerdyce?' he said. 'This is a private office.'

'You can't do this ter me!' Sid lamented, flopping down in a corner chair. 'This could bankrupt me!'

'I think it's called "getting one's come uppance",' said Dorothy curtly, still not looking round at him.

'Look you've got me all wrong,' her father

whined. 'I were only taking the piss out of yer. I wouldn't have seen you go under. Come on, Frank lad, we're both builders, we help each other out in this business!'

'The only help you're gonna get from us is to help you through that door, you lying bastard!' snarled Frank. 'Now get out, Allerdyce, before I call the police!'

Dorothy swung round in her chair and looked at her father. For the first time in her life she felt pity for him. Sid had aged ten years in the last couple of weeks, the ebullience gone from his demeanour. He was broken and she was responsible – and it didn't feel quite as good as she thought it would.

'Why did you do it, Dad?' she asked at length.

It took Sid a while to collect sufficient thoughts to form an answer. 'Why did I do it?' he grunted. 'I'll tell yer why I did it. Because yer'd upset me, me girl, that's why I did it. Turning yer back on all I'd done for yer!'

'No – that's not what I was asking.' She looked at a bead of nervous sweat running down her father's face and knew she'd never had any love for this man, father or no father. 'I want to know why you treated me so badly when I was a child. You know, I can't remember you ever saying a single kind word to me!'

'Let's just say I had me reasons and leave it at that, shall we?' Her questions were making him uncomfortable.

'No, I won't leave it at that,' persisted Dorothy, sensing he had an explanation for her. 'Even the most brutal of men have a soft spot for their daughters. Daughters are most men's Achilles Heel – but you never had a scrap of love for me. Why was that?'

'I said leave it!'

He got up to go, his discomfort was now turning to anger but Dorothy stood her ground. 'Alright,' she said coolly, 'I'll leave it – and I'll leave you as well, leave you out to dry. I was going to do a deal with you to help you out, but you can forget it now.'

'A deal? What sort o' deal?' It was as though a light had been switched on behind Sid's greedy eyes.

'A business deal – but first I want an answer to my question.'

Sid sat down again and rubbed the back of his neck with a beefy hand, ingrained with the dirt of years of hard graft.

'Yer not me daughter!' he rasped, his eyes looking away from her.

Despite this being one of the explanations Dorothy had considered, the reality of it still came as something of a shock to her.

'Oh,' was her immediate reaction. She wasn't disappointed. Finding out she was not Sid's daughter was more of a cause for celebration than regret. 'That's such a relief,' she added cruelly. 'Who is my father then?'

This was a much more crucial question than any she'd asked him before.

'I've no idea,' he said, looking her in the eye. 'And that's the God's honest truth, girl – I don't think yer mother ever knew neither. Yer can ask her if yer like, she can mebbe give yer a few names ter pick from – but mine won't be among 'em!'

'So, why did you marry her? She was obviously pregnant with me when you married her – I'd worked that one out myself.'

Sid's discomfort returned. His hand went back to rubbing his fat neck.

'If yer must know – it were money. It were her money what gave me a leg up in business. She married me cause it weren't respectable ter give birth ter bastards then any more than it is now. I was her only choice.'

Dorothy sat back, satisfied that his explanation was true. 'Right,' she said. 'I think we can do business now.'

Sid sat up in his chair. She had his full attention.

'Seems to me you've lost two things,' she began, smiling at the suspicious look on her father's face. 'A lot of money, but worst of all, your reputation as a businessman.'

Sid looked at the woman he had so despised for marrying a working man and saw in her a strength he couldn't match.

'If you like, we can give you back one of these, your reputation!' she offered suddenly.

Frank sat back. He knew enough not to contradict his junior partner on matters of business. Whatever was in her mind it would be to his advantage.

Sid leaned forward expectantly. Was she throwing him a lifeline? No daughter of his would have done such a thing. He'd certainly never have thrown her one. He'd come to appeal to Frank's better nature, not hers.

'Don't get too excited, Sidney dear,' warned Dorothy, happy now at never having to call him Daddy again. 'It's a lousy deal we're offering – but it's the only one in town, as they say. Your land was worthless without ours, in fact,' she looked at her watch, 'as of an hour ago we own your land. That means we'll have bought the whole shooting match, yours and ours, for eight thousand pounds, not a bad deal when you come to think of it.'

Sid was sitting up now. Despite everything, he could see a lot of himself in her, so could Frank, but Frank wasn't about to tell her that.

'Assuming you still have the connections to raise finance secured against prime building land, we'll sell the whole lot back to you for sixteen thousand.' She looked at Sid, who was doing a quick mental calculation. She was offering him three years' hard work at reduced profits, but he had no option. Anything was better than going under, he knew people who'd put the money up – at a price.

Sid laughed grimly, 'I'll say one thing for you, Dorothy lass. You're a chip off the old block, even if I'm not yer dad!'

'Don't say that, Sid,' warned Frank, 'or the deal might be off!'

Sid stood and reluctantly shook Frank's hand, then offered his hand to Dorothy who took it and eyed him squarely. 'I'm not doing this because you're my step-father or whatever you consider yourself to be,' she said coldly. 'I'm doing it because it's sound business. You've got a week to

294

set the finance up!'

As Sid left the office, Frank turned to Dorothy with a hint of annoyance in his voice. 'I do think you ought to consult me before you make these deals, you sold him it for two thousand less than it was worth.'

'I'm sorry, Frank, but I needed to think on my feet. That telephone call was from the land surveyor about those trial holes you ordered to be dug. Apparently there's a lot of unstable ground on Sid's piece. It'll need piling, raft foundations, the lot. Sixteen thousand's not a bad price as it happens, it gives us eight thousand clear profit.'

'Dorothy, you're unbelievable!' gasped Frank. 'Well, I'd better get meself out there and tell 'em to fill them trial holes in before Sid thinks to dig any.'

'I think my father will have enough on his mind over the next few days to think of anything as sensible as that. He's not as meticulous as you in building matters.'

Frank walked round to her side of the desk and kissed Dorothy full on the lips.

'Mr Sackfield! What on earth was that for?'

'I just felt like it! So, what you going to do about it?' he asked with mock belligerence.

'Nothing, next time just give me some warning that's all.'

'Oh, so you reckon there's going to be a next time, do you?'

'I didn't mean it like that,' she laughed.

She watched Frank as he went back to his chair. He was a nice man. Too old for her of course, mid-forties at least. He caught her staring at him and grinned back at her. 'You're admiring my personal beauty, aren't you,' he joked. 'I get a lot of that.'

'No,' she said tartly. 'I was just trying to work out how much our forty-nine-per-cent was worth now.'

'We going to be bloody good partners me and you,' declared Frank.

Dorothy was wondering just how good. She'd quite enjoyed that kiss.

Chapter Twenty-Two

'Dorothy Bairstow?'

'Yes,' Dorothy's heart sank for the umpteenth time. This wasn't the woman who'd rung her the last time.

'Hang on, I'll just put another penny in then we'll not get cut off,' said the woman.

There was a clang of a coin dropping then the voice came again. 'Any road, I've found her,' it said.

Dorothy recognised the voice from somewhere, then a penny dropped in her brain just as it had in the coin box. It was the toothless woman, Hilda's next door neighbour.

'You've found Hilda?' asked an excited Dorothy.

'Aye. Have you got fifty quid?'

'Does Hilda know where William is?'

'Aye, but she'll not tell me. She'll not tell no one till she's got her twenty-five quid.'

'Right, that's no problem. Where can I meet you?'

'There's a big trannie café on t' Oldham Road. It's about a mile out of 'uddersfield on t' right hand side – yer can't miss it. Tomorrow mornin' at ten o'clock – alright?'

'That's fine, see you then.'

The last penny dropped and the pips went, signalling the end of the call. But Dorothy had heard enough, Susan and Jimmy were hovering over her shoulder.

'I think we're in business,' she announced. 'I'm meeting Hilda Atkins tomorrow in Huddersfield.'

'We're coming with you,' said Susan. The tone of her voice told Dorothy not to argue.

'Good,' she said. 'I'll ring Frank and tell him he's taking another day off.'

Dorothy remembered the cruel laughter of the children when she'd asked if Hilda was married and realised why they'd laughed. Hilda Atkins was a tiny sparrow of a woman who could have been anything between thirty-five and fifty-five. Her eyes darted up at Dorothy and Frank as they walked into the transport café. She was dwarfed by the monumental bosom of her friend who gave them a loose-toothed smile as they sat down at the table.

'What'll you have, ladies?' asked Frank.

'Eee! 'ark at 'im – callin' us ladies,' giggled Hilda's well-endowed friend.

'And why shouldn't I?' protested an indignant Frank. 'Yer as much of a lady as all them prancing about in their fancy dresses an' tiaras down in London.'

Hilda's friend gave him a playful slap on his arm, enough to make him wince. 'Two mugs o' tea and two sausage sandwiches,' she laughed. 'An' if my Walter finds out yer've been chatting me up he'll have yer by yer bollocks!'

She screamed with laughter at her own coarseness and Hilda joined with the shrillest laugh Dorothy had ever heard.

She joined the two women as Frank went off to get served. He looked back at them as he waited for his order to arrive. An incongruous a trio if ever there was one. The tiny wizened sparrow, the fat harridan and the alluring, self-assured beauty.

Dorothy saw no reason to beat about the bush. Jimmy and Susan were waiting in the car and all she wanted was the whereabouts of her nephew. She took two envelopes from her bag and placed them on the table.

'Twenty-five pounds in each envelope,' she said quietly, lest any other customer heard. In 1946, twenty-five pounds was not a sum to be sneezed at. Planting a well-turned elbow on either side of each envelope, she placed her hands together in a protective bridge over them, fingers linked as in prayer.

'Where's William?' she asked, firmly but quietly, her eyes boring into Hilda's.

Hilda's eyes darted round the bustling café, as if looking for eavesdroppers, then back at Dorothy.

298

'Go on! Tell her, yer barmpot – then we can have us brass!' urged her fat friend.

'He's in Oldham!' blurted out Hilda.

'Oldham?' queried Dorothy, as though Oldham was the last place on earth she'd expect them to send him.

'Ashton Lodge in Oldham,' Hilda went on. 'Quicker yer get him outa there the better!'

'It's a shit'ole,' explained the fat friend.

Frank arrived with the tea and sandwiches and sat beside Dorothy at the table.

'William's in Oldham,' Dorothy told him, with a note of triumph in her voice. Turning back to Hilda she asked. 'Why did they send him away?'

Hilda's eyes dropped. 'Yer wrote saying yer were comin' ter fetch him home. If yer'd seen t' state he were in yer'd have had the cops on Parkinson. They'd battered the poor little sod black and blue. So they sent him off ter Oldham an' told yer he'd been adopted – they never expected nobody ter come for him. He were cheeky were your Billy an' they wouldn't stand for it. There were five of us an' Parky an' every one were free wi their fists – even t' women.'

'You weren't,' said Dorothy.

'No, I never hit none of 'em. I reckon they'd enough ter put up with – poor little beggars.'

'Why did you ring me?'

'That snotty cow of a matron sacked me – she said I were being too soft. Reckoned I were letting t' little beggars have their own way too much. I knew yer'd rung – I were in t' office when yer gave old Parky a bollocking. Anyway when they sacked me I were waitin' in t' office for me

299

cards an' I saw your number written down – so I rang yer. I had ter put t' phone down quick 'cos Parky were comin'.'

Dorothy pushed the two envelopes across the table to be picked up by both women with undue haste. Hilda looked grateful but apologetic.

'Yer must think I'm rotten, takin' money off yer like this – but yer don't know how much this means ter me.'

Dorothy stood up to go, Frank had only brought food and drink for the two women. She smiled down at Hilda. 'You don't know how much this means to me, Hilda – you've got my number, give me a ring, I'd like to know how you're going on.'

Then she looked at the fat woman, counting her money, 'It's all there,' she chided. 'But thanks – I don't know how you managed to find Hilda, but I hope it wasn't too much trouble.'

Hilda gave her fat friend a quizzical look, then looked back at Dorothy, 'How d'you mean? Find me?' she asked. 'I'm lodging with her!'

The fat friend gave Dorothy and Frank a cherubic smile, 'When I said she'd done a moonlight,' she explained, 'what I should have mentioned was that she'd moved in with me!'

It took them under an hour to travel to Oldham from Huddersfield along bleak, winding roads. The windscreen wiper fighting a valiant battle against the driving rain as they made their way over 'the tops', as the Pennines were called locally.

'Right, this looks like Oldham,' announced

Frank. 'All we need to do now is find Ashton Road.'

Dorothy, sitting beside him, looked at the road map on her knee. 'I imagine it's the road to Ashton-under-Lyne,' she deduced. 'Look, there's a sign, Ashton-under-Lyne five miles.'

Jimmy and Susan had actually found the journey quite exciting. Especially when a couple of sorry looking sheep had strayed onto the road and inexplicably refused to budge, eventually running into the mist as the four of them got out and shooed them away. After all, the alternative for them was a day at school. Frank pulled in to a petrol station. 'I'll get some juice and see if anyone knows where this place is,' he decided.

Looking through the car window they could see the petrol attendant shrugging his shoulders. He then disappeared into the office, followed by Frank, who came out looking cheerful, sticking a thumb up to the waiting trio.

'Bloke inside knows the home. Not got a brilliant reputation by the sound of it. Anyway it's only about five minutes away.'

Jimmy and Susan looked at each other. Both feeling the same surge of excitement. They were about to meet their long-lost brother. Dorothy blinked away a tear as Frank looked momentarily across at her and smiled at this extraordinary lady he was growing so fond of.

Following the directions he'd been given, Frank turned up a grim-looking road. An empty tram clanked past them, its lights on despite it only being late morning. The rain was slanting down, hammering noisily against the car roof. They

301

stared through the windows at the various buildings slowly passing them by. A row of shops with very few customers. People were either too broke or too cold to venture out and spend their money on such a day. There was a glum-looking Methodist Chapel, a bank, a dentist's and–

'There it is!' shouted Jimmy, who was first to spot the sign, to Susan's mild annoyance.

It stood beside a pair of huge iron gates and said in hard to read Gothic lettering.

ASHTON LODGE HOME FOR BOYS.
Warden. S. Wiggins

Lifting up the latch with her walking stick, Dorothy pushed open the gate and the four of them walked through. It was a large, forbidding place, probably the former home of some cotton mill owner. Built in soot-encrusted stone, it was three storeys high, completely square, completely symmetrical and, apart from a row of weathered gargoyles around the eaves, without a single redeeming architectural feature.

'Looks like a flippin' prison,' observed Jimmy.

'Scary,' said Susan.

Dorothy frowned and said nothing as she led the way along the gravel drive leading to the large double doors and rapped on the peeling brown paint with her stick.

'There's a bell here,' noticed Jimmy, pressing a metal button beside the door.

A loud clanging inside told them the bell was working alright. After a while the door was opened by a small, emaciated, short-trousered boy who, stood and gawped at them as though they were from another planet.

'I'm off sick,' he blurted. 'I'm not supposed ter be at school!'

'Is Mr Wiggins about, son?' asked Frank.

Surprised at Frank's kindly manner, the boy asked nervously, 'Are you t' board man, mister?'

'He thinks you're from the school board, checking on truants,' explained Dorothy.

'No, son. I'm not the board man,' grinned Frank. 'Do you think you could show us Mr Wiggins' office?'

The boy stared at them for a moment, as though needing time for this request to sink in, then turned and walked away, his seg-studded boots clattering cheerfully on the worn parquet floor. A cheerfulness completely at odds with the general atmosphere of the place. No light was switched on to brighten up the dark winter afternoon. There was a stale smell of yesterday's food and no curtains at the grime-covered windows. A well-built young woman passed them, with a cigarette dangling from her mouth, carrying an empty bucket. She gave them a nod and paused momentarily, then shrugged and carried on.

'That were Mrs Abbotson. She's one o' them what looks after us,' explained the boy.

They followed, hoping he was taking them to Mr Wiggins. The boy stopped by a large, panelled door.

'He's in there,' he said in a low voice, before vanishing noisily up the gloomy corridor.

The door opened before Frank had a chance to knock. A surprised-looking man stood there, his face frozen for just a second then switching on

303

the most insincere smile Dorothy had seen for a long time. There were heavy, dark red brocade curtains in this room, but there the colour ended. The walls were painted white, or had been many years ago. There were no pictures or photographs or ornaments of any kind to enliven the boredom. Just a large wooden desk on which stood a half drunk cup of something, a pub ashtray full of cigarette ends and a copy of *Tit-Bits* opened at the crossword page.

'Yes?' he said. 'Can I be of assistance?'

'I do hope so,' said Dorothy, accepting the man's unspoken invitation to accompany him into his office. Jimmy and Susan followed. 'You see, we're trying to track down a boy called William Bairstow and we understand from the last place he was at that he's one of your boys.'

'He's our brother,' explained Susan. 'We were told he was dead.' There was still a trace of bitterness here, 'But we've found out he's not and we've come to take him home.'

Mr Wiggins stroked his chin theatrically. A middle-aged, flabby man, with thinning hair and bad teeth. He had a floppy mouth and mean, piggy eyes, magnified several times through his bottle-bottom glasses.

'William Bairstow? Sorry, there's no boy of that name here.'

'Oh, no!' said Susan, her heart sinking.

'But the Fairbank Home in Huddersfield said they sent him here,' pursued Dorothy, hoping this might give him a jolt.

'I'm sorry, Mrs er…?'

'Bairstow, I'm the boy's aunt.'

'I'm sorry, Mrs Bairstow, but we've only got thirty-four boys here. I do know their names,' he said patronisingly.

Jimmy thought there was a sliminess about the man and he didn't trust him an inch. 'He's only six,' he blurted. 'How can he be missing?'

Wiggins fixed him with a cross between a smile and a sneer.

'If he's lost, sonny, it's not me what lost him. There's never been no William Bairstow at Ashton Lodge. Now if there's nothing else with which I can help you, I've got a lot of work to do.'

Frank glanced down at the half finished *Tit-Bits* crossword on Wiggins' desk and looked up at him. 'Yes, it looks like it,' he said scornfully. 'Thanks for all your help, Mr Wiggins.'

'Not at all,' smirked Wiggins, disregarding the sarcasm.

As they were about to leave the building, the short-trousered boy appeared as if from nowhere to open the outside door for them. 'You sure you're not a board man, mister?' he asked.

'Quite sure,' said Frank, who stuck his hand in his pocket and pulled out a shilling. He held it tantalisingly close to the boy as he asked. 'Do you know a boy called William Bairstow?'

The boy eagerly held his hand out to receive the money, then his face dropped as he realised he didn't have the required information. He pulled his hand away and took a disappointed step back, allowing them through the door.

'Nah, never heard of him,' he muttered.

'What school do the boys here go to?' asked Susan.

The boy's face lit up, a supplementary question, he knew the answer to this one. He held out
his hand, into which Frank dropped the silver
coin.

'Brewster Lane School, just round t' corner,' he
answered triumphantly, taking his prize and
clattering off joyously down the corridor.

'What made you ask that?' inquired Dorothy as
they walked out through the gates.

'Don't know really,' answered Susan. 'There
was something about that man I didn't like.
Maybe we should check his story.'

'He was a slimy creep,' said Jimmy.

'Well summed up, Jimmy,' praised Frank. 'I
couldn't have put it better myself.'

'I see no harm in asking at the school,' decided
Frank. 'Where did he say it was?'

'Brewster Lane,' answered Dorothy. Frank
nodded and narrowed his eyes as he looked at
her. 'You do look pretty in that coat,' he said,
then climbed quickly into the car for the short
journey to Brewster Lane School. Dorothy dismissed his compliment, her mind on much more
important things. Unlike Frank.

As the boy said, the school was just around the
corner. It was 12 o'clock and the children were
pouring out into the school yard for their lunch
break. The rain had more or less stopped and a
game of football got under way. Frank, Dorothy
and Susan fought their way past the players as
they made their way inside, Jimmy waited
outside, sitting on a low brick wall.

'Who says you could sit on my wall, kid?'

The questioner was a belligerent youth, roughly

Jimmy's age. He had a cast in his eye and Jimmy wasn't immediately sure he was talking to him.

'Sorry,' said Jimmy quickly, standing up. 'Didn't know it was your wall.'

'It's not,' smirked the youth, looking at the badge on Jimmy's blazer. 'Where're yer from?' he demanded.

'Leeds,' answered Jimmy, clenching his fists, in readiness for a surprise attack.

'Me uncle's been ter Leeds. He reckons it's a right mucky 'ole.'

'It is,' agreed Jimmy, deciding Leeds wasn't worth fighting about.

'Is it muckier than round 'ere?' asked the boy challengingly.

Jimmy wasn't sure how to answer this one.

'About the same,' he compromised.

This answer seemed to satisfy the boy, who then asked, matter of factly, 'D'yer wanna fight?'

'Can't. I've got me best clothes on.'

Another satisfactory answer. 'My name's Joe Conroy,' said the boy.

'My name's Jimmy Bairstow.'

'Watcha doin' round 'ere?'

'We've come ter look for our kid. We thought he was in an 'ome, but the feller there says he's not.'

'I live in an 'ome.'

'What? Ashton Lodge?'

'Yeah, it's rubbish – worst 'ome I've ever lived in. Have yer been ter see old Wanker Wiggins?'

'Yes,' laughed Jimmy. 'Why do yer call him Wanker?'

'Cos that's what he does. He's allus tossin' hisself off!'

'Yer what? Have yer seen him?'

The boy nodded and smirked. 'If yer do it for him he gives yer more pocket money. He gave me an extra tanner last week!'

Ignoring the disgust on Jimmy's face, the boy went on, 'All t'kids there are nutters. That's where they send 'em all.'

'You're not a nutter,' lied Jimmy.

'I am,' said the boy defensively. 'You ask anyone!' He called to a passing boy of similar age. 'Hey! Devlin, aren't I a nutter?'

'Biggest nutter in school!' confirmed Devlin.

'Told yer,' cackled Joe.

Jimmy nodded, he wasn't going to argue. 'They call our kid William Bairstow. Do you know him?'

'What? Bisto?' grinned the boy.

'No, Bairstow,' repeated Jimmy patiently.

'I've heard of the Bisto Kid,' chortled the youth. 'But he doesn't go to our school.' He laughed out loud at himself and ran off.

Jimmy breathed a sigh of relief at having come away from such a confrontation unharmed and looked up as Frank, Dorothy and Susan emerged from the school, looking disappointed.

'They've never heard of him,' said Dorothy. 'Sounds like old Wiggins was telling the truth.'

'I know,' confirmed Jimmy. 'I've just been talking to a kid who lives in Ashton Lodge. He's never heard of our William either. Tell yer what though. If all the kids there are like him, our William's better off living somewhere else. He was a right nutter!' He was too embarrassed to tell them about Wiggins' disgusting hobby.

Frank drummed his fingers on the steering

wheel, uncertain what to do next. 'Look, Frank,' said Dorothy, 'we're not going back without him.'

'I know,' accepted Frank. 'Trouble is, where the devil is he?' He looked at his watch. 'Look, it's half past twelve, we'd best get something to eat. We'll all think better on full stomachs.'

No one argued with this suggestion. A café lunch was a special treat for the Bairstow kids.

The café was emptying as they arrived and they were shown to a table for four by the window. 'Order what you like, kids,' said Frank, 'your Auntie Dorothy's paying.'

The two of them grinned at this. They liked Frank and his easy-going manner. Susan secretly thought her auntie could do a lot worse, and was slightly exasperated at Dorothy's romantic indifference to him – or to anybody for that matter. No one, it seemed, would ever be able to fill Uncle Tommy's shoes.

Frank was similarly aware of the gap Dorothy was keeping between them. His playful kiss apart, everything between them was strictly business. This was something of a disappointment to Frank as he was beginning to find this unusual woman more captivating by the day, but no way was he going to damage their tenuous relationship by pushing things along too fast.

Dorothy for her part had far too much to think about without complicating her life with such self indulgence. Romance was very much at the back of her mind when Frank's strong hand encased hers across the table.

'We'll not go back without him,' he promised, his solemn grey eyes resting gently on hers. 'No matter what it takes, we'll get him.'

'Thanks Frank,' she smiled. 'It means a lot to us to have you on our side.'

'I quite like being on your side, Dorothy love,' he replied earnestly. But if she caught any hidden meaning she didn't show it. Frank withdrew his hand and ordered steak pie and mash for four.

Dorothy sat for a while, still feeling the remnants of a pleasant tingle in her hand. No man had done that to her since Tommy. Susan had seen it but Jimmy was too engrossed in a dog fight across the street.

'Tell you what,' said Dorothy. 'When we do get him back I don't think he'll want to be called William.'

'Why on earth not?' protested Susan. 'It's a lovely name is William.'

'I think he answers to Billy now,' explained Dorothy.

'*Billy* Bairstow,' repeated Susan. 'Is that that what they're calling him? Suppose we'd have started calling him that by now. Never thought of him as Billy.'

Frank laughed. 'Sounds an appropriate name to me. Apparently at Fairbank Home they called him the *Bisto Kid.*'

Jimmy laughed at first, then the laughter froze on his face. 'That kid at school said something about the Bisto Kid,' he blurted.

'What kid?' asked Frank.

'That kid I was telling you about. The nutter. He said something about the Bisto Kid!'

'What did he say?' demanded Susan. 'Come on, Jimmy. This could be important!'

310

'I know!' protested Jimmy. 'I'm trying ter think, leave me alone for a minute!'

The others sat there impatiently as Jimmy tried to collect his thoughts. 'I told him we were looking for our kid – and that his name was William Bairstow – and he said, "Bisto?" and I said, "No, Bairstow". I thought he was just being stupid, he was a real idiot, you know. Then he said something about he knows the *Bisto Kid*. How was I ter know he might have been talking about our William?'

'You weren't,' soothed Dorothy. 'Now, did he say anything else about this *Bisto Kid?*'

'I don't think so, oh yeah – he said something about, "But he doesn't go to our school".'

'It all fits!' cried Susan. 'That's why they didn't know him at Brewster Lane School!'

Frank turned to a young waitress, who had just arrived with a pot of tea, 'What other schools are there round here where the kids from Ashton House might go, apart from Brewster Lane?'

The waitress scratched her head, 'There's only St Theresa's Primary, but that's a Catholic school. They won't take non-Catholic there.'

'William's a Catholic!' shouted Jimmy. 'That's where he goes! He must do, stands ter reason!'

Frank held up his hands to calm them down. 'The great mystery is,' he mused, 'if this Bisto Kid *is* William, and if he *does* go to St Theresa's, then why did Wiggins say he'd never heard of him?'

Jimmy felt himself blushing now. There was something he knew about Wiggins that they didn't. He wasn't sure what the connection with

311

William was, but he knew he had to tell them.

He took a deep breath. 'That kid at Brewster Road had a nickname for Wiggins.' He paused, feeling four sets of eyes on him. Jimmy looked at the floor.

'They call him Wanker Wiggins!'

Susan was on the verge of chastising Jimmy for using such a word in front of the waitress, but Frank laid a restraining hand on her shoulder.

'Did he say why they call him that, Jimmy?' he asked.

Jimmy nodded, still looking at the floor. 'Because he's always doing it.'

'How do they know?' questioned Dorothy gently.

'They've watched him! Sometimes he gives 'em extra pocket money ter do it for him!'

The last words tumbled out, Jimmy looked up see what effect they'd had. A devastating effect.

'I'd better ring the police,' said Frank.

'No,' warned Dorothy. 'There's something odd about all this. I think we need to find out as much as we can before we start barging in anywhere.'

Susan nodded her agreement, she didn't want anything to jeopardise the situation now they were so close.

'Tell you what,' decided Dorothy. 'We'll have our lunch then I'll go back to Brewster Road school with Jimmy,' she looked at her watch. 'They should be having their afternoon break in about an hour. We'll have a word with this Joe Conroy and get the full story from him and you two go to St Theresa's and find out what you can.'

At two-thirty, the school doors opened to a galloping horde of children eager to enjoy every last second of their afternoon playtime. From their midst emerged Joe Conroy, heading for the gate at high speed and obviously intent on an early escape from the desperate boredom he'd already endured for too long that day.

Jimmy stood in front of him, arms outstretched, barring his way, but Joe didn't appear to see Jimmy and ran straight into him, both of them finishing in a heap on the pavement. Joe was wearing a corduroy windjammer which looked several sizes too small for him, a pair of patched grey flannel trousers tucked into Wellington boots and a balaclava with more holes than wool.

'Why didn't yer stop, yer barmy sod?' asked an irate Jimmy.

''Cos I'm a nutter,' explained Joe grinning up at an amazed Dorothy.

'Remember this morning, Joe?' inquired Jimmy, yanking Joe to his feet, 'when yer said yer knew the Bisto Kid?' Joe nodded dumbly as Jimmy continued, 'Where does he live, this Bisto Kid?'

'With us,' replied Joe, wondering what the mystery was.

'How old is he?' asked Jimmy, excited that the Bisto Kid was probably his brother.

'No idea. He's only a young 'un – he can be a cheeky little bastard though,' grinned the boy.

'Do you know where he is now, will he be at school?' asked Dorothy.

'Nah. I think he's still in t' roof room, been

there a couple o' days. He gave Wanker some cheek – called him a mucky old bugger. Took Wanker ages ter catch him. We was all cheerin' Bisto on. Caught him in t' end though. Gave him a good hiding and locked in t' roof room. It's bloody freezin' up there. I were up there once. He asked me ter toss him off an' I didn't feel like it. I'd never done nowt like that before.'

'Is that why Bisto got locked up do you think?' inquired Dorothy, finding it hard to control her fury.

'Thinks so. That's why Bisto called him a mucky old bugger.'

'This roof room, where is it?' asked Jimmy.

'In t' roof, yer dozy bugger,' laughed Joe. 'Blimey yer a bigger nutter than me!'

He yelled his parting insult over his shoulder as he galloped off down the street to enjoy a couple of hours of freedom before returning to the grim place he had to call home.

They caught up with Frank and Susan in the headmistress's office at St Theresa's.

'It's definitely him!' said an excited Susan, turning to Dorothy and Jimmy. 'He goes to this school!'

'A boy of exceptional ability,' added the headmistress, Sister Frances, 'when he's in school that is. But he hasn't been for a couple of days.'

'We know,' said Jimmy angrily. 'Wanker Wiggins has got him locked up in t' roof room.'

Sister Frances, raised an eyebrow at Jimmy's language, until Dorothy explained.

'Sorry if he shocked you, sister, but I'm afraid

314

the word described what this odious man does – and he apparently does it with the boys in his care! I think a phone call to the police might be in order.'

A shocked Sister Frances immediately picked up the telephone and was already talking to the police as the four of them left her office.

The iron gates were open when they arrived. Not yet closed after the lunchtime exodus of boys. Frank kicked open the door and led the angry quartet down the echoing corridor to Wiggins' office, out of which the short-trousered boy appeared, just as they arrived.

A half smile of recognition lit up his face, fading as he saw the fury on theirs. He wisely decided a retreat was in order and clattered off at high speed towards the front door.

Wiggins was sitting behind his desk, dabbing his forehead with a handkerchief as they arrived.

'No prizes for guessing what you've just been up to, you sick bastard,' roared Dorothy, swinging her walking stick in a long scything arc that hit Wiggins on the side of his head, knocking him clean out of his chair.

On his hands and knees, the man scrabbled across the floor, moaning with pain, clutching at a profusely bleeding ear and searching wildly for the glasses that Susan was callously crunching under her feet. Dorothy hooked her stick around Wiggins' neck, yanking him harshly to his feet; surprisingly strong for a woman, Frank thought admiringly.

'Where is he?' snarled Dorothy.

'I don't know who you mean,' wept Wiggins.

'William Bairstow! The boy you said doesn't live here!' roared Frank, grabbing Wiggins by the scruff of his neck.

'Oh, him? I had to punish him. He's...'

They were interrupted by the breathless return of the short-trousered boy, who viewed the scene at first with shock and then with satisfaction.

'If yer lookin' fer Bisto, he's up on t' roof. He says he's going ter jump off!'

Frank and Dorothy dashed outside, but Susan grabbed the boy and said fiercely, 'Show us how to get to this roof room – quick!'

The boy turned and charged up the stairs with Susan and Jimmy hard on his clattering heels.

Dorothy looked up at the roof and saw a small boy standing beside one of the stone gargoyles. He'd grown so much since she'd last seen him and her heart lurched at the sorrowful sight of this small, pathetic boy silhouetted against the bleak sky. There was fine, saturating rain in the air and the cold wind was tugging at his short trousers and torn shirt. Dorothy could see, even from that distance, that her nephew was crying, she felt sick with fear. The boy was lifting his arms forward, as though preparing to dive. Frank's mind raced. Must distract the boy, make him think about something other than jumping.

'Hello, William!' he shouted. 'I'm you're Uncle Frank and this is your Auntie Dorothy – we've come to take you home.'

The boy hesitated. This was good, thought Frank, anything to take his mind off jumping. 'Your sister Susan's here – and your brother Jimmy,' he continued desperately, looking round, wondering where they were.

'Please William,' pleaded Dorothy, her voice choking. 'We all love you, don't be a silly boy!'

The short-trousered boy had led Jimmy and Susan up to the second floor, then pointed at an iron spiral staircase leading up to the roof. They dashed up it and found themselves in a small dark room, lit only by a tiny window that was banging open in the wind. In front of the window a pile of books had been placed on top of one another. Susan stepped onto the top book and literally dived out of the window, landing in a puddle on the roof outside. Jimmy followed, almost falling on top of her. They could hear people shouting from below. Susan's eyes were drawn to a small figure standing at the edge of the roof. Her baby brother William, about to throw himself off. She could hear him sobbing as she gingerly crept towards him. She stopped.

'William,' she called softly. 'I said I was coming to get you, remember? Well here I am!'

The boy continued crying, Susan moved slowly towards him, frightened that he might slip over the edge.

'Leave me alone, yer rotten buggers,' sobbed the boy without turning round.

She took off her coat and held it out. 'I've brought you a coat, see. We're going home to Leeds in that car. Can you see it? The posh one – parked outside the gate.'

'The police are coming to get Wiggins, the mucky old bugger!' shouted Jimmy.

William liked these voices. These were nice voices. One of them sounded like the voice in his

317

mind, the one who'd promised to come and get him. The other one somehow knew that Mr Wiggins was a mucky old bugger. He turned. Susan smiled and Jimmy grinned. William wiped his eyes and tried to smile back. He knew just by looking at them that these people were his big brother and sister. Then his foot slipped.

Above the wind, Dorothy thought she heard Susan's voice coming from behind the boy on the roof and willed him to take at least one step back from danger. She saw William half-turn round to see who was talking to him, then she saw him teetering over the edge.

'Please God, no!' gasped Frank.

The boy circled his arms frantically to regain his balance, but Dorothy knew he wasn't going to manage it, the boy was falling. Dorothy closed her eyes but Frank's eyes remained transfixed.

An arm came out and grabbed one of the boy's legs, then another arm grabbed the other leg and the boy was pulled back to safety. Frank slapped Dorothy on the back.

'They've got him, he's alright!' he yelled ecstatically.

Dorothy opened her eyes in disbelief and looked up to see the three faces looking down at them.

'Do you know, Frank?' said Dorothy, after her heart had stopped racing. 'I haven't had a minute's flaming peace since they came to live with me!'

'I can well imagine it,' smiled Frank, placing a comforting arm around Dorothy. 'Trouble is, there's three of the buggers now!'

Dorothy was still alternately weeping and laughing as the police arrived to arrest Wiggins, who was still crawling blindly around, looking for his glasses, cruelly taunted by the short-trousered boy, who knew he had nothing more to fear from this evil man.

The journey back to Leeds was a silent journey. Billy, as he chose to be called, sat between Jimmy and Susan on the back seat. He cuddled up to Susan, his small arms gripping her tight as though frightened she might leave him. They'd all said comforting words to him, but everything seemed so inadequate. It was impossible to understand what was going through his six-year-old mind. Impossible to understand the mentality of the authorities who placed children like Billy in the hands of such foul men.

Susan had made a desperate grab for him as she saw him falling off the roof. She managed to get a grip on his ankle, but he was slipping away from her as Jimmy hurled himself forward and grabbed Billy's other leg. Between them they pulled their brother to safety.

Billy's face was still white with shock as the three of them looked down on the weeping face of their Auntie Dorothy being slapped on the back by Frank.

The police took a subdued Wiggins away, watched by Mrs Abbotson and various other members of staff who had appeared from the woodwork to witness their master's disgrace. Many of them had little to be proud of themselves; and their faces were shocked and sombre as they too were led away to various police cars. Frank spent some time explaining what had happened, making a particular point of mentioning the cruelty at the Fairfield Home in Huddersfield.

'For what damn good it'll do!' he said disparagingly to Dorothy, as they watched the convoy of police cars disappear.

Billy had insisted on bringing back with him just one treasured possession. A one-eyed rabbit he'd had with him all the time he'd been in care.

'Hey! That was mine,' cried Jimmy on seeing it. 'I often wondered where it had got to.'

'Well, yer not having it back, yer big bugger!' protested Billy.

'I think you'll need to tidy up his vocabulary,' suggested a grinning Frank.

As the car cruised through rain-swept hills on the bleak road back to Yorkshire, Susan hugged him and crooned to him as she'd heard their mam do. Billy fell fast asleep and didn't wake up until the car pulled in to Broughton Terrace.

'Coming in for a cup of tea, Frank?' asked Dorothy as they began to get out.

'No – I think I'll leave you all to it,' said Frank, 'I reckon you've a lot to talk about and you don't want an outsider like me involved.'

'We don't think you're an outsider, Frank,' argued Susan stoutly. 'Not after today anyway.'

'From now on,' decided Jimmy, 'you're our Uncle Frank – isn't that right, our Billy?'

Billy was much too staggered by the dramatic turn round in his life to make any comment, he just shrugged.

Dorothy waved goodbye to Frank and turned the key in the lock. 'Right, William,' she smiled. 'We've got a brand new bed waiting for you.'

'Me name's Billy,' he said firmly.

'Sorry, Billy,' she laughed. 'You're sharing with Jimmy, is that okay?'

Although the question was rhetorical, due to there being nowhere else he could sleep, Dorothy thought it only fair to let him think he had a choice in the matter.

'Yes, thank you very much,' replied Billy, displaying the disciplined good manners of the institutionalised child.

'Good job yer said yes, or yer'd have been sleeping in t' outside lavvie!' laughed Jimmy.

Billy laughed along with his new brother and followed him upstairs to see his new bed. Dorothy sat on the settee and patted the empty space beside her, inviting Susan to sit down.

'He's had a rough time, hasn't he? You couldn't begin to understand how guilty I feel.'

Susan shook her head. She still had ambivalent feelings towards Auntie Dorothy. It had taken an effort to forgive her for lying about Billy's death. The crime was partially absolved by Dorothy's willingness to sacrifice herself on Susan's behalf, when she laid into Simmo and finished up in jail. But this was different. Billy had almost made Dorothy's lie come true, driven to the brink of suicide by the people Dorothy had sent him to. She saw no reason to spare her auntie any feelings of guilt; after all, she'd been the architect of her brother's miserable existence.

'It's going to take him a long time to get over

what's happened to him,' continued Dorothy sadly. 'Wouldn't surprise me if we didn't have to take him to some sort of psychiatrist. I wonder if he'll ever forgive me?'

'I don't suppose he even blames you,' said Susan philosophically. 'He's just a kid. Kids never question what happens around them. They always think whoever's doing it knows best.'

Dorothy nodded sadly then stared hard at Susan. 'If it's any consolation,' she said, 'I'm not asking you to forgive me, that wouldn't be fair. I can't even forgive myself. What I did was the height of selfishness.'

Susan laid an arm around her auntie's shoulder. 'You're right, Auntie, it was; and maybe I can't forgive you. But I can't forget what you've done for us either, and I know what you've been through. So maybe it's quits.'

'Maybe,' smiled Dorothy, but she wasn't convinced. Nor was Susan.

Billy bounced happily on his bed. 'Best bed I've ever had,' he yelled.

'It's better than my bed,' grumbled Jimmy. 'I've never had a new bed.'

'Hey! Yer not havin' my bed,' said Billy defensively.

'Don't get yer knickers in a twist,' grinned Jimmy. 'I don't want your flipping bed.'

'Good job,' warned his new brother. 'I won't have ter bray yer now.'

'Oh? Yer think yer can bray me do yer? Come on, Bisto, I'll take yer on with one arm behind me back.'

Jimmy wished he hadn't said that, for Billy gave a fierce war whoop and came windmilling into him, forcing Jimmy back on his bed, struggling to hold his six-year-old adversary.

'Bugger me! Billy,' he gasped. Holding his brother's arms tightly and as far away from him as he could. 'Yer a flippin' lunatic. Who taught yer how ter fight like that?'

'Joe Conroy, he were me best mate. Showed me how ter fight.'

'Yer best mate? I've met Joe Conroy – he's twice as old as you!'

'I know, but he's a bit thick. I used to help him with his homework.'

'You! Helping a thirteen-year-old kid with his homework? Pull the other one, it's got bells on!'

'I were teaching him how ter read,' continued Billy, ignored Jimmy's sarcasm. 'He were comin' on alright as well. Have you got any books?'

Jimmy was taken aback. 'I've got a Biggles and some Billy Bunter books in me cupboard, but I haven't got owt for a six-year-old.'

'I like Biggles. They had Biggles in t' school library. I've never read no Billy Bunter books, can I lend one off yer, please?'

Jimmy opened his bedside cupboard and brought out a book, which he handed to his brother. 'There yer go, our young 'un, give us it back when yer've finished with it.'

Billy took the book and looked across at Jimmy. 'Is that what yer gonna call me – "our young 'un"?' he asked, seemingly proud of his new identity.

'Well, that's who yer are, innit?'

'What shall I call you then?'

'Yer call me "our kid", wotcha think yer call me?' replied an exasperated Jimmy. 'Blimey, our young 'un, I hope yer can read better than yer can think!'

Billy grinned, delighted with his new brother. Jimmy studied him for a while, wondering if it was right to ask a six-year-old such a question, but quickly dismissed his misgivings.

'Yer know that mucky old bugger at Ashton House?' he asked, without a hint of tact. 'Why did he lock yer up in that roof room?'

Billy blushed – a Bairstow family weakness. 'Yer won't tell no one, will yer?'

'Scout's honour,' vowed Jimmy, who wasn't a scout so it didn't count.

'He got his willy out and asked me ter touch it!'

'Ugh! The mucky old sod. That's what Joe Conroy told me.'

'I know,' agreed Billy. 'He used to do it to all the kids, but I were t' youngest so he never did it ter me.'

'Till the other day yer mean?'

Billy nodded. 'He got me in his office and told me if I touched his willy he'd give me extra pocket money.'

'Hey! Is that what he called it, his willy?' giggled Jimmy. He himself having graduated to the dick, prick or nob stage.

'No,' grinned Billy. 'He called it his weasel! He asked me if I wanted ter stroke his weasel!'

'Stroke his weasel!' howled Jimmy, screaming with laughter, rolling back on his bed and waving his legs in the air. 'I've never heard it called that, stroking his weasel – that's a good 'un, that!'

Billy immediately saw the funny side of it and joined in his brother's convulsions. After they both calmed down, Jimmy asked, 'Wotcha do then?'

'I kicked him and called him a mucky old bugger. All t' kids were listening outside his office an' they started laughing. He didn't half get mad.'

'Where did you kick him?' asked Jimmy, dying for Billy to give the right answer.

'On his weasel!' he announced.

Jimmy fell back and howled once again, tears rolling down his face. This was the answer he wanted. 'Pop goes the weasel!' he sang. 'Hey! Yer popped *his* weasel for him, our young 'un!'

There was more laughter coming from outside the bedroom door. Dorothy and Susan, on their way to see how the boys were getting along, had stopped to listen in on the conversation. They now clung to each other in sobbing hysterics.

Billy wouldn't be needing any psychiatrist to release him from his trauma. He had Jimmy.

Chapter Twenty-Three

Jimmy and Susan came home from school together on the bus and decided to visit Mam and Dad's grave, and maybe have a look round to see if they could see a headstone that might be a suitable replacement for the stone they'd cracked.

The cemetery was in full bloom. The trees heavy with leaves and blossom, verges alive with summer flowers, graves freshly tended and decorated with sprays and wreaths and messages hopefully crossing across the great divide. Jimmy risked a glance across at where the armless angel looked sweetly down on the spot where the woman had been murdered, and was taken aback at the sight of Len Bateson, on his knees, talking to himself as if in prayer.

'Hiya, Len!' hailed Jimmy, much to Susan's consternation. But Len didn't seem to hear. His mouth was moving and Jimmy plucked up courage to walk over to him. There was a bunch of carnations on the very spot where the woman had fallen.

'It was her fault, she drove me to it,' Len seemed to be talking to the carnations. 'Anyway, like I say, I'm sorry. Not a day's gone by when I haven't regretted it. It should've been her not you!'

Jimmy froze in his tracks when he heard this. Susan who was following him out of some sort of sisterly protection, heard Len as well. She laid a cautioning hand on Jimmy's shoulder and pointed to the tree they'd hidden behind on that fateful night. With bated breath they edged behind the wide trunk, just as Len turned to leave, still muttering words of abject apology. As they heard him walk away they slowly moved round the tree, keeping it between them and the murderer at all times. For now they were as certain as they could be that it was Len who killed the woman.

'We'll tell P.C. Greenough,' decided Susan. 'He's alright is P.C. Greenough.'

Jimmy was unsure about it all.

'Can't yer just ring 'em anonywhatsit and tell 'em Len killed her?' he asked.

'Could do, I suppose,' she mused. 'No, it's better to do the job properly!'

Jimmy couldn't see why, but trudged disconsolately along with her all the same.

Engraved in the deep stone lintel above the door it said simply 'POLICE STATION' as it had for the seventy years it had stood there. The words always struck fear into Jimmy's heart. There were many other words written on the walls. Rude words of criticism by people who were not admirers of the police within. The odd times Jimmy had been inside, mainly in the company of Jackie Crombie, had never been happy ones. He shuffled in behind his sister, who kept telling him he'd got nothing to worry about. The young policeman on the desk did a double take of this pretty school girl walking through the door, with a scruffy young tyke skulking behind her.

'Yes, madam, what can I do for you?' he asked cheerfully.

'We'd like to see P.C. Greenough,' said Susan, 'on very important business.'

'Alan!' yelled the policeman through a door at the back of him. 'Customers for you!'

Jimmy's eyes were automatically drawn to a picture of the murdered woman on the wall, above a request for information leading to the apprehension of the killer. Alongside this was a

327

poster advertising the Policemen's Summer Ball at the Leeds Town Hall, and a photograph of a grinning policeman above the words 'Have You Seen This Man?' All of which somehow detracted from the gravity of the murder they'd come to talk about.

Alan Greenough appeared with a half-eaten sandwich in his hand and his sleeves rolled up.

'Hello, you two,' he smiled, genuinely happy to see them.

'We've come to report a murder,' announced Jimmy solemnly. Susan kicked him because she'd always wanted to say that.

'The woman who was murdered in the cemetery last year,' she expanded. 'We know who did it!'

'Len Bateson,' blurted out Jimmy, who was determined to be the one with the news. Susan kicked him again, harder this time. He was a pest and she wished she'd come on her own.

'You'd better come in,' said Alan, with a mouthful of cheese and tomato, as he lifted up a hinged counter to allow them through.

He led them to a large office full of desks, mainly unattended apart from the unpleasant policewoman, to whom their Auntie Dorothy had taken exception, and with good reason.

'Sit yourselves down,' said Alan, 'and start from the beginning.'

Jimmy eyed the policewoman suspiciously as Susan began to speak. She was sitting at a nearby desk writing something, but kept looking up at Susan as the story unfolded, shaking her head sarcastically.

When Susan came to the second part of the story, how they'd seen him less than an hour ago, talking to a bunch of flowers, the policewoman threw down her pen and sat back laughing.

'They're the Bairstow kids, aren't they?' she called across to Alan.

'What of it?' replied Alan, who obviously had little time for the woman.

'And you believe all that rubbish?' she said pityingly.

'Is there some reason why I shouldn't?' he snapped angrily.

'No, none at all,' she said disparagingly. 'It's your career. If you want to waste your time believing every lying little toerag in the district, it's up to you!'

'You're dead right, Muscroft, it's up to me!'

Susan turned and looked at WPC Muscroft searchingly, before returning her attention to Alan.

'Is she the one Auntie Dorothy told us about?' she asked demurely, but loud enough for the WPC to hear. 'She said there was a fat, ugly one with a moustache, surely there can't be two like that!'

Alan, who had his back to Muscroft, winced in anticipation as Muscroft exploded across the room, grabbing Susan by her collar and dragging her to her feet. Alan intervened quickly.

'Do you mind, WPC Muscroft? You're intimidating witnesses to a major crime!'

Muscroft let go, shaking with anger.

'Thank you,' soothed Alan. 'Now sit down and mind your own business and we'll say no more

329

about it.' He turned to Jimmy and his shaking sister. 'Right, you two, I'm taking you to see Inspector Mansfield, let's see what he makes of your story.'

Jimmy for one was glad to get out of that room. Sometimes he wished Susan would keep her big mouth shut, he was a marked man now!

The following night Alan Greenough knocked on the Bairstows' door, taking off his helmet as he walked in. Jimmy and Susan stood before him expectantly, Dorothy offered him a welcoming cup of tea. She had been forewarned about his visit, Susan having told her all about what had happened in the cemetery.

'Why didn't you tell me about it at the time?' asked a slightly put out Dorothy.

'We couldn't, you were in jail,' explained Susan.

'Oh, right,' said Dorothy. There were some answers you just couldn't argue with.

Alan Greenough faced his two star witnesses with a certain trepidation. 'I thought it only fair to let you know,' he said hesitantly, 'that we've had to let him go!'

'Oh, heck!' exclaimed Jimmy, who wasn't really sure what the implications of this were.

'Why?' inquired a shocked Susan. 'Don't you think he did it?'

'As a matter of fact we do,' admitted Alan, ruefully. 'But his wife's given him an alibi.'

'A what!' exclaimed Susan.

'It's when somebody says you were with them when you weren't really,' explained Jimmy.

'I know what an alibi is, thank you very much,'

objected Susan scornfully.

'She swears he stayed in all that night,' went on the constable. 'So it would be their word against yours, and on the night you say you weren't dead sure it was him.'

'If they say it was him, then it was him!' declared Dorothy stoutly.

'Like I said,' continued Alan, 'it's the Batesons' certain word against their "not sure" word.' He turned to Jimmy and Susan, 'If you two are prepared to swear on oath that it was definitely him that night, then we'll pull him back in.' He looked at them. 'Well?'

Susan thought hard for a while, then shook her head, she didn't fancy swearing something like that on oath, Jimmy breathed a sigh of relief that he didn't have to go to court.

Alan took the cup of tea from Dorothy and took a sip. 'You make a nice cup of tea in this house,' he grinned.

Jimmy returned his grin, remembering who'd made the last cup of tea constable Greenough had drunk here.

'If it's any consolation,' said Alan. 'Bateson doesn't know it was you who saw him!'

'Thank heaven for that!' sighed a relieved Dorothy. 'We've had enough problems recently without having murderers breathing down our necks!'

Chapter Twenty-Four

Frank put down the phone looked across at Dorothy, who was juggling with a mass of figures on a piece of paper in front of her.

'That's it!' He rubbed his hands with glee. 'Allerdyce has completed. The money's in the bank – sixteen thousand lovely pounds. Leaves us eleven thousand in the black!'

'I know,' said Dorothy, not sharing Frank's jubilation. 'I'm just working out what best use to put it to. No point having it in the bank, we're in business to make money for ourselves not for the banks.'

'What have you got in mind now?' asked Frank guardedly. He'd never been so well off in terms of cash in the bank and just wanted to savour the moment.

'There's an eighteen-acre plot in Horsforth we could pick up for five thousand, the owner's desperate to sell.'

'Saw it last year, waste of time. There's room for over two hundred bread and butter houses. The planners'll pass it but the highways won't. They've got this daft idea about two out of three families owning a car within the next ten years. That site leads out onto a dangerous road junction, more houses means more cars using that junction – end of story. That's why it's so cheap. Once the council have improved the junction it'll be a different story.'

'And you're saying the council have no plans for improving it,' said Dorothy.

'Correct,' confirmed Frank.

'Wrong,' said Dorothy. 'The council drew up plans two years ago. What they don't have is money to do the work.'

'Nor are they likely to have in the near future,' argued Frank.

'Correct,' agreed Dorothy. 'Have you any idea how much it would cost to do that junction?'

'Haven't a clue,' admitted Frank, who also hadn't a clue where the conversation was leading.

'Ballpark figure,' said Dorothy. 'Three thousand, possibly less if put out to tender. I picked up a copy of the plans from a friend of mine in the Engineer's Department and dropped it into Gilchrist Brothers for a rough estimate.'

'Why are you telling me all this?'

'Because I want you to go to the council,' said Dorothy, 'and offer to do the junction for nothing in exchange for planning permission for two hundred houses. It's a perfectly legitimate request. They'd need a hell of a good reason to turn it down.'

'Why hasn't anyone else tried it then?' asked Frank, who thought there must be a catch here somewhere.

'Same reason as you didn't. They assume the council wouldn't entertain such an idea. But the council are obliged to look at it, and they'd need a damn good reason to turn it down. I think we should go to the council and confirm that the junction is still their only objection, then make our offer. Once we have their acceptance in writing, we go ahead and buy. Then you sub-contract the junction to the lowest bidder, payment on approval by the council and in three or four months' time we've got a piece of land for two hundred houses for what?'

'Eight thousand,' said Frank.

'And worth how much, would you say?'

'Twenty at least,' replied Frank, gazing fondly at this amazing woman chewing on a pencil at the other side of his desk.

'Dorothy.'

'What, Frank?'

'Do you think? I mean, would you like to, er – Oh, sod it! It's years since I asked a girl out on a date.'

Then realising that he'd done it, he looked at her expectantly. She'd looked back at him with a pretend coyness, teasing him with fluttering eye-lashes.

'Oh, forget it,' he said, slightly embarrassed at the situation he'd just put himself in.

'I most certainly will not!' she replied indig-nantly. 'You can't just raise a girl's hopes just like that, then drop her flat without so much as a "by your leave". Where are we going?'

'Well,' said Frank, taken unawares. 'We could go dancing – do you like dancing?'

'Yes, I love dancing.'

'We could go to the Hippodrome on Saturday.'

'I'd like that, Frank,' she smiled. 'Oh, but, Frank,' she added, serious now.

'What?'

'No strings – I don't want to spoil what we

have. We're friends and business partners – nothing else, never will be.'

'Fair enough,' accepted Frank, disappointed at the finality of her last three words.

Chapter Twenty-Five

'Morning, Jimmy, morning, Susan,' shouted Vera Bateson from across the street as they walked through the gate on their way to school. They felt uneasy. How could she be so cheerful knowing her husband was a murderer?

'Morning, Mrs Bateson,' they replied in polite unison.

'Vera, please. You're old enough to start calling me Vera surely?'

They both smiled nervously and went on their way.

Vera stood and watched them disappear round the corner, then looked up at her husband, staring blankly out of the bedroom window.

'Is Len not going to work this morning?' asked an inquisitive Mrs Byrne from next door, who'd never forgiven Vera for trying it on with her husband at the VE Day party.

'No, he's having a day off sick. It's all that burning rubbish – gets on his chest,' said Vera, who had little time for Mrs Byrne anyway.

Len was an odd job man at the destructor. It was all the work he could get despite having been an engineering draughtsman before the war. His nerves were shattered. He'd lost every decent job he'd been offered due to being completely unable to concentrate on his work. He'd gone from job to job, each one too much of a challenge, until eventually he'd found his niche at the destructor. He was happy in his work, he didn't have to think and he had no responsibilities. The worst part of his day was going home to Vera's constant nagging. She'd been an attractive woman, who'd married Len before the war as some sort of a status symbol. None of her friends had husbands with an office job – a job with real prospects. And now look at him – a labourer at the destructor, the lowest of the low. She knew her friends were laughing at her behind her back but she couldn't do anything about it. So she took it out on Len. He was barred from her bed. She was otherwise well catered for in that department. A couple of local husbands, whose wives weren't up to the job, called in at regular intervals, always leaving a ten bob note on the sideboard as they left.

She'd even got her rent free up to recently, until that idiot Simpson tried it on with Dorothy Bairstow. She wasn't all that sorry, he was repulsive – still fifteen bob a week wasn't to be sneezed at.

Vera had been quite happy thinking she was the widow of a war hero. Her lodger was making her happier still, he'd even proposed and she only just accepted, but the engagement was cut short when Len turned up alive and kicking and threw her fiancé out of the bedroom window.

She walked back into the house and went upstairs to where Len was lying on top of her

336

bed, completely naked.

'Do you mind getting back in your own room!'

Len made no move, he just watched her.

'Is that little thing supposed to get me going?' she laughed scornfully. 'I'm not one of your whores, you know!'

'No! You're me wife. I shouldn't need to go with whores!'

'Well, there's evidently one less for you to go with now. What happened? Did she laugh at you? Did she find you pathetic? Because you are pathetic, just look at you! You're not a man, I don't know why I lied for you last night!'

Len sat up. 'Why did you lie for me?' he asked.

Vera poured more scorn on him. 'Don't you think it's bad enough having a loser like you for a husband without everybody knowing you're a murderer? I didn't lie for your benefit. Just put one foot wrong and I'll shop you just as soon as look at you!'

'You should have told the truth,' smiled Len. 'You should have got me locked up, got me hung – that's what I deserve. Trouble is I'm at your mercy now and I don't like that.'

Vera didn't like the way this conversation was going. She'd never seen Len like this before. He'd never frightened her before. She made for the door but Len anticipated this and moved to block her. A large kitchen knife appeared in his hand. He waved it menacingly in her face.

'Take your clothes off!' he said calmly.

'Stop acting stupid, Len!'

'Take your clothes off or I'll cut your throat!' He had a look in his eye that she'd never seen before and she didn't like it.

'Alright,' she said uncertainly, 'I'll play your stupid game, just this once!'

Without taking her eyes off the knife, she removed her clothes until she stood before him completely naked. He looked her up and down, shaking his head in disdain. She wasn't the woman he'd married. Her breasts were beginning to sag, her stomach was heavier and there were ripples of fat across her thighs.

'What happened to you?' he suddenly snarled, jabbing the knife towards her and forcing her to fall backwards to the floor.

'Please, Len,' she pleaded. 'You can have me if you like, I'm sorry for hurting you. Just put the knife down.'

She reached up between his legs and held him, moving up and down until he was erect. He stared wildly at her, the knife was now pointing at her throat. Vera felt more aroused than she'd ever been in her life before.

'Put it inside me, Len, now!' she almost begged, pulling him down towards her, ignoring the threat of the knife. If he was playing a game it sure as hell was working. If not, she'd worry about that once she'd had her fill of him.

She guided him inside her and he began thrusting insanely again and again with a strength she'd never known before, in him or any man. He went on and on, for what seemed like an age, then he was gasping for breath and she was shuddering to a climax with a molten surge that kept coming and coming as Len collapsed, spent and exhausted, on top of her.

She lay there for a while not quite knowing what to do. Was he still the madman she'd been so scared of just minutes ago?

'Len?' she said gently. 'Could I get up now, please?'

He slowly raised himself to his knees and looked down at her. That strange look still in his eyes. Vera suddenly felt sick with terror. She tried to scream but Len stifled it with his free hand. He raised the knife high above his head, her eyes were glued to it, hypnotised by this thing that was about to end her life.

Len gave a strangled, frustrated yell and brought the knife down viciously, stabbing time and time again at the threadbare rug beneath Vera's head. She was crying with shock, her breath coming in short gasps. Len pulled the knife out for the last time and got to his feet looking down at his wife who was now curled up in a foetal position, sobbing hysterically.

'Get up, Vera,' he said savagely.

She got to her knees and clung to him around his legs, but he kicked her away.

'I told you to get up!' He held the knife to her throat and followed her progress as she slowly raised herself up off the floor.

'Sit on that!' he commanded harshly, pointing to a high-backed chair at the bottom of the bed.

She sat down on the chair as he rummaged in a drawer and took out various scarves and belts with which he gagged her and expertly tied her to the chair and the chair to the iron bedpost.

'What are you going to do to me, Len?' she sobbed, still naked, still shaking with fear.

'I couldn't do it,' he said, shaking his head. 'But it's got to be done – and it's got to look like an accident!'

'I wouldn't tell anyone about you, Len! I'm your wife. I lied to the police, didn't I – you heard me lie to the police!'

'For your own benefit,' he said. 'That's what you told me. You only lied for your own benefit – shop me just as soon as look at me, that's what you said!' He bent down to kiss her. 'Goodbye, Vera,' he whispered, crying himself now.

Len dressed himself and went out to report late for work. A plan of sorts already forming in his head.

Dorothy took a last look at herself in the mirror, gave herself an appreciative nod and left her family their parting instructions.

'Don't be late to bed, any of you. I know it's Saturday tomorrow, but you all need your beauty sleep.'

'Susan does, we're beautiful enough, aren't we, Billy,' cracked Jimmy. He and Billy laughed, then ducked as Susan hurled a cushion in their direction.

'Billy, your bedtime's eight o'clock, not a minute later,' she added before kissing each of them goodbye.

Billy knew that there was no point thinking he'd get away with anything with Susan, she was stricter with him than Auntie Dorothy.

'Just get yourself off, and have a good time,' laughed Susan. 'I'll make sure they behave themselves.'

Frank was already waiting for her in the car as she hurried out, stopping to wave again to the three of them as they came to the window to see her off.

'Do yer think owt'll come of it?' asked a curious Jimmy of his more worldly sister. 'This is the third time he's taken her out in two weeks!'

'No idea,' commented Susan, who thought it was rather nice that her auntie and Frank hit it off so well together.

'It'd be good if they got married,' said Jimmy. 'He's got a great house, has Frank. We could all go live there!'

'I like it here!' declared Billy, who, generally speaking, had never benefited from moves.

'It's not where you live, Billy,' said Susan sagely. 'It's who you live with. Oh, and while I'm at it – washed and pyjamas on, now!'

Billy slunk into the scullery and turned on the tap, before stripping off his shirt. There was no point him giving himself just a 'lick and a promise'. Susan would only make him start again, and he didn't want to miss Dick Barton on the wireless.

At eight o'clock on the dot he was on his way upstairs with his one-eyed rabbit and a glass of milk. He didn't mind though. Susan hadn't found out about his torch and his latest Biggles book, both on loan from Jimmy, who winked at him as he said goodnight.

He was fast asleep when the quiet knock came at the door. Susan looked at the clock and then at Jimmy.

'It's ten-past-ten, who on earth is that?'

Jimmy went with her as he always did when things weren't quite right. Susan turned the handle curiously and they both jumped back as the door was suddenly pushed open.

He stood there, holding the same kitchen knife he'd failed to stab his wife with earlier in the day. The same manic expression on his face and, like Vera, Susan and Jimmy went cold with terror. Neither could speak as he forced them backwards at the point of his knife.

'So, yer thought yer'd shop me to the law, did yer?' he snarled.

'We – we don't know w ... what your talking about, Mr B ... Bateson!' stammered Susan.

'Don't lie ter me!' he yelled. 'She told me it were you, that fat copper. She doesn't like you two, does she?'

'We just said we saw you in the cemetery that's all, Mr Bateson.' Susan could see he was deranged and hadn't a clue how to deal with him.

'You saw me do it! That's what yer told the coppers. You were right an' all – I did do it. I killed that filthy whore – brayed her bleeding head in. Stopped her laughing at me, didn't it?' He started laughing himself now – then just as quickly stopped and his face grew ugly again. He indicated the door with his knife. 'Out!' he snarled. 'Now!'

The three of them walked slowly across the street to the Batesons' house, two hearts beating like hammer drills, the other scarcely beating at all.

The door was swinging open. Jimmy and Susan entered with a feeling of dread, wondering what

342

he'd done with Mrs Bateson. She was nowhere to be seen, up to this point Jimmy hadn't spoken.

'I need to pee, Mr Bateson,' he said pathetically.

Len thought for a bit, then said harshly, 'Piss in yer pants!' but Jimmy had already beaten him to it.

He pushed them roughly to the floor, then bound and gagged them with the same efficiency as he'd tied up his wife, who was still trussed up in the room above them. They were tied together back to back on the floor. Jimmy had one leg tied to the cellar door handle, preventing them from moving across the room.

Len looked down with some satisfaction at his handiwork then turned out the light and left.

Dorothy looked at her watch and then at Frank. 'It's nearly the witching hour, boss, time for beddy byes.'

The Johnnie Goodman orchestra stuck up the last waltz. 'Might as well eh?' asked Frank as he led her back on to the floor for the last time that evening.

'You're a wonderful dancer for a joiner,' complimented Dorothy.

'It comes from all the sawing,' he explained seriously. 'There's rhythm to it you see. Now bricklayers, they're a different kettle of fish altogether. If I was a bricklayer you'd be going home with sore feet!'

Dorothy laughed at this funny man. She'd enjoyed this evening. She felt comfortable with Frank. He wasn't as outrageous as Tommy had

343

been, but there again, even Tommy would have slowed down by the time he reached his forties. As the waltz whirled to a close, Frank bent over and kissed her gently on the lips. Sensing her respond he held her tightly and stopped dancing. Both of them were now alone in the centre of the dance floor locked in a passionate embrace.

Johnnie Goodman put down his clarinet and came to the microphone. 'Could someone bring a bucket of water to the dance floor, please, then we can all go home!'

Frank and Dorothy broke off their embrace to great laughter and tumultuous applause and hurried off the floor with red faces and embarrassed grins.

'Your place or mine,' asked Frank, holding the car door open for Dorothy. He laughed to himself. 'I've always wanted to say that. When I first went courting I didn't have a place. It was more a case of "your back alley or mine"?'

He walked round the car and climbed into the driver's seat. 'Well?' he asked.

'Well what?'

'Your place or mine?'

'Sorry, Frank, I didn't realise you were being serious. No, I must go back. I've left the kids on their own.'

'Are these the same kids who managed very well on their own for all those weeks you were in prison?'

'There's Billy there as well, he's only six.'

'And Susan's there as well. They don't come more capable than Susan,' argued Frank.

'Point taken, but if I don't go home they'll be worrying.'

'They'll be asleep! I'll have you back before they wake up, promise.'

'Do you make a habit of seducing young helpless virgins, Mr Sackfield?' Dorothy giggled; she'd had more to drink than she'd had for a long time.

'Everyone has to have a hobby!'

'Promise to get me back before they wake up?'

'Promise.'

There was a beguiling modesty about Frank which extended to his love-making. Like Dorothy, he'd had no one for a long time and he didn't want to appear too pushy. He lived in a small detached house with an overgrown garden and a garage. So by nineteen-forties standards he was middle class.

He knocked on the bathroom door. She'd been in there a long time, not having had the luxury of a bathroom since she left her father.

'I er, I found a shirt you might like to wear,' he said hesitantly.

'Why would I want a shirt?' The drink was taking its toll on Dorothy, she was feeling daring.

'Oh, right. I'll get into bed then,' he called through the door. He climbed into bed, switching on the small light beside him.

Dorothy had been in the bathroom thinking about the last man who saw her strip naked. Why should this lovely man be deprived of something that the foul Neville Simpson had enjoyed? It was a logic tempered by drink, but Dorothy had recklessly convinced herself of its merit. She swung seductively round the bedroom doorway, smoking a cigarette in a long holder she'd found in the bathroom, dressed in bra, pants, stockings, suspenders – and a trilby hat she'd found in the hall. She hummed to herself as she moved, what she hoped, was gracefully around the room, followed by Frank's startled eyes. One by one the garments flew his way until she, quite brazenly, stood on the bed, looking sensuously down at him as she removed her panties and dropped them on his face.

'What do you think, Mr Sackfield?' she asked. 'Do I get the job?'

'I have to test you on the practical side of things before I make my final decision,' he said, finding it difficult to concentrate on the game she was playing. She threw the bedclothes back and expressed horror at his striped pyjamas.

'Mr Sackfield! You're out of uniform!'

He smiled and pulled her down to him, allowing her to make him as naked as she was. Frank had never seen anyone as beautiful as Dorothy, not even his ex-wife. She paled into insignificance beside this delightful woman, who was now squirming on top of him, easing herself onto him, her breasts swinging playfully against his chest. He closed his eyes and allowed her to carry him away to a pleasure he had never known before.

Billy was one of the few people in Broughton Terrace who hadn't had their sleep disturbed by the spasmodic hammering of a pneumatic drill coming from the destructor yard. But Billy had been used to spending his nights in dormitories full of disturbed boys who often woke screaming and crying and shouting. It'd take more than a pneumatic drill to wake Billy up. He woke at seven o'clock as he always had. Jimmy wasn't in his bed. Now there was a surprise, especially since he now remembered it was Saturday morning and Jimmy never got up early on Saturday morning. It didn't even look as though Jimmy's bed had been slept in.

'Jimmy!' he shouted.

No answer.

He went to the bottom of the attic stairs.

'Susan!'

No answer.

He knocked on Dorothy's door, then opened it slightly, enough to see her bed hadn't been slept in. He dashed up to the attic and burst into tears at the sight of Susan's tidy bed.

'Rotten buggers!' he sobbed.

He ran back down stairs and out into the street, still in his pyjamas, tears streaming down his face. He knew it had been too good to be true.

'Rotten buggers,' he repeated, sitting down on the front step, totally dejected. They'd left him again. He knew they would of course. All the kids at all the homes he'd ever been in had warned him about this. They come and get you but never for very long, they soon get fed up of you and back you come. But there was no way he was going back to that stinking home. No way. Still, it might be okay now that Wiggins had gone. I bet Joe Conroy's still there. He was alright was Joe. A bit thick but he'd never leave you – not like some people. What was he talking about? He'd left Joe, hadn't he? What would Joe think of him?

Dorothy and Frank drove back to Broughton Terrace in a contented silence. For both of them the evening and the ensuing lovemaking had given them something that had been missing from their lives for years. A slight hangover reminded Dorothy of the amount she'd drunk. She smiled to herself.

'I was a bit drunk last night, Mr Sackfield,' she said. 'I hope I didn't do anything naughty.'

'You behaved impeccably, Mrs Bairstow.'

'On a scale of one to ten – how impeccable.'

'Ten.'

'That's alright then – so long as it's under-stood,' she cautioned, 'that our relationship is purely platonic.'

'That's the word all the film stars use,' grumbled Frank.

'Then it's good enough for us.'

Frank gave a reluctant grin – it wasn't good enough for him. His face turned serious as he swung into Broughton Terrace.

'Isn't that your Billy sitting on the step?'

'Billy! What on earth are you doing out here in your pyjamas?'

He hadn't heard the car pull up, too full of self-pity for that. Auntie Dorothy got out and sat down beside him, hugging him to her. She could see he'd been crying. Frank looked out of the van, sharing Dorothy's guilt at somehow causing distress in such a small child.

'I thought yer'd left me again,' he said, drying his eyes and trying to smile up at his auntie.

'Oh, Billy, Billy – I'll never leave you, none of us will!'

'Jimmy and Susan have!'

'What are you talking about Billy?'

'They never slept here last night. I think they've buggered off!'

Dorothy started to correct Billy about his choice of verb but stopped when his statement had sunk in. 'How do you mean? Where are they?'

She was panicking now. Frank got out of the car and followed her inside as she dashed up the stairs and saw what Billy had told her was true. Neither bed had been slept in. They all came back down and realised that the back room light was on, so was the wireless – and the scullery door was wide open.

She started hammering on doors up and down the street. Beyond the destructor wall the pneumatic drill started again. People were coming to bedroom windows and shouting at Dorothy to 'be quiet, we've been awake all bloody night as it is'.

Still in her evening finery she jumped into Frank's car, shoved a bemused Billy, still in his pyjamas, in the back and the three of them drove the short distance to Paradine Hill Police Station. It was WPC Muscroft at the desk.

Dorothy didn't recognise her at first. 'I've come to report two missing children,' she said, unable to control the panic in her voice.

'Name?' said Muscroft, who knew very well what her name was.

'Shit!' groaned Dorothy, recognising Muscroft.

'And would that be your Christian name or your surname?' smirked Muscroft.

'What sort of a stupid question's that?' shouted Frank, who'd no idea who Muscroft was. 'There's two children missing and all you can do is make stupid jokes!'

A sergeant came through the door, 'Alright alright, calm down,' he said. 'What's all the noise about?'

'It's that Bairstow lot,' sniffed WPC Muscroft, as though the very name explained everything.

'My niece and nephew have gone missing, they didn't sleep in their beds last night!'

'Right, Mrs Bairstow,' said the sergeant, taking over the situation. 'When exactly did you notice they'd gone missing?'

'When I got back this morning and found young Billy sitting on the step crying his eyes out...'

The sergeant held up an interrupting hand. 'So, you're saying you weren't home last night? They were left to fend for themselves.' He was looking down his nose at Dorothy.

Frank sprang to her defence, 'Susan is sixteen – and they were left to fend for themselves for several weeks when you people arrested Mrs Bairstow for something she didn't do!'

'Yes, sir,' said the sergeant, suitably chastened. 'Now correct me if I'm wrong, but didn't they go off on their own once before, when they were less capable of fending for themselves?'

Muscroft was standing behind the sergeant's shoulder, a self-satisfied smirk on her face.

Dorothy looked back at the sergeant and said fiercely, 'Alright, alright, I get your message, let's hope nothing's happened to them then. We don't want to give the bearded lady here too much to laugh about, do we?'

Another constable appeared through the door with two cups of tea in his hand, one of which he gave to Muscroft, who was clearly angered by Dorothy's last remark.

'We'll keep an eye out for them, Mrs Bairstow, that's all we can do,' said the sergeant, taking the second cup.

As Dorothy turned to go, a frightening thought came into her head; she paused and looked back at the sergeant. 'You don't suppose it's got anything to do with Len Bateson, do you? My kids are convinced he's the murderer – and so are you lot by the sound of things.'

'There's no way Mr Bateson could know it was your children who informed us about him,' the sergeant reassured her. 'We certainly didn't tell him.'

Dorothy briefly held Muscroft in her gaze, causing the policewoman to lower her eyes, then she looked back at the sergeant. 'I do hope you're telling me the truth, sergeant. Up to now, you people haven't inspired much confidence.'

She turned to Frank and Billy, 'Right then, we'd better try and sort this out ourselves. The people who are paid to do it, have got cups of tea to drink!'

Dorothy hammered hard on the Batesons' door. The three occupants could clearly hear her, but could do nothing about it. Jimmy tried to kick at the cellar door to make a noise she might hear, but Len had done his job too well, even making sure they had their backs to each other so they couldn't communicate. They'd been dozing on and off all night. Frightened, although not absolutely sure what they had to be frightened of. There was someone else upstairs, they both knew that. Every so often they could hear a thumping. Jimmy's legs were chapped where he'd wet himself the night before, Susan had somehow managed to control herself, although things were becoming urgent in that department.

'They're out, Dorothy love!' shouted Mrs Byrne from her next door bedroom window. 'Been out since yesterday morning. I heard 'em having a row, then he went off ter work, though he were supposed ter be off sick – and I think she must have cleared off as well.'

'Thanks, Mrs Byrne,' said Dorothy. She was not on first name terms with Mrs Byrne, who she thought was a busybody and a nuisance.

'That's alright love. Hey! Yer haven't got a cup of sugar I could borrow, have yer?' shouted Mrs Byrne, before slamming the window down in annoyance, because Dorothy was already gone. Her hand was firmly clutching Billy's as she and Frank drove round all the neighbouring streets in vain. Ray hadn't seen them, nor had any of Jimmy's pals. None of them seemed overly worried about their disappearance – such was Jimmy and Susan's reputation.

'Look, Dorothy,' Frank tried to reassure her. 'Knowing them two, they'll be okay. I've never come across two more resourceful kids than them. Why don't you wait at home? I've got to pop into work for half an hour, if they're not back by then, I'll have a good drive round.'

A game of cricket had started up in the street. The Gascoigne brothers had brought a team down from Bridge Street to challenge the depleted Broughton Terrace team. In the end, two mixed teams were picked in the time-honoured 'best gets picked first' method and the game started. Billy watched from his bedroom window, as Dorothy was too scared to let him out of her sight until Jimmy and Susan turned up.

A strange scenario ran through Billy's jumbled brain as he stared across at the Bateson house, which looked oddly quiet. Maybe Len Bateson was keeping them locked up and was torturing them this very minute. Maybe he'd already killed them!

He couldn't for the life of him understand why the police hadn't immediately rushed up there and shot their way in. If he knew Len Bateson had captured his brother and sister, why didn't anybody else? After all, everyone knew Len Bateson was a murderer. Grown-ups could be so stupid. Grown-ups could be so evil – Billy knew more than most about evil grown-ups.

He wished Jackie Crombie hadn't gone down with measles, between the two of them they could have easily rescued Jimmy and Susan. Ah well, he'd better tackle the job on his own. A ball flew high in the air, bouncing onto the Bairstow lavatory roof, then running back down into the rainwater gutter, where it lodged, safely out of the reach of the frustrated cricketers.

They saw Billy leaning out of the window, within easy reach of the ball.

'Nip out an' gerrus t' ball,' someone shouted.

Billy was out of the window and sliding along the slates in a flash. Throwing the ball down before lowering himself in to the hands of a helpful cricketer.

Deciding to make practical use of his unexpected freedom he made his way round to the front door of the Bateson house. Front streets were always quieter than back streets, but what front streets had were coal grates leading into cellars. A small boy of Billy's size could just about squeeze through one of these and providing the householder hadn't locked the cellar door, entry to the house would be easy; and as such properties made poor targets for burglars, security was never much of a priority.

He lifted the grate and went in head first, sliding down the concrete shute and landing more or less unhurt in a pile of coal. The layout of the cellar being much the same as the one at home, Billy managed to find his way, without a light, to the steps, at the top of which would be the door to the Batesons' back room. He pushed at the door and managed to get his face round it to see what the obstruction was.

'Jimmy!' he gasped. 'Bugger me! What you doing here?'

As pleased as Jimmy and Susan were to see their younger brother, it was still exasperating to be asked such a question when they were trussed up like a couple of Christmas turkeys. They grunted at him to take their gags off, and both breathed sighs of relief when he did so.

Eventually freed of their bonds, the two of them stood up and stretched. They wanted to go home, to eat, to pee, but first they had another priority.

'There's somebody upstairs,' Susan reminded Jimmy, he nodded. They'd heard scuffling sounds all night. 'You go up first,' she decided.

'Why me? You're the oldest!'

Susan sighed, she hated this constantly being used against her.

'Right, I'll go up first. Jimmy, you follow me. Billy, you wait here.'

As soon as Susan entered Vera's bedroom she spun round and blocked Jimmy's way.

'It's Mrs Bateson,' she whispered. 'She's tied up – she's got no clothes on!'

Jimmy now bitterly regretted not going first. 'Don't yer want me to help untie her?' he asked innocently, never having seen a naked woman.

'I think I can manage, thank you. Go downstairs and see what Billy's up to.'

A disgruntled Jimmy went back down the stairs, annoyed at his sister's attitude. It wouldn't have hurt her to let him have a quick look. 'How'd you figure out where we were?' asked Jimmy as they dodged across the cobbled cricket pitch, ignoring appeals from the fast bowler to, 'Gerrouta me sodding way!'

'Stands ter reason,' said Billy, who saw nothing but logic in his actions.

Dorothy had seen them through the scullery window and came dashing out to meet them. 'Thank God you're alright!' she pulled Jimmy to her, almost crushing him, forcing him to push her gently away so he could tell her what happened.

'Where's Susan?' asked Dorothy before Jimmy could say anything.

'She's untying Mrs Bateson!'

'She's what?'

'I'd have stopped to help, but Mrs Bateson hasn't got any clothes on – apparently!' he added the last word to emphasise that he actually hadn't seen their naked neighbour. 'Len Bateson tied her up,' he continued. 'He tied us up as well – we've been tied up all night. He's barmy is Len Bateson – and he did kill that woman – he told us he did!'

'Oh my God!' cried Dorothy, letting Jimmy go and dashing across the street to the Batesons' house.

Vera Bateson appeared at the door in a dressing gown, looking pale and shocked. Susan was supporting her.

'She's okay, Auntie Dorothy, we're both okay. Len said he was going to kill her. I think he must be coming back. We'd better get the police!'

Vera sat down on the step. 'Do you know what I'd like right now before we start bothering with the police?' she croaked hoarsely. 'A right nice cuppa tea.'

'You sit there, love, I'll make you one. Them coppers are a waste of time anyway!' comforted Dorothy, coughing as a gust of wind blew smoke over the destructor wall.

'Phew!' yelled one of the cricketers. 'What they burning today? Your old socks, Jimmy!'

Jimmy laughed and climbed up on to the back yard wall of the end house, then up on to the destructor wall to see where the smoke was coming from, pulling Billy up behind him. Billy sat beside his brother, a bit put out that he hadn't yet been accorded suitable thanks for his daring rescue. It wasn't every day that your little brother rescued you from a murderer, somebody should say 'thank you' surely.

They sat together, looking down at the smoke which was coming from a fire at the bottom of the chimney, trying to figure out what was going on. There was an odd crunching sound as the chimney seemed to shift slightly, then a man appeared out of the smoke and looked back at the fire, laughing loudly, but they couldn't see what was so funny.

'Isn't that him?' asked Billy.

'Who?'

'Len Bateson!'

Jimmy peered into the smoke. 'It flippin' is!' he gasped, as the crunching sound came again.

Jimmy grabbed his brother and lowered him down off the wall, making him drop at least six feet to the ground, before he himself jumped down on to the yard wall and then into the street. He looked back up at the chimney and then at the street full of children.

'Run!' he yelled. 'The chimney's falling down!'

Len Bateson laughed to himself as he cut out the

bricks from the base of the chimney with the pneumatic drill. Nobody came to check on what he was doing, he was a law unto himself in the destructor yard. Everyone assumed he was carrying out someone else's instructions. But the fact that his was a menial job, didn't mean that he was stupid. He was brighter than the rest of them put together. None of them had been a Flight Engineer in Lancasters during the war – and they didn't let idiots do that job, it carried the rank of Flight Sergeant. He was the only survivor out of a crew of seven who'd taken off from RAF Mildenhall that March morning in 1944. They thought he was dead. 'No Survivors' was the verdict of the rest of the squadron who'd seen his aircraft explode in mid-air. He was the only one wearing a parachute, a wise precaution as it turned out. He remembered being blown out of the plane, then pulling the rip-cord, then nothing else. He must have been unconscious when he landed, because he woke up in a muddy German field surrounded by ugly women and old men armed with shovels. One of the women was a real Teutonic harridan, he thought she was going to lamp him one with her shovel, which was bigger than anyone else's. It took two of the men to stop her. What was it that woman had against him?

This pneumatic drill made his work easier, even so he reckoned the job would take him all night. It had to be done carefully. The base of the chimney was well over two feet thick, six layers of brick before he got through to the inner lining. He intended to leave that, better not cut through the lining whilst the chimney was in use. As he cut out a section of bricks, he replaced it with cut-down railways sleepers to prop up the chimney until he was ready. There was a pile in the yard he'd cut up into eighteen-inch lengths.

He'd been shunted from Stalag to Stalag. How was he to know his letters weren't getting through? The Germans were on the run and they were taking him with them for company. They'd more to think about than his letters home apparently. Then he'd finished up in Poland in the most God-forsaken hole. He'd never have survived it there. But the Russians came along and liberated him. Their idea of liberating was raping, pillaging and hanging people. They were wanting to hang him because they thought he was German, they'd already strung a few of the Polish prisoners up. Stupid bloody Russians, fancy not being able to tell the difference between a Kraut and a Leeds lad – anyway he didn't stop to argue, he did a runner.

Once he'd cut out two thirds of the way round the chimney, it would be effectively supported by the railway sleepers. He was breaking out the part of the chimney facing his house. His engineer's brain told him that as soon as the props became unstable the chimney would topple towards the street, straight on top of his house and his darling wife, she was the one he wanted dead. Her and them two meddling kids.

Had his engineer's brain been thinking straight he might have worked out that the chimney was in fact destined to miss his house completely and fall right in the middle of Broughton Terrace. There'd be people killed that day – but his darling Vera wouldn't be one of them.

He'd run and walked all the way across Europe. Spurred on by his love for Vera. Two months it had taken him, unsure of what was happening, of who was his friend. The place was full of displaced persons. None of them looked very friendly. Best to assume everyone was his enemy, couldn't go wrong then. He hid in empty houses and barns and woods until he was found asleep by a British Tommy, prodding him awake with his bayonet. They made a fuss of him then alright. Couldn't believe it was possible to walk all that way, they said. Thought he was mad. But he wasn't mad, he did it because he had to – and because he wanted to get back to his beloved Vera.

They'd flown him home as a VIP. Rushed through his demob. First Class rail pass to Leeds, seventy-five quid demob money burning a hole in his pocket and every penny was going to be spent on Vera, his lovely Vera.

Once it was all cut out and propped, all he had to do was build a bonfire around the sleepers, douse the lot with paraffin, put a match to it and stand back. Once the fire burnt through the sleepers, down would come the chimney, bye bye, Vera and the meddling kids.

He still remembered the shock he felt when he found his Vera in bed with that man. He couldn't have timed it worse, both of them naked on top of the bed, he could hear them grunting as he crept upstairs but he didn't allow himself to think it might have been his wife screwing another man. Not his beloved Vera.

Where he got the strength from amazed him even today. He was emaciated from his time in the camps, not to mention his two-month hike. He'd dragged the man up by his hair and hurled him, still naked, through the bedroom window. With his world ruined, he refused to contest a charge of attempted murder, but when the judge heard his story he wouldn't accept his plea. He'd let him go with a ticking off. The poor bloody lodger was still in a wheelchair and serve him right.

When they heard Jimmy screaming with such urgency, the cricketers looked up at the wavering chimney and started to run. Jimmy was charging round like a maniac, pushing and kicking slow movers into action. Dorothy heard him shouting and without stopping to think, bustled Susan and Vera into the back door, through the house, out the front door and along the front street on to Paradine Hill.

She was choking with fear for the safety of Jimmy and Billy as, with a thunderous roar, the smoking edifice collapsed clean along the centre of Back Broughton Terrace. The main road was full of running children who'd only recently been playing cricket. She could just make out Billy, coughing as the dust cloud caught up with him, running beside a boy she took to be Jimmy. Her heart stopped momentarily as the masonry bounced around their heels then she breathed again as they managed to get clear. Children were running and stumbling and crying with fear. Choked by the dust and deafened by the noise. Many with cuts and bruises from flying masonry and nasty falls. Picking themselves up and charging blindly around, sometimes straight back towards danger.

Satisfied that he'd alerted everyone to the danger, Jimmy made his own bid to escape. He chanced a quick glance behind him as the rumbling grew louder. The chimney appeared to be collapsing from the bottom. Disappearing into the ground rather than toppling over. Then everything changed. It was falling straight down on him. The wall at the end of the street burst open and a moving mountain of rubble came bouncing towards him. One brick catching him on the back of his leg as he sprang after his pals, who were all several yards in front of him. Through the dust he could just see Billy galloping along at the back of them. The noise behind him was deafening. He was passing his own back yard when he realised he wasn't going to outrun the collapsing chimney so he flung himself sideways just as the huge tidal wave of rubble filled the area he'd just left. He took cover as best he could beside the lavatory wall then something hit him on the head and the world went black.

Alan Greenough was first on the scene. He was just about to walk into the station when he heard the roar. There was nothing he could do but watch with horror. He knew there'd be children playing in that street, there always were on a

362

Saturday morning.

When the dust settled he was amazed to see it had settled on a great crowd of people of all sizes, some huddled together in the middle of Paradine Hill, some sitting on the Co-op wall. All of them covered in a thick layer of dust, but otherwise unharmed.

'Is that you Mrs Bairstow?' Alan was only a few feet away from Dorothy, but she was so filthy it was hard to distinguish even her handsome features.

'Yes,' she smiled, her white teeth dazzling out from within the grime. 'And we're okay thanks very much!'

The policeman went round checking on everyone, soon joined by his colleagues. Alan looked across at the gang of blackened cricketers sitting on the Co-op wall.

'Do you know if they all got clear?' he asked Dorothy.

'To be honest I don't know,' she replied grimly. 'But I think our Jimmy was at the back of them all and he got out alright.'

'Beats me how they managed it,' said the policeman.

'It were Jimmy mister, he shouted to us all to run, so we did, everybody in the street ran like mad!' The informant was Colin Gascoigne, acting as spokesman for his team, who all muttered their grimy agreement to his assessment.

Alan turned to Billy, who was now standing beside him. 'How did Jimmy know what was happening?'

'It were Len Bateson, he did it,' said Billy. 'Me

an our Jimmy saw him. He lit a fire at the bottom of the chimney, we saw it moving so our kid yelled for 'em all ter run!'

'He tied me up all night,' added Vera, 'and Jimmy and Susan. He said he was going to kill us all! It was him what killed that woman...!'

Alan held up his hands. 'Look, I think you'd all better come down to the station. There's a lot needs clearing up here, and I don't just mean this mess,' he indicated the huge mound of smoking rubble piled all the way up the street. 'I wonder if there's still anybody under all that?'

Charlie Gascoigne took a hesitant step forward. 'There were an old woman sat on t' lavvie when t' chimney came down!'

'Are you sure?' asked Alan.

'I think so, mister. We were all laughing at her 'cos she'd left t' lavvie door open and – she were sat on t' pot with her umbrella up!'

'She allus did that, mister,' confirmed the fast bowler.

'What a way to go!' said Alan.

Dorothy and Susan felt themselves smiling and were suitably disgusted with themselves. As she, Susan, Vera and Alan Greenough left to go the police station Dorothy looked down at Billy. 'Do get Jimmy – tell him to come down to the police station.'

'And Billy,' added Alan Greenough with a twinkle in his eye, 'tell him he's not in any trouble.'

The three of them sat in the front office talking to Alan Greenough and Inspector Mansfield. Dorothy had already told them about her trip to the station earlier and how it had been left up to a six-year-old boy to do their job for them and rescue Jimmy, Susan and Mrs Bateson.

'Had it not been for our Billy and Jimmy,' added Susan, 'you'd have had a street full of dead kids' blood on your hands!'

'On *our* hands?' protested the inspector. 'I do hope you're not blaming the police for the chimney falling down, young lady!'

'You're to blame for letting Len Bateson go,' stormed Susan, angry now at being patronised. 'And he was the one who brought the chimney down – and you told him who informed on him!' she retorted. 'That's why he came for me and Jimmy.'

The inspector blanched, 'I'm sorry, but you're mistaken about that. There's no way we would have told him!'

'That's what he told us,' argued Susan, heatedly.

'He told me the same,' added Vera, who knew she was about to get in trouble for giving Len a false alibi, but the police seemed to have as many problems as her, so she wasn't too bothered. 'The fat one with the moustache, she told him!'

'I might have bloody known it!' shouted an enraged Dorothy leaping to her feet. 'Bring her in here! Let's see what she has to say!'

Without waiting for an answer she stormed out of the door into the main office, shouting as she went, 'Muscroft, you fat-arsed bastard! Come out here!'

The rest of them charged out after her, with Alan in the lead. He caught up with her just as

365

WPC Muscroft emerged from an interview room, wondering what all the fuss was about. Dorothy made a desperate lunge for her, only to be pulled back by Alan.

'Trying to get yourself arrested, dear?' smirked Muscroft, unaware of how much trouble she was in.

'I want her arrested for telling a murderer that my children had informed on him!' roared Dorothy.

Muscroft's face dropped in horror as the magnitude of what had happened was gradually revealed to her by Alan Greenough, who saw no reason to gloss over her part in it all.

Another constable walked into the room with a white-faced Billy by his side. Billy opened his mouth to speak but the words wouldn't come.

'We can't find his brother,' said the constable grimly. 'He might not have got out of the street!'

Chapter Twenty-Six

Frank looked up at the sky, as you do when you think you hear thunder.

'Was that thunder?' he inquired of Alfie Featherstone, his yard man.

'Wouldn't have thought so,' replied Alfie. Looking up at the bright sky, broken by just the odd white cloud.

Frank shook his head and finished off checking his morning delivery of timber, before climbing

366

into his car. It was mid-morning and he'd promised Dorothy he'd be back half an hour ago to look for the kids. He wasn't as worried about them as she was. They'd turn up in their own good time, after all, they were Bairstows.

A clanging ambulance passed him, followed by a string of fire engines, causing him to wonder what the hell was going on. The dust had just about settled when he arrived at the scene of devastation. His heart stopped. Flinging open the car door he rushed around trying to find out what had happened. Had anybody been hurt? Looking at the pile of rubble completely burying Back Broughton Terrace and blocking Paradine Hill, he'd be amazed if anyone had escaped alive.

'Has anyone seen Dorothy Bairstow?' he shouted. But everyone else was shouting as well and no one took any notice.

'Has anyone seen the Bairstow kids?'

Mothers were running up and down Paradine Hill. All they knew was that the destructor chimney had come down in Broughton Terrace, the street where their children were playing.

'Dorothy Bairstow!' he screamed. He didn't realise up until then how much she meant to him. How much he loved her. Please God, don't take her away from me now!

Hysterical reunions were enacted as mothers found their dust-coated offspring wandering around, dazed and dirty. What traffic there was was either backed up the road or making diversions through the nearby streets. An enterprising icecream van had parked nearby. Its cheerful clanging bell mingling with the mayhem going on all around. It was doing a roaring trade as the inevitable spectators began to turn up in their dozens at first and then in their hundreds.

'She's gone to t' cop shop, mister,' squeaked a blackened urchin in eventual answer to Frank's desperate inquiries. The blackened child held out a hopeful hand in case his information was worth rewarding.

A tearful, relieved Frank took a ten shilling note from his pocket and pressed it into the boy's hand before pushing his way back through the crowd.

The amazed urchin thrust this huge reward into his trouser pocket before anyone could see it and went off in search of another desperate adult who might wish to reward him for information.

Billy yelled out to Frank and dashed up to him. 'Have yer seen our Jimmy?' he asked with a note of desperation in his voice.

Frank shook his head. 'I haven't, lad – isn't he with your Auntie Dorothy?'

'Me Auntie Dorothy told me ter fetch him down ter t'police station. I thought he were right behind me when we ran out of t' street.'

'And wasn't he?' Frank felt his heart sinking with dread. He caught a passing policeman by his sleeve. 'There's a young lad missing,' he said. 'This is his brother – I wonder if you could help.'

The policeman bent down to talk to Billy as Frank hurried off.

'Right, young 'un,' decided the constable, on hearing that the rest of Jimmy's family were at the police station. 'Me and you had better pop down to the station. You never know, your

368

brother might have turned up there.'

In the meantime, Frank was dashing down the next street, to the Bairstows' front door. All was normal down this front street, apart from the dust drifting over the rooftops. Just a neat row of front doors and a three-legged dog attempting to pee up against the gas lamp. No hint at all of the mayhem round the back. Thankfully the front door wasn't locked.

Frank pulled open the scullery door and jumped back as the bricks piled against the outside of the door fell around his feet. The outside lavatory had completely collapsed into the yard and the scullery was threatening to do the same. He picked his way to the back gate and surveyed the scene, coughing and spitting as the dust swirled around his head. A fire had started across the street, probably a broken gas main. He could hear the hiss and saw a jet of water shooting high into the air from Mrs Harrison's house. People were beginning to venture down the street, scrambling over the rubble and calling out. A helmeted policeman appeared and told them not to be so stupid and to get out of the place so the firemen could get on with their bloody job.

Frank turned to go back the way he'd come. There was nothing he could do here, then he saw Jimmy's shoe poking out from under the rubble.

'Over here!' he shouted to anyone who might hear, but there were so many people shouting that no one seemed to take any notice.

Frantically, but methodically, he pulled away the broken bricks with his bare hands, toughened by years of hard graft on the sites, and soon uncovered an unconscious Jimmy. Huddled with his face to the ground, his head matted with blood.

Frank began clearing the bricks around the boy to allow him to lift him free.

'Over here!' he shouted again. 'I need help!'

This time his shouts were heard by a fireman who came hurrying and stumbling across the rubble towards the sound of Frank's voice. As he arrived he saw a movement in the scullery wall, below which he saw the crouched figure of Frank removing bricks from around a smaller figure beneath him.

'Watch out!' shouted the fireman. But it happened too quickly. Frank heard the shout and sensed the movement beside him. He instinctively threw himself across Jimmy, just as the scullery wall came down on top of him.

Chapter Twenty-Seven

Dorothy, Susan and Billy stood at the end of the street, watching as the police, firemen and ambulancemen struggled to release Frank and Jimmy.

Susan's lips moved in prayer, Dorothy's quivered in shock. What the hell was happening? Would this nightmare chain of events never come to an end? Frank was brought out first. His face was deathly pale but no one had taken the decision to cover it up which told Dorothy he was still alive. Susan gave him a cursory look. Not that she was unsympathetic, just that she was desperately concerned for her brother. The ambulancemen struggled back over the rubble with the now empty stretcher, cursing that one stretcher was all they'd been allocated.

Jimmy's face was also uncovered, so he must be alive. Congealed blood mixed with brick dust formed a sickly mask on his still face. Susan burst into tears as he was carried past. Dorothy gripped Billy tightly and followed the stretcher to the waiting ambulance.

The driver held up a hand as she and Billy tried to follow Susan into the ambulance. 'Sorry, missis,' he said apologetically, 'we can't carry any more.'

'I'll run you down,' offered Alan Greenough. 'There's a spare car down at the station.'

When they arrived, Susan was waiting and a stern-looking nurse marched towards them, forcing a rare smile to her lips. 'Mr Sackfield's regained consciousness,' she announced. 'He's quite poorly but he's in no danger – you can see him if you like.'

'What about our Jimmy?' asked Susan, ignoring the invitation to visit Frank.

'Jimmy?' The nurse hadn't realised they were waiting for news of two patients.

'James Bairstow,' said Dorothy. 'He and Mr Sackfield were brought in together.'

'I'll go and check.' The nurse spun round and clicked off round the corner, the sound of her feet dying away and being replaced by an approaching pair, heavier these, a man's feet.

The doctor, whose feet they were, made no attempt to smile. The message he had to deliver gave him nothing to smile about.

'Mrs Bairstow?'

'Yes.' Dorothy stood up to receive the news, Susan and Billy on either side of her, each with an arm around their auntie.

'James is on the danger list. We're having to operate to relieve a blood clot on his brain – I'm afraid he's very poorly but we're doing all we can.'

'Is he going to be alright, doctor?' The words were Dorothy's but she spoke for all three of them.

The doctor shook his head. 'There's just no way I can answer you truthfully,' he admitted. Then added, 'I believe he was saved from further injury by someone throwing themselves over him. If James does come through, he can thank that person for his life.'

'Thank you, doctor,' murmured Dorothy.

The three of them sat down again as the stern nurse returned. Dorothy gave her a bleak smile.

'It's okay, nurse,' she said. 'The doctor's just been to tell us about Jimmy.'

The nurse nodded. 'Would you like to see Mr Sackfield now?'

Dorothy stood up. 'Yes thank you, nurse. I'll go.' She turned and looked questioningly at Susan and Billy. Susan looked up at the nurse.

'Is there a chapel in here?' she asked.

'Yes there is, dear. If you wait here a second I'll take you.'

The nurse took Dorothy and Billy to see Frank, leaving Susan alone with her thoughts. Her juvenile mind was flooded with a confusion of events and emotions. Of her mam and dad and Freddie and Ray and getting Billy back and their sudden change in fortunes. She remembered how quickly her mam and dad had been taken away from this world and Uncle Tommy and the woman in the cemetery with Len Bateson and she realised just how fragile life was. But, please God, enough's enough – don't let it happen to Jimmy.

The nurse returned and led her, with a comforting arm on her shoulder, to the chapel. A tiny inter-denominational room with a crucifix, a statue of Our Lady and half a dozen rows of pews. Susan turned to thank the nurse, then asked, 'What do you think his chances are, nurse?'

'If he's still with us in eight hours, I reckon he'll pull through,' answered the nurse decisively. 'As soon as there's any news somebody will come and let you know.'

She clicked off up the corridor as Susan knelt down to begin her vigil.

Frank opened his eyes and attempted a smile, then grimaced at the pain he was causing himself.

'How's the boy?' he asked.

'Poorly,' Dorothy informed him.

'Is he...' He stopped not wanting to say the words.

'We don't know yet,' anticipated Dorothy. 'How're you feeling?'

'Like I've been ten rounds with Joe Louis.'

'They're saying you saved Jimmy's life.'

'So he is going to be alright then?' The look on Frank's face was desperately willing her to say yes. He was fonder of Jimmy than he realised – he was fond of the whole lot of them, especially Dorothy.

Dorothy looked down on him with a tenderness he could have mistaken for love if he didn't know better. 'We'll know more in a few hours,' she replied. 'Susan's in the chapel, praying.'

'I think I'll say a few myself if it'll help. Not that I'm much good at it, I'm a bit of a pagan really.'

'You've done more than anybody up to now.' She leaned over and kissed him softly. He held her in his eyes, unable to reciprocate, but it was surely more than just the kiss of a friend. The memories of the accident were quite blurred, but the memories of the previous night certainly weren't. Billy was standing beside her, otherwise he might have let her know what he felt about her. But this was neither the time nor the place for such things.

Presently he fell asleep and Dorothy and Billy were shown to a relatives' waiting room. Mrs Veitch turned up and offered to take Billy home with her but Dorothy put an arm around her nephew and shook her head. She needed Billy by her side and by the look on Billy's face he wasn't going anywhere until this business was over.

'Thanks, Mrs Veich, you're very kind, but Billy and I are alright here.'

Her neighbour stayed with her for a while in the warm corridor. A young lady sat opposite, her leg encased in plaster, almost obliterated by graffiti some of which bordered on the obscene. Billy was reading this with fascination, then looked away as the girl grinned at him.

'Oops!' she laughed. 'You shouldn't be reading this at your age, love. Me young man did most of it – he's a sailor.'

The two women absentmindedly nodded their understanding. Billy hadn't a clue what she was talking about. Further up the corridor a small boy with a bandaged arm was running a spoon up and down a radiator making a cacophonous noise, unchecked by his illegally smoking mother. Eventually, Mrs Veitch got to her feet and strode up towards them, grabbing the boy by his collar before confronting the mother.

'Are you going ter crack his flamin' ear'ole or would yer like me ter do it for yer?'

Such was the menace in Mrs Veitch's voice that the boy dropped his spoon and flung himself into the protective arms of his shocked parent.

'An' yer can put that bleedin' fag out while yer at it,' added Mrs Veitch. 'We'd all of us like a fag, but some of us have got more bleedin' respect!'

The offending cigarette was immediately crushed underfoot. Thus satisfied that her hospital visit had not been in vain, Mrs Veitch returned to say her farewell to Dorothy.

Billy fell asleep, slumped against his aunt, and Dorothy held on to him. She'd developed a special bond with Billy, probably born from the guilt she still felt at what she'd put him through. An echoing voice summoned the girl opposite. She smiled her farewell as she hobbled off to have her plaster removed, touching Dorothy on the arm in passing.

'He's gonna be alright, love,' she promised.

Dorothy tried to return her reassuring smile and watched the girl limp away.

'God, I hope so,' she said to herself.

Billy's gentle snoring seduced his auntie into the same state. A piercing scream jolted her awake.

'It's okay, love,' a passing nurse assured her. 'Just a young lad having some stitches out.' Dorothy glanced up the corridor at the chairs recently vacated by the annoying boy and his mother. A clock ticked away the hours. Dorothy looked up expectantly at every passing doctor, nurse, porter or anyone who looked as though they might have news of Jimmy. Billy slept through it all, oblivious to his auntie's anxiety.

Susan had fallen fast asleep, slumped over a pew. She'd prayed continuously for several hours, her heart skipping a beat every time she heard footsteps in the corridor outside. The only news she could expect after such a short time would be bad news. She'd held her breath until the footsteps died away in the distance and resumed her fervent prayers.

And now she was dreaming jumbled dreams of her mam and dad. They were both in jail with Auntie Dorothy and the Brigadier was arguing with a prison warder and making them set Dorothy free but Mam and Dad were still locked up and that wasn't fair. And the chimney was falling, making the sky go black with a dusty choking fog and Freddie was running like mad trying to get away and there was Billy standing on the roof, jumping off now and never landing, but the chimney was landing right on top of Jimmy, smashing his head open.

'Jimmy!' she screamed.

And she heard a gentle voice calling her name.

'Susan!'

'Susan!' It was Dorothy.

Susan opened her eyes and looked around, suddenly realising where she was and that Dorothy was shaking her shoulder. She looked up questioningly at her aunt. Her question answered by Dorothy's reassuring smile.

'He's still with us,' she almost sobbed. 'I don't know who you've been talking to, but it seems they were listening. The doctor says he's over the worst. We can go in and see him if we like. Closest relatives first, that's you and Billy.'

Billy hurled himself into his Susan's arms as she looked up at her aunt with immense relief then said, with unbelievable calmness, 'It always works for me, Auntie. I did it once before when he was a baby, I only hope the little pest appreciates what I do for him!'

Chapter Twenty-Eight

As she rounded the corner into the broken limbs ward where her boss was lying with one plaster-encased leg up in the air, Dorothy was surprised to see him and Susan in deep conversation.

'What are you two plotting?' she asked suspiciously. 'If I'm getting the sack I need six months' notice – I wrote that one into my contract myself.'

'Just the opposite actually,' said Frank as Dorothy leaned over to kiss his cheek. If Susan hadn't been there he'd have turned his face round at the last second to trick her into kissing his lips. He'd done that a few times so far and Dorothy appeared to fall for it every time.

'What's the opposite of the sack?' mused Dorothy. 'More work? Short of laying the bricks, I'm doing most of the work already.'

'Frank's helping me to arrange splitting our forty-nine-per-cent four ways,' explained Susan. 'Me, Jimmy, Billy – and you.'

'That's a lot of money you're giving me – and thanks, but you know I can't accept it.'

'You don't have any option,' pressed Susan. 'You're having it whether you like it or not.'

'I am, am I?'

'Yes.'

'I wouldn't argue if I were you,' advised Frank. 'She's a right little madam is that one.'

Dorothy gave Susan a peck on her cheek. 'Okay, I accept. And just to show I'm worth it, I've got the council to agree to us doing that road junction in Horsforth. It'll be ratified at the next committee so we need to get our skates on and buy that land.'

Frank looked at Susan. 'I hope you realise what you've let me in for – she's only been a shareholder for two minutes and she's gone power mad!'

Susan smiled at the pair of them as she left to go. They were good for each other, not just in business either. Maybe one day her auntie would realise that, grown-ups could be so blind at times.

Susan read the invitation twice. The shock of it only sinking in after the second reading.

Mr and Mrs Roger Ibbotson cordially invite you to the wedding of their daughter, Elizabeth Jane, to Frederick Arthur Fforbes-Fiddler at Ripon Cathedral on Saturday 17th August

R.S.V.P.

It was the Tuesday after the accident and Susan had called back to Broughton Terrace to see if there was any post. Whilst repairs were being carried out, Frank had insisted on her and Dorothy and Billy living in his house. A luxury not available to other residents of the street who were having to make the best of things. Not that any of them begrudged the Bairstows, after all, Jimmy had saved many lives that day.

A shout from outside had her hurrying into the back street, now largely cleared of rubble. A crowd of workmen had gathered at the bottom of the street beyond the broken-down destructor wall. She pushed her way through and winced at the grisly sight of Len Bateson's broken body, recently uncovered beneath hundreds of tons of brick, a poetic end. He'd taken Mrs McGinty with him, but hers was perhaps a merciful release from a life of incontinence and senility.

'Best thing he could have done,' commented a burly constable, who stood and surveyed the scene with little compassion for the twisted war veteran. 'We'd have only had to hang the bugger – saves all that!'

The workmen muttered their agreement and stood back as a couple of ambulancemen arrived to joist him unceremoniously onto a stretcher then curse in annoyance as one of them stumbled on the rubble, causing Len's bloodied carcass to fall off.

'Don't hurt him,' shouted one wag. 'He's been through enough already!'

There was a grisly ripple of laughter as Len was replaced on the stretcher and carried to the waiting ambulance. He collected a gob of spit as he passed what was left of Mrs McGinty's back yard. A farewell present from the dead woman's grieving son.

'Bastard!' was all he had to say.

Susan returned to the house and picked up the phone to offer her congratulations to Freddie, hoping the insincerity in her voice wasn't too obvious.

'Susan!' He sounded relieved to hear from her. 'I've just read about what happened to your street – are you okay? How's Jimmy, he was injured, wasn't he?'

'He's out of danger apparently.'

'Thank God for that! What a thing to happen. Hey! He was a bit of a hero, wasn't he? According to the *Evening Post* he ran around warning everybody!'

'He was a lot of a hero – nearly got himself killed. Would have been if Frank hadn't saved his life.'

'Good grief! Look, you must come over this Saturday, we're having an engagement party. Stay the night if you like – I expect you could use a bit of light relief after what's happened.'

Susan hesitated before replying, 'I'd love to come.'

'Brilliant, see you then. Give my love to everyone.'

The phone went dead, as did Susan's heart. Just the sound of his voice brought back a yearning for him. To Freddie she was just a schoolgirl and would always be so.

How she hated being young.

Dorothy gazed down on the sleeping face of her boss. She knew full well how deeply he felt about her, that's why she'd done her best to make light of their relationship. She just didn't know how she felt about him.

It was all Tommy's fault. Had he not been so out of the ordinary, perhaps his memory would be fading even now. But Tommy would always be there. He'd had her laughing from their first date, despite her misgivings at him and Fred bringing along a couple of ferrets. And it wasn't just the laughter, there'd been a magic between them. Something other people didn't seem to have – maybe Fred and Lily – but there again, Fred was another Bairstow. She was only eighteen when she met Tommy – he'd been her first serious boyfriend. Maybe she was expecting too much at her advanced years. She was thirty-four now, practically middle-aged.

And let's face it, Tommy had been no angel. Nothing she could put her finger on, nothing she could prove – or would wish to. But he attracted girls like flies round a jam pot. Tommy had his share of weaknesses, not the least of which was succumbing to temptation. And there were plenty of girls trying to tempt her Tommy. But she was his girl and she knew it. No point trying to tie him down, waste of time anyway. She always felt secure with him – and he did love her. Of that there was no doubt.

Frank opened his eyes, blinked away the sleep then smiled quizzically up at her. A nurse bustled past her and leaned over him, sticking a thermometer in his mouth.

'Welcome back to the world, Mr Sackfield,' announced the nurse. 'The operation went fine.'

'What operation was that?' grunted Frank through the thermometer. His susceptibility to morphine had left him dopey.

'They reset your shoulder, Frank,' explained Dorothy. 'Put some metal in it.'

'Oh, right, sort of reinforcement-like.'

'Sort of,' agreed the nurse. 'How are you feeling?'

'Drunk,' said Frank, after considering his reply.

'Make the most of it,' grinned the nurse, retrieving the thermometer and looking at the reading. 'There'll be no alcohol for you for a while.'

'Thanks nurse,' moaned Frank. 'You're such a treasure.'

Susan had never drunk wine before and she wasn't quite sure if she'd ever get to like it. The party was in full swing. The Fiddler gramophone blasting out Glenn Miller's 'In The Mood' and the parlour was jumping with lively jitterbuggers. Tricky Dicky Dodsworth had been assigned by Freddie to look after her, and this eccentric young man undertook his assignment with an enthusiasm that kept Susan well amused. He was the only surviving son of Lord Sefton Dodsworth, a millionaire landowner. Dicky's two older brothers had been killed in the war and his mother in a riding accident.

He told endless tales of him and Freddie at school. Of pranks they'd got up to, of holidays spent together. All such information about her beloved Freddie was readily devoured by Susan with one eye on the storyteller and one eye on her Freddie. He was still her Freddie, despite Elizabeth. With the optimism of the very young she knew he'd succumb to her charms well before he married Elizabeth.

But no one had warned her of the maudlin effect a few glasses of wine would have, especially on the first-time drinker.

Dicky was in the middle of an hilarious story about how he and Freddie set fire to the chem lab, narrowly avoiding burning down the whole school, when it became obvious, even to him, that he didn't have her undivided attention.

'She doesn't love him, you know,' she suddenly blurted out. 'You've only got to look at them to see that!'

Susan's eyes were brimming with tears and she was staring at a spot somewhere behind him. Aware that his story, although riveting, was hardly likely to bring tears to a young girl's eyes, he followed her gaze to Freddie and Elizabeth, dancing very slowly to 'Moonlight Serenade'. Freddie had his back to them and Elizabeth was facing them, her head resting on his shoulders. She was running her fingers through his hair, an expression of mild boredom on her face.

'You're quite right there, old girl,' remarked Dicky. He turned back, perhaps to explain his observation to Susan, but she'd gone. Dicky shrugged and made his unsteady way to the bar.

The River Nidd slid quietly past the bottom of the Fiddler garden. Quite wide at this point as it meandered towards the Ouse and thence to the Humber. Years ago, the Brigadier had had a small jetty built and it was on this that Susan stood, gazing sorrowfully into the black waters.

Tonight was the end of a dream. She could never imagine loving anyone as much as she loved Freddie. The water looked so tempting. A swim would perhaps soothe her heartache. She loved swimming, although up to now she'd been restricted to ploughing up and down the chlorinated waters of Union Street Public Baths. A fresh water swim would be so nice. Any caution she would normally have felt at such a venture had been dispelled by the wine.

No one was there to see her strip naked and plunge in, leaving scarcely a ripple in her wake. A few strong stokes took her to the middle of the river, looking back at lights of the house, and wondering what Freddie was doing. Had he whisked Elizabeth off to some secluded room to make love to her? How could he love Elizabeth and not her? Surely he could see how she felt about him. There was something about Elizabeth that just didn't fit. Not once did she look at Freddie with the love in her eyes that Susan felt for him, nor did Freddie look at Elizabeth in such a manner. Susan felt some relief in this, although she was at a loss to know what to do about it. Perhaps she should let herself sink to the bottom of the river and end it all – but what would be the point? Freddie would never know why, and would therefore never suffer dreadful pangs of guilt he was entitled to. It would be nice to think he would be so devastated that he would want to follow her to her watery grave. She smiled sadly to herself, floating on her back and gazing up at the stars as, one by one, they winked out through the darkening sky. It was so peaceful. She wished Freddie could be here, swimming beside her. Perhaps they'd make love on the bank. Proper love, not the lusty fumblings she enjoyed with Ray. She'd been saving herself for Freddie – and now she'd never have him. She knew what people would say, 'You're only sixteen, you'll meet someone else.' But she wouldn't, there'll never be another Freddie. The river water diluted her tears as she kicked gently back towards the jetty, a bright new moon mocking her with its cheerfulness. So wrapped up was she in her own thoughts and self-pity that she didn't hear the splash.

'You're wishing he was with you aren't you?'

Susan was shocked to hear Elizabeth's voice so close. She looked around, treading water, and saw Freddie's fiancée, bobbing up and down just a few yards away, as naked as she was, smiling at her.

'Saw how miserable you were,' Elizabeth said. 'Thought I'd join you. If it's any consolation,' she added teasingly, 'I've never done this with Freddie either!'

'I don't know what you mean!' protested Susan, swimming slowly back to the shore.

'Liar!' laughed Elizabeth. 'You're besotted with him. That's why you ran out of the room at Christmas!'

Susan felt herself colouring with anger. Elizabeth was playing a dangerous game. Susan could quite easily drown this gloating woman in seconds, nobody would be any the wiser – and Freddie would be hers.

She was shocked at harbouring such thoughts. Reaching the jetty she hoisted herself up the short ladder and sat on the wooden slats, legs dangling in the water, watching Elizabeth as she too climbed up the ladder, less agile than Susan, her breasts and hips slightly fuller, but no less beautiful. Her dark hair, limp with water now and clinging to her white, porcelain shoulders. Elizabeth sat down beside her, splashing her legs in the water. The two of them naked and lovely in the moonlight.

'Do you love him?' asked Susan. Slightly annoyed at herself for asking such a fatuous question, but somehow she needed to hear Elizabeth say it.

'Not in the same way as you do!' came Elizabeth's surprise answer.

'I don't understand. How many ways are there to love a man?'

'There's your way, and there's my way,' said Elizabeth mysteriously. She laid a hand on Susan's naked thigh and said suddenly.

'I was marrying him for his money!'

Susan absorbed this information with a mixture of anger and relief.

'How could you do such a thing? You'll ruin his life – he deserves someone who truly loves him!'

'Someone like you, you mean?' Elizabeth gave a short laugh. Then added, 'You didn't hear what I said, did you?'

Susan shook her head, not knowing what Elizabeth was getting at.

'I said, "I *was* marrying him for his money" – changed my mind tonight, can't go through with it. Struck me when I saw you run out of the room again. Besides, he fancies you a damn sight more than he fancies me – he's just too stupid to admit it. He's always talking about you – your family as well, but mainly you. It doesn't take a genius to figure him out. Men are like that you know. It's all a question of honour with him, he got engaged to me in a moment of drunken madness and he feels obliged to go through with it.'

Susan found all this too much to take. Elizabeth's hand tightened on her thigh and rubbed her gently, up as far as her damp pubic hair. Although naïve in such matters, it was enough of a signal for Susan to understand. She turned and looked, shocked, at Elizabeth, who held up her hands and smiled apologetically.

'You can hardly blame me for finding you more attractive than men, I mean, look at you!'

Susan froze as Elizabeth leaned across and kissed her fully and sweetly on her mouth, one hand lingering on her breast. A kiss Susan would never know the like of again. Elizabeth pulled away as she sensed the tenseness in Susan's reluctant lips.

'Just thought I'd give it a try,' she said cheekily, 'you never know!'

Susan stared into the water trying to make sense of this odd but beautiful woman splashing her feet in the water beside her.

'How long have you known – that you er, prefer women?' she asked curiously.

Elizabeth laughed at Susan's reluctance to say the word. 'Since I was seduced by my gym mistress at school,' she replied. 'I was fifteen and I enjoyed every minute. I've tried men but it's not the same. I find them all so incredibly unsavoury. Freddie was different, just about bearable. I can see how someone like you would fall in love with him.'

'Does he know?'

'What, that I'm a lesbian? Heavens, no!'

Susan had never heard anyone admit to such a thing before and she was filled with shock and admiration at Elizabeth's openness.

'But he's such a lovely man,' Elizabeth continued, 'I was prepared to make the supreme sacrifice in exchange for the Fiddler fortune. I know it sounds mercenary, but us queers are very much castigated by society. But the richer you are, the more you're accepted. So one has to make the best one can out of life. I'd have had private affairs that Freddie didn't know about, bless him, but I doubt if I'd have been able to do him justice between the sheets. No enthusiasm you see – sad isn't it? Lovely girl like me.'

Try as she might, Susan couldn't help but like this outrageous woman.

'You should try Tricky Dicky,' she said jokingly. 'You'd make a good pair and he is the heir to a fortune!'

'It's an option I'm keeping open,' said Elizabeth, mischievously. 'We'd make an interesting couple, don't you think?'

Susan was grateful that Elizabeth had had the foresight to bring a couple of towels and was more or less dried off and amazingly refreshed in both body and soul as she followed Freddie's soon-to-be-ex-fiancée back into the house.

She watched with unbounded curiosity as Elizabeth took Freddie's hand and led him from the room to a chorus of misplaced ooohs. The party carried on as before, Tricky Dicky demonstrating an agile rubber-legged Charleston to an amazed crowd of modern young things who thought such dances had gone out with Lloyd George.

It was only a matter of minutes before Freddie reappeared: on his own, looking more confused than distressed. He turned off the gramophone.

'Just a short announcement,' he said, drily. 'Lizzie's gone home, the engagement's off.'

He switched the gramophone straight back on but the heart had gone out of the party – for the time being anyway. Susan made her tentative way towards him and took his hand.

'How're you feeling?' she asked.

'Numb!'

'I can imagine, it came as a bit of a shock to me as well.'

'Yes, I gather she told you,' he said, a half-smile playing on his lips. He looked round at the subdued room, then stood on a chair.

'I have another announcement,' he said loudly. 'Anyone not disgracefully plastered within an hour from now will be asked to leave this party!'

This was received with a loud, relieved cheer and the dancers took to the floor once again.

'Did Elizabeth say anything about me?' inquired Susan, fortified by another large glass of wine.

'What would she say about you?'

'You know very well what.'

His eyes softened and he took her hand. 'Susan,' he said gently. 'I've tried my best to get you out of my mind over the last year or so – I know there's something between us – but I'm scared of ruining your life.'

'You could only ruin my life by not being part of it, Freddie Fiddler.'

Freddie took her in his arms and held her to him, kissing her lightly on her lips. 'You're sixteen,' he whispered, aware of the curious eyes dancing around them. 'I've no intention of depriving you of your youth. It's much too precious – I know you don't realise it, but believe me I'm right.'

'The only thing I don't want to be deprived of

is you,' she breathed, pulling him back towards her.

'I think I can promise not to do that.'

He put his hand in his pocket and brought out a ring she hadn't seen for two years.

'You found it! Freddie, it's the ring!'

'I know,' he grinned. 'Came to me where I'd hidden it in the middle of the blasted night. I'd stuck it under an old flagstone in the cellar of the cottage. Rang old Tricky up and we drove through the night to get it.' He held it affectionately between finger and thumb, reflected light playing on his face. 'I must say, it never felt right giving it to Lizzie – came within a hair's breadth though!'

He took her left hand and folded it over the ring.

'There's only one person this ring was ever meant for,' he smiled. 'I'd like you to keep it as a token of our impending engagement. If you ever decide not to go ahead with it, I'll understand. Mind you,' he added, 'I'll want my ring back.'

'I think you can forget that,' gasped Susan, taken aback by this sudden turn of events. 'Does this mean we're enga...'

'Unofficially,' interrupted Freddie, placing a finger on her lips. 'For my part, I know full well there aren't two like you in the world, but I suspect we Freddie Fiddlers are a penny a dozen – I want you to give yourself time. Come and get me when you're ready – I'll be around – no fear of that!'

They kissed once again, this time it was the one she'd been dreaming of.

Frank watched the nurse stride away in that purposeful way nurses have and groaned to himself. Another week to ten days in this damn place. Had to give his shoulder a chance to knit together before they were prepared to let him out. His broken ribs were coming along okay and the lacerations were healing up – if only he hadn't broken his shoulder in three places, he'd be up and about now. Even Jimmy had been allowed home and he'd been at death's door only a week ago. He was still feeling sorry for himself when Dorothy turned up with a carrier bag full of goodies, including four bottles of pale ale, one of which he owed to the chap in the next bed.

'Business first,' she said. 'Sign here and here and here.'

Frank did as he was told, writing his name beside three pencilled crosses.

'What have I signed away?' he asked.

'Nothing, you've just signed a contract to buy the land at Horsforth, at least you have once I've witnessed it.' She wrote in her own name with a flourish.

'Right,' she said. 'Business concluded – what do you want to talk about?'

Frank was sitting up in his bed, propped by a mountain of pillows. He looked across at Dorothy, wondering if this was the right time to ask.

'What are you thinking, Mr Sackfield?' she asked curiously.

'I'm wondering how I'm going to take it.'

'Take what?'

'The feeling of rejection.'

'What are you talking about, Frank?'

'Dorothy – will you marry me?'

Dorothy tensed. She'd been dreading him asking her. She knew it was inevitable – but she just wasn't ready to give him an answer. Not even a maybe. It's even more of a rejection when a maybe turns into a definite 'no'. She looked at him for a long long time.

'I did tell you at the outset Frank that I didn't want to be anything but friends and business partners, so...'

'Don't say it!' interrupted Frank. 'I'd prefer not to hear it. Just forget I ever asked you.'

'Ever asked me what Frank?' she smiled sadly. Wishing she had it in her to say yes to this lovely man.

Frank gave her a resigned smile and settled back. 'What shall we do?' he asked. 'Stay as we are?'

'It'd suit me Frank. This way we can both leave our options open.'

'I don't think I like the sound of that.'

'Sorry.'

She stood up to leave, turning halfway down the ward to blow him a kiss.

'By 'eck! I wish my wife looked like that,' commented the chap in the next bed as Frank secretly passed him a bottle of pale ale.

'So do I,' said Frank, closing his eyes, still drowsy with pain killers.

'Penny for them,' offered Susan as Dorothy gazed out of the scullery window, deep in thought.

'Frank's asked me to marry him,' she said

absentmindedly. Her eyes fixed on a sparrow hopping round the dustbin lid, trying to find a way in.

'That's brilliant!' screamed Susan. 'Oh, Auntie Dorothy, I am pleased for you!'

'I turned him down,' went on Dorothy.

'Oh,' said a seriously disappointed Susan.

'I don't think I love him – certainly not like I loved your Uncle Tommy.'

Susan remained quiet. She had problems of her own and had been wondering whether to burden Dorothy with them. Perhaps now was a good time. A mutual unburdening of troubles.

'I don't know what to say,' commented Susan. 'Except that I think he's a great bloke and you seem to get on so well together.'

'Perhaps I'm asking for too much,' mused her auntie. 'Do you think I'm asking for too much?'

'Auntie Dorothy, I'm sixteen years old, what do I know?'

'Most sixteen-year-olds think they know everything.'

'Well, I'm not one of them – I've got problems of my own.'

This last remark roused Dorothy from her thoughts. 'Oh? What problems?'

'Freddie problems.'

'Oh dear.' Dorothy had told Susan on so many occasions that there was no future in this.

'It's not quite as *oh dear* as it sounds,' retorted Susan. 'He never did get engaged to Elizabeth.'

'Didn't he now? Am I allowed to know why?'

Susan hesitated before replying. 'It turns out that Elizabeth's a lesbian.'

'Wow! I can see how this might put Freddie off – was he heartbroken?'

'More relieved than heartbroken – he found his diamond ring, you know.'

'No, I didn't know.'

'It's a beautiful ring,' said Susan. 'Would you like to see it – he was going to give it to Elizabeth, but obviously that fell through.'

'See it? What are you talking about. Where is it?'

Susan fumbled in her pocket and brought out the huge diamond solitaire. Dorothy gasped.

'Good grief! It's the most beautiful ring I've ever seen.'

'Hmm – I don't think you'd say that if you'd seen my blue diamond,' commented Susan matter-of-factly. 'Still, it is beautiful, isn't it?'

'*Fabulous* wouldn't be too strong a word. What are you doing with it?'

'Freddie gave it to me – sort of an unofficial engagement ring. I'm not to wear it of course – not until we're officially engaged.'

'Oh really? And when will that be, may I ask?' inquired Dorothy, who had learned long ago not to be surprised by anything Susan did.

'We haven't decided. He insisted I get on with my youth, whatever that means.'

'It's something amazingly sensible,' said Dorothy. 'Something that you'd never understand – not until you've finished getting on with your youth anyway.'

'That's what Freddie said. We'll see each other, of course – he's going to university to study medicine. He reckons he'll be waiting for me when I'm ready.'

'I'm absolutely sure he will.' Dorothy regarded her niece with some envy. Easily as beautiful as her auntie but with the glow of youth.

'Trouble is,' went on Susan, 'Ray's asked me out tonight and I don't know what to do.'

Dorothy smiled. 'I think going out with Ray's all part of getting on with your youth.'

Susan gave her a hug that said *I hoped you'd say that.*

'Just one word of warning,' cautioned Dorothy. 'I don't want you doing anything that might get poor Sister Claire into any more trouble – if you know what I mean.' She laughed as she had when Susan had confided in her what Father Helliwell had said. Her niece shook her head with the despair the young reserve for the old. Susan was saving herself for Freddie.

'Hello, Frank,' said the familiar voice. 'Long time no see.'

Frank peered at the face above him through slitted eyes, trying to bring it into focus.

'Oh my God! Elaine,' he gasped. 'How? What on earth are you doing here?'

'Well, I read about the accident and thought I'd pay you a visit.'

'What? You came all the way from America?'

'Not exactly – we came up from Berkshire. We've been living there for the last few weeks.'

'Who's "we" exactly?' asked Frank.

'Me and Kevin.'

'What about *Chuck?*' He said the name with the same sarcasm he'd used when he first heard about his American rival.

'He's still in the States – we're separated. Didn't work out.'

Frank stared at his ex-wife for a while. She'd hardly changed, still a beautiful woman. He'd really loved her once, but now? It had been over two years since he'd last seen her. Her Yank had been stationed here for a while then managed to get transferred back 'Stateside' as they called it. In his case he'd transferred himself, Elaine and their son Kevin. In the meantime Frank had been serving King and country, getting wounded into the bargain.

'Is Kevin with you?'

She nodded. 'I'll get him if you like.'

'I'd like that.'

Elaine went off to bring Kevin. His son would be five years old now. In the last two years he hadn't seen so much as a photograph of him. He'd ask her about that when she came back with the boy.

Kevin didn't appear to know who he was. Hardly surprising as he was only three the last time he'd seen his father.

'Kevin, this is your daddy.'

'No, he's not,' protested the boy with a distinct American accent that unaccountably depressed Frank.

'Don't be rude, Kevin, if I say he's your father he's your fa…'

'Leave it,' interrupted Frank. 'No sense confusing the boy.' He looked hard at his son. The boy glared back resentfully.

'I'd scarcely have recognised him. He's changed so much.'

397

'They do at that age.'

'I wrote and asked you for photographs – why didn't you send any?'

She lowered her eyes.

'Chuck said I mustn't.'

'Watching you twenty-four hours a day, was he?' Frank failed to keep the sarcasm out of his voice. He felt so indignant that this man had deprived him of the chance to see his son growing up. But he dropped the subject, having no strength for an argument. 'So?' he asked. 'Do you have a job?'

'Yes, I'm working as a shorthand typist at the Ministry of Pensions in Reading – and I'm doing a course in business administration at night school.'

Frank nodded his approval of this. 'And what about Kevin?' he asked, smiling at his son but getting no response.

'He just started at the local school,' she turned to their son. 'You like it there, don't you, Kevin?'

The boy remained mute. Elaine looked back at Frank, concern showing on her face. 'You don't look too good, Frank, are you okay?'

'Elaine, I'm in hospital. They don't let you stay in here if you're okay.'

'Oh, right … er, would you like me to visit you again?'

'What? All the way from Berkshire?'

'Actually, I'm staying at my mother's for a few days.'

Frank made no comment. He hated her mother. According to her, he'd never been good enough for Elaine. He had always suspected her mother of putting her up to running off with Chuck.

'I'll pop in tomorrow if you like,' she offered.

'Okay,' said Frank. Not entirely displeased with her offer. She leaned over and pecked his cheek as Kevin looked on gloomily. Frank looked past her at his son, his only child. It would be nice to get to know him.

He watched her walk away down the ward, idly pondering the pros and cons of a reconciliation. If he was reading her signals correctly, it was certainly on the cards. She was a good-looking woman and the mother of his son. And Dorothy had made it clear that she didn't want him. Not as a husband anyway.

Because of her rejection of his proposal, Dorothy thought it better to visit Frank with the frequency of a friend rather than a lover. Three visits during the course of the next week. Elaine had called in every day. Mostly without Kevin. The spark they'd had between them was gradually rekindling. Thanks to careful nurturing by Elaine. Dorothy's visits were causing him more confusion than comfort. He'd thought of asking her to stop coming. Because of her he couldn't think with a clear mind, such was her effect on him. He'd made no mention of Elaine to her, their visits never coinciding, until the day Elaine made her play for him.

She was already there when Dorothy arrived. Apparently she'd been there for some time. Long enough for her to be holding Frank's hand as she spoke to him.

'I was young ... not thinking straight. You'd gone away. I didn't even know when ... or if ... you were coming back.'

Dorothy could only hazard a guess as to who she was. The woman's voice reeked of insincerity, presumably Frank could spot that as well as she could. He was no idiot, wasn't Frank.

'Hello, Frank,' she greeted him cheerfully.

Frank's face creased into an uncertain smile. 'Hello, Dorothy ... Dorothy, I'd like you to meet Elaine, my ex-wife.'

Dorothy gave her a pleasant smile. 'Pleased to meet you, Elaine ... but I thought you lived in America.'

'She did,' explained Frank. 'Broke up with her husband. She's back in England now.'

'Didn't work out, eh?' said Dorothy with convincing sympathy. 'Sorry to hear that. Mind you, I imagine Frank's a hard act to follow.'

'Dorothy's my secretary,' explained Frank.

'And friend,' added Dorothy.

'And very good friend,' said Frank.

'Really?' Elaine sensed competition. 'And how good's "very good"?'

Frank gave a nervous laugh, and caught Dorothy's curious eye. 'Typical woman,' he admonished. 'Trying to read something that's not there.'

'Ooops!' laughed Elaine, with a certain amount of relief. 'It's just that you never mentioned Dorothy before.'

'Why should he mention me in particular?' asked Dorothy, lightly. 'Frank's got lots of friends, I don't suppose he mentioned them either.'

There was an impending friction here. Frank felt caught between the two of them. Elaine sensed his discomfort and decided on a strategic retreat. She looked at her watch.

'God! Is that the time? I must dash. I'll pop in and see you tomorrow evening, Frank. I'll bring our son with me. You and he can get to know each other properly.'

Dorothy watched her go, then looked back at Frank. 'What was all that about, Frank?'

'That's about me being confused. She hasn't actually said it yet, but I'm pretty sure she wants to get back with me.'

'And what do you want to do?'

He gave her a troubled smile. 'What I want is some time to think. I like the idea of bringing up my own son. Kevin's all I've got.'

Dorothy slid a bottle of pale ale under his bedclothes. 'I hope you know what you're doing, Frank. I'd hate to see you hurt.'

'Hurt?' he exclaimed. 'Look at me ... I'm already hurt!'

'You know what I mean.'

'Dorothy, you and me have no future together ... apparently. But me and Elaine used to have something. We were good together, maybe we'll get it back.'

It was Dorothy's turn to be confused now. Perhaps she had no right to pursue the matter. She changed the subject and told him about the land deal.

'Thanks very much, Mr Scanlon, that's just what I wanted to hear.'

Dorothy put the phone down and sat back in Frank's chair with a smile of triumph on her face. The council had formally approved her proposal to improve the road junction in exchange for planning permission for two hundred houses. The fact that Councillor Harry Scanlon had once employed both Bairstow brothers appeared to have had some bearing on the unusual swiftness of the decision.

She picked up the phone again and asked the operator to put her through to a London number.

'McDowd Construction?... Could I speak to Mr James McDowd please? Dorothy Bairstow ... yes, he knows what it's about.' She drummed her fingers on the desk, holding the receiver between her shoulder and her cheek as she'd once seen Humphrey Bogart do. Then she lit a cigarette as she waited. 'Hello, Mr McDowd – fine thank you, he'll be out in a couple of days hopefully, I'll tell him you were asking after him. Right – we're all set. The council approved our proposals this morning, and we're ready to sell to the highest bidder – or to you if you meet our price.' She smiled as the man at the other end grumbled good naturedly at the slick way she'd handled the deal. 'I know, Mr McDowd, it's a tough old world, I don't suppose the previous owner will be too pleased when he finds out. We completed the purchase last night – I got our solicitor to rush it through with what you might call unseemly haste. Yes, I was holding my breath a bit.'

She looked up in surprise as Elaine walked in and sat herself down on the chair opposite.

Nodding her a quizzical greeting, Dorothy concluded the conversation.

'That's right, twenty-two,' she would have added the word 'thousand' but for Elaine's unexpected presence. 'Oh, and, Mr McDowd – I believe it's customary for the purchaser to pay all legal fees.' She laughed at the outburst from the other end. 'Goodbye, Mr McDowd, I'll tell our solicitor to get on with it shall I? Wonderful, pleasure doing business with you, Mr McDowd.' She laughed again at some farewell comment from the other end before replacing the receiver.

Elaine looked at her quizzically. 'So, you're running Frank's business while he's away, are you?'

'Sort of, why do you ask?'

'It's just that...' Elaine stopped, choosing her words carefully. 'Oh, hell! I might as well tell you. It's just that Frank and I are getting back together again.'

'Really?' Dorothy didn't want to hear this.

'Oh, yes. We had a long chat last night and decided to put everything behind us and start afresh. There were faults on both sides of course. There always are when a marriage breaks down.'

Dorothy was wondering how much Frank was to blame for his wife running off with a Yank, but she didn't voice her thoughts.

'He's a good man is Frank when you get to know him,' said Elaine, giving Dorothy an annoying smile. 'I don't suppose I need to tell you this though. With you working for him.'

'What exactly did Frank say about me working with him?'

Elaine shrugged. Not quite sure why Dorothy was asking such a question. 'Nothing much,' she replied. 'We didn't talk about work much. I gather he's doing okay though.' She looked at Dorothy, as though seeking her confirmation of this. Dorothy's face remained expressionless as Elaine went on. 'I seem to remember him mentioning some sort of land deal?'

I bet you do, thought Dorothy.

'A bit above my head really,' continued Elaine. 'Still, I am doing a night school course in business administration. It should come in handy for a business such as this.' She smiled the same patronising smile once again. Blissfully unaware of how dangerous an enemy she was making. 'No offence, Dorothy, but there are some up-to-date methods of running a business that my Frank doesn't know about. It was always his weak point ... but you know that.'

'Do I really?'

There was more than a hint of sarcasm in Dorothy's voice that Elaine didn't pick up on. Dorothy didn't trust this woman. Much as she wanted to see Frank settled down and happy, she didn't like the idea of this grasping bitch getting her claws into him. The very thought of her and Frank together made her stomach lurch.

'Tell you what, Elaine,' she suggested. 'Frank comes out of hospital on Monday. Why don't we all meet round here? I've got to bring Frank up to date on a few things and it'll be a good opportunity for you to get to know his business if you're to become involved in it.'

Elaine's eyes lit up at this suggestion, although

404

she wasn't sure whether Dorothy had authority to call such a meeting. 'Well, I'm not sure whether Frank will be up to it, but I'll put it to him,' she replied, somewhat loftily.

'You do that,' said Dorothy.

Chapter Twenty-Nine

Dorothy pottered round in her bedroom at Broughton Terrace. She'd hardly been back since the accident and the whole house was covered in a thick layer of dust. Most of which had drifted in through the broken windows before the council managed to board them up. Jimmy was outside re-acquainting himself with old friends and neighbours and modestly accepting their admiration of his heroism. Billy was in the front street with Susan, watching a Salvation Army Band gather itself into a circle before playing a stirring 'Abide with Me', making sure no one was still asleep that Sunday morning.

The hymn came to an end and was followed by the customary tuning up noises that Sally Army Bands always made between numbers. A solo cornet struck up above the mild cacophony, forcing them into silence. It was the unseasonable tune that brought Dorothy to the window. A Christmas carol in the middle of summer. And not just any Christmas carol – and not just any instrument.

A huge smile lit up her face as she looked down

on the puffing cheeks of Rita Doidge belting out 'Hark! The Herald Angels Sing'. Within seconds Dorothy was in the street, hugging her old friend, both of them awash with tears.

'When did you escape?' asked Dorothy.

The Sally Army captain gave her a stern look.

'I broke out last week,' rejoined Rita, winking at the captain. 'Got nine months – less good behaviour.'

'Good behaviour, you?'

'Read about you and your lot in the papers,' said Rita. 'So I asked the band to pop round and serenade you – hoped you might be in.'

Susan and Billy stepped forward, curious to meet this unusual Salvation Army lady.

'This is Susan,' introduced Dorothy, 'and this is Billy – Jimmy's in the next street signing autographs, I shouldn't wonder – this is my good friend Rita.'

Rita laughed as she took the hand of each of the children. 'Bit of a hero, young Jimmy – I gather.'

'They're all heroes, Rita, one way or another.' She looked at Billy and Susan with immense affection. 'My cobblestone heroes. God knows what I'd have done without them.'

'Uncle Frank's a hero as well,' Billy reminded her.

'Uncle Frank? Who's he?' inquired Rita nosily, sensing interesting romantic involvement.

'He's my boss, if you must know, nothing more,' declared Dorothy. 'And he saved Jimmy's life.'

'Bugger me! Dolly – yer surrounded by bleedin' heroes!'

'Rita! You promised!' Rita cringed as the Salvation Army captain admonished her for such language.

'Sorry, Henry!'

Rita gave Dorothy a rueful smile. 'I promised ter watch me language, an' I'm tellin' you – it's not bleedin' easy.'

Billy howled with delight at this latest slip and sat on the step as his auntie and her friend exchanged stories and made plans for a future reunion. Dear old Delma had gone off to spend the rest of her natural life in a secure nuthouse, to use Rita's terminology. The band played a couple of numbers as they chatted, then the captain, with a look of mild exasperation on his face, strode across to them.

'Excuse me, madam,' he doffed his cap politely to Dorothy. 'But we need Rita for "Jerusalem," she's our soloist.'

Rita stood up and planted a kiss on the reddening cheek of the captain.

'Dorothy,' she announced, 'meet my fiancé Henry Evans. Takes his job of saving people very seriously, does my Henry.'

'Above and beyond the call of duty,' said an amazed Dorothy. 'Pleased to meet you, Henry.'

Henry doffed his cap once again, then led Rita away to rejoin the band. Dorothy, Susan and Billy waved their goodbyes as they marched off, out of step, down the street to the uplifting Sunday sound of 'Jerusalem'.

Dorothy deliberately positioned herself beside Frank, with Elaine sitting opposite them. Frank's

arm was in a sling and Elaine had gone over-
board, Dorothy thought, with her twitterings of
concern for him. Pity she didn't show the same
concern when she cleared off to America with
her Yank.

'I'm still not sure you're ready for this, Frank
darling,' Elaine cooed. 'Straight from hospital to
here, I really think it's too soon.'

'Tough old bird, our Frank,' grinned Dorothy,
patting him on the back and making him wince
slightly.

'Oh, dear,' sympathised Elaine. 'I bet that hurt.'

'Not really,' said Frank, slightly embarrassed at
being fussed over so much. 'Right, Dorothy –
what have you got for us?'

'Well,' began Dorothy. 'It was something Elaine
said the other day that prompted me to call this
meeting so quickly.'

Frank frowned.

'You see,' she continued. 'I understand that you
and Elaine are getting back together –and I'm
very happy for you. I also understand that Elaine
would like you to benefit from her knowledge of
business administration, which I believe she is
studying at night school.'

Frank's frown remained in place. 'What are you
getting at, Dorothy?' His tone was slightly impatient and drew a small smile of approval from
Elaine.

'Now from my knowledge of business administration, that I learnt at work, it's obvious that
there's only room for one secretary – so I'm
pulling out.'

Her last remark broadened Elaine's smile and

staggered Frank. Before he could say anything, Dorothy opened a desk drawer, pulled out a sheet of paper and pushed it across to Elaine.

'This is our partnership agreement if you'd like to cast a business eye over it.'

'Partnership? You didn't say anything about a partnership, Frank?' Elaine picked up the agreement with marked reluctance.

'Should I have?' asked Frank, puzzled as to where this was all leading. He knew Dorothy had something up her sleeve, but somehow he didn't think it would be to his advantage this time.

'I just thought...' began Elaine, looking at the agreement.

'If you look at it carefully, Elaine,' explained Dorothy, 'you'll see that I and my family own forty-nine-per-cent of the business – but what's more important is Clause Twelve, right at the bottom.'

Frank's frown had become a permanent fixture. He looked at Dorothy but her attitude to him seemed to have changed. This was the businesslike Dorothy, detached from all emotion. The one who'd fleeced Sid Allerdyce out of several thousand pounds.

'In a nutshell,' explained Dorothy, 'it says that in the event of our partnership being dissolved within the first twelve months, Frank's financial position will revert to the status quo as at the time of signing. In other words, whatever the company was worth at that time is exactly what Frank gets out of it. No more, no less.'

'And how much will that be?' asked Elaine. Her concern for Frank's physical welfare now replaced by a greater concern for his financial well being.

'Well, Frank doesn't actually know this, but I had a valuation done on his business before we put our investment in. It wouldn't be an exaggeration to say that Sackfield Builders was in a perilous position. Not to put too fine a point on it, he was facing bankruptcy.'

'You never mentioned a valuation,' protested Frank. 'You didn't show me this blasted Clause Twelve either – or I never would have signed it. I thought it was a standard partnership agreement.'

'Sorry, Frank,' said Dorothy coldly. 'But I had to protect my family's interests.'

'How much was the valuation?' he asked resignedly.

'Two thousand pounds,' answered Dorothy.

'Two thousand pounds? Is that all?' Elaine's face was a mask of disappointment.

'Less legal costs and disbursements,' added Dorothy. 'Frank should end up with eighteen-fifty – give or take a few quid.'

Frank sat back, his face paler than it ever had been during his stay in hospital. Elaine looked at him with contempt.

'How could you let her trick you into this?' she said scathingly.

'I don't know, I didn't realise,' said Frank weakly, taking the agreement from her and looking at the last clause with dismay. Elaine couldn't contain her disgust.

'You bloody idiot, Frank! Eighteen hundred and fifty pounds – and how much does she get?'

'About twenty-two thousand – after this latest deal goes through,' said Dorothy.

'Twenty-two thou ... Jesus Christ!'

Elaine stood up and stormed to the door. 'Just forget me and you getting back together, Frank! You haven't got the brains you were born with!'

Frank watched her go, 'Apparently not,' he said dispassionately.

Elaine left behind her an awkward silence. Each one of them not wanting to speak before they'd marshalled their thoughts properly.

'That's buggered that then!' said Frank at last.

'Well and truly,' agreed Dorothy. 'Still – everyone has their price and hers was a bit more than eighteen-fifty.'

'So it seems,' said Frank, looking accusingly at Dorothy. 'You did it on purpose, didn't you?'

'No! Well – yes actually,' admitted Dorothy, 'sorry!'

'You thought she was just after my money, didn't you?'

'She was.'

'And I suppose you think you're a cut above her, do you?' Frank's voice had an edge to it she'd never heard before, not when he'd been talking to her anyway.

'How do you mean, Frank?'

'You know very well what I mean – I mean Clause bloody Twelve and your valuation.'

'Oh, that.' She picked up the agreement and looked at it admiringly. 'It's a fake, Frank – I only had it printed this morning – good, isn't it?'

Frank snatched it off her. 'You rotten sod! What did you want to go and do that for?'

'To save you from a conniving gold-digger, Frank. She's not interested in you, only in your money. There was no valuation either,' she added guiltily.

Frank's face dropped, he knew she was right. 'It's all your fault!' he said. 'You should never have turned me down.'

'Turned you down? When did I do that?' Dorothy asked innocently.

'When I asked you to – oh never mind – you know very well when!'

'I know nothing of the sort.'

'I asked you to marry me and you said "no".'

'I did not!'

'Yes you di ... how do you mean you didn't?' Frank was confused now.

'Think back – I didn't say no,' she said adamantly.

Frank didn't trust this cunning, devious woman who made his heart lurch just looking at her.

'Why don't you ask me again?' she challenged.

Twisting painfully round in his chair, he looked directly into her eyes. Gone was the detached, businesslike expression. There was genuine affection in these eyes.

'Will you marry me?' he asked.

'Yes.'

'What? Why?'

'Because I love you, why do you think?' said Dorothy.

'I suppose I'd better kiss you or something,' said Frank, desperately fighting back tears of emotion.

412

'I wish you would!' replied Dorothy, who'd already lost that fight.

Dorothy took him in her arms, Frank reciprocating with his one workable arm and they kissed. This time with the love of two lost souls who'd at last found what had been under their noses all the time.

It was a while before a tooth-grating rubbing of dirt from the window alerted Frank to the Peeping Toms outside. Three of them, grinning like Cheshire cats and blowing mute kisses through the grimy glass. Frank grinned and winked at his future step-children over Dorothy's shoulder, then once again kissed their un-suspecting aunt, passionately and unashamedly.

'Soppy buggers!' said Billy happily.

This Large Print Book for the partially
sighted, who cannot read normal print, is
published under the auspices of

THE ULVERSCROFT FOUNDATION